THE MONSTERS WITHIN

WRITTEN BY

DES FONOIMOANA

INK & FABLE PUBLISHING

This is a work of fiction. Names, characters, places, and incidents either are the product of the author's imagination or are used fictitiously. Any resemblance to actual persons, living or dead, events, or locales is entirely coincidental.

First Printing, August 2020

ISBN 978-1-913716-00-4 (HARDBACK)

ISBN 978-1-913716-02-8 (E-BOOK)

ISBN 978-1-913716-01-1 (PAPERBACK)

Cover Designs & Title Page Art: ArtbyKhuggs

Illustrations By: James Mitchell

Ink & Fable Publishing, Ltd.

www.inkandfablepublishing.com

DEDICATION

Good luck guessing which character is based off of you.

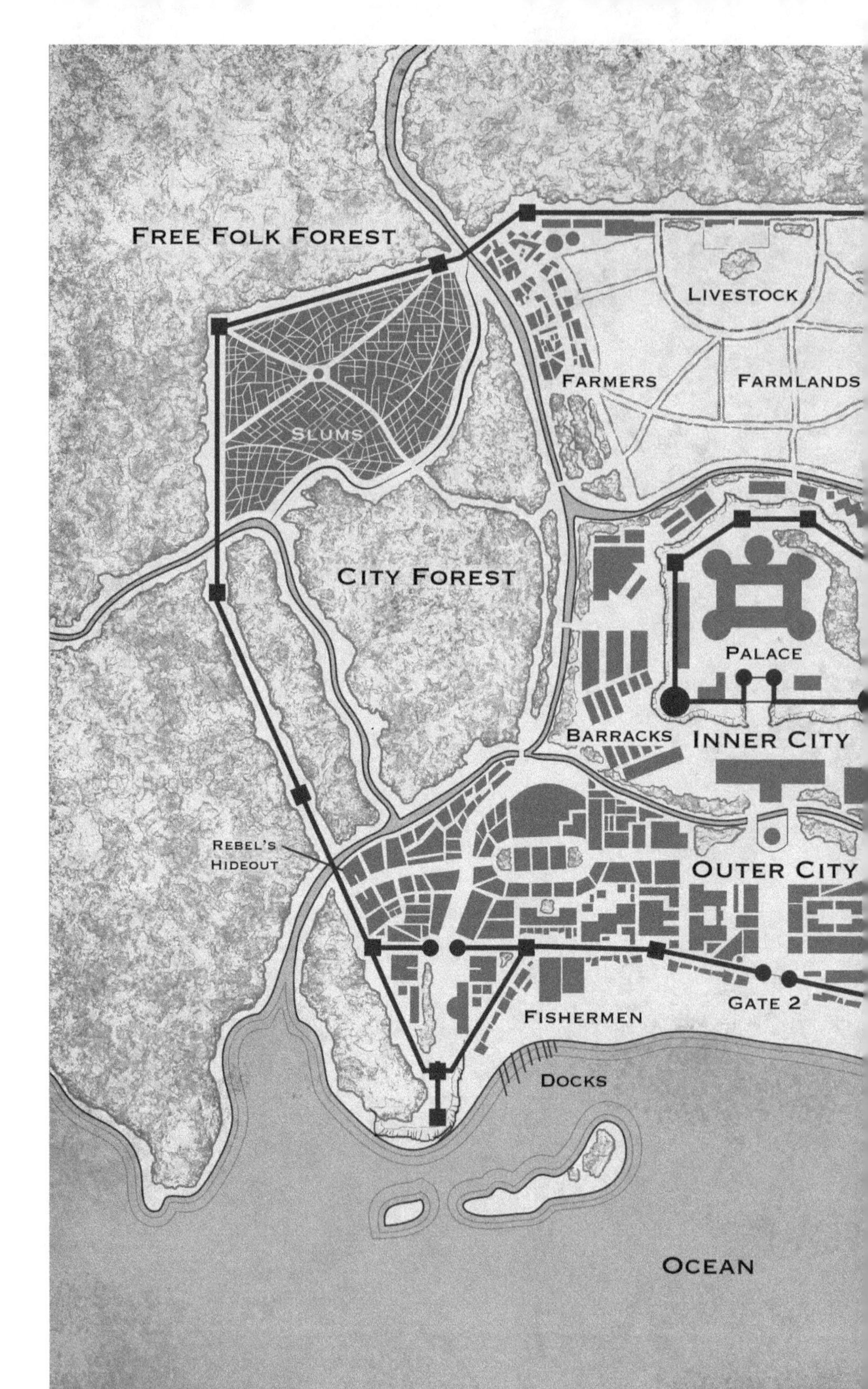

Free Folk Forest
Livestock
Farmers
Farmlands
Slums
City Forest
Palace
Barracks
Inner City
Rebel's
Hideout
Outer City
Gate 2
Fishermen
Docks
Ocean

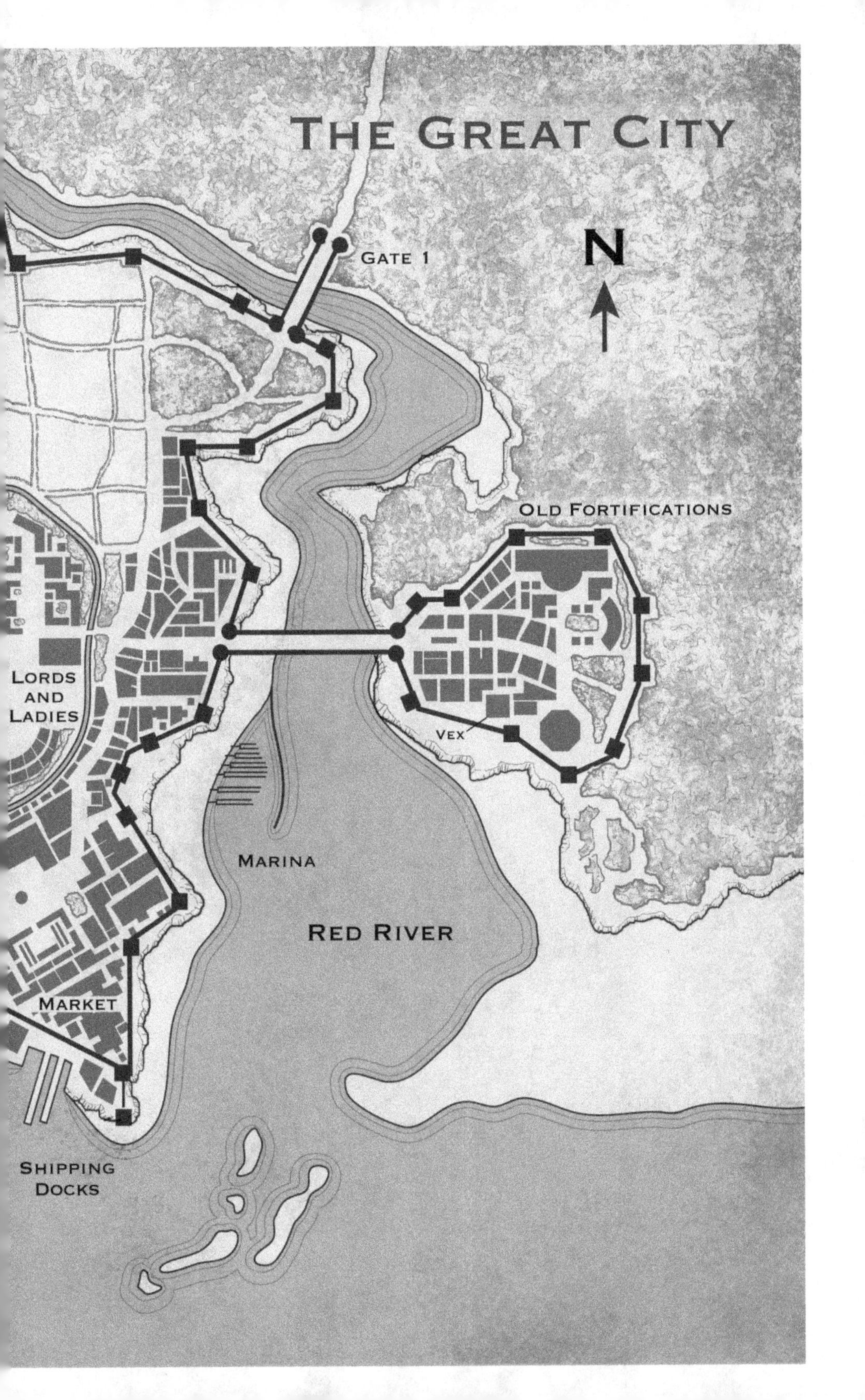

THE GREAT CITY
GATE 1
N
OLD FORTIFICATIONS
LORDS AND LADIES
VEX
MARINA
RED RIVER
MARKET
SHIPPING DOCKS

1

NOW

"*W*hat are you doing here?"

Shadow ignores the question, glancing down at the black drink in front of her. She brings the mug to her lips, staring nonchalantly at the bartender from under her hood. The tavern is vacant besides the two of them, just like old times.

The man with dark hair and sea-foam eyes holds her stare; a disapproving look on his round features. His brows knit so tightly together that she thinks his forehead might just rip this time. That, however, is not her biggest concern.

Shadow is well aware of the risks of being in the Security Zone, the place where the rich and the selfish live. The zone sits underneath the Palace's view—a dangerous place for anyone associated with the Skulls. It's risky and stupid, she knows, and it'll probably get her killed, but she doesn't care. She knew the consequences when she decided to check on her old friend.

"I came to make sure you were still breathing," she murmurs, glancing around suspiciously. "Xero refuses to tell me what's going on this far into The City." She keeps her hood up, hiding her face from prying eyes outside. "Rum, do me a favor? Don't tell Xero that I was here."

"Like I have a choice." He grunts, grinning slightly.

Despite his grumbling, he is grateful to see her—unharmed and still stubborn as hell. He'd been worried for months: unable to see or speak to her due to safety measures. Now that she's doing things her way, he knows that he'll see her more. Still, it doesn't put an end to the fears of her getting caught.

"I'm sorry," she says. And she means it. She hates to worry him, though she has to stay away to keep her friends safe.

Rum gazes at her uneasily. Though she's twenty, he still thinks of her as a kid; his little sister almost. He's stuck in the past, seeing her carefree and youthful in the back of his mind. The desire to protect her is still there. He'll try his best to save whatever innocence is left in the hardened shell that she's become.

"It's too dangerous here. You know it is," he says, stepping closer to her. He grabs a mug from the bar in front of him and begins to clean it with a rag from his shoulder.

"They can't keep me locked up in that damn hut every second of every day," she hisses, eyes narrow and cold. "After the last incident, I was stuck in the Ghetto for three months. I am not an animal."

Rum makes a face. The Ghetto is the poorest part of The City and the most overlooked. Shadow is safest there from King Thanthos and his guards. The 'incident' she mentioned was an accidental shooting involving one of those hunters; a guard who wound up dead.

"It was a safety precaution," he protests quietly, mimicking Xero's excuse. It almost sounds like a question in his mouth.

She rolls her eyes.

"If you don't listen to Xero, Shadow, every guard in The City will come for you. I thought you were laying low."

"I am. It's not that hard to keep a low profile and keep away from the Red Guard. They have bigger fish to fry."

"Bigger than the infamous Shadow? You're a shark in a sea of fish."

Shadow glares at him. He enjoys teasing her, as always. She looks up, about to make a snappy comeback when he cuts her off.

"Get out of here," he orders rapidly. His voice is shaking. "Get out of here, *now*."

Too curious to take any notice of his order, Shadow spins around to see a group of Red Guard men approaching. As the police of The City, they execute the harsh laws that King Thanthos puts in place. Shadow has first-hand experience of their enforcement.

She sits frozen in her chair, eyes wide and heart pounding. If they catch her face, she'll be in trouble. Luckily, her cloak hides most of her features, keeping her from their view. The dimness of the tavern should protect her, and she's matured since she last saw the guards. Maybe she'll be safe, after all.

Fear fights to consume her. One wrong move could get Rum killed and her imprisoned. One wrong move is all it takes to destroy everything.

Rum tries to move casually to the other end of the bar, drawing the guards away from Shadow. She makes a point of sipping her drink and keeping to herself, sharing a nervous glance with Rum before he greets the guards.

"Gentlemen, what can I get for you today?" he says indifferently.

"Your head."

Shadow turns ever so slightly to see who the voice belongs to, and more importantly, what rank he carries.

He's dressed in a black uniform, embellished with silver highlights on the cuffs. The shiny detail continues on the back of the forearms, along the obliques, and down the side of the legs, finishing at the heel. He has metal protectors on his body that shine bright even in the dimly lit tavern, making him stand out. He has a huge gun slung across his back as a warning: don't step out of line. Shadow notices an odd symbol pinned to his broad shoulders, signifying his position. The Commander. His uniform is complete with a helmet, which he sets back on his head as he squares up to interrogate the bartender. "We received news that you've been serving Skulls again."

Rum pretends to be surprised. "Why would I serve those traitors?"

"Funny," the guard snarls back. If his uniform doesn't give it away, his character will—he is clearly in charge. Shadow knows him and his position well enough. The man's name is Jett Torn and he's the new Commander of the entire Guard.

"Funny?" Rum echoes.

"Funny considering you're in bed with Xero Marcs."

Rum frowns. "What are you implying?"

Shadow feels the tension wrap around her throat, constricting her airways. She prepares to step in, ready to ruin everything she has worked for in order to keep Rum safe. Her hand slides to her belt, grasping the dagger that she keeps on her at all times. Patiently, she waits for the opportune moment.

"You best learn where your loyalties lie," Jett growls with heat. The temper on the man is astounding, as Shadow knows. The only thing more impressive than his temper, is his drive—he rose to Commander just months after he lost the love of his life. "You're playing with fire, *Rum*."

"I have no intention of working with the Skulls, Commander," Rum keeps his eyes locked on Torn. "You of all people should know that." For a moment they stand in a silence fueled by testosterone and their egos.

"Perhaps I'll be forced to take you in for questioning," Jett decides then. "What do you think?"

Rum's face goes a shade whiter and Shadow watches as he tries to hide the gulp in his throat. He knows, as does everyone, that going into the Palace is an automatic death sentence. He tries to hide his fear, instead replacing it with annoyance and a hint of bravery.

"Without proper accusation?" asks Rum, trying to stand his ground.

Jett sends him a snide smile. He opens his mouth, as if to declare Rum's fate, but he is cut off.

"Commander, there is a rumble in the market. They are calling for backup," a guard speaks up, drawing the Commander's attention away for a moment. It's long enough for his temper to ease.

His eyebrows knit together at the guard's interjection as he looks back at Rum. "We will finish this later," he warns vehemently. It's a dangerous promise.

With a growl, he and his guards vanish out of the door and back into the daylight, leaving the tavern untouched for now.

Shadow didn't know she'd been holding anything in until she exhaled. A trembling breath escapes from her lips, drawing Rum's attention from the door. He's relieved when he hears the cling of the blade hit the counter. She clenches her hand and stretches it out slowly, coming to terms with the death grip she had on her weapon. It aches.

"If anyone discovers the truth, it'll be him," she mutters, closing her eyes momentarily.

"Don't lose everything you've worked for over me," Rum says suddenly. Shadow looks up and sees the anger settled on his brow. It's clear to her that now, more than ever, she needs to hide the lengths to which she'll go to protect him.

"I'll do whatever I like," she mutters.

Rum pretends not to hear her. There's no good reason he can find to argue with her, and if he does argue, she won't listen anyway. He lifts up a box full of napkins and begins to place them on the counter as silence falls over them.

"Thanthos will do whatever he can to hurt you," she says, keeping her eyes on her drink. It's hard enough to let her own pain seep through, but to keep the fear of losing Rum contained is even harder. "He thinks you're to blame for what happened to his daughter."

"When really, he's the one to blame," Rum says.

Shadow nods. Thanthos Blackthorne is the ruler of The City—a dictator promoted to leader when the last King, his brother, Argos, passed. A wicked and self-righteous King, he tortures and slaughters his own people when he should be protecting them. Worse still, he uses the poorest of his people, as scapegoats for crimes—an excuse to cleanse The City of scum. He built huge, powerful walls to keep The City safe and gain the people's trust, but soon those protective walls became a prison. You don't need to be in a prison cell to be a prisoner in The City. More than anyone though, Thanthos despises the Skulls. They want nothing more than to end his reign and they'll go to any length to do it.

Rum catches the look on his friend's face. She always has been an open book to him. "Alpha's doing well. She's working for the Red Guard now," he tells her.

The Elite are the highest-ranking Red Guards, decorated with navy and silver attire. They are superior in every way to the soldiers, more than the Common Guard who wear the basic black and red attire. With more training, skills, and power, the Elite run The City with an iron fist, and the Common Guard follow.

As Thanthos' right-hand man and most trusted soldier, Jett Torn is the Commander of the entire military. And, naturally, The Skulls' worst nightmare.

Shadow gives him a weary nod.

Rum breathes in deep and exhales a heavy sigh in answer. There is more to this than he's telling her, but he won't tell her everything. Not yet anyway.

"Listen, you need to get back to the hideout. Xero will be looking for you. Come back when it's safe," Rum says, giving her a small smile.

She studies his face, knowing it is time to go. "Let me know if the Commander returns. I'll send word when I can."

Rum nods, watching as she disappears into a crowd. She knows how to blend in, and blend in she does.

~

It's too early to be awake. At least that's what Shadow thinks when she opens her eyes.

She decides to make herself a small breakfast of bacon and toast. Hunger overcomes her while cooking and she steals a piece of bacon straight from the pan. The blistered tongue is worth it.

Shadow lives in the Ghetto near the edge of The City walls. Her hideout is what some might call quaint: there's a bedroom, bathroom, closet, and a living area and kitchen combo. The windows remain blocked, keeping it dark and dank inside. The same as the outside, really. The only light comes from the tiny, ancient TV in the corner that feeds her information on the Palace. The crackling of static might be annoying, but it also brings the only sound. Living in a place like this is the only way for her to keep a low-profile.

Outside, there's nothing more than the boardwalk that forms a circuit around the other houses and back to the center of The City. An almost constant darkness and smog cover the area.

There is nothing beautiful about living here.

She places her food on a plastic, warped plate and sets it at her table with a cup of coffee. Sitting down, her eyes fall upon the TV. Images of King Thanthos flash across the screen as quiet whispers emit from the speakers. She wants to turn the volume up just enough to make the words clear, but that involves getting up and turning the dial. Too much effort. Plus, she's starving.

For the past couple of years, she has lived in this little house alone, keeping to herself. Most of her time is spent wandering around The City or organizing missions with the Skulls. It gets lonely, but she leaves when she can and visits Rum when it is safe.

The Princess comes up on the screen now, attracting Shadow's full attention. She is a young, becoming girl with long, strawberry-blonde hair and green eyes. Her features are soft and round like a child. Gray tattoos that mark her cheeks and forehead, like watermarks, faint and delicate. She is no less beautiful for them.

They are the markings of the Elite.

The Princess' name is Alpha. Alpha is nothing like her father, the King, everyone knows it. But she is too scared to challenge him. This makes her a target of the Skulls whether she wants to be or not. Anyone who doesn't stand against Thanthos are against the Skulls. Alpha's fear keeps her from helping her people and that is not the way a future ruler should be.

Shadow shakes her head in dismay and finishes her toast.

"Shadow," comes a voice in her ear.

She is startled before she realizes it's her discreet communication ear bud, the way she communicates with the Skulls.

"What's going on...?" she asks hesitantly, sitting her lukewarm coffee down on the table. She touches the smooth surface of the table, thinking of the underground market where she bought it. It's a constant reminder of the freedom outside The City walls, outside the Skulls.

She had forgotten about the voice in her ear, until they clear their throat. Xero Marcs is speaking to her—the leader of the Skulls.

"I have someone I need you to meet. I found some answers. We might know what Thanthos has been hunting for," the man says in a rough voice.

Shadow scoffs. "So... what you mean is that you want me to train another minion for you?"

"I mean get here as fast as you can."

It's an order, no room for questions. An order which means she can't enjoy her coffee. Instead she is being forced to go straight to

HQ to speak to Xero and his new pet. She grunts and chugs half of her coffee before tossing the cup in the sink. She steals a few pieces of bacon and switches the TV off, before grabbing her jacket and heading out the door.

A few persistent rays of sunlight manage to break through the thick smog that hovers above the Ghetto. The rest of The City remains free of pollution, but for some reason, this part seems to gather it like a vacuum.

Pulling on her hood, Shadow sets off down the boardwalk, towards the forest that lies between her home and HQ. She sneaks amongst the crowd and slips away unnoticed into the shadows.

Trailing her hand along the deserted alleyway, she finally reaches what she's looking for—the tiny keypad on a hidden door. She's about to press it, when the tiny peephole just above her eye-line opens. A pair of gray, familiar eyes stare back at her.

"Shadow," a voice says, noting her sapphire eyes and golden hair. The peephole is shut and the large, metal door opens, just enough for her to squeeze inside.

She is greeted by Cibor: a large, dark-skinned man with enough brawn and brass to take on an entire army. She knows the truth though—he's really a big teddy bear at heart.

"Hey," she says quietly, glancing around. "Where's Xero?"

Cibor gestures down one of the first halls. Every hall leads to a series of underground tunnels and rooms. This elaborate place was built to house the Skulls and their loved ones, if ever they needed a place to hide. Here, they have enough supplies and weapons to keep them alive and safe.

Shadow nods and makes her way down the hallway, listening out for the sound of hushed voices. Instead, she hears frivolous ones.

She presses the code into the keypad and the door slides open to reveal the room. Inside is a round, wooden table covered with maps and images that hide the walls. A few people—those most precious to the rebellion—sit around it, smiling and joking.

Until they spot Shadow standing in the doorway, that is. Their laughter dies in an instant.

"Shadow, come in." A man with short chocolate-colored hair beckons her in. He is tall and muscular, with scars that line his face and a scowl that rarely leaves. He is handsome in a rugged way; even the way he carries himself is fearless.

The man is Xero Marcs, Leader of the Skulls.

The eyes follow her around the room as she steps inside, moving unconsciously towards Xero as the door shuts behind her. She feels the silence creep up on her.

When she is standing in front of him, he places his hand on her shoulder and gives it an encouraging squeeze. It's something of a comfort to her.

"The tides are changing," he says in a low voice, meant for her alone. He gestures to his right, revealing a young man, probably not much older than Shadow herself. He has dark blond hair, tied back with a bandana, and watchful eyes.

She stays still, studying him for a moment. She attempts to read him through his eyes: the past, the present, and the future. Reading a person's eyes tells her about their hopes, their dreams, their loved ones, and even their deepest, darkest secrets. He avoids her gaze and Shadow knows that it's not a good sign. He is hiding something.

She shifts her weight from one foot to the other. Her eyes flit to Xero, momentarily, who sees her concern.

"This is Dax," Xero introduces him with a terse edge to his voice. "I think he can help us."

"Where did you come from?" Shadow is glaring at Dax outright now. She can feel Xero shooting daggers at her. She might run this guy off before they see what he is capable of.

"Outside the walls," he says curtly, matching Shadow's glowering look.

She crosses her arms, standing her ground. "Really?" she asks, amused. "Outside the walls? That's hard to believe."

"Gives me an advantage," he shrugs. "Thanthos and the Guard don't know who I am."

"That, my friend, makes you a target. This is a political city and without friends, you're as good as dead. Why would an outsider risk it?"

"Shadow," growls Xero deeply. "Enough."

He grabs Shadow's arm before she can protest and pulls her from the room, pushing her into the hallway and slamming the door behind them. She stays quiet, eyes locked on his face. He exhales, running a hand through his hair as paces back and forth.

"I'll forgive you for sneaking into the Security Zone, if you listen," he says pointedly.

"Of course he told you I was there." Shadow grumbles under her breath. She can't help but be angry with Rum for betraying her trust. No doubt to protect her but she is frustrated nevertheless. She wonders when they will finally believe that she can protect herself.

"We've confirmed that Thanthos is looking for magic. The Heir's magic."

Her stomach drops. The Heir magic is beyond powerful. "What? I thought that magic was gone. It's nothing but a myth now, just like every other type of magic." Xero's eyes tell her everything she needs to know. "I thought it was only speculation. What next?" She laughs. "Are you going to tell me that elves are real too?"

Xero scoffs at her, rolling his eyes at the mention. "If anyone should know, it would be you, Shadow."

The comment annoys her. Shadow has spent time in the woods getting to know the souls who call the forest home. The free folk are eccentric, untamed spirits. The people of The City believe that they have magic and fear them. But Shadow has never come across Elves or magical creatures within the forest. The types of magic—Heir magic, Pure magic, and Dark magic—have vanished into history, if they ever truly existed. If they do exist now, those who have magic are secretive, hiding from the world that hunts them.

She hates the prejudice that the free folk face in Thanthos' world. She has hit guards with sticks too many times to count and helped the free folk escape deadly situations because of that hate.

Instead of reacting to Xero's obvious dig at her, she tries to steady her breathing and waits for him to continue.

"My father, Xander Marcs, and Dax's father, Watten Ryer, were friends," he says as if it's some incredible coincidence, "unlikely ones given that his father was much younger, but nevertheless Watten taught my father to use magic and he taught Dax as well. Basic magic from outside the walls."

Outside the walls is unknown, even to Shadow. It's a completely different world to The City. One full of anarchy, bandits, and other hidden dangers. Shadow has only ventured out there a handful of times and found herself in trouble every time. The City is huge on its own, but it hardly compares to the world on the other side of the walls. Mountains, forests, deserts, and plenty of unseen lands exist beyond the pen that Thanthos built. It is a place where myth becomes reality.

"So, you think he can help us find and use whatever it is that Thanthos wants?" She shakes her head in amazement. "I can't believe magic has existed this entire time."

She's suspected Thanthos to be hunting something powerful for a while now, and hearing Xero confirm her suspicions makes her anxious. What does Thanthos know and what will happen if he does find the Heir magic? The City won't last long if he succeeds. Once he has what he needs, the whole world could be in danger.

It's not only Thanthos making her anxious: who the hell is this stranger named Dax who says he can use magic?

"How's his clearance?" she whispers furtively to Xero. She has to know if she can trust him.

"Perfect. Passed every test I had Tools send through the database."

She mulls this over and glances through the small window at

Tools—the lead mechanic and scientist. He is shaking, as usual, and seems to quiver more when Shadow's eyes fall upon him. He gulps and wipes his sweat-soaked brow. Shadow intimidates him, especially as she saunters back into the room toward the glass.

"Every database?" she says clearly, so he can hear.

Tools gives a nod, his silver hair flopping about. "Yes," he replies, twiddling his thumbs. "Every single one. He is who he says he is."

"And who do you say you are, exactly?" She spins round to face Dax, tapping her fingers against her elbow, a single eyebrow raised.

Dax's face drops. How did she not just take his word for it? She is openly accusing him of lying without any proof. "Dax Ryer," he says proudly, "Runner for the Skulls since I was five and ex-inhabitant of the outside world. I'm the best runner you have, in case you were curious, which I'm sure you are."

Shadow snorts. She knows all of the Runners they work with and they're good. They bring supplies like gear and food to the Skulls, usually to those who are forced to hide. Sometimes they bring messages too.

She turns to Xero with dismay. "I want him tested again."

"Of course," Xero appeases. "But I need your word that you'll help him if I need you to. I need him protected."

"Hey! I can protect myself," Dax protests. The Skulls ignore him as they lock eyes in a silent match against one another.

She grimaces. "Fine. May I leave now? I have business to attend to—"

"No," grumbles the leader. "There's more. Come with me."

2

THEN

The screaming starts again; the relentless sound of The City alarm echoing through the Palace, blood curdling howls that rip through the corridors and into the night.

Princess Eirho, barely eighteen, rolls on her side, to gaze at the kiss of moonlight on the building outside. She tries to cover her head with a pillow to block out the alarm. She's trying desperately to make friends with the elusive sleep.

All of a sudden, the door to her room flings open and she grunts in despair. A young girl creeps into the room on tippy toes. She pauses at the foot of the bed, unsure.

"Rho," comes the quiet, gentle voice. "Can I sleep with you?"

Rho purses her lips. She won't get the peaceful sleep she wants now. Her sister, Alpha, kicks and whines in her sleep like a feral dog. But Rho can't turn her away.

"Come here," Rho says, rolling over to make room for her little sister, who's not so little anymore. Rho wonders when her soft-hearted sister will finally be able to handle the alarms and the chaos that comes with living in the Palace.

"What do you think is going on out there?" Alpha says as she buries herself beneath the heavy blanket, hiding everything but her button nose and big eyes.

Rho gives a tired shrug. "I'm not sure. But I promise to keep you safe, so get some rest. Let the alarm lull you to sleep."

Alpha, only thirteen, wants to try but her anxiety keeps her awake and she twists and turns like a log in a river. She kicks this way and that.

After a while, Rho's presence soothes Alpha and she falls into a deep sleep, the sirens becoming nothing more than the background noise to her snoring.

This occurs too often: the sirens going off at late hours of the night. Sometimes it's a common criminal stealing or mugging someone—the reason why Rho is never allowed to go out along the walls. Sometimes it is an altercation in one of the lower-class areas of The City like the Ghetto. Lately, however, the Skulls have been causing problems. They attack the Red Guard, burn government buildings, and vandalize The City with painted threats. It's been happening more frequently, and as much as Rho brushes it off, secretly she's worried about these little things. Every one of them could escalate into something tragic. Her family is in danger and she doesn't even understand why. And because she doesn't understand, there's no stopping it.

There are shouts ringing in the distance, pulling her awake more than the sirens. She wishes their words were clear so that she could know what's happening. It would give her something to think about, at least.

Alpha snores restfully then and drives a foot into the back of Rho's leg. Rho grunts and tries to push herself to the edge of the bed to avoid her sister's vengeful sleep. Another kick comes soon, sending a shooting pain from Rho's calf all the way down to her knee.

Just as she is about to go and sleep on the chair, her door pushes open ever so slightly, and she is met with a pair of eyes the color of the late-night ocean. Those eyes are as familiar to Rho as her own; they can go from a gentle ocean to a dark, rapid current in only a matter of seconds. But when they look at her, they are tranquil waves, soothing her worries. With him, she knows she is safe.

"Rho—" He stops when he sees eyes fall on Alpha sprawled out beside her sister. He takes a step back. "I—um—wanted to make sure you were okay."

Rho moves her hair away from her tired eyes as she sits up in bed. Whenever The City rings with echoes of the sirens, he comes to check on her and tell her what's going on. "I'm fine. I just wish my sister didn't kick like a horse."

He gives her a gentle, knowing smile. To others, his eyes are empty. But Rho detects every flicker of emotion in those azure orbs. "Thank you for worrying about me," she whispers, rubbing her tired forehead. "Do you know what happened?"

He takes a deep breath. "One of my men was beaten."

"By the Skulls?"

"By that worthless bastard, Marcs," he says bitterly. "I'm going to take care of him myself."

"Jett, no," Rho pleads. She surprises herself with how much she cares. She knows, even as she reaches for his hand, that nothing will change his mind.

His eyes widen in surprise and he gives her a peculiar look. "I'm not going to let anything happen unless it's finishing him off, so don't worry, all right?"

She nods, somewhat relieved. Rho knows that he respects her too much to go back on his word. He leaves sullenly and Rho returns to her bed, praying to the Gods that Alpha won't kick her in her sleep.

~

"As much as I would hope for the Resistance to fall, it certainly won't go without a fight," Declan asserts. He inspects The

City below from his perch on the balcony and Rho knows what he's thinking. Lord Snow doesn't see people; he sees small and insignificant creatures. And he will gladly tell anyone who asks.

"What makes you think that?" asks Rho in return, wrapping herself up in her shawl. The breeze wasn't making Rho shudder, being in Declan's presence was the cause of that.

Declan snorts, his auburn hair moving as he shakes his head. "They have everyone fooled, including that moron Lieutenant Colonel what's-his-name."

She wrinkles her small nose in disgust, finding a heat growing inside of her core. Despite the burning hatred building inside, she stays silent.

"He is solving nothing. I suppose the only reason why he has that title is because of his father," he adds bitterly. For someone with such a deep voice, he sounds prudish and snotty. It sends Rho to the edge. "I might suggest to the King to have Torn burned," he continues, oblivious to Rho's thinly veiled rage.

"He is trying, Declan. Lieutenant Colonel Torn has captured more traitors than anyone else under my father's command. His top priority is keeping us safe and stopping the Skulls is second. That's the way it should be and our Elites should be able to take care of that," she counters with a smirk.

Declan seems taken aback, surprised she would stand up for the guard she hardly glances at. She must have shared a total of two words with him her entire life, so her speaking upon his behalf is a shock. "What? So, you care about that half-wit Lieutenant?" She so desperately wants to slap him as she sees a twisted smile spread across his face. How he loves to taunt her.

She gives him a daring look as she tries to steady her temper. "He protects our Palace, that is far more than you are doing."

"Are you implying that he is more worthy than me I?"

"I never said that, Lord Snow, but if the shoe fits—"

Declan's face soon matches his hair; he is furious. Just as he's about to tell her how much of an imbecile she is, a cheery face appears just over Rho's shoulder. Rho understands, then, how deep his jealousy runs.

"Sissy—" Alpha stops in her tracks, gazing at Declan with wide, careful eyes. Her eyes are her most dominant feature and Rho swears if she were any more startled, her eyes might pop right out of her head. "Oh. Lord Snow..." she murmurs, curtsying with her eyes trained on her feet.

"Princess Alpha, we were having a private conversation," he says through gritted teeth. "But I suppose it is a pleasure. What can I do for you?"

Rho sends a covert glare at him. His real self always slithers out before his taught charm. She hates him even more.

"Oh, um," Alpha begins embarrassedly, "Father wants to speak to Rho... He says it's going to rain, Sissy."

Declan's eyes go to Rho, who withholds her bewilderment. King Thanthos rarely calls for his daughters. He keeps them away and under the watchful eyes of the Guard most hours of the day. Rho ignores Declan's look.

The young woman reaches to pat her sister's arm. "Where is he?" she asks.

"He is in the courtyard, alone."

Alone? Rho does all she can to stop herself from sprinting. He is without his guard, and that can only mean one thing; it's urgent.

And more than likely: dangerous.

3

NOW

Xero leads Shadow down the hallways and stairs to his personal room, deep within the heart of the Skulls' headquarters. He types in a code and allows her inside, closing the door behind him.

His room is decorated with maps, pictures, and plans. There's a bed in one corner, a desk, and a shelf filled with personal items. In the center is a large table. An enormous scroll is rolled out, revealing the main outline of The City. He gestures to it.

"This place... we are meant to protect it. By any means necessary." He takes a breath and murmurs, "Why are you against Dax?"

"I'm tired of it, Xero. The last guy you brought in almost blew the entire operation. He got one of our men killed by the Red Guard!"

"He was... inexperienced." He winces at his poor excuse. "Dax, on the other hand, has helped our cause for twenty years, just like his father before him. He's proved his loyalty. We can trust him."

She hesitates, studying Xero's face. She wonders if the idea is a good one and more importantly, she wants to know exactly what he's planning. He notices her scrutinizing stare and clears his throat.

"I think Dax is our only hope. He's the only one that I know who can use any type of magic. Which makes me think he's valuable. But I need you to find out about The Heir's magic and how to get it." He rubs the back of his neck. "Problem is, that might mean going to the Palace and putting together a team."

She feels the weight of the mission being thrown onto her shoulders. The Palace is the last place she ever wants to step foot in again, though hearing the tone of desperation in Xero's voice, Shadow knows she has no say in the matter. After all Xero has done for her, she owes it to him.

There's a war approaching. Thanthos will do all he can to destroy The City and its people, and every day he is getting closer to the power that he seeks. He is well-known for consorting with The Oracles, which means he has a leg up on anyone who dares to oppose him.

"If you don't want to help, I understand, but you know what's at risk here," he turns his back, just enough to fake indifference. He needs her help and they both know it. He also knows that her mind was made up the second that he asked. If she denies him, more people will die and he knows then that he's cornered her.

"I'll help," she says shortly. "And stop guilting me."

"Are you sure?" he turns to face her, his face becoming sly. "And what about Commander Torn?"

"What about him?" she asks bitingly.

"What if you run into him? What if you run into the King or Princess Alpha, or that insufferable Declan Snow?"

"Do you want me to revoke my decision?"

"Your mind is already made up," he notes, "I'm just making sure that you've thought all of this through."

"I'm trying not to think about it," she says. She looks down at her hands. "I'll just act when the time comes. I'll do it on one condition."

Xero looks at her, uncertain.

"I get to be the one who kills Thanthos."

SHADOW SITS ON THE BRIDGE IN THE OLD TOWN, WATCHING THE ducks swim beneath her. They nip at each other, playing tag down the stream. She sits there enjoying a moment of peace, occasionally tossing a piece of bread to an unsuspecting duck.

The whole day has been peaceful, in fact. With the Skulls off her back, and the sun hanging high in the sky, she has finally been able to get some down-time and a chance to enjoy lunch alone.

Something draws her attention to the end of the bridge: a group of guards surrounding someone. She hears dark laughter and what appears to be shoving, so she tosses the rest of her sandwich over the bridge. The ducks swarm it and attack each other as they fight over every last crumb.

She pushes up from the bridge, licking each finger clean of jelly one by one. Her bag goes over her shoulder and she waltzes right into the chaos.

A young girl with wide eyes is being shoved around by a group of dimwitted guards.

"Excuse me," Shadow says as she pushes her way into the middle, grabbing the girl by the shoulders as the guards try to launch her across their little circle. "What the fuck are you morons doing?"

"Hey!" one of them growls. "We're doing whatever the fuck we please. It's none of *your* business."

"If you're feeling so inclined to get our attention, we would be glad to give you some too," another one chuckles darkly.

Shadow moves swiftly in front of the girl —the guards seemingly surprised. They didn't anticipate a challenge. "Touch her one more time and I'll cut your fucking hand off."

The guards guffaw in unison, nudging each other as if it's the best joke any of them have ever heard.

"Please, a tiny thing like you?" a scrawny one chuckles. There are six guards in total—she's triple counted. Two huge ones, three average, and one as short as a child. The average ones might be fast, so she plans to aim for them first. The big guys can come next, and last and definitely least, the shortest one. She won't even break a sweat.

"Okay, try me," she insists.

One of the average guys rises to the challenge. He reaches for the girl's hair and that's exactly what Shadow expected. He clasps her hair in his meaty hand—but only for a second. The next second, his hand is cut clean off.

He screams and his fellow guards rush at Shadow. She expertly dodges them, using her momentum to move around them and knock them out with the hilt of her blade. One by one she drops them with various hits and kicks until there's nothing but a pile of unconscious men lying on the ground.

Totally effortless—just as she predicted.

In the center of it all is the poor girl who stands trembling at the sight.

"Come on," Shadow says gently as she offers her hand. "We need to get you somewhere safe before anyone realizes that these guards got their asses handed to them." The girl takes her hand and they run off, taking a shortcut down the chain of alleys and back to the outer city.

It takes over an hour to get there, but Shadow manages to get the girl to one of the Skulls' safe houses. They slip inside, lock the door, and prepare to hunker down until the guards have forgotten all about this little incident.

Shadow peers outside the window. "So, what's your name?"

"Theta," the girl says in a quivering voice. "How did you do that? You're so much smaller than them! And outnumbered!"

"I've had lots of training," Shadow answers. "Don't let those bastards make you feel weak. I'm Shadow, by the way. Where's your family?"

Theta steps back and frowns. "I don't have any, I'm an orphan," she admits. She pulls her black hair out of her face. She can't be much older than sixteen. "Thanthos killed my family for being Sea Bloods."

Sea Bloods are enemies of The City—enemies to Thanthos because they threaten his rule. Their Kingdom lies to the West and past the horizon where dozens of islands line the water's surface. Any citizens from other Kingdoms are refused. Thanthos is paranoid; he believes those from other Kingdoms are here to spy or to seek the same great power that he is.

"Do the guards bother you often?" The girl nods. "Yes... they knew I didn't have anyone to look after me."

"You do now," Shadow states bluntly. "Let's get you cleaned up and get you something to eat, okay? And I'll get you somewhere safer."

Theta nods gratefully as Shadow shows her where the washroom is. Shadow will clean her up and send her to an older woman in the inner city who takes in stray kids. She takes them in and educates them, all with support of the Skulls.

Shadow gazes out of the window, disappointment flooding her as she thinks about how often this happens. Girls getting harassed and raped by guards; families getting slaughtered for simply being who they are. It's sickening and it's too common.

Too damn common.

~

XERO PUSHES THE DOOR OPEN HESITANTLY AND STEPS INSIDE. He takes his time looking around the room until he finds what he's searching for.

Slowly, Xero moves, closing in on Rum, whose eyes are swollen black and blue. But Xero sees more than the beaten exterior, he sees a burning hatred in the set of his jaw and a pain that goes deeper than the bruises on his skin. The rest of his face is puffed up and as he tries to sit up, he turns his head away from Xero, but it's too late. His punishment has been spotted.

Xero sits at the bar, knowing they are alone. He licks his lips and swallows, watching Rum pull himself up then sets his elbows on the bar patiently.

Rum is a dear friend: reliable, responsible, and loyal to a fault. It hurts Xero to see his friend in pain, but he can't let Rum know. Xero is first and foremost a leader. He reaches over the counter and clutches a bottle of hard liquor in his fist.

"I see that Torn returned."

"How did you know about Torn?" asks Rum. He should know the answer, but he is too frayed to think clearly.

"I could see it in her eyes," states Xero, wiping the edges of his mouth with the back of his hand. He sets the bottle down forcefully and grunts bitterly. "She has lied about this too long. The truth will come out."

"You want it to?"

Xero shrugs. "Not necessarily. But imagine what will happen if the truth is revealed. If The City finds out... Imagine the relief and the hope."

"And the chaos," adds Rum.

"Chaos is inevitable. We should be prepared for anything."

Rum shrugs in a noncommittal way before reaching underneath the counter. "I was told to give this to you," he says and tosses a golden item in front of the leader. Xero fingers it and lifts it to his eyes. *What would I want with a key?* he thinks. It has no teeth and no markings, so it doesn't fit a keyhole. But he knows that somehow, it's a sign from Torn. A significant one.

Thanthos is close to the magic's location, he's sure of it.

With a yell, Xero throws it back. "That bastard!" He takes the neck of the bottle and yanks it to his lips, chugging the fiery liquid that burns in his gut. When he's drained the bottle, he gasps for air and shakes his head furiously to clear it.

"He wanted me to tell you that he'll have his revenge for Princess Rho," Rum adds quietly, seeing the look of utter loathing appear on Xero's face.

"If only that bastard was intelligent enough to realize I never laid a single hand on her."

"You kill King Thanthos' daughter, you can be certain he puts his top soldier on the case," Rum says. He is not trying to insult Xero, or be sarcastic. It's the simple truth. And unfortunately, Commander Jett Torn is King Thanthos' best.

Xero waves a hand before he goes to the door, turning once on his heels to look at his friend.

"Put some ice on that."

~

"Word of the Skulls uprising has sparked further security measures from King Thanthos. More troops are due to be sent around The City in order to serve and protect the citizens. King Thanthos has also issued an order for random searches and the seizure of property. There is no comment, yet, on when the troops will take up their post."

Shadow listens to the ludicrous lies coming from the reporters who either know nothing of The City or are too terrified to report the truth. Thanthos' censorship is out of control. The people hear what he wants them to hear, when he wants them to hear it.

She knows that the people whom Thanthos deem to be useless, or a threat, are being murdered daily. And hope is dwindling fast.

She looks down at the papers in front of her. Xero handed her a map and a few other interesting documents before she left the hideout earlier. She's been trying to scribble down a floor plan of the Palace since she got home. She wants to capture every detail of the inside, recalling it from her memory from her time working there. Tools and Aine—the two brains of the Skulls—are hoping for the map as soon as possible. Shadow hopes to be finished by morning.

Thud.

Her head jerks up, she freezes with her pencil poised. One thing she has learned is to remain still, no matter what. She needs to listen.

Footsteps, she decides. Quickly, she goes through the list of all the people who know where she lives. It doesn't take long; Xero is the only person who knows her location. The only problem is, Xero always calls before he visits, which is next to never. She sure as hell didn't get a phone call and she sure as hell doesn't not recognize those footsteps.

She drops the pencil and goes for the small shelf above the door. Her hand reaches for the familiar feel of cold metal. Within a second, she slams the ammunition into the gun and cocks it, slowly inching towards the door handle.

As anxious as she is, she knows that she has the upper hand. The sound from the television is sure to make whoever it is think that she's distracted.

Moving to the side of the door, she takes a deep breath and calms her mind. She needs to be alert.

In a swift motion, she darts outside to the boardwalk. Shadow waves her hand in front of her face. Nothing. Chills run up her spine as her instincts kick in. When you're unable to see in the shadows, your hearing will increase ten-fold. Every single hair on her body stands on end, ready for an assault.

Shadow feels a large hand clamp down on her shoulder and she feels her body take over. She brings her elbow backward with a sharp jab to the ribs, throwing her attacker off. Hearing them stumble, she spins her gun in her hand before landing a kick square in the person's gut. Shadow sees her opening as the figure doubles over. She slams the heel of her boot with full force into their face, sending them flying backwards.

With her gun in hand, she runs to the figure, keeping low. She kneels on one arm and places her other foot firmly against the windpipe. If need be, she is ready to kill.

The figure struggles to be free until they feel cold metal pressed against their forehead. Shadow watches as they freeze in her grasp like an animal staring into the jaws of a predator.

"Who *are* you!" she demands with narrow eyes, shoving the gun deeper into flesh.

"It's—it's me..." The voice is hoarse, gasping, yes... but there's something familiar about it. A beaten down tone. Yet quick and without delay.

It takes a moment before she comes to the conclusion.

"Ryer, you idiot," she hisses, removing her gun and knee. With a warped sense of satisfaction, she leaves her foot pressed against his throat.

Dax chokes out, having difficulty bringing air into his lungs. She is barely crushing his windpipe. She knows the precise amount of pressure to kill him and this isn't nearly enough.

"What do you think you are doing? How the fuck did you find me?" she says, twisting her boot slightly. The tread tears the sensitive skin at his throat.

He tries to shove the boot away, to no avail.

"Xero sent me... He wants me to stay here."

"What? Why?" she growls.

"I don't know," he admits. "Something about you keeping me safe."

She bites her lip. Out of every person in the Skulls, she does have the best chance of keeping anyone safe. However, it comes at a dangerous price.

"Touch me again and I will kill you," she says, removing her boot.

Dax's hands go straight to his neck, already attempting to massage the pain away. "He didn't tell you I was coming?"

She rolls her eyes. "No. Clearly not, or I wouldn't have tried to kill you." Pausing, she adds, "Or maybe I would."

There is a brief minute of silence, excluding the gentle water swaying underneath them on the boardwalk. The tension is palpable.

"I didn't know you'd be so wound up. I'm sorry. I thought you knew," he says, sitting up.

"He enjoys keeping things from me," she replies. Shadow reaches for the door handle. "Goodbye."

"Wait—"

His toe is propping the door open, effectively keeping her from shutting him out. Ruefully, she realizes he has a metal-toed shoe, and imagines how good it would've felt to smash his foot in the door for trying to stop her. She refrains, of course, but her mind pictures it nonetheless.

"He wants you to get me into the Palace."

She stops in her tracks. Without looking back, she says: "Stay here. I'm going to make a call."

Dax inhales and gives a grateful nod, removing his foot. He waits, glimpsing wearily over his shoulder. The Ghetto is an intimidating place and reeks of garbage. It's the last place he wants to be standing, but here he is. Even the dangers outside the walls seem better than the one streetlight that hovers over him.

After a few minutes, the door opens again. Shadow is clear across the other side of the room, placing something on top of a shelf as she allows him into her home.

He slowly, cautiously, comes inside like a stray dog expecting to be thrown out at any minute. He takes in the quaint place. It's simple but homely. It's not much to look at but Dax sees that she's tried to make her house as comfortable as possible. There's tea brewing and a tidy couch for him to sit on.

"I'm going to bed. You can sleep on the couch. There are blankets and a pillow in the closet. Help yourself," she says passively, going into her bedroom. Then she pauses and looks at him irately. "And whatever happens, do not let anyone in here."

He gives her a salute, which seems to satisfy her. After she leaves, the sole sound comes from the buzzing TV in the corner. It's almost haunting, so he changes it to some news program and goes to the closet.

Dax is greeted with dampness and dust. It is as if the door hasn't been opened in years.

He digs around in the front, spying a sleeping bag. He yanks it out. The bag seems to be in decent shape, so he lifts it up, searching for bugs and shaking off dust.

He reaches in once more for the pillow. His eyes catch something from the corner of the closet.

A small box is marked with a label: *Do Not Touch*. Even Shadow's boxes have her temperament. Curiosity overcomes him and he grabs the box, surprised to find that it's made of ordinary cardboard. He glances surreptitiously at the closed bedroom door. One peek wouldn't hurt. He throws the bedding aside and takes the box to the couch.

This box is calling him, he can feel it. He has to know what is inside, despite the risk of her kicking his teeth in.

Being careful not to disrupt anything, he reaches into the box, pulling out a handful of items. In his hand he holds various papers: news articles, pictures, drawings, and maps. This intrigues him and he begins to sift through them.

Articles involving Thanthos and his daughter are aplenty. There's even an obituary or two mixed in. He discovers images of Shadow and an unknown man, along with darker pictures of a different man—playful and sardonic, yet handsome. The maps must cover the entire city. There are random houses, the Palace, even an outline of the walls. It's almost like a collection.

He goes through quickly, looking for whatever is calling to him. Adrenaline pumps through him and then only calm. He gulps and grabs the envelope marked with dark ink and splotchy letters; it's hard to read in the dimly lit room.

He opens it, dropping the items inside as shock shoots through him.

Dax hurriedly shoves the other pictures and articles back into the box before taking the envelope and stuffing two photos into his pocket. He looks over his shoulder before he puts the box away —Shadow cannot know what he has found. The only person who needs to know is Xero.

4

THEN

Rho sprints down the halls, darting around corners and frightening guards. It takes her mere minutes to reach the courtyard, a sanctuary famous for its beauty. Making her way through the labyrinth of colorful flora and amazing little creatures, she hurries down the stone trail toward her father. She passes through the mighty arbors, over little wooden bridges, and alongside the endless pond that spreads across the vast courtyard.

She stops and looks ahead. A million times she has found this place effortlessly, a million times she has paused in awe. And yet again, she is speechless. There sits an entirely gold bench with twin sculptures of the most magnificent dragons on the back. They are strategically faced in opposite directions; forever vigilant. And between the dragons, sits the great King Thanthos. He sits in a thoughtful silence, letting his thick fingers trace the delicately sculpted dragons and their faces, their detail more astounding than those of myth. Their fangs are too big for their mouths, yet somehow, they fit the snarling lips perfectly. Thanthos is trivial compared to this piece of art.

Thanthos rests his arm on the left dragon's arm and sighs.

Rho holds her breath as he exhales. She is affected by him, as he is her. Her father seems solemn.

She knows this is a grave situation, Thanthos never spends his days on this bench unless it's a private matter; Rho's mother sculpted this bench and all its artistic features from hand.

Thanthos does not speak at first. He traces the crevasses of the glorious seat, pursing his lips in thought. He prides himself on always knowing the right words to say, but when it comes to his eldest daughter, he has none.

Rho decides to speak first, despite tradition and good manners. Thanthos, on the other hand, expects nothing less of his eldest daughter.

"Alpha informed me that it is going to rain, so I came as fast as I could," she begins. He nods, grateful that she remembers the simple code he taught her long ago. "What do I need to do?"

Thanthos smiles then. "Sit, dear one."

Hesitant to obey, Rho sits only after he gestures to the spot beside him.

Rho sees something of sorrow in his eyes. Thanthos doesn't show sorrow to anyone but her, not even little Alpha.

"Listen to me, when I tell you how important this is, Eirho," his face becomes a mask. "Those tyrannical Skulls and their bastard leader have finally reached a point of no return. They killed three of my men and I have retaliated."

The way he speaks the word—*retaliated*—makes Rho feel nauseous.

"What in all the Heavens' names did you do, Father?"

Thanthos doesn't answer immediately. As he opens his mouth to speak, he gives his daughter a sly, sickening grin. "I had Marcs' family skinned and burned alive in front of his own eyes."

The gasp that leaves her throat is hoarse. It escapes so suddenly that she doesn't realize what she's done until anger falls upon the mighty King's brow.

"What?" he bellows, "You think me a monster?"

"No, no, Father," she says, pleading to him with her eyes. "No, they—they deserved it. He deserved to watch them die."

The words hurt her chest, she hates saying them and hates it more that they ring in her head after.

He does not respond, and for a moment Rho thinks of running for her life. As she feels her muscles jerk to move, he smiles and reaches to rub her cheek. The kind touch surprises her and she realizes she has been holding her breath. "You are my daughter, after all."

Rho is lightheaded. She wants to screams and hit him, especially as she stares at his twisted sneer and bright eyes bright as he revels in images of murder. Inside this body is a monster untamable and deaf to the cries of mercy.

Rho is as strong-willed, outspoken, stubborn, and courageous as her father. Her temper can match his. But at heart, Rho is gentle, loving, and merciful.

And Rho is not her father.

His voice brings her back to reality and she feels suffocated. She tries to push the horrific image out of her head. Even though she wasn't there, she swears she can hear their screams in her mind.

"You are the daughter that I trust and love. Alpha is my blood, but she is nothing like me. She is weak and scared. You... you Eirho, are brave and strong. There is a war brewing inside the walls, and outside, as you know," he tells her, some form of his weird fatherly pride sinking through.

Rho knows of the war outside. One of the half-human, half-creature armies is planning on breaking the walls of The City, hoping to take over. That threat is impending, but not as prominent as the other war. Not yet anyway. Inside, the Skulls are fighting Thanthos and trying to usurp him. The war with the Skulls is by far worse. Their 'beloved' King burns their fathers and brothers. Not to mention all the horrific things he has done to this day. She wonders what he will say.

"I am using my many prophets and seers to find something powerful. It is the ancient magic, Rho. It is a mighty gift of ancient fire and blood. And you shall swear not to speak of it, except to me," he warns.

She nods vigorously. "I swear it, Father." *And I shall uncross my fingers now.*

"The Creators of our world put the last of their power into the Heir, my daughter," he explains slowly. "It is unlike anything else. It can give me the magical abilities that I desire. I can rule this city unchallenged… I can rule the whole world!" His excitement heightens as he jumps to his feet. "No Witch or Warlock bears this power. Not one. I need this to fight off our enemies. We will keep searching for it, Eirho. I will find it."

She sits, trying to hide her curiosity tinged with fear. In some way, she's known about this her whole life. She moves to the edge of her seat, both anxious and terrified to hear more.

"I will find it. But in the meantime, I need men. I need support. That is why Declan has lived with us for so long," he states. She looks confused, but he rambles on. "I wish his powerful family in the East to support our cause and to finalize my coronation. That is why you, my daughter, will marry Lord Declan as soon as it is blessed, and I will take back our Kingdom."

Rho has to fight the anger bubbling up inside her. She wants to slap him.

~

"I HATE HIM," MUTTERS LIEUTENANT COLONEL JETT TORN, EYES burning a hole through Declan Snow and his smug grin. He leans against the wall with his arms crossed, his friend doing the same.

"Everyone hates him," Peter Knight agrees, making a face at the Lord. Declan runs his fingers through his hair. "I think it's the fact that he looks like a Princess."

Jett curls his lip up with distaste. "I am sure it's more than that."

Peter chuckles at his friend, so serious, before turning back to the food in front of him. King Thanthos allows his guards to eat amongst the commanding family and their loved ones. Jett and Peter usually lean against the wall, eat their food, and judge the noble people. And every meal is the same: Peter listens while Jett fixates on his hatred for Declan Snow.

Jett nudges his friend suddenly, surprising Peter. "Where were you last night, anyway? I thought we were going for a drink."

"Uh," Peter shuffles feet, his cheeks changing color. "I was training with Cibor."

Laughing, Jett wraps his arm around Peter's shoulder. "Good, you could use the extra practice."

Peter forces a laugh, elbowing his friend back as a small relieved sigh escapes his lips. It's not long until the façade drops, and Peter has a grave look on his face. With a low, trembling voice he says, "Can I ask you something?"

"I don't know, can you?"

"Hey, Captain Grammar, it's a simple yes or no."

Jett smirks wildly. "Yeah, go ahead."

At his words, Peter grows serious. "Is it true that Marcs' family was skinned and burned?"

Jett blinks in surprise, that wasn't the question he was expecting. He swallows hard, concentrating on the scrape mark on his boots. How can he put this? Jett sighs, defeated, all he can do is nod and give a feeble, "Yes". Peter looks as if he has been punched in the gut, his face turning ghost-white. When he signed up for the Guard, he never thought that Thanthos would allow such brutality. And it makes him sick to his stomach.

Jett sees his friend struggling yet he cannot help but watch Princess Eirho talking to her ladies and sister. What he wouldn't give to know the secret in her eyes? Why do they tear up in the moments she thinks no-one is watching? He watches as she looks out of the large windows with a delicate frown on her face.

Peter reaches for a glass, accidentally clinking with another one beside it. This draws Jett's attention back.

With a weak smile, Peter reaches for a pitcher full to the brim with alcohol. It will serve as his refillable glass for the evening, if he can help it.

Jett swats at him. "You keep drinking like that on the job, you'll be excommunicated. We might as well just start calling you Rum, now."

Peter smiles at him half-heartedly and takes a big swig.

Jett doesn't even notice the smile, for his eyes are resting on Eirho's face once more. She is mesmerizing, losing him in her vivid eyes, mirroring the waves of an ocean. She is a Goddess among mortals. He wishes he were royalty more often than not, that way he could be sitting at her table. He comes from a line of nobles, sure, but he will never be able to sit at a table with Thanthos and his daughters, even if he knows he belongs there. Never.

Eirho wishes she didn't have to sit at this table, faking laughter and joy while the people around her tell boring stories and construct lie after lie. She would do anything to be outside under the blanket of stars, riding her horse into the forests. These people are liars and cheaters, plus a handful of them are proclaimed murderers. Her mother would loathe her sitting in the company of such people, but her father fits in with them all too perfectly.

Her eyes flicker away from the table for a moment, spotting a familiar and comforting face. He stands tall in front of the throne room doors. Jett Torn is unlike any other man she has met in this world, she decides. He is witty and compassionate, playful and strong. And much more. She recognizes the risks that he takes whilst working and the dark things that he must do for her father. Despite that, she sees the good in him and knows he's not that man. Her Jett doesn't revel in such horrid tasks. He is still perfect to her.

Glimpsing towards the door, he catches her eye. He understands exactly what he needs to do next.

5

NOW

Outside on the boardwalk, Shadow fastens her cloak, hiding from any inquisitive eyes. A thick fog surrounds her, giving her a veil of protection. And since Shadow slipped away at dusk, most of The City is asleep. Her journey to the other side of The City shall be safe.

She left Dax alone so that he could speak to Xero and the Skulls; the leader had requested him after all. His journey will be safe too as Shadow sent a scout to watch his back, just in case. Her mind is whirring with questions about Dax. She pushes the thoughts away for now, focusing instead, on the task at hand.

Below her, the creaking boards broadcast her arrival to anyone hiding in the shadows, though no-one comes to face her. Guards are scarce here which is even more evidence that Thanthos doesn't care about his people. It makes no difference to him if the Ghetto populace lives or not. He lacks compassion for his people, especially the lower class. Most of whom have already been killed by his hand. Only the strong shall prevail against Thanthos.

Shadow's mind goes to Dax once more, fear plaguing her. Moments before, she had opened her bedroom door to discover her things all jumbled around. The box she kept in her closet was not where she left it, the front door was wide open, and Dax was nowhere to be found. She had panicked when she recalled the private items inside the box, scrambling to check the contents. Dax took a couple of the photos with him but why? She prays that he won't use what he learned against her. That still didn't explain why he chose those two photos specifically: one of King Argos and one of the Palace interior: the ballroom to be precise. And no matter what she does, Shadow can't shake the feeling that Dax isn't quite who he says he is.

She traverses the inner heart of The City with ease, moving as one with large crowds before slipping off and taking the narrow, hidden passages that she knows best. It's all about instinct and awareness.

Within minutes she is sneaking by a group of guards and heading into a tiny shop filled with various trinkets and an array of colors. Everything from dolls and toy cars, to remedies and books line the walls. Blankets and rugs are strung about in a disorderly fashion—somehow only adding to the character and the uniqueness of the shop.

Moving through a curtain of beads, she peers at a thin-faced brunette sitting on a stool, reading a book that is clearly over a thousand pages. She's clearly engrossed and Shadow hesitates, not wanting to interrupt.

"She is in the back," the girl says, without warning. She doesn't glance up, not even for a second.

Shadow narrows her eyes and fights her way through a wall of blankets into the back room where bookshelves line the walls. She walks alongside the shelves, counting the books until she finds the one that she's after. Shadow pulls the golden-lined book toward her and there is a shift in the room.

The bookshelf to her right spins half way around, leaving just enough space for her to squeeze through. As she does, she hits a button that places the shelf back to its original spot, leaving her in the pitch black.

Shadow shuffles her feet through the long corridor and down a set of stairs, treading carefully in the darkness. Her memory is the only thing guiding her. Why they don't put lights on the whole wall she'll never know. The further she walks, the lighter it gets, until a single candle is sitting on a hook next to her head. It's half-melted; an indication of how much time has passed. Shadow knows just by looking at that candle, what kind of scene she'll be walking into.

She types a code in the keypad below the candle and places her hand on it. A vivid blue light scans her hand, followed by a beep. Slowly but surely, a steel door opens releasing a flood of sound. The clattering of tools and grunting sounds mix all too easily with the fragile whimpers she can hear now. Whoever it is gave up fighting a long time ago. Shadow drops her eyes and swallows hard. She removes her hood before stepping through the door, listening as it closes with a final *clunk*.

Walking down one last passage, she walks into a circular room that unnerves her more than the rest. This is where all the dark secrets are uncovered. A dazzling chandelier hangs above the table in front of her. The beauty of the crystal offers a stark contrast to the shaking figure strapped to the table. Shadow feels sick as the overpowering smell of blood and body odor floods into her nostrils.

A sneering, older woman stands next to the table holding a long, razor-sharp knife in her pale hand. As always, she has a look of masochistic glee. Fortunately for Shadow, the woman seems pleased to see her.

Shadow's alarmed eyes stay glued to the figure on the table. The man has rust-colored hair and eyes that are glazed over with pain and suffering. Cuts line his body like paint lines a canvas. He has become a piece of art to this woman. Creeks of blood no bigger than a pencil drip down the cuts and onto the table in pools.

He is paralyzed with pain.

"I see you are hard at work," Shadow comments.

The woman wipes the knife on the apron wrapped neatly around her waist. "He's a difficult one, but I'm breaking him. What brings you here?"

Shadow glances around the room. Different tools used for torture hang menacingly on hooks and ledges in the wall. Dotted between the metal instruments are photographs of beautiful men and women in a range of positions and attires. Everything is made of different metals and decorated with a purpose. It's a sadistic yet beautiful gallery of crimson, black, and gold.

Shadow snaps out of her trance. "Has he told you anything?" The room is elegantly done and it troubles her that it is being used for such wickedness. Such necessary wickedness.

"He said something about 'vengeance for Princess Rho'."

Shadow clenches her teeth until a pain starts to radiate her along her jaw. She releases it, feeling stiff and uncomfortable. "Vex, clean him up and clear his memory. You know that Torn will tear down every house until he finds him."

"We don't want that," Vex replies dryly. She returns to the side of the table. "Give me the rest of the day and I'll free him to the streets."

"At least let this one have his pants back."

Vex laughs darkly and sets her knife across the muscled, ghostly, white chest of the man. Shadow watches aghast as his body fights desperately to move away from the advancing blade with no success. He is helpless. Vex combs through her raven and silver hair with a thoughtful look on her face. As she reaches the end, just below her shoulder blades, she turns to face Shadow with a sudden frown.

"I need a higher-ranking officer, Shadow. These Privates know nothing of what is happening in the Palace, apart from the fact that Torn is in control." She crosses her arms. "Maybe you should bring him to me."

Shadow sends her a vicious glare but Vex doesn't bat an eyelid. "No-one is allowed to lay a hand on Torn—no-one but me."

Vex rubs her pointed chin in mock consideration. "Should I respond or let it go, I wonder?"

"Let it go, Vex," Shadow warns. "I've got a bone to pick with Torn. But that's not why I'm here. I came to pick your memory."

"Let me guess... Tools' records are proving positive again. The recruit you have is coming out clean as a whistle–but you think I know more about whoever is in your mind." Shadow nods reluctantly. "I see. And might that someone be Xero's newest pup?" Vex smirks knowingly. "Give me a name."

"Dax Ryer." Shadow doesn't hesitate.

Vex inhales and hums softly to herself. Humming is a way for her to clear her mind and sift through memories.

Within a few seconds, the humming ceases and she averts her gaze.

Shadow can't help but tap her foot feverishly, an annoying nervous habit that she swore she had dropped years ago. "His father took him out of The City to keep him safe for multiple reasons; Dax's father knew that his son would be important. And he was right. Dax will cause a lot of events to occur. Some in this time, some in the next."

"What does he look like?" Shadow says with narrowed eyes. She's always been skeptical of vague riddles. She tries to see a hidden meaning in Vex's words but it's no use.

"The young man is who he says he is," Vex says, "and if you are still skeptical, check his history yourself. Now, I'm afraid that I must get back to work. Bring me a higher-ranking officer, if you would."

Shadow assents. She eagerly leaves the room, abandoning the powerless man to the mercy of the mad woman.

She fears that he'll never see the light of day again.

~

"I DON'T UNDERSTAND WHAT HE WANTS WITH MAGIC," DAX ADMITS, looking to Shadow for answers, as she averts her gaze to Xero. She hopes that Xero will take the reins on this one; she has absolutely no desire to speak about Thanthos. "My magic can hardly lift anything, it's useless." Dax looks to Shadow again, his expression unreadable. "I don't even know how I have it! My parents weren't gifted and my father said it skips generations. If all magic is like this, then why would Thanthos want something so weak?"

Xero called them here to talk to them about the next plan of action and discuss their next move.

"The Heir magic is far more powerful than the Pure magic that you have, Dax. He wants unopposed power. Which is why he's been slaughtering our people for ages," Xero says bluntly. He swallows hard, feeling an unquenchable dryness in his throat. "He wants The Heir magic because it's unlimited. With that, he can do whatever he pleases."

Shadow nods in agreement. "Yes, but Thanthos doesn't understand the consequences of its deep, ancient magic. It's protected and gifted by The Creators because of how dangerous it is. I'm sure that The Oracles he uses are involved with Dark magic."

Both men look to her, astounded. How could she know something like that? The Oracles were meant to help the people use their magic for good, but they are no longer the good forces that The Creators intended them to be. The Oracles are enveloped in darkness.

"Consequences? What consequences?" asks Dax.

Shadow shrugs indifferently. "I just don't believe it's a good idea, that's all. He doesn't know what he's dealing with. And neither do we."

Xero flicks his wrist as if brushing her worries aside. "The magic may be a myth for all we know, yes. But there is a Sorcerer that knows all about magic," Xero explains to Dax, seeing Shadow's eyes light up. Her hunger to escape the walls overwhelms her and soon she's clutching her thigh to control her excitement.

"I'm assuming we've abandoned any plan of taking over the Palace, right now," she says.

Xero nods. "For now. The Palace has upped their security. We have to find a way around it first. We need to see what the Sorcerer has to say first. There's no point running around blind. A childhood ally told me that he's back home."

Shadow is ready to take action, she is desperate to speak to the Sorcerer. Speaking to him might be the key to learning more about magic and where to find it. Shadow needs to get rid of Thanthos and save The City.

Maybe then she can have her old life back.

~

"I SAID NO."

"Xero I'm serious! You can't just brush me off your shoulder. I *have* to go. You'll have to stop telling me what to do at some point," Shadow whines. "That old geezer won't talk to anyone but me."

"He will."

"For a price, and even then, he won't give them the whole truth," she counters. "You know that. Why would you let me go to the Palace but not the forest?"

Deep down Xero knows that she is right. The Sorcerer favors Shadow over everyone else and trusts her. She has visited him ever since she was a child, although with Xero's recent babysitting, she hasn't been able to visit as often as she'd like.

Xero looks over at Cibor slumped in the corner and struggling to keep his eyes open. He'd be no use. He turns to an eager Dax, practically bursting with energy. Could Dax get the answers they needed? No, Xero decides. There's no-one else he trusts more than

Shadow. The Sorcerer will welcome Shadow and only Shadow. And that hardly leaves him with a choice.

"We need help from all sides if we're going to take down Thanthos. We cannot expect to do it alone," she points out now, her face determined and resolute. "You have to let me go to him."

"No." Xero hates to give in.

"You have no right to hold me here. You know I can get out of the cells faster than you can reprogram them. And unlike you, the others will refuse to keep me locked up." If she just keeps pushing, she knows that she'll get what she wants. First, however, Xero has to grant her access to the weapons.

"And the other half would want to keep you locked up, Shadow! Having you go past our perimeter is just asking for trouble. Anyone lurking outside the walls automatically draws attention and you will more than likely be caught."

"I can escape."

Dax moves to stand next to Shadow. Xero looks at him in despair. "I support her, Xero. And I want to go with her."

Xero throws his hands up in defeat, looking dumbfounded between the two of them. He looks pleadingly to Cibor for help, but the mighty man leans against the wall defeated by sleep. Xero knows which side Cibor would choose.

Shadow smiles at Dax when she sees Xero's resignation. Even as he stands by her side, she still doesn't trust him. Trust is earned, not given, in her mind.

Despite her constantly challenging Xero, Dax notices that Shadow seems to have nothing but respect for her leader. He looks out for her, and though they fight about everything, she'll do whatever she can to help him and their cause. "She is supposed to be watching out for you, kid," Xero says. His voice is softer now, more tired in tone. "Not the other way around."

"She will, but can't I watch her back too? Maybe the Sorcerer will be pleased with me." Dax puffs his chest out. *That definitely won't get you far,* Shadow thinks to herself. He is beyond arrogant when it comes to his own talents. Not that she'll mention it now. Xero will support the decision if she stays quiet.

After a long pause, Xero nods. He shoos them away like pests and mutters something about weapons before retiring from the room. Shadow sighs with relief and Dax smirks wildly.

He better lose that smirk before they visit the Sorcerer.

~

SHADOW RACES FROM THE ROOM, SPRINTING DOWN THE LONG corridors to her personal chamber. She keeps nothing there but a blanket, a few books, and some paper; that is all she needs. When she types her code in and steps into the room, the warm scent of vanilla surrounds her. She smiles.

Her target is a book hidden along the shelves of her near empty room. When she finds it, she touches the cover gently, tracing a rose carved into the front. It was a gift from her mother long ago, before she died. It's her favorite book and she never leaves The City without it.

She puts the book in her bag and runs to leave the room. She's so excited about leaving The City that she doesn't notice Dax standing right outside her door.

"So, how do we get to this Sorcerer?" he asks, arms crossed. "Is he in The City?"

Shadow laughs in his face. "Why is it, do you think, that Xero fought not to let me go?"

Dax looks blankly at her and shrugs, "Because it's dangerous?"

"It's more than 'dangerous', kid. It's outside the walls."

His jaw drops, just for a second. Hell, he hadn't been back there in years. It's a wild and merciless place. A place that he had hoped he would never have to return to again. How ironic that he unknowingly signed up for a return trip.

"Read the fine-print next time," Shadow says, zipping her bag up. She busies herself with a quiet inventory of her weapons and tools, in preparation for the journey ahead Dax gulps. Out there, there is a danger unimaginable to any person who strays too far from The City. That has to be why Thanthos is fighting so viciously to find the magic. Nobody, not even the wickedest of men, would want to remain unarmed and vulnerable to the threats outside.

Dax's mind races until he feels dizzy and nauseous, pressing himself against the stone walls for balance. He breathes steadily and pretends that the world out there is nothing more than empty, boring lands.

Shadow grabs at him. She is thrilled. He wonders if she knows what she is getting herself into. Of course, she does. Something tells him that she's been outside many times.

When they're packed and armed with the best weapons, Xero meets them once more, still reluctant to let them go. There is still a futile glimmer of hope inside of him that Shadow will change her mind and stay. He owes her one more gift before her trek.

Shadow breathes in awe as she accepts a final weapon from the silent and stern leader: a thin, elegant blade, with a hilt made of diamond and dragons carved into the blade. It has been passed down between every leader as a sign of honor. And now rests in Shadow's hands. She feels a sense of power flood over her as the blade rests in her palms.

"Forgive me for not gifting you with this before," Xero says, his voice hoarse. "This will help you out there if you need it. I hope it won't come to that. Please... be cautious."

Shadow nods and puts the sword away carefully before fastening it around her waist. "Thank you, Xero. You know how much this means to me. I promise to treat it well."

He smiles. "Cibor and Rencher will help you out of The City. Call us if there's any problems. We will expect you back by tomorrow noon."

It won't take that long; she has her shortcuts. In the back of her mind, she wonders if Dax is trustworthy enough to take on her secret routes.

She makes her decision as Cibor and Rencher appear from the corridor. Cibor towers over her easily, whereas Rencher is a couple of inches shorter than her— which makes him tiny. Rencher wiggles his nose, causing his square-framed glasses to bob comically up and down. Finally, he pushes his glasses back on to the bridge of his nose and looks attentively to Shadow. With a flare of his nostrils, he offers his hand out.

Hesitant to take it, Shadow finally thrusts her hand out when Cibor shoots her a glare for being rude.

"Nice to see you again," he comments, his orange hair brightening in the light. "Haven't seen you since the last Hanging."

"Hanging?" Dax cuts in.

Shadow waves her hand at him, casting his question aside. This isn't any of his business. "Yes, can we leave now?"

Cibor nods and pushes Rencher in front of him, giving Shadow a look of understanding. The fiery-haired man just can't keep his mouth shut. How did he become a Skull?

Rencher and Dax start up a conversation about the Ruins of The City versus the old docks and Cibor and Shadow hang back. "I want to take the West route," she murmurs. Her eyes narrow as she scans ahead. "I think it'll be quicker."

He nods, reading between the lines. Cibor is one of the few people she can trust no matter what and she is happy that he's the one who is leading her out of The City. Trustworthiness and the ability to make someone feel safe are the things she admires most in an ally, and a friend. She hopes to do the same for Cibor.

Shadow has known Cibor since she was a teenager, longer than any other Skull, including Xero. Cibor tutored her in sword-fighting and hand-to-hand combat; lessons her mother loathed and her father adored. Shadow needed to be able to protect herself and that is exactly what she learned to do. Cibor was one of the first people to make her feel comfortable at the Skulls—back when she got involved. He would entice her with stories of the mighty leader, Xander Marcs—Xero's late father. The stories told of a man battling for the wellbeing of the helpless and vulnerable, against a wicked man who kept the throne. Shadow would feel inspired by the stories of heroism and defiance, and soon she knew what path she was going to take. If it wasn't for Cibor, she wouldn't be here.

~

FOR A GOOD HOUR THEY WALK, DISAPPEARING INTO THE TREES OF The City's miniature forest, a place known as the Bush. Though it seems harmless, the forest has many wild and dangerous animals that lurk in the Bush. They watch the travelers steadily from their vantage point in the trees. When the Great City was built, they placed a wall at the edge of the free folk Forest: a forest vaster and more mysterious than even this one. Few men or beasts would enter. Yet another reason to seek haven within The City. Rencher and Dax remain uncertain of the forest, having dropped back behind Cibor and Shadow, who traverse with ease. Many moons have guided them through the Bush, either leading them to safety or to an escape route. The creatures of the Bush pale in comparison to the Great King of The City. They don't fear the animals—animals are predictable. Thanthos is not.

The thick trees block out the moonlight and the whispers in the branches only excite the imaginations of the two fearful men. Twigs break and leaves crumble—they are being followed. Shadow pays no heed to the creature tracking them, though Rencher is spinning in a constant circle with his weapon held high.

Cibor finally snaps. "Lower that fucking weapon down, Rencher. Nothing will get your head bitten off faster in here than waving that weapon around. And I promise, these creatures aren't friendly. Though, if you shoot me, your death will be much more painful," he growls.

Shadow smirks when she sees the frightened man shiver. "I

don't like guns to be pointed at me, Rench." She says, "Remember what happened to Valys."

Valys was the Skull who held a gun to Shadow's head after a disagreement. The big man ended up face first in the ground, pleading to be let go. All those lessons with Cibor certainly paid off.

"Yeah, you really don't want to piss this lass off," chuckles Cibor. "She is a feisty woman with wit and skill to back her."

Dax sends an inquiring stare to Shadow. He is left hanging just as the group arrives at the edge of the wall.

"Is the Sorcerer actually capable of magic?" Dax blurts.

Cibor shakes his head, laughing. "He's more of an herbalist, but the people think that he uses magic for healing and medicine."

Shadow shrugs. "I've always found him rather magical."

Dax scratches his head, wondering how an herbalist outside the walls is supposed to help them.

"Well, here we are, the one exit," Cibor announces, gesturing to the mighty oaks. Two trees wrap around themselves, weaving effortlessly in a graceful and eternal dance. They grow a bit more every time he comes here, even in the coldest of months.

Shadow walks towards the tree, digging in the dirt around it. She finds a brass key and she takes it to a rock by the roots. Shadow traces various patterns in the rock with her finger and the rock slides to the right, revealing a small hidden door. It is the passage to the outside of the wall.

Cibor takes a quick peek around while Shadow lowers her stuff into the dark hole and sends Dax in first. Rencher keeps his weapon drawn and shakes when the breeze moves the trees around.

"Thank you," she whispers through the rustling. Cibor stops to listen to her, knowing from the tone in her voice there is more to be heard. "I promise to come back in one piece. Keep Xero distracted. Also, make sure the door is shut tight."

The big man's eyes flash for a second—their secret code for keeping an eye out for danger. "Of course."

Cibor watches as his past student vanishes into the rabbit hole, landing into the dirt and darkness below.

"Safe travels," he says, the wind carrying his voice into the tunnel.

Shadow looks to Dax, who is pressed against the wall, staring dead ahead into pitch blackness. Sighing, she lifts her things over her shoulder and begins to walk, squeezing Dax's shoulder in reassurance. Dax soon follows suit.

The tunnel is just large enough to stand up in and touch the cool, earthy walls. It's easy to maneuver without lighting as Shadow is guiding them. She's long since memorized every step. "How long has this tunnel been here?" he asks quietly, trying to make conversation.

"Longer than I know of. I'm assuming since the walls went up," she lies. There is an entire network of tunnels under The City, but he doesn't need to know that. These tunnels are a refuge and escape route for the innocent people of The City. That is something she cannot risk.

Dax refrains from blurting out any more questions. It is abundantly clear that she's annoyed.

For the remainder of their journey, he keeps his mouth shut tightly.

~

SUNRISE BEGINS TO FLOURISH OVER THE EASTERN SKY: ORANGES, yellows, and pinks all merge together to create an ocean of color in the sky. The clouds, white and sharp, cut like waves in the sand, the orange slashes through them like a storm. Yet the yellows and pinks bring a calmness to the sky, and Shadow is happy to be awake for such a marvelous show of Mother Nature's power.

The pair reach the depths of the free folk Forest, after trudging along the beaten trail for what seems like hours. Luckily, they traveled through the night and are at the summit of a gigantic network of trees, the biggest ahead of them. They can see the finish line: a small cottage woven into the trees. The windows are carved into the tree trunk, the doors are made of bark, and stairs to the house are made of stepping stones. Even the limbs and vines have twisted to form a roof over the cottage. The cottage was created through ancient magic and song. It is a wonder that amazes Shadow each time she sees it. Behind her, Dax is in shock, never having seen anything like it. He rubs his eyes, thinking that his eyes are playing tricks on him. It's all very much real.

They are nearing the door of the cottage when a puff of smoke appears. Not long after a small man, a dwarf perhaps, steps through the smoke. He glares openly at Dax, clearly suspicious. Dax looks nervously at Shadow.

"Well, what do we have here?" asks the old man, stabbing a short and fat finger into Dax's arm, applying enough pressure to make him jerk back in pain. "Timid and skinny as a pecker's leg."

"Oakenstaid."

The Sorcerer stops his interrogation and turns to Shadow, his eyes widening with excitement.

"They let you out of the walls!" he exclaims cheerfully with a huge grin. "Now, I would not have paid heed to a friend approaching. Hmph! But this man is no friend of mine," he says defiantly.

Shadow smirks, gesturing for Dax to take a seat on a fallen log until they finish their meeting.

"Come into my home," says the Sorcerer, taking Shadow's bag and leading her up the stone steps. He ushers her in and slams it shut, a sure sign to Dax that he must stay put.

Shadow takes her jacket off while Oakenstaid puts her things on a wooden rack to his left. He heads into the kitchen as Shadow takes in the familiar smell of bark and a smoldering fire. She looks around her in awe. The furniture is carved from fallen trees, artistically engineered to fit the quirky home. The main room is covered in intriguing items, from potion bottles and spell books to shrunken heads and lizard legs. It's busy but welcoming, much like Oakenstaid.

"Oh, how I have missed your companionship, Shadow. Alas, I know that you are not here to see an old friend!" he says as he goes to his fireplace and sets a pot of water above the licking flames. "I know you well enough to know that the sole way Marcs would let you past the prison walls is to seek my guidance. Tell me about this mission." He takes a seat in his tall, oak chair, waiting for a response.

Shadow sighs and sits opposite. "You're right, I wouldn't be let out without purpose." She reaches into her pocket and sets a tiny envelope onto the table. "We heard Thanthos that is too damn close to what he's hunting. An ancient magic, to be precise. I want to know how to destroy the magic and stop him."

The Sorcerer runs his hand down his beard thoughtfully.

"The people bow to him with fear, that is without question. He has locked free folk up in cells to rot and starve, and he has run anyone that is against him out of The City. There is a restlessness in my woods. Even the Ancient Ones are hidden from him—who is challenging him now that they have gone, Shadow?"

"I am," she answers determinedly. "He may not know it yet, but a true ruler exists in Alpha and the Skulls and I want to put her on the throne. Thanthos wants this magic so that he can rule without opposition."

The old man nods and rises from where he sits to check his pot of water. He grabs various ingredients from the shelves nearby, mostly plants and seeds, before pulling a beard hair off and tossing it into the large pot. He stirs it and whispers some foreign and archaic words before he turns to Shadow.

"You know what is needed for me to summon your answers."

Without a care, she moves toward him with her arm extended. He grabs a blade from near the pot and grips her wrist in his icy palm. His eyes close and he mumbles more gibberish. The words jar in Shadow's ears, sounding inexplicably harsh and intense.

Shadow tries her best to relax, knowing what is coming. She closes her eyes as Oakenstaid slices the blade down the sensitive flesh of her arm. The blood pours from the wound in rivulets, cascading into the pot below. The fire rises as each drop of blood hits the pot.

Oakenstaid shoves her arm away suddenly, pushing her back. His eyes are huge and frantic. Shadow opens her mouth to ask him what's wrong but he stays silent as he studies her. The blood trickles from her wrist to the floor as she stares at him in shock.

"You are not wrong about being his opposition, Shadow. I did not realize I would find such a... grave truth."

"Oakenstaid, what's that supposed to mean?" she demands. She nurses her arm against her body, applying pressure to the wound. "Tell me what you—"

"No. I cannot divulge this secret. You must decide how this story ends on your own, Shadow," he tells her solemnly. He grabs another bottle of something and pours it into the mixture. It goes black and fills the room with smoke, disappearing a few moments later.

She stands frozen in place, unable to process his reaction. Suddenly, she comes to a realization. "Does that mean you know how to destroy the magic? Where can I find it?"

Oakenstaid sighs. "This dark and powerful magic is contained inside of something," he says. "It is in a secret location, sealed away. Something *among the roses.* I cannot see where it is as there is a spell protecting it, but it is what Thanthos is after. You need to discover where the magic lies."

"How? Where do I start?"

"I cannot say. Fate is intertwined too deeply with this." He takes a deep breath, clearly upset that he cannot say more. "You have a destiny greater than you think."

Swallowing hard, she nods. He won't tell her why she is on this path, but she believes that she has a deeper purpose. And knowing the ancient magic is sealed somewhere… she knows that she must be the one to find it.

"Oakenstaid, thank you," she says softly.

He looks up at her with surprise, guilt plaguing his features. "I wish I could tell you more. I really do, but this path is for you alone. If I dare trifle with the powers at play, the future to come... I could alter it terribly."

She searches his face. This has to mean that everything will turn out for the best. Or at least the best outcome there can be. This means there is a chance they'll be able to take Thanthos down.

"What you've told me is enough. I know what I need to do."

He takes a deep breath and hands her a bandage for her arm. "Always trust your gut."

She chews at her lip, wishing she knew what fate has in store for her.

Oakenstaid never offered an outright answer to her question, never giving her the fear of what is coming, but her heart is pounding like a war drum. She knows something is coming.

6

THEN

Eirho sneaks down the hall, away from the cacophony of voices that seem to chase after her. All the laughter, gossiping, and music is giving her a headache. The cool and tranquil garden has never been so inviting. She slips her shoes off, placing them near the gate as she welcomes the feel of cold stone on the bottom of her aching feet.

She pushes further into the labyrinth of foliage, slipping through the bushes toward the fish pond. She tugs the bottom of her dress up as she sits, spying those gigantic far-set eyes breaking the water's surface.

She struggles in her pocket to dig out some bread from the feast. She saved it for the fish; their wide mouths are waiting expectantly. Breaking little crumbs off, she tosses them into the water, hearing gulps and splashes as the fish take the food and swim down into the depths of the pond.

"Rho."

She cannot keep herself from smiling at the sound of his voice. Jett sits down beside her and rests his arms on his knees. His beams at her and she giggles.

"You seem to be in a good mood," she notes as he places her hand in his. Her hand feels so small, cocooned like this. So warm and safe.

"I get to be with you," he reminds her. "That's enough to put any man in a good mood."

"Except for Declan," she says, rolling her eyes.

Jett purses his lips. "How's that going? Babysitting him, I mean." He feigns a casual tone.

She swallows and stares down at her feet. She doesn't know how to tell him, or even if she wants to. He will find out eventually and it is best if it comes from her. Realizing she has no choice; she removes her hand from his after giving a tight squeeze. Guilt is already sinking into her.

"Jett, I have something to tell you."

His smile fades as he notices the sudden turn in her voice. Whatever she has to tell him, it can't be good. "What's wrong, Eirho?" he says in a low tone. "What happened?"

All she can do is offer him a weak, halfhearted smile.

"Declan is my betrothed."

Jett pulls his hand away, looking at her in disbelief. Pain courses through him.

"What?" he whispers, his voice breaking.

"My father told me today that he wants me to marry Declan," she says, avoiding eye connection. "I have to do it."

"You don't *have* to do it," he argues. "You can tell him about us. About how we want to get married."

"He'll kill you," she says. "My father would rather us sneak around while he uses Declan to gain military alliances. He wants power. And he won't let anything get in the way of that."

"I thought you loved me." A cold statement. Eirho feels Jett's words pierce her lungs.

"I do love you. I'm in love with you," she pleads. "But if I want to keep you safe… I have to do this."

He watches her with big, confused eyes. As much as he wants

to understand what she means, he can't. "You don't do this to someone you love, Eirho."

"I don't have a choice," she whimpers, the brim of her eyes filling with tears. Her heart breaks inside of her and the pain seeping into the cracks. The way he's looking at her now... it's killing her. Jett Torn is a broken man and it's all her fault.

He stares at the pond, not feeling strong enough to look at her. If he looks into her eyes now, he will see his pain mirrored back in her eyes. This brave, intelligent, wonderful woman should not have to know the pain of sacrificing love for duty. She should not be bullied into marrying some man who will never love her the way that she deserves. Jett wants to be the man who treats her well, that arrogant son-of-a-bitch Declan doesn't. It makes him sick to his stomach just thinking about it.

Eirho reaches for his hand again, pulling it close despite his protests. She needs to feel his touch emblazoned on her skin. She wants to remember every inch of him as this might be the last time she can touch him.

"I didn't mean for it to happen, Jett," she says quietly. "You know I've loved you since I was a child and I will never love anyone else."

"I know, Eirho, but seeing you with him... Knowing he is touching you... Being the face you see before you sleep and the first thing you see when you wake. It's not only about loving each other. It's about all those possibilities... those moments that we could've had. All that will be stripped away the second that you marry him. Those moments I've wished to have for as long as I can remember." With a shaky breath he yanks his hand back and presses his thumb into the corner of each eye. Eirho sees the tears pool around the tip of his thumb and her heart breaks a little more. Every hope he had for the two of them is fading with every word she speaks.

All she can do is lean her head on his shoulder, craving his reassuring touch. She needs him to make it through.

"I want to be there for you too, Jett. I want to be the person you share your heart and soul with. I want to be the one who takes care of you when you're sick and sees your first gray hairs growing. I want to have a family with you," she whispers into his neck. His smell is an intoxicating perfume. She breathes in deep and her head spins. "I have to keep you safe, though." She pushes herself upright. "This is how I do that."

Jett turns to face her with a stony expression. After a while, he pushes himself up and rises to his feet. He doesn't know what to say. Jett stares at her long and hard, his face indecipherable. With a deep breath, he turns and strides out of the garden, leaving Eirho alone.

"ALPHA, WHAT ARE YOU DOING?" ASKS RHO, WATCHING HER SISTER AS she digs through a small box. Rho has been pacing the Palace, hoping to find Jett so that they can speak again. When she realizes he is out, she gives in and decides to see her sister.

"I want to paint, but I can't find my brushes," she answers in a sad tone.

Rho grins and reaches to the top shelf in Alpha's room. She grabs another small box and hands it to her younger sister.

"Your brushes are in here," she tells her.

Alpha snatches the box and runs to adjust her easel. She searches for the perfect brush and dips it onto a palette of colors that she mixed herself. When Alpha was a child, Rho had taught her how to make her own shades from a mix of colors.

Rho sits on the window seat watching her little sister paint. Alpha is a rarity; she's strong and intelligent as well as kind. Unfortunately for Alpha, though, a kind heart is a weakness in the eyes of others. She's a gentle soul stuck in this unforgiving world. Even her own father wants to harden her. *That's the way it's always been,* Rho thinks, as she gazes at the busy Palace yard below. Her father thirsts for war. Mankind loves chaos and loves to create it. The City has been in more wars than she could ever learn about during her tutoring. And considering what she knows of the rest of the world, everywhere is the same.

"Sister," Alpha pipes up, painting a thin, long line across her canvas. She tilts her head as she makes a thicker line in a deep orange.

"Yes?" Eirho replies, looking away from the world outside. She smiles, seeing Alpha's sunrise appearing on the canvas.

"Is Father making you marry Declan?"

Eirho chokes. Reality is getting closer and closer and it's making her uncomfortable.

"He wants me to, yes. To make our Kingdom stronger," she explains. "To create an alliance."

"But you don't want to marry him," Alpha notes. "It's obvious."

Eirho chuckles at the statement. She didn't realize that her feelings for Declan were that clear. She makes a mental note to hide her disgust better in the future.

"He's a jerk," Alpha says, shaking her head. "He is cruel to people. I've never seen you act that way, Eirho. You treat everyone with kindness, regardless of who they are. Declan treats them like they're dirt on the bottom of his gold-lined boot."

Eirho lets out a huge laugh. "Yes, Alpha, I know. He is a selfish and arrogant man. Maybe some of my wonderful qualities will rub off on him."

"Oh, I doubt it." Alpha bows her head, defeated. She doesn't want her sister to marry that awful man. She wants to make it better.

"Don't worry too much, Alpha. I'll be fine, you'll see," Eirho tells her. "I'm going to go train with Cibor before I get in trouble for being lazy. Could I see your painting when you're done?"

Alpha grins and nods wildly, unable to contain it. She cannot wait to show her sister the final product and make her proud.

Eirho walks across the room, pausing momentarily to place her hand on her sister's shoulder. She gives it a careful squeeze before she leaves the room.

7

NOW

"What did the Sorcerer have to say?" Xero questions, raising his eyebrow as he slides a glass of water over to Shadow.

"He wasn't as helpful as I'd hoped, but he did say that we're searching for a location. He said that we should look through history books and things like that for something *among the roses*." Shadow shrugs. "He seems terrified and excited about the outcome. From what I could gather, it will turn out in our favor," she explains. As soon as she's done, Shadow grabs the water and gulps it down in seconds. She's left with an unquenchable thirst even after drinking. It's her own fault, really—she forced her and Dax to walk through the night until they made it back to The City.

Xero collapses into his chair as if his feet have given out. "I will speak to Aine and Tools. Let's just try to find any ancient scripture that might show us where we should be searching. I'll task the brainy duo with figuring out the mystery."

"What will you have me do?" Shadow inquires.

"Train Dax. If he is going to be an asset, we need him ready. Scout as usual, keep an eye out. You know the drill, Shadow." He waves his hand around impatiently; he wants to get to the point. "And keep yourself out of sight. Jett Torn's sight specifically."

She rolls her eyes. "Got it."

~

"WHY DO YOU LOOK UNCOMFORTABLE AFTER EVERY MEETING?" Shadow asks.

She is walking back home with Dax after touching base with the Council again. They discussed the various locations around The City that Thanthos has been targeting. He has searched old museums, chapels, and even the sewer. Nothing of interest has popped up yet but Xero wanted everyone on the same page.

Though Shadow has been pawning Dax off on others with every chance she gets, she's curious to know what he's thinking. Is he getting training? Is it magic training or combat training? She wants every bit of knowledge that she can get.

Dax shrugs in response, trying to make it look like she's wrong. He doesn't like the fact that she can read him so easily. He decides to ignore Shadow's question and ask one of his own.

"What do you think will happen if Thanthos finds the location of the magic?"

"I think Thanthos has been torturing and slaughtering our people for years, in the sheer hope of killing the one who has the magic. That tendency to murder doesn't just go away. He'll kill hundreds more; he's not going to stop now. He will awaken great darkness if he gets his hands on it," Shadow knows more than she is letting on. More than even Xero knows. The time she passed in libraries as a teen was spent gaining knowledge of magic and uncovering ancient history.

"Great darkness?"

"I don't know what it means exactly, but I know it won't be good. It'll result in a war within our own walls and I think it's happened already. As he searches for the location, things are only getting more chaotic." She ignores some chatter through her earbud, watching as Dax takes in all the information she gives him. "I need to speak with Tools and Aine before we head back. I have to give them the information I got from Oakenstaid."

"When will we begin looking for the Heir magic?"

"*We* aren't looking for anything. Cibor will be by to teach you some moves. Make certain you pay attention to what he says or he will kick your ass," she tells him, stopping as they reach the door. "I'll be back before dark."

~

AINE PULLS HER BAG UP HIGHER ON HER SHOULDER AS SHE JOGS through crowds of people. She's trying to keep up with Shadow as she makes a beeline for the bridge to Old Town—the first original section of The City. Aine is hoping to avoid Vex—the Skulls' fierce and merciless information gatherer. Or torturer if Aine is honest.

"Where are we going?" she questions, watching as Shadow pulls her cloak hood down, once they see the welcoming sight of the bridge. The guards avoid Old Town, so she is free to show her face here.

"There's a museum a few blocks from your favorite Skull. They have a secret room with ancient books and scrolls. If you pay them enough, they'll let you in. I don't have too much money... But I can be very persuasive."

Aine watches Shadow's fingers pull her cloak back, revealing the hilt of a gun. Shadow's skill in manipulation is one of the reasons why the Skulls have been successful in recent years.

As they cross the old cobblestone, they enter a town with tall, thin buildings made of wood and old stone. It was once a great city. Now it's a small corner of The City, harboring fugitives who are turned away from regular society. Aine grows increasingly uncomfortable as they duck under the crooked sign, knowing exactly the kind of people that she will see.

The misfits of The City love to live in Old Town. Greasy men with only a couple of fingers ogle Aine and try to squeeze her backside. It makes her skin crawl. She clings to Shadow by who refuses to deal with any nonsense.

They walk in silence for a while until they reach a quiet, empty street. Shadow walks up to the old museum and gently pulls on the door. It groans in pain and Aine flinches at the sound. Shadow yanks the door open and layers of dust coat them both. How long has it been since the business had any customers?

Aine hesitates for a moment, but against her better judgement, she follows right behind.

"This place is terrifying," she mumbles as she takes it all in. Cracked bones, strange concoctions in jars, and various pieces of the past line the room. Peculiar paintings and pottery works, including those in the shape of male genitalia. Everything seems to be musty and covered in a thick layer of dust. It looks as though no-one has maintained it since the building was built and that could have been millennia ago.

"Who dares to come into my museum?" A voice grunts. A man limps into the main room, his eyes sunken and narrow. His face is molded into a frown as he looks the women up and down with blatant distaste.

"I'm Shadow," the braver woman says, bowing slightly. "This is Aine." Aine gives the old man a slight wave. "We have come to buy some of your older books, sir."

"Ha!" He snorts abruptly, causing Aine to jump back. "You expect me to just give you a key to the past? What is in it for me?"

Shadow sighs, knowing what will need to be done. Aine steps behind her, peeking over Shadow's shoulder. This odd, little man is giving her the creeps.

"I don't have a lot of money," Shadow admits, handing him a small bag of coins. "But I can promise that I won't have your skin peeled off your body if you allow us to look at the books."

Aine is stunned as the man's anger erupts.

"You threaten me? You stupid bitches," he sneers, grabbing a bottle from the counter within his reach. His plan, undoubtedly, is to smack Shadow over the head with it.

The man goes for the obvious choice. He swings wildly at her face with the bottle. Shadow reaches out and launches it back behind her. She takes advantage of his confusion and slides a blade out of her sleeve. Soon, the man is pinned to the counter with the blade at his throat.

The blade is cold against his throat, threatening to pierce the sensitive skin. He shivers at the realization that he could die at her hands.

"I don't want to hurt you," Shadow tells him indifferently. "But I need the books. I will offer you safety from the Red Guard and the rebels and I'll make sure that the Skulls bring you supplies."

"The Skulls put you up to this? Xero Marcs will hear about—" He cuts off when she digs the blade into his neck, leaving beads of blood.

"He didn't make me do this. You did this all to yourself," she promises. "So, do we have a deal?"

The man grumbles, but to Aine's surprise, he nods. He gestures toward a large painting, twice the size of Shadow, on the wall with a gold trim. Shadow jerks her chin at the painting and removes the blade from his neck. He walks to the frame and gives it a quick push, causing it to jolt and move to the side.

"Down there," he mumbles.

"Thank you," she says, "but you're coming with us."

The man is startled as she grabs him by the collar and pushes him down into the basement. This way he'll have no chance to lock them in there. Shadow reaches into her pocket and grabs the rope, snatching his hands up and tying them together before he can react. She had this planned ahead of time.

"No funny business, tiny man," she says, making him lead the way in the dark and down the stairs. He stomps loudly to the bottom, glaring behind at Shadow.

"To your left, there's a switch."

Shadow flips it and the light buzzes from above. It takes a second before the room illuminates. The bright light reveals towering shelves and rows of books spreading in every direction. Shadow and Aine are in awe. The room is full to the brim: books, scrolls, and other scriptures are stacked on top of shelves or in piles on the floor.

Aine bounds in, eager to begin searching.

Shadow gestures the man to a tiny stool at the bottom of the stairs. "I need the oldest books you have."

"Far back, in a small shelf," he says wearily.

She nods towards Aine who runs down the rows to find the books she needs. When she comes to the small shelf, she realizes there are only a few books, the rest are scrolls.

"Put them in your bag," Shadow orders as she keeps a close eye on her hostage.

Aine listens and sweeps the shelf into her satchel. Everything about this makes the timid woman queasy.

"You bitch," the man says. "That's my personal collection."

"I promise, we will return them," Shadow says. "But, right now, we need them."

He sends her a dangerous glare as Aine hurries back with the bag weighing her down.

"I got everything off the shelf," she tells Shadow. "Nothing with roses stuck out, though."

Shadow nods and goes to release the man, motioning for Aine to rush up the stairs before her. She's disappointed that Oaken-staid's words haven't connected to anything they've found yet.

"I would say I'm sorry, but I'm not," she says, cutting the rope loose. She winks at him and hurries up the stairs after her friend. They sprint out of the building before they can be stopped.

8

THEN

"You're being too aggressive, Princess," Cibor says as Eirho feels the sweat dripping down the side of her face.

"I'm sorry," she says hoarsely. "My mind is not where it usually is."

He raises his thick eyebrow, watching as her chest rises and falls heavily as she pants. Her skin is pale and her energy is draining quicker than usual. She is not her normal self.

"How about we take a break? I'm thirsty anyway," he says nonchalantly.

Eirho is relieved as she reaches for her jug of water, chugging the cold liquid. The cold fills her chest and stomach as she flops on the ground to lie against the grass.

Cibor sits next to her, watching as she tries to catch her breath. Normally she is fast, sharp, and full of passion for fighting. Now she is angry and distracted. Eirho has never been like this.

"Are you okay?" The trainer searches her face for clues.

She just laughs. A short, empty laugh.

"I know something is going on," Cibor nudges her. "Torn isn't himself. Won't even talk to Peter, or so it seems. And pain radiates from every pore that you have. Did you two end your secret fling?"

"Could you say it louder for the people who will stone him?" Her voice catches as she lets out a shaky breath. She realizes how cruel she sounds and the guilt emerges. Cibor has done nothing to upset her, so there is no reason for her to take out her frustration on him. "I'm sorry, Cibor. I was hoping that fighting would take the anger right out of me, but I'm still furious."

"Do you want to tell me what's going on?"

"I am set to marry Declan," she whispers bitterly, the pain of each word sinking into her. She has to marry a man she does not love and that she will never love. Knowing he will be cold to her is only half of the struggle. The other half is thinking of what cruel ways he will torment her to amuse himself. "I told Jett a few nights ago. He hasn't been inside the Palace since."

Cibor takes a deep breath. He has been her mentor, her friend and the one person that she trusted with her secret. All the pain she feels, he feels too. He has been by her side since she was a child and now, he has to watch as she throws her happiness away.

"I didn't want to hurt him," she says. Tears begin to mix with the drops of sweat that cling to her cheeks. They fall in a crooked path down her face and into the grass. "I thought I could find a way to be with him, but now I feel stuck."

"Your father is making this happen, isn't he?" he says. "He's forcing you to do this for him so he can use the alliance for more power."

Eirho closes her eyes, feeling her eyelashes stick together with tears. She has to face the obstacles ahead of her, one at a time.

"Please, do not let anyone hear you say that," she says. "They'll kill you, Cibor. Just… Let it be. I can deal with Declan."

"But you can't deal with Jett. With his suffering."

"He's suffering because my father is power-hungry."

He looks across the courtyard, watching as the gardeners discuss adding a new pond and line of trees in. One of the few joys in Eirho's life is being able to control what happens in the garden. It is her safe place, her sanctuary. It is the one thing that she has power over in her life.

"This garden is becoming beautiful," he notes, wanting to give her a compliment that might brighten up her day. "It's a great place for us to practice. Gives you lots of focus, you know... and comfort. Plus, I think Declan hates flowers."

She begins to laugh. A warm, genuine laugh. "He's allergic," she says. "I guess I won't have a garden when I live with him. I'll have to collect cacti from the South."

"That'd fit perfectly, since he's a real prick."

Eirho chuckles loudly and sits up, wiping her face on her grass-stained sleeves. She grins at him, thankful to have him at her side. He always knows how to make her laugh. Talking to him allows her to look forward to the future and appreciate the present.

"Too much?" he asks playfully.

"Just enough," she says. Her face becomes grave. "Do you know what I can do to fix things with Jett?"

Cibor considers this for a moment. "I could lie to you and say yes. I could make up a story, even. But the truth is, you just have to think about how he is feeling. Think about it. You're going to move away with a man who will never treat you the way Jett knows you deserve. That boy has always made it clear that his path in life is to be by your side," he tells her softly.

Pulling her knees to her chest, Eirho wonders what she could do to fix a problem that she had no hand in creating. The King has left her with a mess she might not be able to mend.

"What if I tell my father that I refuse to marry Declan?"

Cibor chokes on his drink, coughing and spluttering. "No, Eirho. I know it's unfair, but you know how he'll react! It will be dangerous and—and—"

"—I cannot allow him to win. He can make alliances in other ways. Money, favors, whatever else. Making me do that... That will cause more issues than it could resolve," she tells him determinedly. "I will find a way to make this fall through the cracks."

He swallows roughly as he pictures exactly how King Thanthos will react. Cibor knows of his wickedness and the sole reason he stays under that man's eye is because of the love he has for Eirho. She is a sister to him. Seeing her go through this torment and thinking of how it could become worse makes him sick.

He decides that his best bet is to talk to Peter Knight, one of his most loyal friends.

"Promise me that you won't do anything drastic, Princess," he finally says, "because I think I may have a way out of this."

PETER SPENDS MOST OF HIS TIME IN HIS ROOM, DRINKING AND listening to music when he should be on duty. Generally, Jett forgives him and covers for him. Peter conspires ways to get out of the Guard. Maybe a broken bone or getting shot. Anything would do it, he hopes.

There's a sudden knock at his door. Peter panics and spills his glass and drink on the floor. As he hurries to the door, he settles on the excuse that he's taking a lunch break.

"Oh! Cibor," he says, relaxing as he sees the giant man in front of him.

Cibor steps in without a word, obviously agitated. Peter's relaxation is replaced by anxiety once more. Cibor waits until the door is closed before he speaks in a low, quick tone.

"Now is the time," he says. "I have to get her out of the Palace. I need you to talk to her, Peter."

Peter hold his hands up. "Slow down, Cibor. Who? What is it time for?"

Cibor grunts at him. "Eirho is being forced to marry that asshole Declan. We have to do something about it. I think we can get her out and keep her safe with Marcs."

"Fuck," he growls, putting his hand on his head. "Jett is going to be devastated. Does he know?"

"Yes, she told him already. If you want to save your best friend, we have to get her out of that place. We have to keep her safe. She wants to refuse Thanthos' wishes. Do you understand what he will do to her and Jett, if she denies him?" Cibor bites his lip hard, trying desperately to think of all of the things that he can do to make things better for her.

Peter goes to fill up his glass again, the bottle taunting him. Cibor sees him and steps in front of the bottle, glaring down at him.

"What the hell?" Peter grumbles in a low tone. "I'm thirsty."

"You're thirsty for a way out. I will pay off the head of the Guard if you help me get her out of there."

"I want to, trust me. But how?"

"Eirho is an intelligent, strong woman. She's similar to her father in many ways, but she's not evil. She knows that Thanthos is wicked and she wants to break free from his cruelty. We have to persuade her and now is the time. She wants to take her life back, especially while she is being forced to marry that monster, Declan." Cibor explains.

Peter inhales. "What do I do?"

"You're Jett's best friend, Peter. She will listen to you if you talk to her. Tell her that this is how she saves him. She will understand," he says. "We can get Jett out too."

"I can try to get to them both."

Cibor shakes his head. "We have to get her out first. Jett can come after," he promises. "Will you help?"

Peter gulps and considers what this means. "Yes," he finally answers. "I'll do it."

"Good. Let me find out how long we have. I'll send you a note. Also, Jett wants to see you later tonight."

Peter only nods, wondering what he's just gotten himself into.

9

NOW

Dax cannot peel his eyes away from Shadow, who moves about the small house at a rapid pace, moving from one side to the other in a flash. Since they returned to the house, she has been busy and distracted, barely saying two words. He doesn't know what's wrong, but he's curious to find out.

The only problem is: she refuses to let down her mighty walls. Yes, she's civil to him and she has yet to kill him, but that's the extent of it. He tries to make small talk and every time he tries, she finds a way to change the subject. Getting to know her is much harder than he anticipated. Shadow is a private person to say the least and it is offensive to not have someone immediately love him.

The way she repeatedly avoids his questions only makes him prod harder for answers. There is a dark past to Shadow, one full of mysteries. Dax is dying to find out more, if only she would let him.

"So, aside from fighting against a corrupt tyrant, what do you like to do for fun?" he finally asks. Dax feels the tension in the air as she stops dead and stares at him. His courage dwindles to ash.

After a minute or so, Shadow gives him an answer.

"You're here because Xero ordered it. I don't want you here and I don't want to share my private life with you. You're already in my home, what more do you want?" Shadow cringes at her bluntness. She wouldn't have to be so hard if he got the hint. Maybe honesty will get him to listen. Being nice to him is just wearing her out.

"We are on the same side, Shadow. Hell, we're practically roommates now. Shouldn't we know some stuff about each other?"

She bites her lip and rolls her eyes with exaggeration. This kid is relentless. "I refuse to give information to people who might use it against me."

"Why would I?"

"When and if it's time to trust you, I'm sure I will."

Dax crosses his arms in a huff. Why won't she open up? He refuses to be stuck in a tiny house with a person who won't even give him the time of day.

"Can we talk about the Skulls, then?" he placates, hoping she might crack.

Moving through boxes and drawers, she nods. "Why not? What do you want to know?"

"How did the Skulls get started?"

"Thanthos came to power after his late brother, Argos, some 20 odd years ago. So about 19 years ago, Xero's father, a brave man by the name of Xander Marcs, created the Skulls. Xander despised the way that the King ruled and how merciless he was to his people. Luckily, he wasn't alone in thinking that," she tells him, digging through a drawer in the kitchen. "He began by bringing in trustworthy allies who shared his mindset, creating the Resistance group known as the Skulls. It's only through Xero following in his father's footsteps that the Skulls grew into the network it is today."

"How did the Skulls get their name?" he asks, excited to be having a conversation.

She places her hands on her hips and looks around purposefully. "Well," she starts, "the first crusaders in the world rose against a great evil and as they battled, they placed the skulls of their fallen soldiers on their horses. They believed that it would give them the power to defeat whatever evil lay ahead. They believed that their deceased members remained with them to guard them and help them when they needed it the most. And so, they started to coin the name 'Skulls'."

Dax sits in awe, surprised to be given so much information. It may not involve Shadow but he is happy she is sharing *something* with him. Dax sees his opportunity to ask her and he goes for it. "I noticed how close you are to Xero, he's like a father to you. Why is that? And how did you find the Skulls?" he blurts, hoping she will take the bait and answer one of them.

She shoots him a poisonous look from across the room, planting her hands on her hips. "That's a story you're not ready for and not something I want to discuss. Any other questions?"

He meets her stare with a terse look of his own. He thought he had her.

"What's the worst thing about Thanthos? Why's he so bad?"

She looks at him blankly.

"I lived outside the walls, remember. We didn't hear much about him," he explains with a shrug.

"Thanthos is a bastard." Shadow begins. "There is simply no other way to put it. He is cruel; he loves to torture, maim, and kill. And he'll kill anyone who stands in his way. His goal, besides gaining power, is to create a perfect, mindless army to serve him. He has been cleansing his Kingdom of 'imperfection' for years. His reach goes beyond The City. He knows those 'perfect' people will follow him if he makes them feel important. If that's not enough, if the imperfect want to live, he makes them pay heavy taxes."

"And if they can't pay?"

Shadow pauses. "Show me your magic, Dax."

He is taken aback. In the weeks that they've spent together she has never shown any interest in his magic. Dax, resigned, walks over to the table and holds out his palms facing down. Shadow is still as he tries to focus energy through his hand. His hand seems to pulsate, a dim and orange light coming from his hand and onto the table top. He moves a piece of paper. Barely. His power is just strong enough to make her believe it's real.

Shadow has seen enough.

"That will not stop Thanthos," she says.

Dax's eyes widen. He knew it wasn't much but he thought it might help somehow. He managed to survive as an outsider, he didn't realize he'd need more to survive in Thanthos' world.

"Can the Skulls defeat him?"

Shadow hesitates, standing up straight and looking out through the tiny crack in the curtains. She flits back and forth, in her mind, debating how to twist her answer without giving anything away.

"I can."

Dax is alert now. He wants to ask how, but he knows from her sharp tone that question time is over. He does not get any elaboration. Even if he tries, she won't tell him.

~

"DID AINE AND TOOLS FIND ANYTHING?" SHADOW ASKS, WATCHING Xero pace.

He doesn't answer her and instead grabs a pile of maps and notes, scouring through them at. He doesn't notice that she is sitting there, patiently waiting for a response.

When her patience wears off, she speaks up: "Xero. *Xero*."

He shakes his head and his clouded expression clears. He glances over at her. He huffs, annoyed at the distraction.

"What is going on?" she says firmly, hoping to elicit a coherent response. "You're starting to worry me, Xero."

Glaring at her sternly, he tosses the papers aside and presses his palms onto the large desk. He averts his gaze as he tries to form the words. "Thanthos had an entire village slaughtered last night."

Shadow tenses up and anger begins to simmer as she thinks about those innocent families. The Skulls are too busy deliberating on their next steps to keep The City safe, whilst another massacre occurs. Yet again, nothing has been done. Men, women, and even children were lost at Thanthos' hands. She bows her head for them, feeling sorrow overcome the rage in her heart.

"I think Dax is Thanthos' nephew." Xero blurts. Shadow laughs in surprise.

"You—you think Dax is Argos' son?"

King Argos was Thanthos' older brother. He was a strong and kind man, with an appealing face and caring leadership. A man who sought prosperity for his city and its people. He would feed the poor and wash the feet of the disabled. The people loved him; his family loved him. It was a tragedy for the people when he suddenly passed away. He passed before his nieces, Princess Eirho and Princess Alpha, were born. It wasn't so tragic for Thanthos, though. Thanthos claimed power immediately after his brother's death; he finally got what he wanted.

"From what I've known of Dax's family, he could be the true Heir to the throne. Before his father, Watten Ryer, died, he divulged to me that he wasn't Dax's biological father. Dax's mom left The City to go beyond the walls and brought baby Dax with her. Watten simply adopted Dax. Dax's mom would always say he was destined to do something great, and my friend, Watten, believed her," he says. "That's why I believe he's The Heir."

Shadow swallows hard, feeling the air escapes from her lungs. All this new information is overwhelming as she tries to wrap her head around it.

"Hold on. So.... just because his mother thought he was special, that makes him The Heir?" Shadow rolls her eyes at him. Everyone's mother is obligated to say they're special. Why would Dax be any different? He is probably the least special of all. No offense to him.

"No, Shadow. She spent a lot of time sneaking around the Palace gardens when Argos was alive. There were rumors that she was one of his lovers."

"Well if Dax is related to Thanthos, he could be working for him, Xero. I'm right not to trust him," she points out, crossing her arms over her chest. She refuses to trust this stranger.

"Dax doesn't know about any of this. He thinks that Watten Ryer, the man who raised him, is his only family now," Xero says.

Shadow scoffs at him. Xero's words don't make a difference—she is already set on one thing: "I don't trust him. I'd never heard of him before all this and suddenly, you want him to know the inner workings of the Skulls."

"You let me worry about that. You focus on Thanthos. He hasn't stopped murdering. A village by the docks was burned to ash last time. You can imagine the hell they faced at his hand. We must retaliate."

"Were the Red Guards involved?"

"Only the Elite."

She puts her head in her hands and holds her breath, trying to distract her brain from thoughts of innocent people being tortured, mutilated, and murdered.

"Jett Torn did this."

"No," Xero replies, stunning her. "He wasn't part of this. My sources say he was nowhere around. If he was, it would give us more fuel to feed the flames."

"We have enough kindling, Xero," she says evenly, running her hand through her thick honey-colored hair. She takes a moment to relax. "So, I know you have a plan with all this."

Xero takes a seat and slides the map towards her. "Aine and Tools seem to be onto something. They are keeping a close eye on Thanthos' movements. I have a strong feeling that Thanthos already knows where the magic could be. For whatever reason, he is buying time before he tries to use it. When he does, you will be on his heels, ready to kill him. The others will take down the guard towers as well as the Palace defenses. We will take The City if you can handle Thanthos."

"Of course I can. But I'll need more information. Where will he be going? How many men will be in his company?" The list inside her head grows as she considers every possibility.

"We have time to figure out those details," he says. "I promise. For now, you need to keep this mindset. You must be ready to kill. And I need you to make certain that Dax is protected."

"I'm babysitting him?"

He rolls his eyes at her. "I just need you to keep him safe. Cibor says that he will train Dax and Tools wants to help him learn the layout of The City," he explains to her.

"Do you still trust him?" she demands, unable to stop herself. She doesn't know Dax, doesn't particularly like him, and everything inside of her is saying that she shouldn't let him in. She has a very bad feeling about all this.

Xero furrows his dark brows "You need to put your trust in him, too."

She decides to ignore that. "What will we do with Alpha? I thought she was the true Heir."

"Alpha will do just fine but, but she isn't the true Heir. We will capture her and hold her here until everything passes."

"I wish your plans were more specific, Xero," she tells him with a sigh. "I don't know who to be supporting as our leader."

"Support anyone but Thanthos," he says, standing up on his feet. "Are you taking this evening off since Dax is with Cibor?"

She nods. "I'll be heading home for some wine and sleep."

"Stay safe," he says. "And don't take any risks."

"I won't, *Mother*."

He glares at her and places the map in her slender hand. Instead of replying with a cutting remark, he squeezes her shoulder and leaves the room without a word.

~

"HERE, TAKE THIS," RUM HANDS SHADOW A BOTTLE OF LIQUOR. "Have a swig."

She chuckles, twirling the bottle and watching in fascination as the alcohol swirls like a tornado. "Are you trying to get me drunk and stumbling?"

He smiles at her, leaning back in his creaky chair. "Obviously you can stay if push comes to shove."

"Push might come to fall," she laughs, pulling her feet onto the seat so that her knees are tight to her chest.

"So," he says in the moment of silence, knowing something is on her mind. "What's going on?"

She stares at her feet and gives a soft, nervous smile. Rum is one of the few people that Shadow can truly feel comfortable around and he is grateful for it. The weight of the world is on her shoulders and he's more than happy to lend an ear.

Despite what Xero said the plan was for taking down Thanthos, Shadow has her own plan. She decides not to tell Xero. She will dance and flirt with the truth No doubt he'll figure it out anyway.

"I am sick of having to hide, I am sick of being treated like a child. If I could do what I want and invade the Palace myself, Thanthos would be out of power before nightfall. What are we waiting for? Killing guards hardly wounds the beast," she says in a huff. She closes her eyes to find some peace again. "I feel torn."

Rum nods once. "I know you do. And I know you feel like a caged animal, because let's face it: you're feral." He laughs and Shadow joins in. "I think Xero's waiting because he wants to follow Thanthos to the magic."

"But why would he need that?" she questions. "Oh..."

"Yeah." Rum replies. "He wants to destroy it."

Shadow scrubs her hands across her face in frustration. "That magic is better left alone."

"Good luck convincing Xero. Anyway, those damn guards keep sniffing around here. I'm losing my patience. Torn needs to stay the hell away." Rum slaps his large hand across his knee. The later it gets, the more willing he is to express his feelings. Drinking alcohol might have helped.

"Good luck keeping Torn away," she says, smirking at him. Having a laugh keeps her sane in these dark times. "He's drawn to you like a moth to a nightlight, Rum. Can't have one without the other."

"You are insane," he tells her, frustrated. "Not to mention, gross."

"Out of every Skull I know, he loves to pick on you the most."

"You're right, maybe he is in love with me. Wouldn't that make a great love story?"

Chuckling, he leans his head back against the wall of his tiny apartment. The apartment sits just above the tavern, offering him a short commute between home and work every day. At least he'll get home safe when he drinks too much.

Shadow is still giggling at the thought of Jett Torn proposing to a bashful Rum. It's the little things that get her through the worries; like how Xero has waited years to attack Thanthos. So many more deaths will come if he doesn't act soon.

"Honestly though, I wish he wasn't such an asshole. He comes in once a week to break my precious stock. I have to hide them from sight now, so his men will leave me alone," he grunts. "One day he might just decide to kill me."

"I'll take care of them, if you like."

He sits up with shock. "Absolutely not! Are you insane? It's dangerous and you know it. Why do you insist on flirting with the idea of putting yourself in harm's way?" He pauses to take another swig of his concoction. "Now that I think of it, you're the reason why I drink, woman."

Laughing, she pats his shoulder. "And you're one of the few good reasons I'm here."

He inhales. "Yes, I saved you. But I wasn't able to save Princess Rho and that's precisely why Jett Torn wants to kick my ass every day of the week. Thanthos thinks I killed her," he admits, lowering his head. "I wouldn't and couldn't kill a soul. I have trouble killing flies."

"I have a feeling she would've forgiven you," she notes with a smile. "Still, try to continue to evade Jett's ridiculous temper."

"You know he was calm before all this. Before he lost her. Then he went nuts," he says, making a face. "It's insane what love can do to a man."

"Yes, I can see it in your eyes when you look at Cibor."

Rum shoots her a hard stare. He wants his true self to remain a secret. Once he acknowledges it, he'll have to face the facts.

"How are things going with Dax?" he interjects, subtly changing the subject.

She watches him closely for a long moment before she answers him. "He's a pain in my ass, if you want the honest-to-Gods truth."

"Oh, but he seems like such a swell guy."

"I don't trust him, for one. And I have to keep him at my tiny shack in the Ghetto, because for some reason, Xero thinks he's safest there," she tells him. "He asks too many damn questions and he eats all of my snacks."

Rum chuckles. "Well, we all know how you dislike that, right? Don't sweat it too much, he'll be out of your hair in no time."

"A few months, if my prayers are answered by The Creators," she grumbles. "Either way, I'm glad I can still sit on your floor and get ridiculously drunk. It's a nice feeling."

"Why do you think I do it every day?"

10

THEN

Jett sits in his small apartment, gazing out of the tiny window. His view is beautiful. The window looks out on the large river that twists and turns into The City. He is a few stories up so he can see everything below him. Sometimes the view makes him feel mighty and other times, small. Today, he feels invisible.

The past couple of weeks have been spent staying in his room, ignoring the outside world and trying to decide how to move forward. But no matter what he does… he can't do it. He doesn't know how.

The woman that is destined to be his wife, created for his soul to fit with… She's going to be gone. In no time she'll be dressed in white—the color of a virgin. A special gift she shared with *him*. They'll powder her face, curl her hair, and send her to a living Hell. She will be forced to make Declan happy. An impossible task.

Jett tortures himself with thoughts of her crying alone. Thoughts of him being powerless to help her; to hold her. What can he do to keep her safe? Even if she didn't want to be with Jett, even if she wanted to be with someone else, at least she would be happy. In this situation, she loses whichever way she rolls.

Sleep is a stranger to the Lieutenant, only visiting when his mind is quiet. This silence is rare and so he sits all day and looks out of the window, trying to decide what to do.

He reaches for the bottle of wine just as there's a knock at his door. He takes a deep, weary breath and walks over. He hesitates before he opens it, though when he does, he is taken by surprise.

"Princess Alpha," he exclaims. "What are you doing here? Shouldn't you be in the main Palace?"

"I wanted to talk to you, Jett," she says in her sweet, little voice. "About Eirho."

He inhales deeply and veers away, knowing that the same pain is accompanying Alpha. "Why don't we go walk around the garden and talk? I just need to grab a jacket."

She nods feverishly and waits outside the door, wrapped in a shawl. He grabs a jacket from the chair and throws it on, stepping out into the hallway. It doesn't take long for them to get to the garden. Jett is grateful for it because he can't stand the awkwardness between them. Judging by the determination in Alpha's eyes, he doubts she even notices.

"What is going on, Princess?" Jett says as they breach the courtyard; garden right ahead.

"I wanted to check on you. My sister told me what happened," she says in a quiet tone. "She is devastated."

Jett stops in his tracks. "What? She told you about *us*?"

"I guessed," Alpha grins. "It's easy to spot if you pay attention. Plus, she's been crying a lot. And I asked what was bothering her."

A bead of sweat drips down his neck. He thought they had been sneaky and they were keeping everything concealed, but now Alpha knows. He panics, praying she won't tell Thanthos the truth.

"I will not say a word, I promise," she says, reading his mind. "I would never do that to my sister. And I definitely wouldn't tell my father. I have a plan and I wanted to talk to you about it."

"A plan?" he echoes.

"Yes. I know this betrothal is awful especially since she is being forced to marry Declan... but I have a plan to keep you two together, at the very least."

He watches her closely; desperate to understand. Jett can't believe it: little Alpha is scheming against a tyrant. Incredible!

"Okay, tell me how I get to be with your sister then," he leads. "What do I need to do?"

"I know you want to be together and you might not be able to be married, but I think I can persuade my father to send you with Eirho."

He raises his eyebrow.

"Eirho is his favorite, that much is clear. She's more like him... I'm not," she admits softly. "But you are also one of his most trusted. You're not a Commander yet, so losing you wouldn't be a terrific blow. But you are worth enough to him that he would trust you to protect her. And if not that... to gain information for him."

Jett stops, watching her in surprise. He is amazed by her brilliance. "You think he will use me protecting her as a cover, while I gather dirt on Declan's family so he can have control over them."

Alpha nods with excitement as he pieces together what she is saying. "Yes! Yes. Exactly, yes. We have to decide who can suggest it to him, though."

"I can," he suggests.

"No," she scolds. They walk into the rose garden where statues sprout up, covered in vines. They seem to dance through the colorful grounds. It's just the way Eirho designed it: eccentric and gorgeous.

"Why? He might listen to me," he offers, checking furtively over his shoulder to make sure that no-one is following them.

"Eirho needs to be the one to tell him," she says. "She has to be. He listens to her more than he listens to anyone."

He knows arguing is useless. Thanthos trusts his eldest daughter more than anyone. He adores her. Using Eirho against him would be smart.

"Do you think you could talk her into doing it?" Alpha asks, frowning. She doesn't want her sister to deny herself the chance to be with Jett, just because she's trying to protect him. Taking a deep breath, he considers the question. There is something inside of him that says she might fight this. She wants to protect him.

"I don't know" he says, rubbing the side of his neck. "I don't know if she would want to be with me or try to protect me. I think she might tell me it's too dangerous."

Alpha nods, agreeing despite herself. "I think you're right. Maybe we don't tell her. Maybe we see if you can accomplish this on your own."

"Maybe. I hope your father will listen to me."

"So do I," she says. "I just want her to be happy."

"Trust me, I know how you feel."

"THE KING WILL SEE YOU NOW," A GUARD TELLS JETT. HE HAS BEEN pacing up and down the hallway, waiting to go into Thanthos' room. His room hasn't changed one bit since the last time he was here. Jett remembers the musty smell and pristine condition like it was yesterday. Thanthos' books are aligned neatly on the shelves and not a single piece of dust lies anywhere. Thanthos' pickiness and need for perfection screams psychotic

Jett walks through the doors, greeted by a cloud of spiced cologne and mildewed books. The unique smell of Thanthos.

"Ah, Jett, come in," Thanthos' sly voice calls to him. He is doing his best to be charming. "Have a seat."

"Thank you, my King," Jett says, taking a seat in a huge, polished chair across from the even more impressive chair that

Thanthos sits in. Jett sits back in the chair and waits for Thanthos to speak.

Thanthos places his quill down and beams at his prized soldier. "You will make Commander in no time," he says. "Is that why you're here today?"

"Thank you, my King, but no. I was hoping to talk to you about Princess Eirho and her betrothal," he says, holding his breath.

"My lovely daughter? Yes. She is set to marry Lord Declan Snow. He is a great man, much like you, Jett," Thanthos tells him. "What would you like to discuss?"

Jett gulps as he watches Thanthos grab a small vial from a drawer and place a few drops of the liquid into his tea.

"After the wedding, Declan will take Princess Eirho back to his homeland. She will be going to a new place and who knows what dangers might be there," he explains.

Thanthos waves his hand to cut Jett off. "Please, Eirho has been trained all her life to be strong and powerful. She can take care of herself."

"Yes Sire, however, that is not the only reason for my asking."

Jett knew that Thanthos wouldn't buy into that argument. That's why Jett saved his best hand for last. He knows Thanthos well. The only way to get Thanthos to agree is to sell it so well that he's manipulated into buying the story that Alpha planned. He takes a deep breath to prepare himself.

The King is intrigued, raising his dark eyebrows. "Continue, Lieutenant."

"It will be a great new alliance, Your Grace, but we cannot be too cautious. I would go with her and as well as keeping an eye on her, I will make certain that there is no foul play. I can spy on them to fit your needs. And if they show any sign of causing you problems, we will know exactly how to *destroy* them," he says, imitating Thanthos' most wicked smile.

Thanthos chuckles darkly and pounds a fist on the table,

causing Jett to jump slightly. Jett definitely wasn't expecting that reaction and he's not sure how to take it.

"I admire your thinking, Lieutenant Torn. You're strategic and intelligent. I think your idea will help our Kingdom thrive. You have my support," he says, with a glint in his eye. "And if those bastards try to oppose us, we will skin and burn them *alive*."

~

"I LOVE THE GROUNDS," ALPHA SAYS TO HER SISTER AS SHE PAINTS A new canvas. "You created such a wonderful sanctuary."

Eirho chuckles at Alpha's ever-growing vocabulary. "The garden has lots of secrets, some of which you might never know."

Alpha groans in protest. She hates when her sister hides things and teases her. "Could you tell me a few?" she pleads.

Eirho laughs musically as she skims through her book. "It seems that there are secret tunnels under the Palace."

"You've seen them?"

"No, but my handmaid used to tell me stories that she heard around Old Town and in the Market."

"Do you think they're real?" Alpha exclaims frantically.

"I tend to wonder if they exist or if they're a folktale," she admits, flipping to the next page in her book. "Before she passed away, Mother always told me stories, too. I was about your age and somehow I still remember them."

"What kind of stories did she tell?" Alpha's interest is piqued. She drops her brush and sits down quickly, buzzing with excitement.

Eirho cannot help but smile at the reaction. "Mother believed that The City holds so many secrets, especially secrets below. She always said that the heart of The City is underneath us. Said there's untold magic down there."

"Does Father know about it, too?" Alpha questions. Her eyes are filled with wonder.

"No, never. She said we must never tell him. She told me it would be too dangerous if he knew," she confesses, averting her gaze. She can remember her mother's warning like it was yesterday. Her warnings about Thanthos stuck with Eirho and she sometimes wonders if those warnings lead to her mother's untimely death. Although she wants to tell Alpha what occurred, she decides to keep it to herself. One day, Alpha will know.

"Why would it be dangerous, Sissy?" she quizzes with fearful eyes.

How does Eirho tell Alpha about the darkness their father carries in his heart? How can she explain the power he is seeking? She doesn't know what to say or how to say it. It would devastate her sister. She needs to see him in a good light, to keep the innocent image of Thanthos as a protector and savior. Not the monster that he really is.

"Uh," Eirho stalls as she thinks of a good lie. "I think she thought he could be put in danger if he came across whatever's down there. She never told me exactly what she believed was under there, but she spoke of it with fire in her eyes. Mother knew more than she would ever say."

"Do you think she loved Father?"

The question takes her by surprise. She would love to say *Yes, they were soul mates*. But the truth is their mother loved their uncle Argos more than she could ever love Thanthos. Her betrothal to Thanthos was forced and customary, but her heart went with Argos. The one thing that kept her with Thanthos was her two daughters.

"I think that she loved him for giving her us," she says. "Mother's greatest love was us, Alpha, especially you."

Alpha's face turns into a glowing smile. She had been only a year old when their mother was taken away from them. The things she can recall are the hugs and the laughs that brought life to any room. Her mother's portraits line the Palace so Alpha can remember her beauty. Alpha mirrors both her mother's looks and her grace.

Eirho, on the other hand, is almost a copy of the late-Queen, Saryss, their aunt. Long, honey-colored hair that glistens in the sun, almond-shaped green orbs framed by long eyelashes. Freckles dance across her nose and over her high cheekbones. She is tall and strong, her body built to survive. Everything about her is elegant yet powerful.

The sole difference between Eirho and her Aunt Saryss is what lies behind their eyes. Saryss' eyes carry wisdom and solace, whereas Eirho's are vibrant, eager, and hungry for something more. Eirho learnt long ago to camouflage the spark that glows inside of her with a calm and graceful composure.

Alpha knows she and her sister are different. Her features have the softness of childhood and her hair is a deep scarlet hue. Her eyes are also green, but deeper, like the forest. She is shorter and thinner, her body deceptively quicker than her sister's. Alpha, at her core, is driven by peace and passion; painting is one of the few outlets to express this. Even her spirit is different: it is softer and gentler. She is content with the things around her. Their unique souls are what make them a great family.

"Mother adored you," Eirho continues, smiling as she relives the memories. "She would praise your beauty with every chance she got. She loved your hair and insisted on brushing it every night."

"Is that why you brush it now?" she inquires, watching her older sister nod.

"She would have wanted me to."

Alpha warms at the thought, despite never knowing her mother. Her heart aches for the things that could've been; dressing for balls with her mother and strolling through the garden with her. Alpha never had the chance to talk to her about crushes, or the changes in her body. All the things that Alpha needed a mother's support in, have passed. Eirho is the only person she can lean on, and even then, it is not the same. Eirho tries, but it is not always easy.

"Thank you, Sissy, for taking care of me," she says. "I hope I can repay you."

Eirho smiles. "Being your sister is payment enough."

11

NOW

Shadow unlocks the door of her apartment, steeling herself to deal with Dax. She steps through and places her bag down, letting out a huge sigh as she does. Rum drained her emotionally, bringing up the past and, unintentionally, making her regret the things she has done. He did not do it intentionally of course, but she is exhausted no less.

Dax is sitting on the couch, watching television. He is enjoying one of Shadow's snacks and watching the only channel she gets—the news.

"Where were you?" Dax asks, peering over the back of the couch.

"Rum and I were talking," she answers. "Skulls' business." Lying to him feels *oh so good,* she has to admit. He is prying and irritating. For whatever reason, he thinks that he deserves answers.

He furrows his brows. "Is that the skinny guy that owns the bar?"

"Why does that matter?" She snaps, feeling defensive and suspicious.

"I don't know. Xero was asking where you were after Cibor and

I were done training." He pauses. "Aren't you supposed to be training me?"

"Ha! He wants the others to train you while I do my own thing. In a couple weeks, I'll be patrolling the market again and won't see you for a month, hopefully. It will be too difficult for me to travel back and forth. You'll have to stay with Xero." She shrugs like there's nothing else she can do about it.

"Why can't I go with you?"

"Maybe you can when I do the pick-ups. We will see if I like you by then."

He grunts at her response, clearly unamused. "I had hoped you would already."

She walks to her bedroom door and opens it. "Don't bother me tonight, Dax."

~

"THANK YOU FOR THAT," ZED SAYS WITH A CHUCKLE, LEANING HIS head back against the pillow. He glistens with sweat as he smiles widely, closely his eyes to enjoy the moment.

Shadow looks down at his hard, naked chest and smirks. "I needed it, too. Trust me. Living with that nosy asshole has taken all of my patience away." She unhooks her legs from around his hips and lies beside him, absorbing his heat.

"Xero's bright idea?" he inquires, raising an eyebrow. "Is that why I had to come in through the window this time?"

"Yeah, he's here to keep me preoccupied so I don't cause trouble," she says. "How's your job?"

"Oh, you mean being an Elite member and being Jett's lapdog? It's fucking great," he says in return. He offers a lighthearted laugh. "Just wish he wasn't such an ass."

She smiles. "Any news I should be aware of?"

"Other than Jett being an asshole? No. All I've heard of lately is about Princess Alpha and that snobbish Declan Snow getting married. They tied the knot this past week."

Shadow sits up, horrified. "She had to marry that monster?"

"He's certainly unpleasant, but you're forgetting what the rest of the Red Guard is doing. We've been forced to burn houses to the ground with families inside, Shadow. Thanthos made us lock a church from the outside and burn everyone during prayer. Shadow, I'll never get that out of my head. He is getting worse. If the Skulls can stop him now, they need to." Zed's eyes are sad and dark, reminiscing on the billowing smoke that carried screams and tears with it. He will not be able to relieve himself of the cries for mercy.

"Did Jett order it?" She feels her chest tighten with guilt as she considers more lives lost to Thanthos' hunger for power. First the village massacre, now this.

"No, he wasn't even there. Thanthos is the one behind all of this madness, as I'm sure you know by now. Jett is not my favorite individual, but he never participates. I think he hates it just as much as anyone else."

"I'll speak to Xero as soon as I can. I think he might be on a mission tonight, but he should be back tomorrow morning. I'll drag my new sidekick with me to talk to him."

"Does the sidekick not know you call me for late night shenanigans?"

She laughs and shakes her head. "If you could not call it that, I would appreciate it."

He smiles warmly and pushes himself up. "I have to get back on patrol. Thanthos will be doing mass invasions looking for Skulls soon, so be careful. I'll do what I can."

"Thank you, Zed. You're a great ally to have."

He leans down and grabs his pants, slowly pulling them over his hips before tightening his belt and checking that his weapons are in place. His shirt slides on quickly. Shrugging his jacket over his shoulders, he flashes her a smile.

"You only say that because I know how to use my mouth."

She rolls her eyes once again and laughs. "Okay, pretty boy. I'll see you next time you do your rounds."

"You got it," he says as he opens the window again and squeezes out, shutting it behind him.

Shadow stays in the bed, covering herself up and soaking up the leftover heat. Her mind is stuck on all the lives Thanthos has taken and what she will do to make things right.

~

"REMEMBER WHEN I WAS TRYING TO TEACH YOU HOW TO SHOOT properly and you let it kick back into your face?" Cibor roars with laughter.

"I had a black eye for a week after. My father was enraged," Shadow replies, rolling her eyes. "After that mistake, I picked it up fairly quickly."

Cibor smiles, his eyes crinkling in the corner, the years of his life starting to show on his youthful face. Shadow notes the little lines that are slowly spreading from his eyes and she's glad to have the chance to see the years grow on him. It's nice to know that he still smiles with his eyes.

Xero walks tall and proud, his sharp features hidden behind his hood. To Xero, it's unusual for Shadow to mention her father: family is a taboo subject for her. He and Cibor are the only ones to hear about the man she called Father many years ago. Even through all the darkness she faces, Shadow finds a way to make the light appear more vivid and lovely. Life is as beautiful as the pain is ugly.

As much as they bicker, Xero cares for her, and he admits how much he needs her, both as a Skull and a friend. No, maybe not a friend. Maybe now, for as many teardrops and blood drops, they have shed, maybe they are family. Maybe all three of them are family now.

Xero slows his walk and falls between the pair who are reminiscing about better times. He wraps an arm around each of their shoulders, stretching slightly to reach Cibor. Shadow leans into his arm and for a moment she is quiet and calm. On his other side, Cibor swings his tree-trunk of an arm around and squeezes Xero, who squirms and regrets his decision instantly.

"I was trying to have a moment, my friend. Not be strangled to death by your constricting biceps. Damn!" Xero shakes his head.

That laugh comes straight from the big man's belly again as he pats Xero on the back.

"My Elite informant told me that there will be raids soon. We need to get things locked down in the next couple days," Shadow stops. "Here we are."

Xero and Cibor stop behind her, gazing at the scene before them.

Music, flashing lights, and a bustling number of people are barely contained inside the small tavern. A jazz band is playing and the people swing back and forth, regardless of how drunk they are. It's the nicest tavern they have and the reason is simple: it is in the Inner City.

The rich folk of the Inner City can treat themselves to bottomless drinks and an endless banquet here, all the while there are people starving in the Slums. The biggest, brightest sign of them all is a fire-colored sign that says: T's. It hangs high above the ground floor, almost as tall as Cibor.

Guards patrol around, becoming easily distracted by alcohol and drunken ladies.

"I feel inclined to blow this joint up. Why the hell does Noah want to meet here? He better not have switched at the last minute," Xero growls furiously. His hands take stock of the weapons he carries, checking each one.

"They would never expect us to walk into a place like this, that's why it is perfect. C'mon." Grabbing their arms, Shadow pulls them inside and past a careless guard who leans over the railing, whispering sweet words to some cute girl.

Cibor seems uneasy in this place. It's rare for him to feel on edge and Shadow is tempted to send him outside. Knowing they shouldn't be separated, she finds the quietest booth at the very back of the wild tavern, instead. They sit and remove their cloaks, waiting for their informant to arrive.

"I have never seen so many naked women in my life," comments Xero, his eyes drinking them in "Not even in the brothels around the market sector."

"You must lead a boring life," Cibor tells him, trying to keep a straight face.

Shadow smirks at the joke as Xero shoots Cibor daggers. Xero crosses her arms and leans back.

A few minutes pass before they are approached by a Red Guard. He is tall and stocky; he would definitely give Cibor a fair fight. Everyone tenses, ready for trouble, until he removes his helmet. The man sets it down on the table and takes a seat beside Shadow.

"What do you think?" he says, laughing. It's Noah, their informant. He's one of the few guards who works with the Skulls and he is the only one to prove his loyalty time and time again. He never gives them false information or causes problems. Xero is hesitant to trust him, despite his long history with the Skulls. Shadow, on the other hand, is eager to hear him out.

"It is frustrating that people are dying while this party occurs, but there's not much we can do," Shadow mutters as she studies the entire tavern. People are dancing on little stages, a band in performing what looks to be their best show yet, and bartenders seem to effortlessly create drinks from thin air. Confetti, lights, and sounds—it's certainly a place to remember.

"If you do blow it up, can you give me a call first? I don't want to die here. People will talk. It's sleazy, you know," he murmurs, shaking his head.

Xero leans forward and plants his elbows on the table. "So, what do you have for us?"

Noah isn't listening; he's too busy staring at Shadow's, admiring her fair skin and big eyes. She's a distraction for sure.

"Thanthos is sending Alpha on random missions, *outside* the walls," he tells her, scooting closer to her. "I'm not sure what she is after, but I think it's Dark magic."

Xero and Cibor exchange uncomfortable looks before adjusting in their seats—Xero leans forward as Cibor moves back. That's not news they wanted to hear.

"Thanthos has upped all patrols in the Palace, 'cause of the missions and also 'cause it's nearly the anniversary of Princess Eirho's death. He always acts leading up to it," Noah continues determinedly. His eyes dart around the room nervously, before he leans closer.

"If you want information, you need to get Alpha," Noah says. "She's the closest to Thanthos and she knows what he's searching for."

Xero and Shadow exchange glances, each knowing what the other is thinking. They have to find a way to capture Alpha.

"Thank you, Noah. Anything else?" Shadow asks.

He nods. "Yeah, I think Thanthos is sending spies around The City. Like I said, he's already upped the patrols and searches, but spies could cause the Skulls' to crumble. I know he's gonna be raiding and imprisoning people again. A mass raid and murder. So, you better watch your backs."

Shadow nudges Xero with her foot and he growls at her. Cibor laughs. "Thank you, Noah."

He smiles from ear to ear as he stands up. Within seconds, a scantily clad woman appears at his side. "If you'll excuse me, I'm going to unwind. You all stay safe," he says, bowing his head and waltzing away to a grand evening of debauchery.

Xero clears his throat. "So, Aine and Tools have been searching within The City. Are we on the completely wrong track if Thanthos is searching outside the walls?"

"Do we have any scripture that tells us about the outside?" Cibor inquires thoughtfully.

Xero shakes his head. "Not that I'm aware of."

"It could be Noah being given false information," Shadow cuts in. "It could be a diversion to throw us off the scent."

"I thought you trusted him with your life," Xero says dramatically.

Cibor raises his hand to call over the waitress. He'll need a few more drinks to get him through the arguing.

"Shut up," she says. "I'm sure Torn knows there's some traitors in his midst. No doubt it's him planting seeds."

"She's got a point," Cibor says. "Jett's an ass, but he's also smart."

"Maybe, but if he knows that Noah is working with us, he's as good as dead. And if we don't have useful information, what good is he?" Xero asks sourly.

Shadow chooses to ignore that snarky comment and think ahead to their next plan of action. "Xero has a good point. We need to stop focusing on Thanthos for a minute and capture Alpha."

"And how do you plan to do that?"

"I'll meet her face-to-face."

12

THEN

Eirho takes her afternoon snack onto the balcony, eager to eat. Alpha is spending time with her friends whilst Thanthos is away on business in various parts of The City. Eirho is left alone which means she can snack all she wants without sharing.

Eirho spent her free afternoon picking raspberries from the Palace grounds. She arrives back in her room to enjoy a bowl, savoring the sweet yet tart taste of the fruit. She hears her room door open and turns to see Jett's face peering around the door. He scans the room to make sure that they're alone.

Surprised, Eirho sets her bowl down and stands up to meet him.

"What are you doing here?" she demands fearfully. It's dangerous for them to meet during the day; anyone could see them. "You shouldn't be here—"

"—We need to talk, Eirho," he interrupts, making sure that the door is locked behind him. If anyone tries to come in, he'll climb out of her window to escape.

She watches him closely as he paces the length of the room. He hopes she'll agree to this, but it is hard for him to know how she'll react.

"What's going on, Jett? Are you all right?"

He takes a deep breath, nodding. "I'm sorry I haven't spoken to you in a couple weeks. I was devastated, Rho. But I have an idea... of how we can be together," he says.

"You know we won't be able to. I'll have to marry Declan and move far away... And you have to fall in love with someone else." Eirho reaches out for his hands despite herself. The thought of Jett being with another woman causes her eyes to well up and a rock to form in her throat. Somehow, she manages to stay resolute. "I don't want you to be alone."

Jett shakes his head vigorously. "No, absolutely not," he protests, "I will love you forever and always, Rho. That's why I've come up with a plan. Your father has agreed to send me to Snow's Kingdom with you, so I can be a spy for him. I will be his link into the Kingdom. But this way, I can keep you safe. And we can still be together."

Eirho is stunned. She can't fathom having Jett by her side, where he will be in constant danger. If they sneak around and end up getting caught... Not only would there be a war on their hands, but Jett would be killed. The idea is too painful. She has to deny him.

"No, I won't let you do it," she protests, taking her hands out of his. "You won't be safe there. I can't keep you safe. If anything were to happen, you'd be their first choice of hostage."

"Rather me than you."

"No! Jett, I refuse to have you with me. I'll request a different man. I'll do whatever it takes to make my father rise against it," she says angrily. "I don't want any harm to come to you, why don't you understand that?"

He frowns. He knew she'd fight the idea but he didn't expect this. "And I don't want any to come to you, Rho, but you need to understand how much I care for you too. I can keep you safe and make you feel loved. If I stay here, I'll never see you again. I'll never touch you again or kiss you... Or make love to you." His voice trails off as he realizes the full force of what will happen when she leaves without him. His heart breaks.

"I know how strongly you feel about this, Jett, and I swear I would do the same thing if I were in your shoes. But you have to realize that, ultimately, it's safer for both of us to be apart."

"Why the hell do you want to get rid of me so badly?" he yells.

She stares at him, dumbfounded. "Jett, I'm not trying to get rid of you. I'm trying to keep you safe," she says, attempting to soothe him. "I love you with everything I am. You're the only person I want to be with, but we can't. Sometimes fate doesn't allow it and we have to accept that this is the way things are. All that matters to me is you're safe and alive. As long as I know that, I can't complain."

"Without you, I'm better off dead."

"Jett—"

He interjects immediately, "I want to be with you, is that not obvious? We've had to keep our relationship a secret for *years*. I can't even hold your hand if anyone is around! It makes our relationship seem shameful, when I want nothing more than to show everyone the woman who inspires me and makes me happy, the woman who makes me be a better man. And even though I can't have you completely, I would risk my life just to be around you. You need to give me that much."

"Jett, I don't know what to say," she admits in a low voice. She takes a deep breath. "The only thing I can say is... No."

He searches her face for any hint of doubt, but he can see that her mind is made up. All of a sudden, the weight of the world is bearing down on him. He shakes his head and leaves the room in silence. It doesn't matter what she says. He'll go with her anyway and keep her safe. It might mean that he will never touch or kiss her again, but at least he will know that she is okay.

~

PETER IS NERVOUS, AND RIGHTLY SO. CIBOR SEEMS PRETTY convinced that Eirho will willingly and painlessly join. Although that doesn't stop him from worrying about the entire thing blowing up in his face. He prays that Cibor is right and nothing bad will come of Peter speaking to her. With Thanthos and Alpha elsewhere, Jett clearly frustrated by something, and Declan prancing around The City and flirting with other women, Peter deems it a perfect time to talk to Eirho. He knows she'll be out in the garden, reading or writing.

There she is with her bare feet in the pond and her hair in a wild ponytail. He approaches her like a jumpy mare, trying not to spook her as he inches closer. He clears his throat to draw her attention, but she is too involved in the book.

"Princess," he says, standing erect when she turns to look up at him.

She smiles brightly, thankful to see someone who doesn't make her feel sad or guilty about things that are out of her control.

"Peter!" she greets excitedly, gesturing for him to sit. "How are you? How's your stomach? Jett mentioned you weren't feeling well."

"I feel better, thank you," he replies as he takes a seat next to her. He slides his boots off, then his socks. He loves to stick his toes in the cool pond water, watching as the koi fish brush the surface. They nibble at Peter's toes, causing him to squirm and laugh like a child.

She points at an all-white fish who is hungrily waiting for more. "That's Cerberus, Guardian of the pond. He likes to bite everything, even if it is not edible. He won't hurt you though, don't worry."

"He is vicious," he teases. Peter eyes the fish, tilting his head as he watches its big dark eyes flutter back and forth, watching him. "How are you doing, Princess Rho?"

It feels nice to have someone ask her how she is for once. It should be something that happens often, but it's a rarity in this place.

"I'm doing as okay as I can be," she mumbles back, staring at the dancing koi in the pond. She decides to tell him about her relationship with Jett—after all, things can't get any worse. "I keep hurting Jett."

"What happened?" Peter inquires. He wonders briefly if this will be easier than he expected. Maybe she'll guide him into it instead of him guiding her.

"Surely, you know by now that I am betrothed to Declan Snow," she says bitterly. When he nods, she continues. "I told Jett which I thought was the right thing to do. I couldn't lie to him or hide the truth. I had to tell him. Now he's hurt, understandably so. He's trying to find ways for us to stay together. He wants to leave The City with me and move to Declan's Kingdom as my guard and my father's spy. I told him I wouldn't let him. I can't keep him safe, Peter."

The ache behind her words makes him feel guilty for not speaking to her sooner. Here he is with the perfect plan; a way for Eirho to escape this evil prison and be with Jett. Yet he just can't pluck up the courage. He lets the conversation go on, waiting to find the right moment.

"I know he is hurting, but he's not stupid. You know how realistic he is. Give him some time and he will realize that it is safer for you to be apart," he tells her. "How do you feel about being away from him?"

She rests her chin on her knees and pulls them close to her body. A slight breeze causes her hair to twirl around her face but she doesn't notice. Her eyes are intent as she figures out how to put her emotions into words. As strange as it sounds, Eirho hasn't had time to consider how *she* feels about all this despite it affecting her the most. Her mind has revolved around Jett and how he's handling it.

"I love him," she says simply. "There's no other way to put it. It hurts, it kills me. I would give anything to be with him..."

"Why can't you be with him?"

She laughs derisively, lowering her knees so that she can look him in the eye. "My father would never allow it. Jett comes from a powerful family, but not powerful enough. I am a currency to my father. He wants nothing more than to use me for his own personal gain. Everything that man does is wicked."

This is easier than I thought. She's basically setting me up to ask. Maybe she will join us, Peter thinks. "What if there was a way you could be with him *and* have your freedom from your father?"

Eirho scoffs. "In my dreams maybe," she says. "My father won't let me leave without marrying Declan and he definitely won't let me be with Jett."

"What if I know a way to resolve that?"

"Peter, what are you talking about? You're acting odd," she says, cocking her eyebrow.

He bites the inside of his lip, blood pooling into his mouth.

"What is it, Peter?"

It turns out that there is no right moment to tell her, so he blurts it out before he can stop himself. "You can join the Resistance, Eirho. You can work with the Skulls to make The City a better place." He grins with relief.

"WHAT?" Eirho gasps. "Why would you suggest that?"

"I know it sounds insane for me to tell you of all people about it, but it's the only way. You can both be safe and be together, with the Skulls. We can get you away from your father, Princess," he assures her. "This is the only way to keep Jett safe and keep him here."

She lets her hands fall from her lap to the ground beside her as she works to unravel what he has just told her. Her secret lover's best friend is a Skull. He is part of the group that works night and day to destroy her father and his evil. This man is supposed to be her sworn enemy. They are supposed to despise each other. So why doesn't she feel that way? She doesn't hate Peter— she's relieved.

Finally, she feels the weight of her father's evil lift from her shoulders. Peter sees it too and he knows he is in—he has won her favor. Eirho smiles despite herself. Now that she has a way to help stop Thanthos, the idea does sound intriguing. Still, it's dangerous, impossible even. How could she hide within The City walls? They would have to make her live on the outside with the bandits, the gypsies, and the chaos.

"Peter, it sounds great," she admits with a nervous smile. "But it wouldn't work. My father would send both Guards to hunt me down, until every person was dead and The City was burned to the ground. If Jett and I disappeared, it would raise suspicions. They would know that we've snuck around all these years."

"If you help us, we'll make it work. The Skulls will find a way to keep your secret safe. Xero Marcs is an intelligent man, he always thinks of something."

"I don't know," she mumbles. "I don't think it'll work, Peter. I have to leave Jett and marry Declan. I have to do this for my Kingdom and my loved ones. Don't worry though, I'll take this conversation to my grave."

He stares down at his feet. "Promise me you will at least consider it, Princess. Please."

As she looks into her friend's eyes, something tells her she has to give him hope. She nods in response.

"I will consider it, Peter. I promise."

13

NOW

After traveling all the way across town and past the Security Zone, Shadow finds herself in the rolling, green pastures of farmland, stepping up onto a broken-down porch. The porch wraps around a small, worn hut where a family of seven live: a mother, a father and their five young children. Over the years, Shadow has grown to love the family as if they were her own. When she's not on missions or on house arrest as per Xero's orders, she comes to talk politics with the father, learn to cook with the mother, or play a variety of games with the kids, to give their parents a brief break from their hectic life.

Shadow doesn't get the chance to knock before the mother, Quinta Gustus, is at the door, throwing her arms around Shadow. Laughing a pure, rare, happy laugh, Shadow engulfs Quinta, grateful for another safe week for the family. Soon, Trenton, the father, is there to wrap his arm around Shadow too. They're only a few years older than her but they are wise beyond their years.

"My, how we have missed you!" Quinta announces with a grin, gesturing for her beloved friend to come inside. "Tell me, all is well?"

"Let her sit first, Quinta. She looks exhausted," Trenton tells her, seeing the exhaustion in her face. "Busy day at the office?"

Shadow rolls her sapphire eyes at him with a chuckle. "Always. I brought you both a gift," she says, removing a tiny coin bag from the concealed pocket in her cloak.

Quinta is close to tears when she hears the jingle of the money. She bites her lip to hold the wave back and hugs the other woman tightly.

Trenton pats Shadow on the back, giving her shoulder a tight squeeze. "Thank you, thank you from the bottom of our hearts. I don't know how we can ever repay you."

"Don't be ridiculous. I would do anything for my favorite family."

"And what about us?" teases Trenton. He reminds Shadow of a young tree, struggling to stand against the mighty winds that threaten to blow it over. No matter how much he struggles, in the end he will stand tall.

"Where are the little ones?"

"School, of course."

She nods, forgetting about such normal things. Nothing in her day-to-day life would be considered normal. Nothing about her life even resembles normal so she is comforted by seeing it in their lives.

"Rye just turned eight. Hyra and Todd will be ten soon. The rest are just a handful!" Quinta exclaims tiredly, sneaking a genuine smile in. Motherhood has blessed her more than anything; it gives her hope in the darkest of days.

"Good. There's presents for all of them outside."

Trenton hands Shadow a jar filled with fresh milk. It's the only drink that leaves her feeling comforted. "We have been attending church..." He trails off numbly.

Shadow takes a sip, while she waits for him to continue. He seems hesitant. Alarm bells begin to ring in Shadow's head.

"We have witnessed terrible horrors, Shadow," Quinta adds in a quiet voice, physically shying away from the windows and doors as if someone may be listening in. " Thanthos is growing crueler."

"I was hoping that wasn't possible," she replies wearily. "What is he ordering now?"

The couple are taken aback by Shadow's indifference. How could she feel that way? Shadow acts like his cruelty is commonplace. Every day the Gustus' live in fear and every day The City trembles, but Shadow remains untouched. Every day the parents regret their decision to leave their Kingdom, the Kingdom of the Sea, to come to The City. They thought that their children would grow up in a kind, prosperous world with Argos as King, but that soon changed after his death.

"The family just down the road lost three members last week... Oh it was terrible," Quinta gasps, her eyes glistening. She pulls her curly hair into a ponytail which falls down her back in chocolate kinks. "Their son was wheelchair bound; he could barely walk."

"You said *was,* Quinta." Shadow clenches her jaw. Shadow isn't indifferent any more. Anger simmers in her gut and she struggles to mask her emotions.

"He was born with a disability," Trenton explains, his back now turned to the two women as he prunes his plants. "Poor boy never walked. He was 'imperfect' and you know Thanthos won't stand for that."

Shadow rubs her forehead, pinching at the bridge of her nose with calloused fingers.

"The guards came to take the boy to his death while we attended prayer. The father and the eldest son jumped in... both were shot in the head. The son had to go first so the father could watch. Then the guards tied the boy down... slowly cutting off his skin and... chopping his other limbs off." Trenton wretches and swallows hard, releasing a jagged breath.

"Anyone who tried to intervene was harmed... It took three days until he finally died," Quinta comments, taking a biscuit from the center of the table and setting it on a napkin in front of Shadow. "He was the same age as Rye."

Silence ensues, leaving the three to ponder how The Creators could let this atrocity happen. Thanthos needs to be killed, his minions as well. *They deserve the same treatment, if not worse,* Shadow thinks.

Trenton breaks the long moment of quiet. "Last month, they burned my cousin's house to the ground. Sickens me, really."

"I'll bring more money for you to distribute soon," Shadow promises. "That's the least I can do, until I kill Thanthos myself."

Quinta closes her eyes and keeps them shut, a lonely tear rolling down her face as her mind replays the disturbing events. As a mother, the death of any child is a heavy weight to carry. This is one that she will carry for the rest of her life.

"Was Commander Torn there when it happened?" Shadow questions, desperate to know.

"He never is, never. As mean as he is, he isn't as evil as they say. I don't think he can stomach it. Either that or he makes his men do it for him," informs the father, snipping a special herb. He places it on Shadow's napkin. Shadow crushes it between her fingers and sprinkles it onto her bread. It tastes like honey when she bites into the crisp biscuit. She misses this simplicity.

"Only a monster can stomach this torture," Quinta says, disgusted. "Curse Thanthos."

"I concur," Trenton chuckles, approaching Quinta and giving her shoulder a tight, assuring squeeze. "If King Argos still breathed, we would be safe. I miss that compassionate man."

"I am certain most of The City does," Shadow grins. "But... as luck would have it, we have a bloodthirsty King in control. And I am determined to kill him myself. Time is slipping through my fingers. I have to get the Skulls to act. Now."

"I know the other Kingdoms fear him and refuse to intervene. Does Xero know that you've decided this?" asks Trenton, dubiously. He knows Xero well enough to know that he considers every single angle and agonizes over every detail. Shadow, however, is swift and impulsive at times, causing tension to generate between the two.

She shakes her head firmly. "No, he does not. And he doesn't need to. He would only try to stop me."

Trenton and Quinta share a proud look. They know how strong she is; Shadow gives them hope.

"We should refocus," suggests Quinta as she wipes her eyes and gets to her feet. "Stay for dinner, our children have missed you dearly."

Shadow gives her a kind, soft smile, a rarity. With a nod, she accepts, knowing from the beginning she would be staying for dinner and long through the night. It will be a relief to spend one evening in someone else's life, away from all the chaos and the terror of her dark world. Surely peace can find her for one evening.

~

"AUNT DOE, WHERE HAVE YOU BEEN?" HYRA WONDERS AS THE FAMILY sits down at their wobbly wooden table to eat.

Shadow misses that nickname. "I have been keeping you safe," she answers. "It's at the top of my list."

Rye frowns at the reply. "Shouldn't we see you more then?"

Quinta chuckles with Shadow, who can only nod in agreement. She wishes that visiting was easier, though she knows Xero would never allow more time with the family than she gets now.

"You're right, Rye. One day, I will spend more time with you all. Just wait, you'll see," she tells him, smiling to the other kids as well. "You have my word."

Quinta and Trenton give each other knowing glances. They pray it will change one day soon. "Momma says you keep bad guys away," Oak, the eldest daughter, speaks up. Her wide eyes follow

Shadow's movements, growing more alert each time that Shadow visits. "Is that true?"

Shadow chuckles warmly and looks to Quinta who blushes a deep pink and grins back.

"I try my best," she answers, filling Oak with joy. "You're twelve right, Oak?"

Oak nods her head feverishly. Her sisters, Brook and Hyra, raise their eyebrows at her, wondering where this is going.

"In six years' time, I'll train you to help me. If you'll accept my offer, that is." Shadow knows that she would train the girl to accomplish anything her heart desires. She swallows a spoonful of soup, hungry for the warm broth.

Oak brightens up and the whole room seems to glow. Even the darkened corners of the cottage beam with her light and she stretches high in her chair. "Yes, Aunt Doe! Yes, please! I accept!"

Shadow is happy to hear it. She finishes the rest of the food: it's not much, but it's enough to make her feel full. This family's kindness is exactly what Shadow strives to create in The City. She hopes, when all the killing stops and all the love begins again, that she can honor them in the best way she knows how: justice.

Time goes by too quickly in the home with all the laughs and jokes, especially bonding with the children. They play games and tell her funny stories, never for a second revealing an inch of the dark world they have been born into. It's an inspiration to know that they can find such happiness in this miserable world.

Shadow admires their strength.

When the children's eyes grow heavy, Shadow knows she must leave. She gives them hugs and kisses, promising that she'll return. She also slips them each a neatly wrapped box to open after their prayers have been said. They thank her with wide smiles, tight hugs, and little kisses. Then, as quick as they can, they run into the bedroom and place their boxes on the hay bed before speaking their prayers.

Quinta kisses Shadow's cheek and gives her a long, loving hug before making her way to the other room, blowing out a candle as she passes.

Trenton remains in the main room of the house, standing by the door as Shadow waits to speak to him in private. He speaks in a voice only she can hear.

"Thanthos has no mercy," he says, rubbing his tired eyes. This world is a living nightmare for Trenton; he can't sleep because he is too busy worrying about his family.

"Trust me, I am well aware of that man's sick missions," she replies sternly, feeling a hard shell encasing her again. The smiles are fading quicker now. "Are you scared he will find your family out here?"

Trenton rubs the back of his arm, sighing as he does. "Quinta and the children will be slaughtered if he finds out they're Sea Bloods. Besides, Rye is weak. I fear a disease is overcoming him... and if Thanthos finds out, that will be the end of it."

Unfortunately for the people of The City, many of the other Kingdoms and lands refuse to intervene with the terrors that Thanthos causes. They are too frightened to threaten him and outright refuse to spark a war. This leaves the people to fend for themselves against the Red Guard, which is why the Resistance is so vital in the fight against Thanthos. Very few have been courageous enough to rise against him.

"I'll keep more patrols in the area and I'll come more often," she says solemnly. "I swear to The Creators and the graves of my loved ones, no harm will come to your family. I can't protect your neighbors or your friends, but I promise to protect you and those little souls. I'll kill anyone who lays a finger on them."

Trenton looks at the resolution in Shadow's face. He can tell by the dangerous glint in her eye that she means every word. She is the match that will burn the sadistic King to ash. She will light the entire forest on fire if she has to.

"Thank you, Shadow. Thank you."

She places a reassuring hand on his shoulder and squeezes it tightly, just like he would for her. "Goodnight," she says.

"Farewell."

Into the night she goes, closing the door softly behind her.

She pulls her hood up to cover her face. Shadow blends seamlessly into the dark lands around her. The sound of wolves howling in the distance makes an eerie soundtrack; no-one dares to go outside the walls where the wolves are as big as horses. The wolves do a good job of keeping people inside the inner part of The City, just how Shadow likes it.

Shadow's mind is heavy with bleak thoughts as she travels closer towards the inner city and out of the farmlands. She decides to take the long way home and explore the night. The fresh, crisp air will soothe her lungs and relax her tightened muscles.

Seeing the Gustus family and connecting with them reminds her that even though the world contains darkness, it doesn't mean that the world is darkness. Visiting them gives her something to look forward to. If there were ever a family to represent Good, it would be the Gustus family.

When she was fifteen, she first came across Trenton Gustus, a defiant man who spoke out against all cruelty and was often beaten in the market square for it. He was a feral young man, who would gladly fight all those who opposed him. In a way, he was much like Shadow is now—untamable, determined, and hungering for more to life. From the moment she caught wind of him, she knew he would be a powerful ally to have.

It was not until she was eighteen that she met him again, an older man with more to lose than before. Like most men who have families, Trenton settled down. He gave up his weapons to carry the scars that sweet Quinta would kiss in the darkness. Shadow admired them both, seeing how they used love to deal with all the obstacles they faced. Shadow saved them from an attack a long time ago and from that moment, they became friends.

Once every week, Shadow would visit her old friends,

discussing the goings on around The City. They would share memories and laughter. Soon, the sound of laughter was mingled with the patter of tiny feet. Shadow visited three times a week and watched the babies while Quinta napped and had some time to herself. Sometimes she would help Trenton in the fields so he could finish up early and enjoy his babies. She was always around.

That was before Xero banned her from most interactions outside of the Skulls. Shadow fights him on the subject daily — not that she takes any notice — he's not her master after all.

And in the brief time she has to herself, she spends as much time with the Gustus family as she can.

Shadow mulls over the things that Trenton told her and she wonders, distractedly, what she should do next.

"What the—" Suddenly, Shadow is being grabbed from behind and spun around, a knife slicing across her face.

The figure holding the knife swings in at her and she ducks before doing a hard-hitting backflip into the overgrown grass. "*Shit*." She sure as hell didn't see this coming.

Shadow grabs a fistful of dirt to sway her attacker and darts to the side. She spins and deftly swings her foot out, kicking them full in the face. The assailant stumbles back clumsily, giving her enough time to kick them to the ground.

Shadow feels a warm liquid running down her icy skin, and soon she tastes drops of iron at the corner of her mouth. Enraged, she pulls her pistol out, aiming it at the face of whomever lies in front of her.

"Who the hell are you and what do you want?" she demands angrily, her hand trembling as she clutches her weapon.

The figure, shrouded in a thick, black cloak, says nothing. The size of the figure makes her realize it is a man attacking her. Shadow moves out of the tree line to get a better view of her attacker. The dagger glows in the moonlight, revealing bright jade gems and a long, curved blade. Shadow hasn't seen anything like it.

The figure makes a quick movement with their free hand and Shadow reacts too late.

Sharp stings lace her arm and hip as small throwing knives whiz past her. Another knife slices her shooting arm causing her to drop her gun just long enough for the figure to flee.

Shadow won't let them get away with that. She snatches up the tiny blade they left behind and steps back, ready to throw the weapon. She launches it, slicing the victim in the back of the knee and they fall. Her blow wasn't deep but it'll give her an advantage. She knows she has been followed and she knows that the Gustus family will be harmed because of her negligence. She should have known she wasn't alone.

A low moan fills her ears—her predator has become her prey. Their life is in her hands and she hasn't decided how forgiving she wants to be. She picks up her pistol and cocks it, steadily approaching.

"I didn't want to kill you," she says, remorse flooding her tone. "But—" She's about to pull the trigger when a hard kick to the ankle sends her tumbling down.

She lands on her wrist, causing a sickening *crack*. Shadow watches as the figure runs away. Shadow searches for her gun but she only has time to grab it and shoot at the person. And she misses her shot.

She struggles to get up as pain pulses through her body. When she gets up to chase them, they've vanished into the dense forest. She wipes her mouth with her tattered sleeve and puts her weight on her good wrist and ankle. She finds a throwing knife a few yards away, with her gun. She gathers everything and she hobbles toward the Gustus' home. She feels blood pouring down her chin as she makes a call to Xero.

"I've been attacked," she says. She turns off the communications on her watch.

~

"Thank you for patching her up," Xero tells Quinta, who nods with a pained smile as she washes her bloody hands in a warm bath of water and cleansers. His hands plant firmly into his thighs as he stares at Shadow, who ignores his eyes as long as she can. He sits across from her, groaning as if he is aching.

Trenton exhales loudly from the corner of the room, where he and Cibor are studying the blade for any signs of ownership or clues as to who attacked Shadow.

"I wish we had the other blade you described. No signs of a mark or special wrapping," Trenton tells the leader, his fingers tracing the blade carefully, analyzing every detail. He scrutinizes the workmanship, though he cannot find any specific indicator. "This is a common assassin blade, sold at one of the larger flea markets, I presume. It looks nice and sharp, but you could have kicked it just right and the blade would have shattered. It is not made for true combat. It is more of an ornament."

Shadow leans back into the cold wooden wall behind her. Her mind is swimming right now and she needs to stay upright. It took her fellow Skulls a couple of hours to arrive. She had plenty of time to plan for whatever Xero had to say.

"I imagine this wasn't a coincidence," Cibor pipes up. "They didn't want to hurt her, they wanted to wound her. To slow her down."

"It worked, obviously," Xero says sharply, his eyes cutting into Shadow deeper than any knife ever could. He lets out a quivering breath as he studies her.

She gives him the middle finger in reply and tries to stand tall, Cibor rushing to help her. She holds her hand up to stop him and though it stings, she manages it. Her eyes bore into Xero and she swears for a moment he nearly shies away.

"I have some cuts and sprains. I stabbed, bruised, and shot at whoever attacked me. I wasn't helpless, I was caught off-guard. Which as you know, never happens," she tells him, grumbling. Her voice is dry and hoarse. "I think it was someone in the Skulls. No-one else would have been able to get so close to me… to track me without me noticing."

With a concerned motherly look, Quinta leaves to fetch Shadow some water from the well. Trenton and Cibor accompany her for her safety.

Xero waits until the two of them are alone to scold her. "We can discuss the possibility of a spy later. Shadow… Are you blind to the fucking danger you are in? There are people now who will kill you. I can't let you get hurt."

"You haven't."

"Shadow. I am banning you from coming to see the Gustus family until we can be certain you are safe," he says in a final tone. "I am sorry."

"You can't do that. You're not my father, or my lover, you're not my fucking master, Xero! You can't control me. I don't care how many cuts or sprains or stitches I get—I am not stopping seeing this family. And we are putting patrols out here to protect them. You know it was Dax," she growls, slamming her hands down to push herself up. In her momentary anger she forgot about her broken wrist. She ignores the searing pain and looks him in the eye. "If you dare try to stop me, I will let the world know the truth."

Xero explodes. He leaps up from his seat in one fluid motion and flings his chair across the room. He storms off like a child and slams the door shut behind him. Cibor raises an eyebrow at Xero when he stalks past, shrugging to the husband and wife that walk with him. "Nothing new," he murmurs with a chuckle. He goes inside and gives Shadow the water they've retrieved. She gulps the water gratefully and hands back an empty bucket.

"Thirsty?" Trenton asks, smiling at her.

"Immensely," she answers, thanking them after. "Cibor, we need to get back."

"You're right. C'mere, you get to ride shotgun." He squats down for Shadow to hop onto his back, where she almost bumps her head on the ceiling.

"Thank you both, for your kindness. We appreciate it very dearly." Cibor says with a smile.

"I'll be back, soon," Shadow promises from her new seat.

The pair walk to meet Xero outside where they travel in darkness all the way to the headquarters.

14

THEN

"Father wants to speak to you," Alpha says, peering from behind the door at her elder sister. She watches as Eirho places her book down and stands up, reluctant to go speak to him. "He says it's urgent."

Eirho nods in return, her mind still reeling from her conversation with Peter. She doesn't know what to think yet, but she promised that she would consider it. And Eirho prides herself on keeping her promises. Absentmindedly, she pats her younger sister on the head and drifts down the long corridors, as she weighs out all the possibilities of her future.

It takes a few minutes to reach the throne room, giving her more time to ponder. When she reaches the room, she jumps in surprise as guards are posted on either side of the big doors. The only time the guards are there is when Thanthos brings his devious work home with him. She begins to question the real reason why he called her here.

"Princess," the guards say in unison, slowly opening the doors for her.

She grows suspicious as her anxiety kicks in. She steps

forward, bowing her head to the men and makes her way over to her father. He sits on the throne with a wicked smirk plastered on his face and an unsettling darkness in his eyes.

"Eirho, my favorite daughter," he announces, standing up. He holds his arms open for a hug, waiting for her to get closer.

Eirho gulps as she scrambles up the steps to give him a hug. "Father," she says.

"Have a seat beside me," he orders. "We have a busy day ahead of us."

"What will we be doing?"

He bellows at her naiveté. "You are much like me, Eirho. So brave and strong. You're fearless, I know. You're also going to be the next ruler when I pass on. You have to be prepared for what you could face, daughter."

The way he speaks sends shivers down her spine like wildfire, making her stomach grow instantly nauseous. There is something coming; her body is screaming that something's not right. She doesn't know what it is but she fears it already. Maybe he knows about the conversation she had with Peter. Maybe she willingly just walked to her death; she wouldn't put it past Thanthos to kill his own daughter.

"Sit, sit," he says, waving his hand around.

She swallows. "Yes, Father."

He gazes across the large room, checking that everything is in place. For what, she cannot guess. The fear begins to build and she wonders with a twinge of panic if she'll be walking back out of those doors.

"Now, daughter, I know the sirens keep you awake and I know that there are things in The City that cause fear and terror. The Skulls are the biggest cause of that. They're our enemies—mutilating our men and tearing us apart. As a leader, I must keep our people safe as I must keep you safe."

Her attention is seized by the sudden bang of a side door bursting open. Two guards march through dragging someone with them. Eirho's eyes widen in horror and she gasps inaudibly as she realizes what is about to happen. Luckily, her father doesn't hear.

"The Skulls burn our men, torture them, and slaughter them with every chance they get," he snarls, his eyes growing lighter with amusement as the guards come into view.

The man in between them is covered in cuts and bruises, his skin is pale and his hair is matted with blood. He's weak, beaten, and worn down. His torso is bare and covered with wounds, both old and fresh. As they yank the man closer, he coughs up blood onto the ground at Earth's feet. The guards wait until Thanthos nods before releasing their grip on him and dropping him to the ground with a hard thud. He lands on the center of the floor over the giant rose that is carved into the ground.

Eirho clutches the arms of her chair, fighting the urge to reach out for this man.

"We caught this *Skull* fighting against the Kingdom," Thanthos announces to her, spitting the word Skull with a vehemence. "And we will assure that his punishment will be painful and most deserved."

Eirho trembles. "What might his punishment be?"

Thanthos laughs, mistaking her trepidation for glee. "That is for you to decide, Daughter. Whatever punishment you deem fit. Whatever death this traitorous monster deserves."

"And if I don't?"

"I will choose a punishment for Alpha."

Eirho's eyes dart to him, praying that this is just some sick joke but she can tell by the fire in his eyes that he's serious. Dead serious. He's prepared to kill his youngest daughter just to make Eirho murder a potentially innocent man. He's forcing her to cover her hands in blood.

"What?" she whispers.

"You do what must be done as a ruler or I will murder your sister."

Eirho holds his intent gaze before she shifts her gaze to the poor man with his face pressed against the cold floor. He has done this to her many times before in one way or another but he has never used Alpha against her. Now he is truly testing her.

"Pick his death."

Time seems to stop as she considers her options. She knows that either way, this man will die, but she doesn't want to be the one to kill him. He could have a family—a wife and children. He could love to draw, or sing, or dance. He could be passionate, or wild, or smart. He could be all of those things. And yet Eirho is being forced to destroy every aspect of him. This is what it is like to be a monster.

Knowing that she has no choice, she slowly begins to consider his death. She wants it quick and as painless as possible. There will be no more suffering. Fire will be too painful, and stoning. She can't have him shot with an arrow— that would take too long. Her eyes fall upon the holster of one of the guards.

"L-let me be the one who kills him," she mutters.

Her father looks at her with utter delight.

The man on the ground opens a swollen eye, watching her with whatever awareness he has left. His eyes are glazed with fear. And under that fear, Eirho sees empathy. He knows that she doesn't want to harm him, that she'll do what she can to make it easy. He is simply pleading for mercy.

Thanthos grows impatient. He growls, looking to his men. "Burn him alive, *now*."

The men have the necessary supplies ready. One of them drenches the man in gasoline whilst the other readies the matches. The man on the ground moans in response, knowing how excruciating this will be. He watches her the entire time, trying to accept this fate.

The guard lights the match and throws it on him.

Eirho jumps up and races frantically to the blazing man on the ground. His screams pierce her ears until the pain is too much and he can scream no more. He withers on the floor, the flames engulfing every inch of his body—the smell of burnt hair and flesh filling the room. Eirho barges past the guards and grabs a gun in the process. She directs the gun at his head, feeling the power of the weapon weighing her down. She wants to turn the gun on her father, on herself even, but that will end up worse for the people she loves. Eirho thinks, briefly, how it's a peculiar sensation to know that you have complete power over someone's life and only you can take it away.

He lets out another cry that burns her ears and brings tears to her eyes. The guilt is immense.

She pulls the trigger, his body falling limp in the flames as it becomes engulfed. She covers her nose and steps back, her heart racing in her chest; her body shaking uncontrollably. She has to think quickly before Thanthos is engulfed in anger.

"I said I wanted to do it," she spits at her father, throwing the gun on the ground in disgust. She knows that her father won't see the tears of sorrow. All he will see is anger and he believes it is from the fact that her kill was taken by someone else's hands.

She is right. He laps it up like the sick masochist he is— he even clasps his hands together in pride at his daughter. Eirho is already out the door, getting as far away from that atrocity as she can.

As soon as she breathes in the fresh air, she begins to sprint. She runs out of the courtyard, across the garden, and out along the barracks. Her heart aches in her chest as she sucks in a jagged breath.

Eirho charges through the large doors and up a flight of stairs. She darts down another long hallway, desperate now, and bangs on the door at the end. She heaves from the intense run and the lingering image of the burning man. When her patience runs out, she opens the door.

Peter is stepping towards her, about to grab the doorknob. He takes in her devastated appearance. "Princess, is everything okay?"

"I'm in."

~

"IF YOU WERE WELL-READ YOU MIGHT UNDERSTAND THE PRESENT issue," Declan snubs Eirho, rambling about something frivolous.

Her mind is a million miles away, so she simply nods and waves her hand. His words are of no importance to her. She is too focused on other things going back and forth in her mind. She tries to think about what will happen when she meets Xero Marcs: her father's worst enemy. And every few moments, the face of the burning man flashes behind her eyes, making her feel sick once more.

Declan is irritated that she refuses to give him the attention he craves. "You are certainly a looker, Princess Eirho, but your head is full of air," he says.

She ignores him, naturally, and stares across the yard. Jett Torn is bringing something over to them, his gaze averted from Eirho.

"My Lord," he greets. His hand goes across to the left side of his chest, pressing firmly in salute.

Declan waves off the gesture impatiently. "What is it?"

"I was told to speak to you about the trip to your Kingdom," he says, ignoring Eirho's wandering gaze. "We have a lot to prepare."

"You're coming with us?" Declan questions.

Jett nods. "Yes, sir. I'm being sent to protect Princess Eirho and be at her service. King Thanthos demands it," he assures Declan.

Declan gives a big sigh. "Fine. Have a seat, uh—" He searches vainly for the name of the man who stands in front of him. He draws a blank which shows just how self-centered he is; Jett has to introduce himself at least twice a week.

"Lieutenant Jett Torn," he prompts, taking a seat between Eirho and Declan.

Eirho watches him closely. He can plan all he wants, but she knows that they won't end up at Declan's homeland of Azura. She wonders how Jett would react if he knew what she had planned.

"I need to know the route to your land, Lord Snow, as well as the local customs and the layout of the castle. I need to be able to protect Princess Eirho," he explains. Jett hides his emotions well—only Eirho hears the passion in his voice.

Declan seems pleased by this. "Good. Eirho is an ignorant woman. She needs all the protection she can get." Eirho fights the urge to leap over Jett and strangle him. "I tried to have an intelligent conversation with her, but she just looked straight through me and stared at the wall behind me," he grunts, crossing his arms.

Eirho watches Jett's reaction, sensing his temper grow hot underneath the calm exterior. She half-expects him to snap, but all she sees is a subtle clench in his jaw as he adjusts in his seat. She realizes then that Jett is more determined than ever to go with her, not just to protect her, but also to remind her of her worth. The thought makes her soften a little.

As Declan and Jett discuss the details, Eirho can't help but wish she could fall into Jett's arms. She imagines holding him again, taking in his warmth. She wants to spill her heart to him and tell him all about Peter's offer and the murder she committed. Jett would know what to say. He would know how to make things right. But no matter how much she wants to, she knows she can't tell him.

"I will allow you to guard her 24/7, Torn," Declan says. "Excluding when I have my time with her. She will fulfill my needs as often as I desire. She better understands that or she faces dire consequences." Declan shoots Eirho a warning look before turning back to Jett. "Wives must pleasure their husbands. That's all they're good for."

Jett is ballooning with rage. He would give anything to reach across the stone table and wrap his hands around the weasel's neck until his eyes pop out. All he can do is force a smile.

Eirho is past being shocked by his disgusting sexist attitude. She simply rolls her eyes. She'll defy him all she wants and there is nothing he can do about it.

"I need you to make certain she is loyal and clean for me,"

Declan adds on with a toothy sneer. "I also need her to do her duties—the duties she has as my wife."

That term: *my wife*. It makes Jett's skin crawl. No woman should be forced to endure such a repulsive man, especially Eirho. Perhaps one day, Declan will find himself asleep in bed, never to wake up again.

"I'll do as you say," Jett lies.

Declan nods, satisfied. "I will have my guards go over the castle plans with you when you arrive. After that, you'll occupy Eirho and keep her in line. Understood?"

Jett nods forcefully. "Yes, sir."

Eirho rolls her eyes at Declan for the millionth time.

All of a sudden, Jett's hand is under the table and Eirho's eyes widen when she realizes he is giving her thigh a soft squeeze. The beating in her chest soothes at his touch and she feels whole in that moment. Even this small, secretive touch brings her comfort and hope. She will always have him and things will always be okay... she hopes.

"Now, leave. I have things to discuss with Eirho, privately." Declan barks his orders.

Jett visibly tenses but he stands nonetheless. He salutes both of them before leaving, thanking Declan in the process. Eirho follows him with her eyes, grateful for his touch and sorry that he had to leave.

His touch will stay forever imprinted on her skin.

15

NOW

"You act like I stabbed myself, Xero," Shadow grumbles, making a face at her leader.

After they left the Gustus' house that night, she hadn't been able to reach Xero for a week. Xero vanished into the dark, leaving the Shadow and Cibor to travel back together. In the end, Cibor had escorted her home and Xero was nowhere to be seen. He took Dax wherever the hell he went and left the others to tend to things on their own.

Xero exhales through his nose. "That's what you take from this? Shadow, I'm furious with you for putting yourself in a position where you could have been killed," he snaps back.

Shadow doesn't react to his words. The others will be joining them soon.

Cibor sets his personal communication device down on the table, along with a bottle of ice-cold glacier water— something that he specifically leaves The City's walls for. The others trickle in after Cibor. The table is full of leading members of the Skulls: Xero, Shadow, Cibor, Bender, Vex, and River. Xero looks at each of the members in turn, giving them an acknowledging nod before moving onto the next.

Bender is the oldest member, having served alongside Xero's father. At nearly ninety-years-old, he is a patient intellect who strategizes every move. He knows what has and more importantly, hasn't worked for the Skulls. His main goal is to better the organization.

Quite a few years younger at 33, River is another member of the Skulls' Council. Despite his impulsivity and temperamental nature, he's a vital member of the Skulls. River has the mindset of a warrior, having served in the Red Guard for many years, before seeing the darkness that Thanthos cast upon The City. Similar to Bender, strategy and success are constantly on his mind. Which is probably why he's the trainer for the newest recruits, making sure they are fit for Cibor's intense regime for seasoned members.

When Xero's eyes fall upon Vex Laurimore, he smiles darkly. She is a genius, both in science and mathematics, and, of course, torture. Thanthos' Red Guard mutilated her family and she is set on returning the favor. Gaining information to use against the wicked King is just a useful perk of the job. Vex doesn't kill her victims, they are sliced, diced, made to forget, then publicly humiliated by being sent naked into the streets. A proper crime for such dark servants. The naked part is just a bit of fun for Vex. Though you wouldn't think it, the old woman has compassion where it's due and she teaches the other Skulls to hold their tongue, or else get it cut out.

Xero takes a seat at the head of the table, far across from Cibor. The solemn leader remains silent. He is unchallenged by the Council. Due to his kindness, his mercy, and his sense of caution, they stand by his side. The leader has had a few struggles in his position, all of them have been because of one person: Shadow.

Trouble herself sits beside him, observing every single detail around her. Her mind is forever turning, gathering information and using it to her advantage. She holds a lot of power over most of the other Skulls, but now she is with her equals; those that she respects and can have a good bicker with. Though she is usually on edge, for a brief moment she actually relaxes.

"Welcome," Xero says, after taking in the people around him. "Thank you for gathering on such short notice."

Every head nods in return, alert and ready to hear what he has to say.

"I have some pressing things to discuss with you all," he says, sighing.

"We have a traitor in our midst." Shadow interrupts. Not exactly what he wanted to talk about but as usual the agenda is thrown out the window and the more pressing matter is brought up.

"What is it you have to say, Shadow?" he asks reluctantly.

She shrugs and appears indifferent, tapping her fingers on the wooden tabletop. She clicks her nails over and over, staring fixedly at her own hand.

Xero is annoyed by her silence and he gestures to an intrigued River.

"Do we have any leads, Xero?"

"No," Xero admits. He elaborates begrudgingly, "As you all know, Shadow was attacked last week. We are assuming there is an enemy in our ranks, one who has been tracking her. We don't know who it is yet, but we hope to find out soon."

"We know who it is," Shadow growls, her brows drawing together.

"Who are you thinking?" Vex asks, arching her thin eyebrow.

Shadow snorts at Xero's stupidity and leans back in her chair, cautious of her new wounds. "Dax, obviously. Everything was fine until he came to help us. Isn't that right, Xero?"

Xero scrunches his face up in disagreement. "We are not blaming an innocent man, Shadow. There is no need for that. The only reason that you dislike Dax is because he's new. You need to trust him." Xero retorts.

"Hold on Xero, she has a point," Cibor cuts in. "He lives with her; he knows where she is going. And he has only been with us for a few months. How well do we actually know him?"

Xero's irritation grows as he sees the rest beginning to suspect Dax. He loathes being wrong. He knows that Dax is a good man and Shadow has no real reason to suspect Dax of anything.

"You have no proof," he tells Shadow in a fierce voice. "You can't blame him without reason."

She rolls her eyes at him. "I have a serious feeling that he's not who he says he is. You can disagree with me all you like, but I know his fighting style."

"How do you know his fighting style?" Bender asks, confused.

Shadow stares Xero down, wanting nothing more than to stand up and give him a hard smack on the head to wake him up. "The first night you sent that asshole to my hut, I thought I was being attacked so I fought him before I realized who it was. And then I fought that man last night. They were the same exact size and they both fought offensively."

"Bullshit, that's not a rarity," Xero shouts, shoving his chair out behind him and walking to face Shadow.

"You have a point there, Xero. But maybe she's on to something," Cibor notes. He has been spending his time training Dax so Cibor knows Dax's strengths and weaknesses as a fighter better than anyone. Shadow's description sounds accurate to him.

"Do we have any other evidence?" wonders Vex, studying Shadow's face as she shoots daggers at Xero. They are always competing, always fighting. She wonders if it is because they are too similar and equally strong-willed.

"Not yet," Xero says through gritted teeth.

"What are we gonna do about this?" Bender questions. He is good at guiding the conversation when tensions rise, leading it towards a more productive outcome.

Xero growls under his breath and sits back down at the head of the table.

"We are upping our patrols. I trust Dax and he will be staying at the hideout with Shadow until further notice. I can't have him being persecuted without proper evidence. We will interview our members, check alibis, and keep an eye on them. If anyone is lying, we will catch them. Tools and Aine are working on logs for each member as we speak."

"And what if Shadow's theories are correct?" Vex asks.

"If they are—which they won't be," he includes bitterly, "we will take action and discover how he managed to infiltrate the Skulls. Then he will be executed."

"What do you mean 'discover'?" Shadow snorts. "Please tell me how it's not obvious that you brought him in here."

"Shadow," Cibor warns in a low tone. Now is not the time to go for Xero's throat. They need to simmer down, take a deep breath, and reassess.

Xero leans forward. "Believe whatever you want, but I know his family and I know they wouldn't do this."

"His family is not him. Might I remind you of a similar incident?" She is fuming now. The anger is brewing inside of her, making her hot and clammy.

"Enough," River snaps, standing to his feet. "We have a plan. Now we have to go ahead and implement it. You two can argue the logistics of it later. Besides, Shadow, shouldn't you be preparing to take Alpha as a prisoner?"

She glares at him. "Shouldn't you be minding your own damn business, River?"

Vex is the quickest to intercept River from jumping over the table at full force.

"You think you know fucking everything, don't you? You fucking smartass," River growls as Vex holds him back, rolling her eyes at his childish words. "No wonder you're the target."

"Sounds like you're admitting to something," Shadow replies nonchalantly. That pisses River off more and he kicks the table, pushing it towards her.

"*Shadow*," Xero snaps. "Knock it off."

She ignores him. "I will do what I need to do. The rest of you can have your little tea party," she says as she stands.

She winces from her wounds as she moves about, smiling at River confidently despite it. This isn't the first time they've bickered. River is cantankerous to a fault and she enjoys frustrating him to no end. Eventually, he'll apologize out of guilt and she'll apologize out of obligation, not because she means it. A flaw of hers, no doubt.

Cibor catches her eyes before she leaves, begging her to keep her temper in check from now on.

She is not willing to keep that promise.

~

"So, what's the story with Jett Torn?" questions Dax as he stands outside with Xero while he smokes.

"He's an asshole," says Xero, breathing in the smoke. He's not a smoker, he just smokes when he's stressed— which is a lot.

Dax chuckles. "Come on, you sound like Shadow."

"Fine," Xero says, "Jett Torn is the Commander of the entire Guard, including the Elite. He was born into a rich, aristocratic family. He grew up with the late Princess Eirho, and eventually he had a secret affair with her. When she was killed, he grew into an even greater asshole."

Dax conceals his amusement and looks down the darkened alleyway. He is happy to get some information from someone, and coming from Xero, it means a lot. The leader of the Skulls is much more open than Dax would ever imagine.

"Do you think he still loves her?" Dax asks.

Xero is surprised by the question, but he doesn't show it. "I'm not sure," he admits. "I'd like to think he does, but I think his anger is far more powerful than it once was. I don't know if love could soothe it after all that he has been through." He stops suddenly.

"Not that I'm making excuses for that arrogant son-of-a-bitch, but that's what made him worse."

"He couldn't be that bad if he loved her, right?"

"He's bad. Perhaps on a different level from Thanthos, but I would still kill him without a second thought," Xero states.

Dax ponders that answer. "Too bad she isn't alive. Maybe she could stop all of this."

"Yeah, it's quite a shame," Xero says quietly. "She might be just as bad as her whole damn family."

"You think?"

Xero nods, inhaling more smoke into his lungs. After dealing with Shadow today, he needs something to bring him back down. No-one gets him fired up like she does.

"What's Shadow's story?" Dax asks, leaning against the wall. He kicks up a pebble, propelling it across the vacant street.

"Ah. Just the person I didn't want to talk about," Xero sighs. "But sure, I'll humor you. Shadow came from a fucked-up family. Didn't really have parents her whole life and spent most of it being betrayed by people. It probably explains why she's so sour now, but I do understand that. She had a sibling, but I'm not sure what happened there. Cibor found her and we took her in, giving her a roof over her head and offering safety in exchange for her loyalty. She's a pain in my ass, but she's one of the best we have. I don't know if her defiance is worth that title anymore, though. She refuses to listen."

Dax considers all of this as the question comes to his head again. After putting it off for so long, he decides to ask. "Why does she hate me so much? Is it because of my magic? It would be a whole lot better if I had The Heir magic... My magic would be useful then."

"She doesn't trust easily," Xero explains. "She's stubborn and anxious. It doesn't surprise me that she dislikes you but I hope that her feelings will change."

"Oh, I'm certain that they will."

16

THEN

"You'll write every day?" Alpha says, asking for what feels like the millionth time.

"Yes, I promise. I will write to you about everything," Eirho promises as she potters around the room, folding her clothes and putting them away. She refuses to have the handmaid's help; Eirho wants to spend as much time with her sister as possible.

Alpha takes a deep breath and looks at Eirho with her most serious face. "Okay. I'll do the same, I swear it."

Eirho laughs lightly as she places her favorite dress in her bags. Tomorrow she will be escorted to the wedding, making a stop in town to attend some pre-ceremony rituals in one of the older spiritual buildings. She wants to look her best.

"Have you seen your dress yet?" Alpha asks, dying to know what it looks like.

"Yes, Declan picked it out," she says. "He has better taste that I thought he would, but it's just a dress to marry a stupid man."

Alpha sighs at this, remembering the reality of their life again. Her sister is going to marry a monster, and live in a strange place, far, far away where only Jett can comfort her and keep her safe.

Thinking about Jett reminds her that he is going away, too. And the thought makes her brighten up.

"Are you happy Jett is going with you?" she asks with a smile.

"No," Eirho admits. "I don't want any harm to come to him. I don't want him to live the life that he will with me. I want him to stay and be happy, maybe even wait until you're old enough and he could marry you."

Alpha shakes her head feverishly. "Jett loves you, otherwise he wouldn't care that you're leaving. He would spend any time he could with you and no-one could ever change that, Eirho. Jett loves you."

Eirho looks away, as tears threaten to spill over. It is hard to be strong and pretend this isn't killing her. She wants to marry Jett; she'd always planned on it. Imagining him waiting for her in a handsome suit with a smile on his face, is her haven.

Now, she is forced to walk down the aisle to someone who will never love her.

"I'm sorry you have to deal with this, Sissy," Alpha says, her eyes distant and immeasurably sad. "I wish I could come with you."

Eirho walks over to her, placing a gentle hand on her cheek. "No, Alpha. You are safest here."

"I would be safer with you," she whispers, lowering her eyes. Her heart aches at the thought of her family being torn apart.

"We will be together, always," Eirho promises. "Even if we are not next to each other, you'll be in my heart. You always are."

Alpha takes a deep breath, trying to calm herself. "It's not the same," she says.

"I know, but we have to work with what we have. I'll do what I can to visit often and I'll send letters," Eirho promises, holding Alpha's hand tightly.

Alpha can't deny her tears any longer. They stream down her face, trickling onto her chest as she thinks of her sister being so far away. In Alpha's eyes, Eirho is the only family she has. She's the person who loves her, looks out for her, and cares for her, unlike her father. Her father couldn't care less and Alpha realizes exactly what will happen when Eirho is gone. She doesn't think Eirho has realized it yet.

But of course, Eirho knows what is coming. Her plan with Peter ensures that Jett will stay here to take care of Alpha, leaving at least one person to take care of her while Eirho is gone.

"It will be okay, I promise," Eirho says, pulling her in for a tight hug, wishing in that moment that she would never have to let go.

~

"TODAY IS THE DAY," JETT WHISPERS TO EIRHO AS SHE INHALES, going to the room to prepare with the maids. She can hear the strain in his voice: how forceful his words are. He's trying his hardest to seem upbeat and happy, but Eirho can tell that this is draining him.

"Yes, it is," she answers with a weak smile, before slipping into the room to get ready.

Jett waits outside, trying not to let his mind stray too far. He will be the first to see her and the one who gets to escort her to the carriage that waits outside, that's all he needs to focus on right now.

"My Princess!" One of the handmaids bustles around the room, eager to make the perfect seat for Eirho. This wedding is a great day for them; it's a blessing.

Eirho smiles at the women and takes a seat in the large chair at the center of the room. At least five handmaids bounce around, each holding items to style her hair, powder her face, and get her clothing ready for the big day ahead. All Eirho wants to do is hold a smile and pretend like this isn't a huge ordeal.

"We will do big curls and braids, Princess," a handmaid named

Sarah says excitedly. She places a bag of equipment down, prepared to tame Eirho's wild hair.

"That sounds lovely," Eirho notes.

Another handmaid, Bronyx, grabs a container of powder, ready to doll up Eirho's face whilst her hair is being done.

"Isn't this such a grand occasion?" Sarah asks, brushing through Eirho's honey hair. "You're so beautiful, I can barely imagine how you will look today!"

Eirho smiles at her compliment. "I'm excited too."

"I cannot wait to see Lord Declan's face!" Molly, another, giggles. She is busy inspecting the wedding dress to make sure it's in perfect condition before she hangs it up.

The only person that Eirho wants to see is Jett. She can't wait to see his reaction, though she knows sadness will soon follow. He will deflate after realizing that she will never be his entirely, no matter the circumstances. But the idea of his excitement growing as she walks out, clad in white with pearls and curls, makes her smile. Her imagination gets the best of her as she pretends that Jett Torn is her husband-to-be. That fantasy is the one thing getting her through all of this.

"He will be very happy," Bronyx grins, patting carefully at Eirho's face. "I will use eyeliner, blush, and an array of soft pinks and browns today, Princess. I hope you like what I do."

"Your makeup is the best in The City, Bronyx, you have nothing to worry about," Eirho assures her. "Please, don't worry. I'll look lovely with all of your help."

They seem pleased with her response and they begin to get to work, each of them focused on their individual tasks.

Eirho is locked away in her head for what seems like hours until Sarah giggles lightheartedly and tells her that she's ready.

Eirho rises, the handmaids help her put the dress on over her head. They tighten the back, gently, allowing her space to move and breathe. She's grateful for that, knowing the extra movement will help her plan.

The ladies make their final touches and sigh over how beautiful she looks, admiring their handiwork. Once she is ready, they carefully turn her towards the mirror, revealing the outfit, letting her take in the view.

"You are so beautiful!" Sarah exhales.

Bronyx looks her up and down approvingly. "You will be the talk of The City! Every man will wish they were marrying you," she says with a smile.

Molly hugs herself, sighing dreamily as she pretends that she's Eirho. The other handmaids chatter happily amongst themselves, agreeing that all their hard work has paid off.

"You are ready to go," Sarah tells her, placing a gentle hand on her back and walking her to the door. "We cannot wait to see the wedding."

Eirho smiles politely. "Me neither," she lies through her teeth.

Molly dances over to the door, opening it and peeking out. "You should come look at her," she says with a wide smile to Jett.

Jett jumps in surprise, but he breathes deep to find his strength. He steps inside and the air is sucked out of his lungs immediately.

His eyes fall upon Eirho's soft smile, her hair in big beautiful curls. And her face! Her cheeks are full, tinged with color and her gorgeous sapphire eyes are outlined in black, making them stand out. Her dress flows perfectly over her curves and cascades to the ground in a pool around her feet. The dress has long, delicate sleeves that leave her shoulders bare. Jett thinks she is always beautiful, but seeing her in this light—dressed up to be a wife—makes his heart feel full. She is the most beautiful, incredible person, and seeing her like this makes him tear up. He swallows hard, fighting the lump in his throat.

"Isn't she beautiful, Lieutenant?" Molly grins. Sarah gives Molly's arm a squeeze as they admire their handiwork.

"She was already lovely, but we really topped it off," Bronyx says proudly.

Jett is speechless, his heart pounding in his chest. He is incredibly nervous all of a sudden, his palms are sweating and his breath catches in his throat. He remembers, out of any memory, when he first saw her all those years ago. Bright-eyed, fiery, and kind, she had immediately interested him when he saw her stand up to the Commander at the time. Immediately he was enticed with her, seeing a fearlessness that he admired within her. Tears are tickling behind his eyes.

"Lieutenant?" Molly says.

He pulls away from his thoughts, looking to her for a split second before his eyes return to Eirho.

Eirho's eyes lock with his, pulling him closer to tears.

"She is gorgeous, as usual," he says.

The women giggle, blind to the emotion in his voice. They are too pleased that he likes what they have done to notice. They prance around, laughing like children.

"Are you ready to get going, Princess?" Jett asks in a soft tone.

Eirho nods once as Jett comes to her side, offering his arm. She slides her arm through his as they walk out of the room, a silence falling over them until they are in the hallway, alone.

Jett reaches up to rub his mouth, trying to figure out how to say what he feels. When they are far enough down the hallway, he stops, pulling her close to him as he decides what to say.

"You are the most beautiful woman I have ever seen," he tells her. A genuine smile spreads across Eirho's face. "I wish I could be the one to marry you," he says, his voice growing more serious.

Eirho glimpses around and takes his hand in hers. "I wish it was you, too. More than anything in this world."

Jett squeezes his eyes shut to fend off the tears. The hollowness of his gut fills with anger and he desires nothing more than Eirho when he sees her in that dress—looking like an angel with her wedding attire on. He's not quite sure how he should feel.

"I am so sorry you have to sit through this," she says.

"No, don't be," he cuts her off, he can't stand to hear her say it. "I know you're doing this for your family, your Kingdom. I understand."

She bites her lip, wishing she could be a more selfish person. Maybe then, today would have a different ending than the one she knows is coming.

"You will always be the one who has my heart, Eirho," he tells her. "No matter how many wicked men you have to marry, or how many duties you have to fulfill, I will still love you. More than anything or anyone else."

"And I will always love you," she says in return. "There is no-one I could love more."

He squeezes her hand tightly and they begin to walk again, silence overwhelming them. They make their way down the corridors and to the carriage that waits outside, many different workers in the Palace and those in the various stages of guard waiting to see them off to the church and the ceremony.

Jett holds out a hand to help her inside the carriage. Once she is settled in, he crawls in after her and closes the door. It will just be the two of them as they make their way to the church for her pre-marriage rituals.

Jett seems distracted, watching the outside world go by through the thin opening in the curtain.

Eirho can't handle it any longer. Suddenly she leans forward and grabs his face in her hands. She plants a deep and meaningful kiss on his mouth. This takes him by surprise and he almost pulls away, but he kisses back until she lets go.

"Never forget that you're the one I love."

Jett puts a hand on her face, rubbing her cheek gently. "I promise I won't."

She nods in response and leans back in the seat. There will be a long road ahead and she needs him to know that he is the world to her.

17

NOW

"We need to stay away from the market, so we'll go alongside the older buildings here," Shadow instructs Aine. They have a busy day ahead of them, patrolling and running supplies to other safe houses.

"I think we might blend in with the market," Aine says. "And Dax kept telling me Alpha has been hanging around that area, so we may want to check it out."

Shadow shrugs, deciding it is worth a shot, even if it is Dax's suggestion. She hasn't been near him since before she was attacked at the Gustus' house, and she hopes to keep it that way. Though it is a little odd that he was so persistent. Shadow can't help but think, *it's almost as if he wants us to get caught.*

If the women find any trouble in the market, it'll be easy to escape. Shadow begins to walk with Aine at her heels. They go through busy crowds of people, slipping through unnoticed for the most part.

It is only when one group refuses to budge— no matter how much she threatens or shoves— that Shadow stops to glance up and see what's going on in the center of the market square.

Her heart stops beating when she sees the stage.

Surrounded by a crowd of nosy people, in the center of the town square sits a wooden stage. A line of men and women dressed in black stand in the back of the stage, a tall post erected in front of them. Two men stand near the post: one is dressed in all black with a hood. His figure is familiar; he's the executioner. The other is dressed in black and silver, clearly a high-ranking soldier. The Commander. He's scowling, though there's something else in his eye.

There's not enough time to find out what. Shadow is about to turn around when someone begins to speak.

The man in the black hood reads from a long scroll to the expectant crowd. They're rising on the tip of their toes now, craning their necks, desperate to see the action. As the executioner reaches the end of his paper, a man is brought out from the back of a wagon and shoved to his knees on the wooden platform.

The man's skin is painted with dried blood, days old by the look of it. The blood has matted his hair into solid clumps and a rainbow of bruises line his face. The man is a sorry collage of aches and wounds— Vex would be proud. Shadow feels sorry for him when she looks down to see him dressed in only long, brown pants, revealing a puzzle of open wounds on his pale back. It's clear that death isn't far away.

Shadow is staring intently, hoping to discern who the man is. All she sees is a mass of dirty hair. Beside her, Aine stares transfixed by the horror unfolding. Her hand reaches for Shadow, pulling her close.

"On this day, we sentence you to death, Peter Knight. May The Creators have mercy on your soul," the hooded man declares. The hooded man lifts him up to his feet and yanks him to the noose.

Shadow snaps. Peter Knight is Rum's real name.

A scream bursts from Shadow's mouth and she pushes through the crowd, yelling to the guards the entire way. She bears inhuman speed now, her protectiveness fueling her inner fire. She is at the noose in a second. She's willing to risk everything if it means that her friend will be safe.

"Don't you dare lay another finger on him! I will kill you!" She is shouting in a blind rage now. Her blood continues to boil as she takes in the horrific sight of her beloved friend.

Aine doesn't know what to do. She tried to catch Shadow's arm twice, but she was too late. Shadow was already up the stairs, falling to her knees next to Peter before anyone could grab her. Aine stays frozen to the ground, watching helplessly.

"How dare you do this?" Shadow growls, cradling Peter in her arms. She looks around her, her eyes boring into the audience. "You sick bastards!" The audience gasps with excitement.

"If she loves her friend so much, she can prove it by dying next to him," the Commander says to his men in a taunting voice. He motions them forward.

In an instant, she is pulled to her feet by two huge men. A rope is looped over her head, going from loose to snug in a matter of seconds. She kicks and struggles, feeling the naked flesh of her neck rub against the rope. It is painful, though not enough to make her stop.

"Let us go," she demands, trying to tear away. "You will regret this."

The Commander laughs, deadpan. "Why would I regret killing a street girl?"

Shadow bites her lip, readying herself for the plunge. She shakes her hood off as best she can with her hands bound behind her back. The hood falls, revealing her striking sapphire eyes and the golden waves that cascade down her back. "Because you remember me." A whisper that only Jett can hear. "Princess Eirho."

Jett scoffs at her—he has heard this lie many times before from criminals searching for immunity. It no longer phases him in the way it once did, he almost expects them to say it. This time is different. He takes a good, long look at her and feels her eyes drawing him in. He'd know those eyes anywhere.

"Rho—" he gasps, in disbelief. He removes his helmet to get a closer look. The guards don't understand what's going on, all they know is that something has shocked their commander. They begin to raise the call for help, reaching for their radios as Jett approaches Shadow. "It *is* you."

He reaches out to touch her face with his calloused hand, but stops suddenly aware of the audience. Instead he removes the rope, his gloves brushing her skin and causing her to hold her breath. He wants to drink her in, but he resists. There'll be time for that later. Now is not the time for weakness.

"Get these people out of this square and take these two into the dungeon! Now!" The anger in his gut returns as he instructs his men to take Shadow to the wagon, being as careful as ever now. He struggles to keep calm, but his heart is racing. "And nobody but me lays a hand on her."

The guards nod and prepare to haul the prisoners away. They know the consequences of disobeying him. Where Shadow was placed gently in the wagon, Peter was thrown in like a doll, causing fresh blood to trickle from his wounds.

Shadow isn't tied up, so she grabs Peter to soothe him. She digs through her hidden pockets to find a special ointment that Tools gives her whenever she runs out. When she finds it, she rubs it wherever she can see wounds on his body, despite his muffled protests.

"Shh... it'll help." Her voice hurts from screaming, her body is aching and her head spins uncontrollably. What has she done? Everything the Skulls have worked for is destroyed. But she couldn't let Peter die. "It will be better than this mess I just created. I am sorry."

Peter coughs and grimaces as he tries to lift his heavy head. "You should have let me die. Now it's all over..."

"No, no it's not," she promises, fearfully. "Not yet. I'll get you out of here first, even if I can't follow."

"What you just stopped can't be as bad as what will come. It'll only get worse now," he says, wincing as the wagon hits a series of bumps on the uneven, cobblestone road. Peter slams against the wooden floor on impact.

"I can take whatever they throw at me, Peter. I'll be okay. I couldn't take you dying for me; for a lie. They thought I was dead. They thought you killed me. And, I just proved them wrong. Your name will be cleared."

Peter closes his eyes as her words remind him of why she left her old life. She was trapped, mistreated, and used. There was no happiness inside the Palace walls, none whatsoever. Her father took it all away. Yet she willingly made a sacrifice to keep Peter safe. She revealed her true identity and now she has to return home.

Jett crosses Peter's mind shortly after. The now vicious Commander was once the only solace for Eirho, providing her with love and safety. He can't even imagine what will happen now, what Jett will say. He has dealt with the angry Commander more times than he cares to think about and he wonders if Shadow will be safe. He can no longer guess. All he can hope for is that Jett will protect her secret.

And then there's Thanthos, the twisted and manipulative leader. Who knows what he would do? There is no grey area with him, there's only black and white. He will either welcome his eldest daughter back into his home with love and gratitude or he will have her executed for her lies and betrayal.

Shadow has risked everything for Peter, even her own life. He hopes for her sake that her sacrifice doesn't go to waste. He feels sick to his stomach thinking about it. Maybe the Skulls will save them and Shadow will escape unharmed, at least until the inevitable war ensues.

Shadow prays softly to herself as the wagon bumps along, her hand gripping Peter's tightly. When her father finds out the truth, everyone she loves will die. If Jett tells him she is alive, her work will be gone, all her efforts destroyed. She hopes that a tiny light still shines inside the blackness of Jett's heart, maybe the old him will show her mercy. It is the one hope she has left.

18

THEN

"Are you ready for this?" Jett asks as the carriage stops in front of the remarkable church. A crowd of excited people are eagerly awaiting their Princess.

"As ready as I'll ever be," Eirho grimaces. She peers out the curtain, seeing the colorful stained glass and the ivy carved into the arches of the ancient building. Knowing what will come next for her, there's a feeling of dread in her stomach that she cannot ignore.

Jett leans over one more time and kisses her carefully on the mouth—a sweet stolen moment. "Let me come in with you."

"No!" Her voice comes out harsher than she intended. She takes a steadying breath to compose herself. "I need you to keep watch out here. Times are getting dangerous; anything could happen out here. I'll be okay inside, I promise."

Despite her assurance, he can't shake this anxious feeling, but he knows better than to fight her on this. He opens the small door and slips out, helping her out after.

He opens the church doors for her and bows as she walks inside. A familiar smile forms on her face and with one look, she reminds him of a thousand different memories and feelings. The nights they shared together, the days where all they could share were looks and secret touches... It will never be the same. As she turns around, Jett knows that she belongs to someone else now, and even though he loves and cares for her, he knows it will not be the same. Though his love will never change.

"Princess, please come in. I will guide you to the back room," says a petite woman, curtsying for Eirho and taking her through the white, stone church to the chapel room.

Eirho steps inside, the emptiness of her life starts to sink in. She is met with rows upon rows of pews and only one person sitting in silence. A man sits with a bowed head, his dark tussles falling forward. The woman closes the door behind Eirho and locks it.

After staring longingly at the locked door to where Jett stands, Eirho prays that this will turn out how she expected. She lifts up her dress and saunters down the aisle to where the man sits. She takes a seat in the row behind him, gazing up at the images of The Creators that brand the church: the mesmerizing warrior Gods of the First Days.

"Princess Blackthorne, it is a pleasure to finally meet you," the man says in a low, cautious voice. He sounds genuinely pleased to see her.

"It is a pleasure to meet you as well," Eirho says, leaning back and watching him from the corner of her eye. She feels apprehensive about sitting here with him; she remembers the stories about him killing her father's men and standing against the tyrant, King Thanthos. She is both scared and exhilarated.

"I'm Xero Marcs, in case Peter and Cibor forgot to mention that," he says.

"They mentioned it." She pauses, wondering how to fill the sudden silence. "Do I need to introduce myself?" she asks in a teasing way.

"That won't be necessary. Everyone knows who you are. Do you have any questions before we get started?"

"What happens after this?" she says softly, thinking of Alpha and Jett more than herself. Their lives will be forever changed, tainted by the choices she makes today. Maybe it'll be for the better, maybe not.

"Well, we have a decoy body. Some young woman who passed away from starvation." Xero shrugs like it was nothing. "We will take your dress and put it on her body. We will have to destroy every means of identifying the body. Oh, and we will leave your jewelry unharmed. My men and women are working hard to prepare her right now," he explains, checking his watch.

"How much time do we have?"

"About fifteen minutes," he answers. "Enough time for us to talk."

"Where will I be going?"

"You will be joining Cibor and I at the Skulls' headquarters. You'll be given a room and be taken care of by those closest to me. Most of the Skulls will not know who you really are. I have a backstory and a cloak ready. Once the backlash blows over, you will be given your own house in the ghetto *if* we deem it safe enough, as well as a new identity. You will be watched closely and kept under wraps. We can't have this secret getting out." He folds his arms and finally leans back, peering at her over his shoulder. "Wow, you really are beautiful. I'm sorry we are ruining your special day," he says with a grin.

She snorts at this. "Please. You're doing me a favor. Declan Snow is a selfish, greedy man who doesn't even know the definition of kindness. Or any other pleasant word for that matter."

Xero's laughs heartily. Something tells Eirho they will get along well for the most part.

"Do I get a new name?"

"Yes," he says. "Any name you want."

She rubs her chin. "How about Shadow? It sounds right. And since I'll have to stay in the shadows to hide from everyone, it fits."

"I agree," he says. "Shadow it is. Now, tell me about the people you are leaving behind."

This question takes her by surprise. Why would he want to know about her loved ones? Is this some kind of test?

"My sister Alpha is incredibly important to me. I love her so much. But as long as I'm around, our father doesn't pay her any attention. Maybe she'll be able to find herself while we work to defeat him. And Jett Torn," she says, watching as he cringes. It's clear that he despises Jett. At least she knows the feeling's mutual between them. "I love him with all my heart. And I know what will happen. If he has any ties to the Skulls, he will be killed. So, it's safer if he doesn't know and perhaps one day, when we defeat my father, Jett and I can be together. Fate hasn't been kind to us, though. I'm hoping I can change that."

Xero seems pleased enough with those answers. "Good," he stands up and throws her a bag that was down by his feet. "You have to change. Now."

She stares at him, confused. Does he really expect her to change in front of a stranger?

"C'mon, I'm not going to look, or touch. Just do it so we can use your dress on the decoy and let's get the fuck out of here," he says. He goes to the back door as Eirho rushes to take her dress off the best she can.

"Marcs! I need your help," she calls when it gets stuck over her head.

He exhales and hurries over, untying the lace at the back. He closes his eyes before grabbing the bottom and pulling it over her head. She thanks him and tears the rest of her things off. When she is finally naked, she places everything onto the bench and roots through the bag as Xero keeps a lookout. Eirho hastily pulls on a pair of dark, denim pants and a cloak. She wipes her make-up off the best she can and lets her hair down, before tying it up into a ponytail.

She feels guilty for all the hard work the handmaids put into her earlier in the day. She wishes she could enjoy it for longer. She wishes she could enjoy it with Jett. Her future is written and Jett isn't in it, so she pushes the thoughts away and pulls her hood over her head.

A couple of people file in through the side door, and a couple more come in carrying something charred that she assumes is the body. Her eyes connect with Cibor's as he slides in through the back door.

"Tools, Aine, place her between those pews," Xero directs. "Cibor, get *Shadow* out of here."

"You got it," he says, giving her a tight, reassuring hug. He searches her face. "Are you ready for this?"

Eirho nods skeptically.

"I'll be by your side the whole way. You know I won't let anything happen to you, or your loved ones. Both Alpha and Jett will be safe, I promise," he says, smiling at her. "Remember, we're here to make this world better."

"Yes, you're right," she replies. "Let's do this."

Cibor looks to Xero, giving him a nod. He takes Eirho's arm and guides her out. "We have less than five minutes," he says as they rush outside.

"Hold on," she grabs his arm. She stops for a moment and peers back, seeing Jett standing in front of the carriage, waiting patiently for her to return, so handsome, loyal, and kind. Xero Marcs might disagree, but she knows that there's a kindness in his heart. This last look will mean everything to her. This is the way she will remember him for a long time, if not forever.

Cibor gives her shoulder a pat, motioning toward an alleyway. It's time for everything to change.

~

JETT TAPS HIS FINGERS AGAINST HIS ARMS, IMPATIENT FOR THE rituals to be over so he can steal a few minutes longer with Eirho. Any time he gets with her before the wedding is a blessing. At least he can talk to her, see her, and pretend, just for a while, that things aren't so complicated.

He hears chatter in his ear bud as preparations begin for the wedding and he blocks it out. Security will be posted all over The City and the surrounding area, protecting the partygoers from any danger. The Skulls are the first on the suspect list. Though Jett isn't completely against the idea of ruining Declan's special day.

"Lieutenant Torn, come in," a voice buzzes in his ear.

He only pays attention because he recognizes the voice of his best friend. Peter is waiting for a response, reluctantly, Jett clears his throat and presses the button on his sleeve.

"Yes, Peter, what is it?" He straightens up and glances around the church.

"We have everything set here, sir. What is your location?" Peter inquires.

"Princess Eirho insisted I stay by the carriage," he answers, trying to hide the disappointment in his voice. "I'm on the street across from the church, waiting for her."

Peter does not answer immediately and Jett can hear Peter talking faintly to someone in the background before he speaks to Jett again. "So, you're outside, away from the church?"

"That is correct."

"Perfect, Lieutenant. I'll see you shortly."

Jett doesn't reply. *Peter is acting more peculiar than usual,* he thinks. Jett pushes it out of his mind for now. He needs more time to think; how will he save Eirho from the cruel sentence of marrying Declan Snow?

As he looks up and down the street, he feels the earth shake beneath him.

He is thrown to the ground.

Heat is radiating from the church. He looks up and his eyes

burn from the dust, his ears ring, and the church is engulfed in smoke and flames. It is being devoured by the fire.

"No—no—NO!" Jett doesn't know how loud he's screaming but he can feel the vibrations in his chest; the explosion has deafened him. He scrambles to his feet and runs straight to the church. He knows deep down that Eirho is either severely harmed or gone with the flames already. He stumbles blindly across the cobblestone, fighting the smoke and tears.

"Lieutenant, no! Stop, please!" The driver of the wagon is on the ground, cowering from the explosion, giving him the quick advantage of grabbing Torn by the ankle. Jett shakes him off and sprints toward the collapsing structure. "You can't go in there! Call medical crews, call someone, please. You're the only one that can call."

Jett's eyes are wide and he slowly turns to look at the driver. He presses the button. "Attention Red Guard, attention Elites. We have an emergency at the church, there has been an explosion. Princess Eirho is inside. This is an attack on the Blackthorne family. Respond immediately," he orders as firmly as he can. His radio buzzes into a frenzy as everyone responds.

The driver tries to stop him once again. "Lieutenant, it's too late. It's too late, don't go in," he pleads. His voice is strained with his effort to keep Jett away. Each one fights to overpower the other and soon they both become tired.

Jett falls to his knees as every inch of the building is consumed in the flames. He knows there's nothing left inside but his heart still tells him to try. He looks around, trying to find a source of water. There's a pump outside one of the buildings. He darts over, grabs a bucket and fills it before throwing it on the flames in a useless bid to save the woman he loves from a fiery death.

He does this incessantly until the Guard comes. Peter is with them, his face pale as he grabs Jett in his arms, hugging him tightly and trying to soothe his pain. Jett fights with all he has to pull away from his friend, but he's too exhausted.

"Jett, Jett, they're going in there to find her," he says, holding him back while the firefighters disappear in the flames. "You can't go in; you have to be okay. You have to be all right for her, it's what she would want. Calm down."

"Fuck all of you! She's in there! We have to get her out! I have to save her, Peter!" He doesn't know he's screaming the same thing over and over; he's in another world.

"They're looking for her," Peter promises, hoping his words will calm him. "Our men will check the church as well. You know they will. It will be okay."

Jett is vicious as Peter's words slap him across the face. "It won't be okay! She's hurt... She could be... dead," he says, the reality hitting him like a brick. He freezes.

Peter helps him to the ground, shielding him from the chaos around the church. Jett is rocking back and forth, muttering that he can still save her— that he should have gone inside with her. Peter holds him tighter.

He cries silent tears as he tries to free himself from Peter's grasp, but Peter calls on the other guards to help move Jett into the wagon, blocking him inside until he settles down. As soon as he's inside, he breaks down. He cries snotty tears, he screams and shouts, crying for help... His entire world is gone. He just knows it. His hope fades and his heart crumbles into nothingness.

Eirho is dead.

19

NOW

Rum, a.k.a. Peter, lies unconscious, blood pouring from his wounds. Shadow works feverishly to tear off pieces of her cloak to wrap his wounds. If she is forced to go to the Palace, she fears that Peter will be treated negligently and he'll die. She uses whatever knowledge she has to help his wounds clot. He seems to be getting hotter. Shadow feels the heat from his skin radiate on hers and she grows more worried. She clambers around the back of the cart, looking for anything cold she can use as a compress.

"Oh, Peter, I'm so sorry. I didn't want you to have to go through this," she says with a big sigh. Her only hope is to use her true identity to gain leverage; she has to make sure that they treat Peter with kindness and mend him back to good health.

Suddenly, the cart halts and the momentum throws her forward into the front of the cart. Unsurprisingly, she smacks her head hard. She hurries to sit up as she hears angry shouts coming from outside. Shadow rubs her head, peering through the cracks in the cart. There's nothing to see but the flash of men running around. She thinks she hears fighting and cursing, but it's hard to tell.

The door of the cart flings open and she moves to shield Peter's body from the unseen harm. "Well, guess your cover got blown," Xero grumbles.

Shadow scurries to give him a tight, relieved hug. "Peter's in bad shape, we have to get him to the headquarters. I've done what I could, but without medicine and—"

"Cibor, I need you and Aine to take care of this," he calls. Cibor is fast, appearing at Xero's side in a second. He gives a pained look as he lifts Peter up with ease and moves him to the Skulls' wagon cautiously.

Xero helps Shadow out and dusts her off. She's worried, combing the street for where Jett and his men might be. The indifference in Xero's eyes quells her nerves, though it only makes her more frustrated.

"He's fine," Xero assures her. "We knocked him out—much to my own amazement—and threw him in the back of our cart. The other guards are going with Vex for some debriefing." Seeing the look on Shadow's face, he says: "Don't worry! We'll keep Jett with us so he is closer and we can obtain information ourselves."

She exhales, wondering what will happen next. Xero guides her to the Skulls' cart, helping her inside and climbing in after her. The slamming of the door makes her shake. They sit in silence for the duration of their trip home.

~

OVER THE PAST COUPLE OF DAYS, XERO HAS KEPT A CLOSE EYE ON Shadow, checking on her frequently. When he couldn't be there, he ordered Dax to watch her, and when he tried she tended to hide from him. Despite him being annoyed at Shadow, he wants her to be okay. She refuses to leave her room in the headquarters for anything except to check on Peter. The words that she does speak are short and direct. He can't imagine what she must be going through.

Xero has to keep an eye on Cibor as well. He is making himself sick with worry over Peter's condition — he's been pacing frantically for hours. Aine assures him repeatedly that Peter will be fine after he gets some fluids and rest, but Cibor isn't so sure. Xero does what he can to make Cibor leave Peter's side and make Jett give them information.

"He is being rather difficult," Cibor tells Xero, after grilling the Commander in the interrogation room. After seeing the look of disdain on Xero's face, Cibor knows full well that the leader of the Skulls already has a fire in his gut for that man.

"What a surprise," Xero grunts. "He's been here for two days and he won't even speak to us. Unless it's an insult, that is."

"Maybe you should talk to him," Dax suggests, curious about the look of pure amusement on Xero's face.

Xero smiles slyly. "That'll be the day. He won't listen to me, nor will he talk to me. He might even try to kill me. There's only one person who can break him at this point."

Dax is about to open his mouth in question when Shadow glides in, placing a soft hand on Dax's shoulder and giving him a smile full of apprehension.

Before Shadow can go into the room, Xero grasps her hand tightly, keeping her in place.

"You don't have to do this," he assures her.

She sighs, exhausted. "It's not for me. It's for him."

Xero releases ruefully and watches as she keys in the master code and walks down the short hallway. She unlocks the final door to the cell where the Commander sits.

She hesitates at the door, arguing back and forth with herself. In the end, she bites her lip hard enough to shock her body into obeying. When she turns the handle and shows her face, she hears

Jett's mouth drop, just for a second, before it turns into a deadly grimace.

Crossing the floor, she pulls out the chair across from Jett and takes a seat, folding her hands in front of her. He watches her cautiously, trying to hide his emotions behind a scowl. Shadow swears he looks as if he may shout, laugh, and cry all at once.

Shadow leans back in the chair, getting comfortable. He is as appealing as the moment she first laid eyes upon him: the stereotypical tall, dark, and handsome man. But Jett has something else—a dangerous smirk that draws her in. His eyes are nature's finest piece of art and she has to fight the urge to stare and become mesmerized.

She has to remind herself of all the things she's done and all the things that have changed.

"I hear you are being difficult," she says nonchalantly.

He curls his lip. "Why the hell should I speak to you?" he asks, utter revulsion sounding in his voice.

"I'm the only one here who won't hurt you."

"Won't hurt me?" he says incredulously. Shadow knows his temper. She can see the years of resentment and sorrow overcoming him. "I hope you are mocking me, Eirho."

Eirho, she muses. It's been years since someone called her by that name. Her real name. The name her parents gave to her the day she breathed her first gasp of air.

"You hurt me worse than anyone. As if your death wasn't enough! Here you are, deceitful as well. You lied about your own death. To me!" his voice increases in volume until he's practically shouting. His words hurt, but she knows she deserves it. Shadow senses the self-loathing he feels for speaking to her this way. Regardless, he continues and she lets him. This way, he can let out years of stored emotion. It's almost therapeutic.

"I did," she murmurs, crossing her arms.

"Your deception hurts the most. You're a traitor, not only to your family and your Kingdom, but also to me," he whispers bitterly, eyes narrowing. His words twist like a knife. He is right, after all, but there is more to the story than he knows.

"I have no Kingdom," she challenges. "I am no heir."

He tightens his jaw. "Fantastic."

"I'm sorry."

"At least say it like you mean it," he mocks. "Or was that a lie too?"

"I was protecting you," she replies, feeling her own temper beginning to flair. She has to stay calm and focus on getting him to talk. About something useful.

He laughs. He actually laughs. Shadow feels her heart beat faster with anger. "Protecting me?"

"If you knew what I was doing and my father found out, you wouldn't be dead. No, Jett. Death is what you would wish for. Every single day."

"I can take care of myself, unlike the Princess who ran away."

"I didn't run," she protests. "I've been here the entire time."

He sneers. "You loved to run, Rho. Or... is that your name now?"

"The Skulls call me Shadow."

"Shadow? Why? Are you Xero's personal pet? His little Shadow? Do you follow him around like a dog? "

She feels the jealous bite behind his words. He honestly thinks she is in love with Xero, that she has been the entire time. He is envious and hateful, spiteful even. Shadow's lip bleeds profusely as she digs her teeth in to keep from lashing at him. Jett can see the struggle on her face.

"I hope he takes you on walks."

Shadow does all she can to keep from reacting. Of course he's hurt by her actions.

A low sound comes from his throat. "Out of everyone you could've deceived, why was I on that list?" He is solemn now, leaving his distasteful remarks to turn sour in the back of his mouth.

"I was protecting you," she says quietly. "I know I handled it the wrong way, but you clearly don't understand what my father is capable of."

"Protecting me?" he hisses. "Betraying and protecting are two different things. Your father could never hurt me as badly as you have."

That stings. Shadow is tempted to reach out and slap him across the face. She wants him to attack her, but she knows he would never. She merely wants a good reason to punch him.

"Certainly seems like it, what with all those fucking whores you brought into your chamber," she says.

Jett inhales sharply.

Outside, Xero, Cibor, and Dax share a fearful look. Cibor pulls out his stun gun and Xero moves to the door, ready to stop a physical fight.

"I saw how you reacted when I 'died'," she continues bitterly. "Night after night... You had a different prostitute in your bed. You most certainly acted as if you were hurt."

"I thought you were dead!" he objects.

Shadow snatches some paperwork from the tabletop—maps and written reports—and chucks them at Jett's face. He doesn't block them, just turns his head to the side as they hit him. He purses his lips and watches her anger unfold.

"Oh, you definitely mourned for me," she says, grabbing the paper in her quivering, pale hand. She flings it at him—books now, and pencils that had been placed on the table. Jett allows her outburst and flares his nostrils out. A pencil skims his left brow and he blinks softly. "I hope it was a good fuck," she says shakily. "I hope you got your kicks out of it."

"Well, I didn't," he protests then. His tone is less quarrelsome now. Maybe he's realized how badly she hurts too, maybe he wants to resolve things. Shadow doesn't even notice.

"I should have been an obedient, silent princess and married Declan."

Jett cringes as she picks up the final book and slams it into the desk. She goes to the door, waiting for Xero to let her out.

"Have fun taking traitor dick," hisses Jett just before Shadow steps out the door.

Xero exhales and snatches a fierce Shadow in his arms, holding her as she struggles and kicks, trying to free herself. She wants to attack that arrogant jerk.

"Calm down, dammit," Xero scolds, tightening his grip. "You can't kill him, we need him."

She knows it's true. She stops struggling and Xero releases her, slowly. When she knows she's free, she walks swiftly to where Jett sits and leans over to put her mouth to his ear.

He holds his breath when he feels the warmth of her mouth on his neck, trying to stop the goosebumps and the engulfing memories.

"Tonight, I'll make sure to call out his name. Loud enough for you to hear my moans from your cell," she says, making Jett's skin crawl. She marches away, refusing to listen to another word.

Shadow barges past the men outside without a second thought.

Xero sighs and glimpses at Jett, who looks at him wearily. Xero almost apologizes. Instead, he lets the door shut and he turns to Cibor.

"Well, that was a lot less bloody than I expected."

Cibor can't help but chuckle as he locks the door.

Xero looks to Dax, who is standing in shock. Apparently, he's never witnessed the unforgiving wrath that is Shadow's temper.

"Do you think he saw me?" Dax asks, worriedly. He seems out of breath and anxious.

The leader cocks his eyebrow.

"Won't he tell Thanthos that he saw me?"

Xero nods then, tiredly. "If he escapes— which he won't. But he didn't see your face, don't sweat it."

The younger man nods and rushes away from the holding cell, trying to keep his feet from running as he passes through the corridor.

20

THEN

"Okay, give me the details. How's everything been going since you moved in?" Xero questions as he scoots a tray of fruit towards Eirho, her stomach growling in excitement. She shoves berries into her mouth hastily.

"I'm alive," she says through her chewing. "That's one thing. It's been an interesting transition. I'm lucky to have Peter and Cibor here."

Xero hums his agreement. "Are you missing your family yet?"

"I miss my sister," she says softly. "I think of her all the time. Seeing those… newspaper clippings of her crying…" She lingers on the idea, thinking of her poor young Alpha having no-one to care about her, or comfort her. What a twisted older sister she must be for abandoning her.

"It's only normal to miss them," Xero assures her. "Perhaps one day you will see them again."

"I hope. Jett can certainly take care of himself. He has good friends and a family. But Alpha has no-one. She's all alone and stuck with my wicked father and pompous Declan Snow." She takes an angry bite. "Couldn't we just assassinate them? Put my sister on the throne."

Xero smiles. "If only it were that simple. It's not easy to get in the Palace."

"You should've let me kill him without all this fake dying," she grumbles. "I'd poison him for good measure."

"You wouldn't have been safe. You know that."

"Maybe not, but I could have stayed with Alpha. Who will keep her safe now?" She grimaces at him.

Xero pats her arm comfortingly. "We have people on the inside keeping her safe."

"Have *them* kill Thanthos."

"It's not that simple. It's hard to get close to him or get him alone. Aside from that, if he leads us to the magic, we can destroy it once and for all," he explains to her. "There's always a reason for what we do."

She sighs. "You promise the Skulls will keep her safe?"

"I swear on my life," he tells her. "Any information or photos they can sneak to us will be given to you. You can watch her grow up."

"From afar... that's not exactly comforting. Having a long-distance relationship with someone who is only minutes away is much harder than if they were a thousand miles away." She crosses her arms and sulks, pouting visibly.

"I know it's hard, Eirho." He stops himself. "*Shadow*," he corrects, "but you're doing what is right. The City will be a better place because of you. You will be making an important change."

"Is it worth the risk? The risk of never seeing the man I love again? Or my sister?"

"You know it is. Otherwise you would be sitting in your fancy room in the Palace right now and not some musty old room with me," Xero points outs. "I know it's tough, but we are here for you, Shadow. And after what your father has done and continues to do, you know you're right where you belong."

"I suppose you have a point," she admits. "It's just tough."

"Sometimes the right thing is the toughest. You're not alone though. The Skulls have your back. Rum and Cibor, especially." He flashes her a smile. "You're not alone anymore."

"I was never alone," she says. "I was just a prisoner."

"I mean... Imagine if you had married Declan."

She groans loudly. "Gross. Please don't remind me of that. I dodged the worst mistake of my life there."

"That's no lie," he laughs brightly. "Alpha would be proud of the woman you are becoming."

"What makes you so certain?"

"You pointed out the newspaper articles. She loves you dearly, no matter what."

Eirho pushes the tray of fruit away and leans back. "She's such a sweet soul. I have no idea how my merciless father helped create her. If the world was full of Alphas... we would be better off."

"Well, it's funny you should mention that. I was thinking maybe our ultimate goal should be putting Alpha on the throne," he offers, seeing her face light up. "You're right, she would be compassionate and just. The true Heir to the throne. Not the hollow throne that your father sits on."

"I think she would make a wonderful queen. I love that idea," she says fondly. "Queen Alpha."

Xero chuckles. "It's settled then. We have a goal."

~

THE MOONLIGHT IS BARELY VISIBLE IN THE DENSE HEART OF THE forest. Traversing the trail proves more difficult than usual when the broken cobblestones and tree roots hide in the dark. Even with the faint moonlight and his men's torches, Thanthos has a hard time seeing the ruins in front of him.

Walking up the crooked stairs, he looks over his shoulder at Jett Torn, who stands quietly with the others. He has barely said a word since Princess Eirho was killed. Thanthos motions for Jett to follow him into the home of The Oracles.

The Oracles are strange creatures. When The Creators made the world, they gave a group of elves the power of foresight and turned them immortal. Centuries have passed by, leaving the elves wrinkled, beaten, and hungry for death, after the dark requests of men twisted their minds. Jett is hesitant but follows after, his hands on his guns. Though he has heard whispers of their existence, he has yet to visit the ancient place of the Elvish seers. It's no secret that Thanthos uses them to do his dark bidding.

Admittedly, Jett doesn't know much about The Creators, but he knows they're referred to as the Gods who started the world. They created humans, animals, plants, and even magic. Even though magic has faded, traces of The Creators can still be found in dark, hidden places such as the free folk Forest.

Thanthos gestures again and Jett moves to his side, watching the purple flames of the fire. The night appears darker around the fire. He shivers when he sees six figures moving around in slow poses, chanting under their breath. He can see their pointed ears and their yellow teeth, along with the scars and spots that cover them. Being immortal has not treated them kindly and neither has having magic.

"Do *not* let them touch you, Commander Torn," Thanthos warns, his lip curled in a snarl. "Chances are I will have to find a new Commander if they do."

Chills run up the back of Jett's neck, growing colder when he sees Thanthos bow to The Oracles. What kind of hell has Thanthos gotten them mixed up in? Jett's heard of people becoming ill or suffering excruciating pain because of The Oracles, but the way Thanthos voice bellows tells a different story.

A low gurgle comes from one of the creatures. It steps forward sniffing at the unwavering King. Another loud sound leaves it, this time a cackle.

The others begin to dance around, snorting and laughing

maniacally. With each sound the violet flames rise to the treetops, gaining power from their madness.

Jett steps away, wary. These creatures are disgusting with their rotting skin and their stench of darkness, yet the King seems to love them. Or rather, they repulse him, but he loves their power and what they can offer him.

"King Thanthos," one of The Oracles hisses mockingly. "Are you not in mourning? Why do you visit now?"

"I want to know if the magic is finally mine. If I can rule without challenge," he states. Thanthos shows no fear as he steps forward. "Is the magic mine?"

"A selfish one," an Oracle hisses. "Not mourning her death."

Another one sneers and reaches for Thanthos. Jett goes to hit it, but Thanthos stops him. "The true Heir is still alive. Keep searching, *King*." It spits the last word derisively.

A long-haired Oracle approaches Jett. "Ah," her voice lulls, "a heartbroken man. Your misery tastes *delicious*."

Jett avoids the Oracle's gaze quickly, the heaviness of reality weighing on him. The wound is still so fresh it burns, why does this monster have to bring it up?

"Fear not, young man, you will find love again," it cackles, scurrying back to its friends.

Jett clenches his jaw, unable to escape from his own nightmare. Even these old Elves taunt him and remind him of how hollow he feels. When he lost Eirho, he lost everything.

Thanthos is too fixated on his own questions to notice. "How do I find the magic?"

"You cannot ask such a question without a gift," one of them chides, clicking its tongue. It inches closer to him. "Do you have a gift, King?"

Reaching into his satchel, Thanthos reveals a clear pot with a cork lid. A dark crimson liquid swirls around in the glass as he hands it to them.

"The blood of virgins," he says. "A dozen of them."

Jett cringes. Thanthos is toying with dark magic. Knowing what Thanthos does is sickening. He wants to run away from this forsaken place or kill Thanthos and be done with him. But all he can do is stand and watch, or risk being put on the executioner's block.

The Oracles laugh darkly and throw the container into the flames. It bursts and images begin to dance in it. A giant rose appears, the marking of The Creators. It looks like it's somewhere in the forest.

"You should hunt north of the walls, King," the long-haired one says. "Deep in the meadows, you will find the first piece. From there you will find more. When you find the last one, you will be led to the place where gifts are given."

"But be warned," another adds, "you will not get the gift easily. You face a dangerous challenger. If you are not careful, you will lose."

Jett likes that idea, hoping that Thanthos will lose soon enough, expelling him as King.

"As for you," a hoarse one snarls and gets closer, smelling Jett, "you will face betrayal unlike anything you've ever known, but things are not always what they seem."

He steps towards the creature. "What—"

The Oracles leave, laughing loudly and disappearing into the mist.

Thanthos exhales angrily, spinning to face Jett. "Send a group of men north of the wall. Tell them what to look for. Go, Torn, now."

"But it's dangerous, Sire," he protests.

Thanthos grabs his collar. "Do it or you will not live to fulfill the future that The Oracles sought for you. Go!" He thunders, pushing Jett back.

Exhaling angrily, Jett marches back to tell his commanding officer. He knows that this mission may just be a death sentence.

21

NOW

"Do you want to talk?" Xero says, sitting on the end of Shadow's bed.

She sits hunched over with her face in her palms, lost in a labyrinth of memories. For years, she imagined how good it would feel to see Jett again, how ecstatic and relieved he would be. She pictured her Jett, not this angry, resentful chaotic man. He loathes her more than anyone else.

"I want to go back and save Peter before any of this went to shit," she replies, covering her eyes. She wants to sleep, but sleep is the last thing on her mind. "I can't believe he hates me this much. I thought he'd feel better after six years."

Xero sighs. "Of course he doesn't, I know that. He's processing things, trying to figure it out. He thought you were dead for years, Shadow! And now the truth hits him in the face? Imagine how that feels," he offers. He hates Jett Torn, but he does what he can to bring Shadow back down, he needs her.

"He'll refuse to help us after seeing me. He thinks I'm a traitor, but how can he not see what I rose up against? He should know

Thanthos' evil better than anyone." Her thoughts just keep pouring from her mouth as she attempts to organize them.

"Your fake death fueled his drive, Shadow. He wanted revenge on us when he thought that the Skulls had killed you," Xero points out. "Give him time and he will calm down. It shouldn't take long before he wants to talk to you again."

She looks over at him with tired eyes. He thinks for a second that she may have been crying, but he looks away. Shadow isn't vulnerable. It makes him uncomfortable.

"I let him hurt for all these years. I thought I was protecting him, but I doubt he sees it that way," she admits. "I'm sure he thinks I was just being selfish."

"That Commander thinks very highly of you. Look at the change your 'death' caused. He's an evil bastard now because of it. Just tone him down a bit," Xero says.

"I'll try, but I don't know if I can focus enough to capture Alpha. And I need to do that as soon as possible, if we want to get ahead of Thanthos." She pauses, her eyes growing wider. She looks like she could throw up. "Imagine how *she'll* react to seeing me."

"They both need time," he says. "You would be hurt and furious too, Shadow. Anyone would. Even me."

She scoffs. "Xero Marcs has feelings? Are you doing okay? Did you bump your head?"

"Shut it, I'm fine. You'll have to speak to him again, soon, though. You're the only one who can convince him to help us. I can't do it," he grumbles with annoyance, his voice growing low and mocking. "Even though I'm the best with people."

She laughs and rolls her eyes; Xero is hardly good with her. "Once I can muster up the courage, I'll speak to him. But I need someone to meet up with Noah and finalize the details for capturing Alpha."

Xero rubs his chin thoughtfully. "I'll figure something out. After you're done with Torn, talk to Aine and Tools. They've been dying to share some new information with you."

She nods. "Thank you."

"Anytime. I'll see what information Noah has for us. When I get back, you'll have 24 hours to capture Alpha," he states. "We are running out of time."

~

JETT GLARES AT THE FLOOR OF HIS CELL. DESPITE THEIR EFFORTS IN making the bed more comfortable—with another blanket and some extra padding—it was still cold and uncomfortable. Instead of sleeping on the bed, he is on the ground with his back against the wall, wondering exactly whose idea it was to make his stay more comfortable.

He's stuck in a whirlpool of thoughts that pull him deeper and deeper into himself. Everything he believed is now a lie.

Jett also needs to sort through his feelings. He loves Eirho with his entire being—that's indisputable. But now, he has to face her again after six years. She left him alone in this chaotic world, letting him think she was dead. He didn't want to face the world solo, he wanted to be by Eirho's side.

If he thinks about it for too long, it makes him sick. She's been working with the Skulls all this time; beating and killing his guards and plotting to overthrow Thanthos. He wonders, briefly, if she's with Xero Marcs and thinks that maybe she always had been. Jett contemplates the vast number of men that have probably fallen in love with her. How many has she given something back to? The thought is unsettling.

He hears the light, careful tread of boots coming down the hallway and it pulls him out of his slump. A moment later, Shadow is standing at the cell door. He stares at her through the clear, cell wall in confusion as she waves her hand over the scanner that unlocks the door and slips inside. She makes sure that the door locks behind her before she walks over to him in silence.

"What are you doing?" he growls suspiciously.

Shadow reaches into her belt and pulls out one of her pistols. She places it tentatively on the ground and slides it toward his hand in one quick motion. She sits across from him, challenging him to take it.

"What the fuck are you doing?" he says, eyeing the gun.

"I'm giving you the chance to have your revenge," she says, indifferent. She leans her head against the wall and takes a deep breath, readying herself.

He picks up the gun, admiring it in his hand. It's cold and heavier than he expected, but he flips it back and forth, weighing his options. He flicks the safety off the gun and aims point-blank into Shadow's face. Shadow flinches pressing backwards into the wall, squeezing her eyes shut. She jumps as the gun hits the floor with a loud clatter. He tosses it forcefully, spinning it towards the other side of the room.

Shadow opens her eyes, raises an eyebrow, but leaves her head on the wall. "You could have killed me and escaped," she notes. "Why didn't you?"

"You must not have believed me when I said I would always love you," he grunts. He crosses his arms over his strong chest.

"But I betrayed you."

"Love is unconditional."

She takes a long breath and holds it in as she considers this. He could have even held the gun to her head and forced his way out, without hurting her. So, the question still stands: *Why didn't he?*

"Don't think I didn't feel the weight of my choices every single day," Shadow murmurs.

"I hope you felt it every second," he says scathingly.

She lifts her head up, trying to read those fathomless eyes without being pulled into them. He's as handsome as she remembers, if not more. Now he is older, more handsome and manly. She senses the fire burning inside of him. As she looks into his eyes, she sees his ache brought to life. Shadow wonders which pieces of him are missing.

Jett pulls his knees up and rests his arms on them, trying to seem relaxed despite the urge to hide himself from her.

"I thought you'd be with Xero," he mutters.

She lets a laugh escape, realizing the twisted world she lives in. At least she can find humor in it. "I will never be with Xero. I was trying to hurt you."

"Why?"

"You were pissing me off," she nonchalantly. "And remembering how you brought all those women back to your room..." she trails off. "It's burned into me."

He gulps. "I never touched them, Eirho. I couldn't bring myself to do it. And I wasn't going to kill Peter, not really. I was trying to lure Marcs out. How was I supposed to know you'd come instead?"

Her eyes dart to him in surprise and instantly, she feels a twinge of guilt. She *could* bring herself to do it. A couple of times. After seeing the throngs women go into his quarters, she couldn't contain her anger. And to know he was setting Xero up... she doesn't know what to say.

"So, what happens now?" he asks tiredly. All these emotions are exhausting.

"Xero will do whatever he can to gain knowledge on Thanthos."

He scoffs. "I'd like to see that asshole try."

"That's another reason why I gave you the gun," she says, sighing. "They'll kill you."

"Let them."

It hurts her to see him so careless. She doesn't want him to feel lost and alone. He can't go through life thinking that the only way out is to be murdered by the Skulls. And it's all her fault; this is what she's done to him, regardless of what she's hoped for. This is the reality.

"I'll never let them," she replies. "I'll let you out."

"Stop trying to do me a favor, Eirho. What's done is done and you'll never be able to take it back." The second the words leave his mouth, he feels the guilt swoop in. He knows how much they'll hurt her. And even after all she did, Jett still cannot imagine hurting her. "Eirho—"

She puts her hand up and pushes herself from the ground. "I guess I'd hoped that my actions wouldn't have such severe consequences," she says, walking to the door. She waves her hand one last time over the scanner and steps out, locking it behind her. "Goodnight, Jett."

~

AINE SCURRIES AROUND EXCITEDLY, PULLING ALL OF HER PAPERS together with hope of showing Shadow everything she's learned. Shadow will be pleased, she's certain of it.

Xero is already in the room when Shadow comes in holding a mug of some peculiar drink. He takes a seat at the table and reclines back, studying Shadow as she stands across from him.

"I am so excited! We have learned so much, Shadow!" Aine exclaims, a big smile drawn on her face. She seems to dance around the room as she gathers all her materials.

"Tell me, what am I searching for?"

Aine opens a folded piece of paper on the table, spreading it out to reveal a scribbled drawing of The City and other markings on the sides. "From what the old texts are saying, I think you might be shocked."

Shadow stares at the images on the paper: strange color patterns, outlines of animals, and unique gems decorate the page. Everything Aine has gained knowledge of is right there in front of them.

"Well, What is it?" asks Xero, raising his eyebrow impatiently.

"We believe the magic has to be unlocked," Aine explains. "We found literature saying that the magic could be sealed away until an heir releases it. No doubt from a special place."

Shadow steps forward, her curiosity getting the better of her. "What type of special place?"

Aine pauses and frowns, clearly at a loss. "We don't know yet. It has to be some sacred, magical place where The Heir can tap into their gifts, but we don't have a clue where it is. I'm assuming it's somewhere in the kingdom."

"Thanthos is already searching then," Shadow says, grumbling to herself.

"Which means we have even fewer opportunities to kidnap Alpha if she's so damn busy," Xero complains. "And whatever she knows is crucial to stopping Thanthos."

Aine is hesitant but she chimes in. "There *is* someone else who might know. Well, they may not realize it, but I'm certain they could help."

Xero looks at Aine, patiently.

"I noticed that the Elite guards have been revisiting specific places around The City. Commander Torn might know where they are. We can use what he knows to zero in on a better idea," Aine suggests, looking between the two of them, waiting for a reaction.

"Could you see if he'll tell you?" Xero directs the question to Shadow.

She has her arms crossed. "He won't tell me shit. I will capture Alpha on my own, but be prepared for the backlash."

Xero purses his lips. In his head, he goes over all the options and the way he would do things, but he knows, ultimately, it's Shadow's mission. And she will do it her way.

"I'll bring my sister in, Xero. But keep this quiet. I don't want anyone to betray us."

Aine is surprised to hear Shadow say it. *Sister* had been a forbidden word, until now. It's new, different; she knows things are changing. And the threat of a spy makes Aine anxious.

"One more thing," Aine says before Shadow can leave. The other woman stops and turns and they share a secretive glance.

She places a picture on the table, revealing a vibrant, red rose. *Among the roses,* Oakenstaid had said. It's all connecting now. "This image keeps popping up. Keep it in mind."

Shadow and Xero note the rose, Xero taking the image in his hand and putting it near his pile of papers on the table. He needs to save this for later.

"Thank you, Aine," Shadow says. She is too focused on getting her sister to think about the rose right now. Her mind is stuck on Alpha's face as she leaves the room.

22

THEN

Peter knocks on Jett's door. It's been a few days since Eirho's body was buried and Jett has stayed cooped up in his room the entire time, locked away from the outside world.

When he hears nothing but a groan, he sticks a makeshift pick in the lock and jimmies the door to open up for him, slipping inside before anyone asks to see the grieving man. Jett sits facing out the window, almost oblivious to the other man in his room. Peter sits on his bed—it's been untouched for days.

"Damnit, Jett have you been sleeping?" The room hasn't changed since last time he visited. "Man, I know you're hurting but you've got to take care of yourself."

Jett doesn't say anything, he simply stares out the window, without really seeing anything.

Peter isn't sure what to do, he shakes his head and goes to get a glass of water from the small kitchen. He brings it back to Jett and places it on the table next to him, hoping he'll drink it.

"Come on, man." Peter puts a kind hand on Jett's shoulder, but he gets no response. He doesn't know how to get his friend to acknowledge him, let alone talk to him. "Please, I'm really worried about you."

Jett doesn't even blink.

"She wouldn't want you to be like this, man. Eirho would want you to be happy, she would want you to try to move on." That will either get his attention or piss him off—Peter is just hoping for some kind of reaction.

He finally moves, turning to stare at Peter. His eyes are sunken, glazed over, and bloodshot. Somehow his face looks thinner, his entire body actually. It's as if Eirho wasn't the only one who died that day.

"Do it for her, Jett. Take care of yourself for her. She loved you so much," Peter says, trying to console him. "Please."

A tear pools at the corner of Jett's eye. The droplet cascades down his cheek and stains his shirt.

"I wanted to spend the rest of my life with her," he whispers. "And now I never will."

"I know, man, I know. I'm so sorry you're going through this," Peter says, keeping a hand on his friend's shoulder. Peter wants to break down and cry. That damn guilt of his actions, what he and Eirho have done to his best friend, his brother.

"I loved her. She was my soulmate and I couldn't even openly grieve at her funeral," he whispers again, his voice hoarser and shakier this time. "I let her down. I should have protected her, Peter. I should have checked the church."

Peter tightens his grip. "I know, Jett, I know."

With that, full tears stream down Jett's face. "How do I fix this pain? How do I bring her back?" The desperation in his voice breaks Peter's heart.

"You let time take its course. You live for her, Jett. That's what she would have wanted. You live the life she couldn't."

"I feel like I died with her. Only, I didn't. I'm stuck between this world and the next," he says. He looks out the window, his entire face is covered with the wet stickiness of tears. "I don't know how to fix this."

Peter grabs the back of his head and pulls him into a hug, grasping him tightly. "I'm here," he says between Jett's sobs. "I'm here. I'll help you through this, I promise. We'll make it through." He cries too, as he holds onto his best friend and feels Jett's pain radiating into him.

I'm a fucking monster, he thinks, anguished. *I'm the worst friend ever.*

"It's okay, Jett, it's okay. We will make it through buddy. I promise."

~

PETER ARRIVES AT THE SKULLS' HEADQUARTERS TO FIND EIRHO STILL awake. Her door is shut but a small sliver of light is shining from under the door. Peter knocks heavily, pressing his forehead into the door. He hears the sound of a book being set down on a table and the swish of her feet on carpet before she opens it, gasping when she sees his face.

"Oh my God, Peter! Are you okay?" she asks, giving him a tight hug. "What happened?"

Peter nods to the room, wiping his face. She brings him inside and he flops onto the bed as she closes the door. Eirho sits next to him and takes his hands in hers, searching his face. She wonders what happened to make him so upset. She's never seen him this way.

"What happened? Peter, what's wrong?" she pleads, rubbing his hand with her thumb, tracing light circles on his palm in an attempt to comfort him. When she looks closer, she sees that his eyes are not only red and swollen from crying, but someone has punched him as well. "Peter?"

"We made a mistake, Eirho," he gasps through his sobs. "We hurt him so bad. I'm the *worst* friend in the history of friends. He hasn't slept, hasn't eaten. Nothing. I don't know. I fed him and made him walk around the apartment with me, but he's so upset. I shouldn't have made you do this."

She holds his face in her hands. "Peter, *stop*. You didn't make me. I chose this," she says. All of a sudden, Peter bursts out:

"I—I told him the truth! This is stupid, Rho. We should have told him from the beginning."

She freezes, letting go of his face. "You did what?" She falls back onto the floor in shock. "Peter..."

"You weren't the one who had to see his face and who had to comfort him. He was so sick, Eirho. So sick. I had to do it or else he was going to kill himself slowly," he exclaims through his tears. "I had to tell him!"

"W-what did you say? What did he say?" Her question is asked in a fearful tone. She is terrified to ask him, but she has to know.

Peter laughs at the question. "I have a black eye! He wanted to kill me but he stopped himself," he says, looking down at his hands. "He stopped. And he hugged me and he cried with relief."

"Is he going to tell Thanthos?" she whispers.

"No, he's not. He's going to play the game, pretend to be his lap dog. He's going to blame me and ban me from the guard so I can finally get out! He's going to help us." He sighs with relief, grateful he had someone he could tell. "I just feel so bad for hurting him and for betraying your trust. And my eye hurts. It really hurts."

She smiles at him. "It looks like it hurts," she chuckles. "But we can't tell anyone. Ever. It could put his life at risk and our own. Peter, this is our secret. Do you understand?"

He nods. "Yes. I'm so sorry. I didn't want to hurt him. I just really couldn't stand to see him that way. I'm too weak."

"No, you're not. You're just compassionate and you care about him. I care about him, too. He's mad I didn't tell him, isn't he?"

"Furious. But he understands. And he'll do what he can to keep people from getting slaughtered under his watch. He'll get them out of The City," he tells her, taking a tissue from her proffered hand. "Thank you."

"Peter? How much do you trust Xero?"

Peter freezes at the question. "What? Why?"

"Something isn't right, I know that, but I can't put my finger on it. We have to be careful; we have to tread with caution. You and I are against the world right now." She puts her hands on his shoulders. "You and I."

He nods in response, understanding what she means.

"We will play Xero's game and we will go after Thanthos, but it's going to take some time. We have to live as if we have no connection to that life anymore. We have to keep ourselves and our loved ones safe," she says. "We have to play and we have to win."

23

NOW

"Vex, I need you to get high up. A bird's eye view preferably," Shadow says covertly into her headset. She looks around the dark alleyway at the others; her backup. Ultimately though, their success is down to her alone.

"You got it, Shadow," Vex whispers eagerly into the headset.

Shadow hears the soft movements of Vex in her ear. When Vex settles in, it's time for her to set the plan into motion.

Reaching into her pocket, she double checks her supplies. Rope, tape, a taser—anything that might help. This is a dangerous mission and she only has one chance. If she messes up, the entire plan is compromised and the Skulls will be in danger.

"I see the caravan," Scout, a fellow Skull, whispers into the headset. He is peering with binoculars across the wasteland as the sun falls beyond the horizon. "We have approximately ten minutes."

"Perfect," Shadow says. "We'll hit the caravan before they reach the wall. I need the rest of you to dart them as they arrive. I will take care of Alpha."

"I'll take left and Scout you take right. Everyone else, offer us cover in the event that we miss," Vex orders, taking a deep breath. "Don't worry, I never miss."

"Is that so?" Scout asks, clicking his tongue. "You think you have better aim than me?"

"We are about to find out," Shadow intervenes swiftly. She leans her back against the stone wall, taking deep breaths as the reality hits her. She is going to take Alpha prisoner, her own sister—or so she hopes. If Shadow doesn't, the war will start before they make it back to The City.

"Are you ready?" Xero's voice sounds in her earbud. He's concerned and on edge; the little tremble in his voice gives him away. No-one else seems to notice, but Shadow knows him too well. She swallows hard, trying to keep her own voice steady. "Ready to succeed."

He makes a noise—disbelief, fear, relief? Shadow cannot tell this time.

"T-minus sixty-seconds," Scout announces. "On your call, Shadow."

She takes a deep breath and closes her eyes. She covers her face with her hood, listening to the sound of the cars rolling in as the dust and rock crunch under the wheels. Her heart stops and her senses heighten: the feeling of her gun against her leg feels like an ache, the wind causes her to stumble, and finally, she can smell the gas from the cars and hear the faint, careless laughter of the Red Guards under Alpha's watch.

When she hears the cars begin to brake at the unusual roadblock, she snaps out of it.

"Now!" she orders into the mic, hurling herself over the wall and onto the ground. She sprints to the back car, seeing the others follow suit. Within seconds she has the door open and is crawling into the backseat of the car that Alpha had been in. *Had been.*

Shadow looks up frantically, seeing Alpha racing across the ground towards the wall. She rolls and jumps out of the car before taking off running, her feet stinging from the pressure she's putting them under. Shadow has to double Alpha's speed to catch her before she slips back into The City's walls.

Alpha peers over her shoulder, nearly stumbling as she sees her attacker only a few feet behind. Shadow sees her chance as they close in on the wall, an opening to capture her sister. Alpha has been trained —without knowing what hit her, she goes into fight mode. She rolls under Shadow and swings at her. Shadow dodges the attempt and grabs Alpha's arms to pin her down. This gives Alpha the opportunity to kick her back, leaping up as Shadow slams into the ground.

"You bitch! What do you want!" Alpha shouts, taking a fighting stance.

Shadow doesn't respond, she reacts. She needs to get Alpha into custody and fast. She charges her, avoiding the oncoming hits and landing a blow in Alpha's stomach. Groaning, Alpha swings and busts Shadow's lip, it doesn't faze Shadow in the least. Before Shadow can seize the opportunity to take control, Alpha knocks her in the nose with her head.

Shadow grows annoyed as the blood stains her face. She holds Alpha down with her body weight and jabs two fingers into the pressure point at the back of Alpha's neck. At the last second, Alpha moves and Shadow misses. Alpha frees a hand and smacks Shadow across the face, causing her mask to fall.

Alpha freezes at the sight. She *knows* this woman. The face—the wide sapphire eyes.

"Eirho," she gasps, her body going limp. "How?"

"I don't have time to explain everything, there's a lot that you don't know." Shadow assures her, wiping the dirt and blood from her face. "But for now, I need you to come with me."

A new rage overtakes Alpha and she knocks Shadow off.

"You traitor! You're working with *them*! You're a damned Skull!" Alpha screams as she reaches for her weapon, only to find it laying on the ground, a few feet from them.

Shadow follows her gaze from where she sits. She spots the gun and dives to grab it. Alpha is only a second late and digs her heel into her sister's hand.

"You left me for those bastards!" Alpha says as Shadow winces and shakes her hand. She kicks the gun out of reach whilst Alpha is distracted. "How could you do that! We all thought you were dead! You destroyed us! You destroyed Jett and you destroyed me! You're a selfish monster."

"I was trying to save you," Shadow murmurs. "I wanted to keep you safe from our wicked father."

Alpha jumps onto her, smacking her in the face with all her might. "You selfish bitch! You left me with him!" she growls, towering over her sister as she hits her repeatedly. Shadow reluctantly guards her face, knowing she deserves this. The anger, the pain, the hatred. She is not innocent.

"I know, I know," she whispers through the blows. "I'm sorry, Sister."

"No! No, you're not you—"

Without warning, Alpha goes limp and falls onto Shadow. Scout stands above her with a gun clenched in his hand; he used the hilt against Alpha's head. He shakes his head at Shadow and lifts Alpha up, binding her hands together and picking her up.

"That was unnecessary," Shadow growls as she pushes herself up, spitting blood.

"You were letting her beat the shit out of you," he snaps back. "I didn't want to watch you let her kill you because you didn't want to fight back."

She glares at him. "It's none of your business."

"Just get up and let's get going," he says, adjusting Alpha's body against his chest. "We need to get out of here."

~

"LET ME HAVE IT," SHADOW SIGHS AS SHE WIPES THE BLOOD OFF HER face with a cold rag. The cuts sting as she cleans herself and she does her best to hide it. "I can see it on your face."

Xero scoffs at her behavior. "You would've let her kill you."

"I'd rather she kill me than the other way round. At least I deserve it."

"Enough," he says viciously. "She is being treated until she wakes up. Stop feeling sorry for yourself and see what you can discover."

Her eyes follow him as he walks to pour himself some tea. He sips it lightly and looks back at her, questioningly. "You know something, don't you?" she asks quietly.

"Well, I'm just considering who attacked you and who didn't. I think we have a better chance of your sister knowing more useful information," he points out. "I know Thanthos has been trying to use her for his games, since you didn't stick around. She's even more compelled than Torn. And he hates your father as much as us."

"If Jett hated my father so much, then why did he support him?"

"He was trying to forget you."

"I don't blame him," she admits, her gaze lingering on her feet. She wanted to forget, too. "Alpha made it clear what damage I've done. You can't blame me for wanting to take that away. Killing me would've been a relief for her."

"Killing you would have made her feel worse," he retorts sharply. "Get out of that mindset or we will *never* defeat Thanthos. Do you want him to continue to murder the innocent? To rape, and burn, and mutilate?"

Shadow winces involuntarily. "I've been wanting to stop him but you've refused to let me out of this cage."

"I've been waiting for the right moment," he snaps back. "I refuse to let you go in there blind. How will I know that you're actually able to kill your own father?"

"I don't understand, Xero."

"What don't you understand?" he asks, pursing his lips. He crosses his arms slowly, bracing himself for an onslaught of accusations.

"Here we go again! You think that Dax should be the one to do it!" Shadow throws her arms up in defeat. "I don't understand why you would trust Dax over me. I can't believe you'd question my loyalty, after everything I've given up for this. I've sacrificed my home, my life, my family, and my soulmate. I missed my sister growing into a woman. I missed so many milestones in her life and yet you think I would play along for years, only to bail at the last minute." Just when Xero thinks she's done, she starts again: "I don't understand. Is it because your fathers had history and you want to respect that? Or maybe you found hope when he came along, and now you can't handle it 'cause you know he's shady. I'm just hurt you don't trust me to do it, after everything."

Shadow sits, shocked that she said so much. She tries to control the tears that threaten to fall. She has given everything to Xero and this mission, and now he does not trust her.

"I—I'm sorry," he utters. "I want this war to be over. I want to put Alpha on the throne, Thanthos in the ground, and I want the magic in the right hands. Our people are dying daily and we're powerless to stop it. It's a fucking massacre. I had hoped he could help us, but I guess that's not going to happen."

Shadow inhales and hangs her head low. The pain is overwhelming—she can't tell if the tears are from sadness or pain, or maybe a mixture of both. "We don't need him," she says, "I'm prepared to do the unspeakable. I will kill Thanthos myself, so long as you put Alpha on the throne. Let me be the one to kill him."

"I can't let you do that. It's a suicide mission," he tells her firmly, his brows knitting together. "I won't let you do it alone."

Shadow shakes her head in disappointment as she stands. "I'm going for a walk."

Xero opens his mouth to say something, but Shadow has already left.

~

"AH, YOU'RE AWAKE," VEX COOS AS HER VICTIM OPENS HER EYES, wincing at the bright light. "So nice of you to join the conscious."

"Where—where am I?" Alpha whispers, turning her head slowly, taking in her surroundings. She tries to sit up, but she soon realizes that she's tied firmly to a table. Her head is pounding.

Vex reaches over and touches Alpha's face gently. "You're in the custody of the Skulls, dear. In the infirmary," she reminds her, studying the bump on her head. "Minor concussion, but you'll be okay."

"My fucking sister," Alpha growls, her wrists rubbing against the restraints. She puts all her strength into making them budge, but it's no use. "Does she want you to kill me? Is this how I go? Tied up to this damn table!"

"I'm not going to kill you," Vex responds in a soothing voice. She rubs some cream onto Alpha's head as she twists and turns. "If I hurt you, your sister would kill me, believe it or not."

"How about *not*? She betrayed our family," Alpha growls back. "I wouldn't trust the nose on her face."

Vex hums with amusement, a slight grin on her face. "Oh, but she did what she needed to do to save you. It's no secret that Thanthos wanted you dead while Princess Eirho was alive. You were too kind, too gentle. You were weak to him."

"Shut up! If you're going to kill me, just do it!" Alpha hisses, sweat glistening on her forehead as she tries to free herself.

"Shadow would have my throat," Vex muses. She looks down at Alpha, watching her carefully. "Are you hungry? I can have the cooks bring something to you. You will need to drink at least."

Alpha's eyes grow dark as she watches Vex. "I'll die first."

"Okay, we will give you nourishment through an IV," Vex says indifferently. As she goes to grab the line, Alpha grunts in defeat.

"Give me a damn straw."

Vex chuckles to herself as she fetches water for her prisoner. She fills a glass and offers Alpha the straw, who drinks reluctantly and glares at the other woman as she does so.

"Ah, see? Not so bad. We want you to be well again," Vex notes gingerly. She takes a seat on a stool beside the bed, staying quiet for a long moment. "We aren't going to hurt you. We want your help."

"You are keeping me prisoner—why should I help you?"

"I will allow Shadow to explain that. For now, you need your rest. You won't be any good to us if you are ill," Vex tells her gently. She offers her another drink. "You are safe here."

24

NOW

Cibor dabs the cloth into the cool water, wringing it out before he lays it carefully on Peter's forehead. The younger man stirs at the cold and reaches for Cibor's large hand, giving it a squeeze. He's grateful to have someone as kind-hearted as Cibor to take care of him.

"How are you feeling?" Cibor questions anxiously.

"I'm better," Peter answers in his strained tone. "I will be okay, I'm just achy now. Thanthos didn't make my stay at the Palace very welcoming."

"I'll *kill* him."

Peter shakes his head in protest at the idea. "He will kill you. Only The Heir can kill him now."

"We don't even know who The Heir is. Until we know more, that isn't going to happen." Cibor says, frustrated.

"From what I know, The Ancient Ones, a.k.a. the first people that The Creators made, disappeared when Dark magic came around. They left one person to protect what was left behind and challenge the bad guys," Peter explains, taking his time to get the words out. "Someone of royal blood I'm sure. The Heir magic is rumored to be locked away. Thanthos was raging about it being kept from him."

"How did you find this out?"

Peter shrugs slowly. "I heard things while I was locked up. You know I love eavesdropping," he chuckles. "Argos' gift wasn't given to Thanthos when he was killed so Thanthos thought it was locked away somewhere."

"So Thanthos knows it's being protected from him," Cibor clarifies as he stumbles through his thoughts. The new information is overwhelming, no doubt, but it gives him hope. No-one at the headquarters has mentioned this yet.

"Yeah. The true heir of magic will be able to unlock it, no-one else," he points out, sighing into the cool, damp air of the room. "He doesn't even know. I think he sent Alpha outside the walls to find information and he discovered that it could be protected."

"The True Heir," Cibor whispers, hearing the wonder in his own voice. "I fear he might have found a way to take it from The Heir."

Peter nods. "Considering no-one is certain who The Heir is, I think we need to start researching," he says, sighing. "We need to trace Argos' interactions and lovers. There's a bastard in his line somewhere."

"Why would Argos leave a bastard behind without training them? He knew they would have powers," Cibor points out. He engulfs Peter's hand in his, giving it a squeeze. "And he knew Thanthos was evil."

"I don't know. Maybe he was trying to protect The Heir? Maybe he knew Thanthos would kill him for the power and he didn't want The Heir to suffer the same fate?"

Cibor settles back in his seat as his; he tries to relax his tense muscles. "That makes sense, unfortunately. But who could The Heir be?"

"I think our best bet is to talk to the people who actually lived in the Palace. Shadow, Torn, and Alpha. One of them has to know the truth about Argos."

Peter grimaces at the thought of his old best friend. Torn might be an unbearable asshole, but imagining him chained up in a cell makes him feel sorry for him. They were like brothers once, after all. Sometimes he can't help but still think of him as one.

"They'd know without realizing, I'm sure," Cibor says. "We have to make sure they don't catch on."

"Let me talk to Torn," he says. "He can't hurt me anymore than he already has," he continues swiftly when he notes the worry on Cibor's face. "I'll be fine, babe."

Cibor nods reluctantly, unable to deny Peter when he calls him anything sweet.

"I want to speak with Shadow, too. We have loads to discuss," Peter adds with a small smile. "Like why she risked everything to save me."

"Tread lightly. Torn has turned her into a bigger mess than usual. She left the headquarters early this morning after a fight with Xero."

"I'll find her."

Cibor sighs wearily. Seeing Peter in this state makes him feel sick, and thinking of him getting involved with Shadow when she's already highly strung, makes him feel worse. He takes Peter's hand and brings it to his lips, kissing it gently.

"I'll bring her to you. I need you to rest," he whispers softly.

Peter's eyes twinkle. "Thank you, Cibor."

"Anything for you, my love."

SHADOW SUCKS HER CHEEKS IN AS SHE WATCHES THE SECURITY footage. Jett Torn paces the length of the small cell before sliding his back down the wall and sitting on the concrete. At least he's safe, even if she can't gather enough courage to talk to him again.

He's still just as she remembers—handsome, brave, fearless. That sharp jaw, those bright eyes, that crooked smirk. He is a force to be reckoned with—a force that could destroy her.

"Shadow?"

She jumps, slamming her screen face-down onto the counter. She hopes she hasn't shattered this one while trying to hide the fact she has been watching him. Spinning around, she sees Peter leaning against the doorway, wrapped up in bandages. For once, she can't read the expression on his face.

"Why aren't you resting?"

It's been a couple of weeks, but she worries about his wounds—and the scars that will last a lifetime. He went through a lot because of Xero, Thanthos, and even herself.

"I wanted to talk to you," he answers as he enters her room and shuts the door. "Have you spoken to Alpha yet?"

She studies him. "No. I haven't. I don't know what to say."

"I know you've spoken to Torn," he announces, sitting on the bed. "I know you blocked out the video footage," he adds when she gives him a sharp stare.

"It was hard for me to not talk to him," she grumbles. He knows her so well. *Damn you, Peter Rum Knight.*

Peter smiles. "Well, you're in love with him."

She bites her lip sharply, chills creeping across her skin. There he goes again.

"And that will never change. He feels the same way, you know." Peter watches Shadow sift through her emotions. After a moment of silence, he says softly: "I never got to thank you for being so stupid."

She nudges him playfully and shakes her head, a smile tugging at her lips. "I couldn't let Torn kill his best friend because of me."

"I know he felt betrayed, but you know he didn't want to kill me. He is mad at me for helping you get into the Skulls but he wanted to kill Xero. Guess he never anticipated you would come to save me instead."

She raises her head and looks into his eyes. "I'd do anything for you, Peter."

"Even if it kills you, apparently," he comments, rolling his eyes. "No wonder Xero locks you away in your tower."

She sticks her tongue out at him and grins. "You've been my friend through everything, Peter. Through both lives and all the obstacles that I've faced. I can't let those assholes use you as bait or hurt you in any way."

He takes a deep breath. "So, how did things go with Jett?"

"He told me that he can't hate me. I deserve it, Gods know I do. I'm wicked and selfish. Things would be easier if he hated me the way Alpha does. She instantly wanted to tear my throat out. But Jett… he's not like that. He could never be influenced by anyone, and he still holds onto the person I used to be."

She pauses, trying to remain composed, despite the emotions that rip through her core. The memories of Jett— of loving him, of betraying him. She can't help but feel guilty. Long ago it seemed like the best idea and now that she sees the consequences, she questions her decisions. Maybe she should have done things differently.

"How could anyone want to be around someone like me? I'm a monster, Peter."

"You're not," he argues. "That's why he loves you. That's why he never stopped. Commander Jett Torn loves you with his entire being."

She purses her lips, shoving the thoughts away. "Anyway, you didn't come to reminisce about lost love. What did you want to say?"

"When I was in the Palace, I learned something. Thanthos should have been the next in line for the magic and since he never got it, he thinks the magic is locked away somewhere. But I think there's a bastard somewhere, Argos' true Heir. Thanthos wouldn't give the full knowledge to anyone while I was in there, but he would give pieces. If I picked up enough while I was in captivity, imagine what Jett knows. And Alpha. By Gods."

"Does that matter? Jett is hurt—I doubt he'll ever talk to me again. And Alpha's ready to kill me. Vex had to double the straps," she grumbles.

Shadow's decisions are catching up with her, no doubt about that. How could she ever do the things she has if she wasn't a monster? What possessed her to do them? The pain she has caused is an endless well.

"He will open up," Peter says. "And Alpha... she's just masking her hurt. All that rage comes from her love for you."

"If she talks to me, I'll die of shock. It seems she's become a stubborn old bat like me—and my father."

"Your father is a monster. You're not. Never compare yourself to him. You know how to love others. He doesn't."

Shadow nods slowly. "And that's why I'm in this mess. Imagine if I didn't have emotions. I would be sitting pretty in the Palace right now." A smile spreads across her face.

"And I would be dead," he rolls his eyes. "Please, Shadow. You're the only one who can get them to talk. You're the one shot we have at taking down the evil."

It takes a moment for her to realize the full force of his words. Finally, she nods.

"I'll try." His face lights up. "I'm not making any promises, Peter. Alpha would rather kill me at this point and Jett would rather let himself burn."

"I know. All I ask is that you try."

~

"GOOD GODS KID," XERO GROWLS, USING THE BACK OF HIS HAND TO wipe the sweat from his forehead. "Have you been practicing?"

Dax smirks playfully at him and massages his knuckle. "Cibor's been training me. After I heard that he trained Shadow, I wanted in."

"Did she inspire you when she pinned you to the boardwalk?"

Dax lets out a mocking laugh. "She's skilled, I won't deny that." He turns serious. "When I heard she gave up herself to save Peter, I didn't realize how quickly things could go bad."

"In the world we live in, your worst nightmares could become a reality in a matter of seconds. Thanthos is eager to burn The City down." Xero sighs and cleans himself up with a rag, reaching for a canteen of water. "It's better to be prepared than to be sorry."

The younger man nods in agreement, brushing his hair out of his eyes. "So, what are you going to do about Commander Torn?"

Xero tries not to laugh. "Shadow refuses to let Vex torture the truth out of him. But it's not like he's willing to talk to her either."

"She seems distant now. I mean… she was already miles out there, but this is worse."

"Yeah. She thinks I don't trust her to kill Thanthos when the time comes. Torn being locked up in a cell is changing everything."

"*Do* you trust her?"

Xero is taken aback by the question and he studies Dax for a long moment. "I don't trust her to kill Thanthos and I can't force her to kill Jett."

"But you're using that to your advantage."

A smile emerges on Xero's face. "Yeah, maybe I am."

SHADOW PRESSES HER PALM AGAINST THE COLD, METAL DOOR.

On the other side is her beautiful, strong, and kind, baby sister. The same sister that wants to tear her head off and feed it to the royal fish.

She sighs. What a lifetime of mistakes she's made. She grips the door knob, psyching herself up to turn it. The door knob reads her fingerprints with a confirmative bleep and Shadow twists the handle and pushes the door open.

Shadow sees her sister first. Bare feet on the table, staring at the ceiling. Her strawberry hair is darker now and it falls around her, bringing out the blue in her eyes. She is still, peaceful. As young and gorgeous as Shadow remembers. Her baby sister is a woman now.

It only takes one look at Shadow's golden hair for Alpha to ignite.

"You fucking traitor. I hate you," Alpha fights her binds, twisting and yanking hysterically. If the binds were any weaker, Alpha's hands would be planted around her sister's throat.

"I know," Shadow whispers. "I know I deserve all that. And more."

"I can't believe you were the one to kidnap Jett. Is he alive? Did you finally kill him off?"

Shadow purses her lips. "I would never hurt Jett. And I would never hurt you."

"Yeah, you would rather lie to me and betray me. Maybe you wouldn't physically hurt me, but you'd tear my emotions apart."

Her bitter words stung. Shadow flinches.

"Too bad I didn't get the chance to kill you." Alpha gibes.

"I wish you had."

Alpha seems surprised by this reaction and she recoils.

"It's not like I don't deserve it, Alpha. There's not one day that goes by where I don't wish I was dead. I know what I've done. I know the damage. I know that you're angry. I wonder if it was worth it sometimes," she admits, feeling her emotions take over. "I've tried a handful of times to take my own life. But if I died, how would I protect you from that monster?"

"Ha. The monster is you, Eirho. Or whatever your murderous buddies call you," she scoffs, feeling vengeful again. The betrayal she feels cut deeply.

Exhaling, Shadow presses a button under the table that elevates the top half of the table. This way, Alpha can sit upright and Shadow can see her sister's reaction to what she's about to say.

"Before my wedding, Father ordered me to kill a man. He tried to make me murder an innocent person because he thought he could mold me into a merciless killer, he was so focused on me being like him. He had done things like that before.... But that time he threatened to hurt you. I allied with the Skulls that night. I wanted to bring you and Jett, but Xero wouldn't let me. It was too dangerous to take a man who hated the Skulls so deeply and a child. But none of that matters now. I see that he decided to use you as his pawn instead." Shadow paces in front of the chair, Alpha's brows furrowing deeper as she listens.

"I'm not a pawn. I'm a loyal daughter!"

"Did he make you kill men? Women? *Children*? Did he trick you into being a killer to please him? To allow him to have control?" Shadow snaps back. When Alpha is too stunned to respond, Shadow presses further: "He did. I bet you remember every face. Every smell. Every scream. I bet you can't sleep 'cause they haunt you."

"Shut up, Eirho."

Shadow places her palms on the arms of the chair, inches close to her sister's face. "Those nightmares, Alpha, are precisely why I want to stop him. Why I'm going to *kill* him."

"You can't. You can't get inside that Palace!"

"Oh yeah? I could beat myself up. Say I escaped. No-one on the inside knows that I'm alive. Otherwise there'd be alarms blaring and The City would burn to the ground. Father would take me back in and I could *slit his throat*. For all the times he cursed you—forcing you to slaughter the innocent." She speaks slow, drawing her words out to allow their full effect. "I know how he is. I know he's hurt you. He probably put you so close to death you could hear the Heavens. I'm not ignorant to what he's doing inside the Palace. I have eyes and ears in that place."

"He made me stronger, built me up when you left us. He gave

me a chance to succeed in ways you *never* would have. You're weak. You let those bastards manipulate you, like some puppet."

"That's exactly what's happened to you."

Alpha pulls at her restraints. "I fucking hate you. I wish you really had died in that fire."

Those words puncture Shadow's heart. Somehow, she manages to keep her façade going, if only for a bit longer. "Maybe so. But if you didn't love me too, you wouldn't have this fire in your heart."

"Whatever love I have for you is dead."

"No. I've watched you for far too long to believe that. You visited my grave last month. You cried and wished and prayed. You care, whether or not you can accept it."

"Stop trying to manipulate me," she shouts in return. "Stop trying to make me feel guilty!"

Shadow crouches down and looks her dead in the eye. "I want you to understand two things. One, we love each other more than life itself and we always will. And two, I did this to give you a better life. Maybe not the past few years, maybe not the next few... but I will get you out of his clutches."

Alpha narrows her eyes until only her pupils are visible. "Fuck you."

With a long inhale, her older sister stands and smiles. "I'll be back in a couple days. Think about what I said."

Alpha pulls against her bonds one more time before Shadow exits the room. She rushes to shut the door as sobs wrack her body and tears stream down her face.

Alpha's words threaten to break her.

JETT STARES AT THE CEILING. 374 SMALL TILES STARE BACK AT HIM. He has counted them over and over again to make sure. Yep, still 374 tiles looking back at him. He sighs tiredly. The books that Shadow shoved under his door have been read more than once. At this point, he's bored enough to wish someone would torture him for some excitement.

If he ever gets out of here, he'll make certain the Palace dungeons don't have any lines or squares to count; after a few days, the prisoners will be out of their minds with boredom. They'll be singing the information he wants to know.

"Old friend."

"Peter," Jett grumbles as he starts his count over. "To what do I owe the visit?"

"I wanted to see how you're doing," Peter offers, cocking his eyebrow, speaking through a small box for Jett to hear him. "You seem to be getting by well enough."

"374 tiles. Trust me, I've counted them over and over."

A chuckle leaves Peter's throat before he studies the man in front of him. Jett had been kind, strong, and brave. A loving man, a loving friend. There was a time when Peter could recite Jett's favorite colors, his dreams, his fears. Everything Jett was, Peter knew. He knew how he'd react to good news and bad news. He knew, just by looking at his face, when he had been hurt. Every little thing about him, Peter knew. They were brothers.

Now he's a stranger.

"Are you going to give us information?" Peter asks. "Or are you gonna carry on being stubborn?"

"I have a few more weeks to count tiles before I completely lose my shit," Jett assures him. "You have a few more weeks to wait?"

Peter shakes his head. "No, it's only getting worse out there; it's dangerous. And Xero's threatening to torture you."

"Why is he only threatening?"

"Well, Eirho refuses to give him the opportunity. She hasn't gone home. Or slept." Peter shrugs.

Jett adjusts slightly. It would have gone unnoticed by anyone else, but Peter can see that the idea of Jett's first and only love making herself sick over him, is bothering him deeply.

"How are you doing? Now that you've seen her again?" Peter pries, hoping he'll open up.

"It's sickening," Jett admits. He pushes himself up on his elbows, staring his friend dead in the eye. "For a long time, I blamed you for being a part of all this even though you were the only one who told me the truth. And I let them use you as bait and they would've killed you. I should never have done that."

Peter frowns. "We've been in two different worlds. And my death wouldn't have been your doing entirely."

"I would have killed her if she didn't show her face," he mutters, disgusted with himself. "I would never want to hurt her."

"Oh, I know. She knows that too. Otherwise she would have never told you," Peter points out. "She still trusts you after everything you've been through."

The Commander is speechless as a long moment of quietness swells around them, the awkward feeling of their past settling in. Jett wishes he could go back and change everything.

"Look," Peter finally speaks up with a sigh. "For what it's worth, I am so sorry we lied to you. I'm sorry I lied to you for the time that I did. It killed me to see you hurting, which is why I caved and told you. I'm the worst friend."

"You're not. You were protecting her. I haven't been able to see that, but I've had enough time to count tiles and think." Jett swings his legs to the edge of the bed and stands tall. His body is as broad and towering as ever. Peter— not much shorter— suddenly feels insignificant next to Jett. "I'm sorry I hurt you. That's one of my biggest regrets in this life. Thanthos wanted me to use you as bait to get Marcs out of his hole. And I was still so angry at you for lying to me, so I told myself that it was okay."

"I deserved it for lying to you," Peter says, resting his head against the clear glass just above the speaker. "I wish I hadn't made the choices I did. In the beginning, I swore to Rho I wouldn't tell you. She wanted you safe. She kept Xero off your back and kept you alive the whole time."

"Are you here to persuade me to be with her again?"

"I can't," Peter admits, causing Jett to take a step back. "Because you've never stopped wanting to be with her."

Jett doesn't say anything, he simply stands there waiting for the rage to surface at Peter's words. Yet there's no rage, only a sense of sorrow as he realizes that Peter's right. Even when he saw her face at the hanging, he still protected her. And now, he still wanted to hold her despite knowing that she faked her death to separate them.

It comforts Peter to know that he can read Jett the same as he could back then.

"I don't expect you to forgive me, ever," Peter tells him. It hurts him to acknowledge the pain that he caused his friend, but he knows he deserves the resentment. "But you should consider forgiving Eirho. Everything she did was to protect you, even though it killed her. I know it'll take time, but your love for her isn't going to disappear. Hers never did."

Jett clenches his square jaw as he listens to Peter's words. There was a dark time where he would rather have choked Peter to death than talk to him. Even after Peter told him the truth, Jett's rage only grew as he knew his best friend—his brother—was helping the Skulls. Jett tried to scare him into stopping, attempting to threaten him. Nothing worked and Jett's disdain only grew.

Yet here he is. Wishing he could share a drink with Peter, yearning to talk about everything and to embrace him like old times.

"The thing I hate most is that I can't hate either of you at all. Though my anger is mostly for her... you were trying to be a friend and I almost killed you." He hesitates. "I hope you took care of her."

Peter gives him a gentle grin. "I did. For you."

"Good." Jett stretches his arms out, feeling an ache inside of them. He's been lying around too long; he needs to exercise at least. "I'm happy for you, by the way."

"Huh?" Peter asks, confused.

"I know you're with that big guy. I could see it on your faces the first couple weeks I was dragged in here." He gives a smirk. "I always knew, you know that, right?"

Peter feels his face grow hot and he presses it against the palm of his hand. "Of course you did. Why am I not surprised?"

"I know why you never told me. You didn't want anyone else to find out," Jett says. "Thanthos would burn you at the stake."

"Would you?" Peter asks anxiously. He hopes that his friend still has the same compassionate heart that he had before, all those years ago.

Jett laughs at the idea. "No, of course not! You love who you love." He shrugs. "I know love isn't a choice. If it was, I'd have moved on from all of this a long time ago. You should be able to be who you are without fear."

Peter feels relieved at the thought. *Someone supports me. There's good in the world.*

"Things are changing. I hope they change in your favor," Jett tells him. Peter doubts Jett at first, but he can see the sincerity in his eyes. "I hope you guys defeat him."

Peter nods. "So do we. Goodnight, Jett."

"Goodnight."

THANTHOS STALKS ACROSS HIS THRONE ROOM, TRYING TO KEEP A level head though it doesn't last long. "My daughter and Commander are *missing*?" he echoes. "And you have *no* clue what happened to them?"

Officer Marcus O'Malley nods, trying to hide the fear that courses through him. "Yes, Your Highness," he forces himself to say.

"And how exactly did my men allow this to happen?"

Marcus swallows hard and looks over to Declan who is glaring daringly at him. "I don't know, my King. General Leon only sent me as the messenger."

Thanthos advances on Marcus, getting so close to him that Marcus can smell the stench of alcohol wafting from his breath. It makes his eyes water.

"Tell General Leon he has *two days* to find Alpha and Torn. Tell him to start in the Slums. Tell him it will be hard for him to make reports to me without a tongue."

The adrenaline pumps through Marcus as he looks into the eyes of The City's most infamous killer. He nods shakily. "Yes, my King."

Thanthos snarls. "Leave!"

It doesn't take Marcus long to bow and vacate the room, leaving Thanthos and Declan alone as his footsteps waver in the hall.

Declan saunters over to Thanthos, crossing his arms. "Do you think the Skulls are getting smarter or do you think they ran off together?"

Thanthos snarls as he tries to process the fresh information. "Either way, we will blame the Skulls."

"What happens if the General can't find any evidence?"

"He will." Thanthos affirms "Even if I have to plant the evidence myself."

25

NOW

Shadow stops herself from scanning her hand, despite the ungodly desire to talk to Jett. She sees him asleep on the bed, his arm slung over his eyes to block out the light from the corridor. He never could sleep anywhere that wasn't pitch black.

Sighing with sadness, Shadow turns to walk away. It's no use. It was a stupid idea anyway.

"Wait."

She freezes about three cells down, peering over her shoulder, unable to form words.

"Come here, Eirho."

An invisible hand seems to push her to him. She lingers for a moment before stepping into view.

He's sat up, sleep making his eyes heavy as he tries to rub it away. He watches her as he stands, trying to massage a knot out of his lower back. It takes him only two strides to reach the door of the cell, a yawn escaping his mouth.

"What happened?" he asks groggily.

"We captured Alpha. A few days ago. She... she hates me." She pauses. "Even more than you."

Jett lets out a jagged sound. "Gods. Thanthos will turn The City to ash." He sees the tears pricking at the corner of her eyes and he leans one arm on the clear wall between them, his other hand at his side. "I can't say you don't deserve the hatred, Eirho, but I'm sorry that doing what you thought was right led to all of this." His warm palm touches her hand suddenly, sliding through the small opening where he is given food three times a day. This action—the touch— causes her to freeze in his grasp. He presses his forehead against his other forearm, still against the wall. "And just to be clear, I don't hate you."

She scoffs. "How could you not?"

"Fuck, Eirho, it would be so much easier to hate you and write you off. But I've had weeks to think in here. I can't hate you, no matter how angry I am," he says with despair. "And Alpha doesn't hate you either. She's mad. I mean, how would you feel?"

"Furious," she admits, gazing down at his hand on hers. "But I wouldn't be able to hate you either. Even when you try to kill my friends."

Jett shakes his head. "He was my *best* friend. He was like a brother to me."

"And you think he'd betray you by killing me?"

"To be fair, I didn't think you'd fake your own death so you could play house with our enemies, either."

She takes her hand away and crosses her arms, suddenly uncomfortable with the entire situation. "Fine. I deserve that. But, they're not our enemies. They want to take my father off the throne just as much as we do. Before he finds the Heir magic and gains unlimited power."

"Xero should start shitting himself now. Thanthos is getting close. Close enough he might not look for his own daughter."

Shadow's face drops. "He *what*?"

"Yup," he responds. "There's some prophecies and riddles and loads of other ancient crap he's been raving about. I'm assuming you caught Alpha outside the walls?"

"How'd you know that?"

He exhales. "He's been sending her to the forests and the mountains to look for clues. He's been hunting down witches to find The Oracles, and *they've* been leading him to some puzzle pieces, I guess. Some ancient bullshit he would never tell me about."

She straightens up. "Why are you telling me this? Is this some kind of trap?"

He groans. "I'm angry that you lied to me and I'm angry that I wouldn't have known if Peter hadn't confessed. But I wouldn't set you up, Eirho. I don't want you to die."

Confused, she opens her mouth to protest, but he interjects.

"I can see you've been crying. No doubt from Alpha's words," he sums up. "But I can't save you while I'm in here, so maybe you can save yourself."

"I'll never understand you."

"You do more than you think."

She sighs at his words, hugging herself now, trying to hide the bareness of her soul on display. It's too late; he can read her like a book he's memorized.

"Goodnight, Jett. Thank you."

"Goodnight, Princess."

A grateful smile passes her lips as she walks away. Shadow feels his touch like a burn upon her skin and her heart begs her to stay.

ANOTHER MEETING, ANOTHER BORING DISCUSSION WHERE SHADOW ends up doing whatever she wants after anyway. Xero should seriously consider not inviting her. For the first half hour she ignores most of the murmurings about The City until Cibor speaks. It's a rarity and it pulls her attention from cleaning her nails with a knife.

"There's a ball coming up, some masquerade event," Cibor announces to the table of Skulls. He towers above them as he shares the news. "In two months, Thanthos will be throwing the biggest celebration The City has ever witnessed."

"Sounds like a trap," someone says, clearly scared by the idea.

"Or an invitation," Shadow muses slyly. All eyes turn to her. The disapproval on Xero's face is clear as day. A memory of the photo Dax took—of the ballroom—flashes in Shadow's mind. There's something important there, she's sure of it. "I mean, we all know that Thanthos is hunting for us because of Alpha and Commander Torn. It's an invitation for us to reveal our faces. It'd be a terrible shame if we weren't able to RSVP."

Xero puts his palm on the table. "You want to walk into a trap?"

"Yes. He'd expect all of us to be there, he wouldn't expect a lone skull. And I want to be the one to go in. I would finally be able to get close enough to kill him."

"And how do you anticipate a supposedly dead ex-princess waltzing into the Palace will turn out? Especially after the disappearance of his right-hand man and his youngest daughter," Xero challenges.

The normally vocal members stay quiet for this one. Getting caught between Shadow and Xero during their battles is dangerous and no-one gets out without being gutted. It's safer to let it run its course.

Shadow grins. After she saved Peter, each member of the Skulls discovered her true identity in the weeks that followed. It led to hours of interrogations and tests to make certain that no-one would betray them. Not to mention countless hours of keeping an eye on suspicious members.

Since Xero can speak freely about it now, he tends to err on the snarky side.

"I'll have a mask on. Besides, I think I'll be able to get Jett and Alpha to help us." That's a lie. She can't force them and they don't exactly seem willing at this point. Jett seems to have accepted his fate and Alpha has tried everything to escape—short of gnawing her own arm off. If only she could make them see how Thanthos truly is. And why she had to make the choices that hurt them.

"You better. We can't afford any mishaps," Xero scolds her. "Have either of you been able to get information from them?" He looks between her and Vex.

Shadow glimpses at Vex anxiously, hoping she didn't have to hurt Alpha to get anything.

"Alpha is stubborn, but she is faltering. I've been allowing her to listen to conversations I have with the others. The conversations about Thanthos killing the poor and slaughtering misfits. It'll take time, but she knows he's wrong," Vex explains. "I've been able to allow her out of the binds. She's been mostly good."

Until she sees me, Shadow thinks.

Xero looks to Shadow.

"Jett says Thanthos is close. He's been seeking help from The Oracles for pieces of some puzzle," she says, wishing in that moment she had more information. "I'm assuming it's a riddle or a key to the magic. That's really what Alpha has been hunting down. I don't know much more at this point."

"A puzzle?" Aine repeats thoughtfully. "I'll look into it. I can't promise much though. We know as much as we ever will until we follow Thanthos."

"I can help if you need it," Shadow says.

Xero shakes his head, dismissing her offer. "No. You have to find out information from Alpha and Torn. Cibor will find out more about the ball."

"I can set up a meeting with our informant, then," Shadow says.

The leader shrugs. "Fine. You can take Cibor and Peter this time. Aine, if she isn't busy. Shall we break?"

"Fine," she snaps, just to spite him.

"I'm going to search the library," Aine says. "I'll radio when I can."

Xero nods, grateful for her hard work. Aine is resilient, regardless of what is thrown her way. They wouldn't be half as knowledgeable without her.

"I'll set up a meeting for this weekend," Shadow says to Cibor as he leaves. Everyone else follows his lead, excluding Xero and Vex. They stay behind with solemn demeanors.

Shadow rises from her seat and Xero makes her sit back down. She breathes slow and deep—she knows what's about to come.

"Are you going to make me say it?" Xero questions when Shadow stays silent.

"It's more of a dare."

"This is a serious matter," Vex pipes in. "If Alpha and Torn refuse to talk, we will be forced to take extreme measures. Though I promise not to cause defects."

"No," Shadow snaps. "If you torture them, I'll turn myself in."

"I understand how you feel, but we need answers. If you can't find them, I will make Vex find them or Dax." Xero glares at her, challenging her to speak against him. She refuses to humor him and sits quietly. "If you want to go to this ball, you better find out information or someone else will be in charge of killing Thanthos."

"Oh, like your little boy toy?"

"Dax should be your protégé but you've been too busy causing chaos. He could be a valuable player."

She rolls her eyes. "Keep your slimy paws off Alpha and Torn. I'll find out the information we need."

Vex begins to realize how awkward a showdown between the two stubborn Skulls is. Come to think of it, she'd rather be tortured herself than sit through this uncomfortable situation any longer.

In one swift motion, Shadow stands, shoving her chair into the table. She glowers at him. "I'll talk to them tomorrow. I'm going home tonight."

"Tell Zed that Jett says hi."

Shadow nearly smashes her fist into his face. Instead, she grabs her things and takes the long way home. The Security Zone has never been so appealing.

~

"I'M SORRY I'VE BEEN GONE," SHADOW SAYS, SITTING NAKED NEXT TO Zed. "It's been a hectic couple of months."

"I understand," Zed sighs. He trails a finger over her thigh. "I have to say, you're much better than the brothel workers."

She hits him playfully with a pillow. "Sleaze."

He chuckles and leans his head on his arm. "Torn and Alpha are both MIA right now. Thanthos is more worried about whatever project he's got going on. He pretends to care, but we all know he's full of shit."

"What makes you say that?" She inquires innocently.

"He's too worried about his party. Some big celebration in his honor." He rolls his eyes. "Statues and pictures and even little prints of his face on every napkin. I don't want to wipe my mouth with his scowling face."

Shadow chuckles at the thought and leans back onto the bed.

She frowns as she hears the turn of the door knob. Dax is coming in. And she has a bone to pick with that guy. He had the audacity to go through her things, which she may have planted to see who he was working for, and take some pictures. Annoyed, she slides out of the bed and storms toward the bedroom door—stark naked.

"Shadow, what are you doing?" demands Zed, sitting upright. "Are you crazy?"

Ignoring him, she yanks the door open and marches up to Dax as he shuts the front door behind him. He turns to see her standing there and his jaw drops. He's definitely more distracted by her body than the fact she might slit his throat.

"Why are you here?" she asks irately, not bothering to cover herself.

"I—uh—um—Xero sent me. He wanted me to keep an eye on you," he tries to look away, his cheeks hot.

"You can tell Xero to do his own dirty work," she says. "You have your own place at the headquarters and I am not letting someone who stole my personal items stay here. The envelope with the picture of Argos and the ballroom. They were the two good memories I had from when my mother was alive and you stole them. Thieves aren't welcome in my home. Leave."

Dax attempts to open his mouth—to snap back, but he can't find the words. She caught him but he has nothing to say. Though that's probably because she's completely nude in front of him and he cannot turn away fast enough.

When she turns to walk back into her room, he sees something that takes his breath away.

Scars spread across the skin on her back in dark welts like the branches of a tree. There is hardly any skin left untouched, as if someone wanted to mark her forever; to claim her as their own.

She closes the door.

He swallows hard, deciding that it's best for him to leave, even though he has so many questions.

"Had enough of your roommate?" asks Zed.

"Had enough of the Skulls entirely." She finds a spot next to him, giving him a playful smile. "Where were we?"

He cocks his eyebrow and leans over to kiss her shoulder gently. "Round two?"

26

NOW

"Absolutely not."

Peter tilts his head, trying to decide how to feel about Cibor's reaction. Whether to be mad at him or grateful that he cares enough.

"You're not going inside that Palace again. I forbid it," Cibor says from his spot, surrounded by his notes and plans for the ball. "Not after what happened."

"Shadow will want me to go in with her. And Xero said he would rather not have her go alone. Why don't you trust me?"

Peter's words leave him feeling winded with guilt. He shakes his head and reaches for him, touching his arm gently. "Baby, I do trust you. I just don't want to lose you. I almost did. You can't blame me for that."

Peter knows he has a point. Hell, he would feel the same way too if something happened to Cibor. Regardless, he wants to help Shadow. He wants to keep his friend safe.

"Shadow almost sacrificed *everything* to save me. I—*we*—at least owe her this. You know we do," he reasons. Peter's soft hands slip into Cibor's rough, callused ones. He wishes he'd known Cibor sooner. He could've had many more years of feeling this.

"She knew what she was doing," Cibor tells him. He knows it's stupid trying to justify not helping her. Cibor does want to repay Shadow for rescuing Peter— that act alone is worth more to Cibor than anything else in the world.

"Cibor, c'mon," Peter says. He inches closer. "You want to help her. You want to keep her safe."

The taller man sighs, giving in. "I do," he says. "We're all family. I just can't imagine losing you. I mean, look at what happened to Torn. I don't want to turn out like him."

Peter can't help but laugh. "You're nothing like him, don't worry. He's a product of that toxic environment and the Shadow's choices."

"Choices she *had* to make."

"Oh, I know. I'm not saying that she should have stayed with Thanthos." Peter looks horrified at the idea.

"Thank the Gods she made a better choice," breathes Cibor.

Peter nods. "And we're all about to see the end of it."

"I hope we win, Peter."

Another nod.

"We can finally settle down, buy a nice farmhouse, have a family of our own. I want chickens too," Cibor says gleefully, his excitement makes his boyfriend smile. "Wake up together, fall asleep together. Get mad at you for hogging the blankets."

"You steal the blankets more than I do," Peter protests. "You have more square footage to cover."

Cibor chuckles in his deep, warm way. "You're right. That is why I'm so stunned you manage to hog the blankets."

"Ha!"

"We can adopt some orphans. A boy and a girl."

"Maybe I want seven kids. Or maybe twenty." Peter teases.

Cibor takes in a lungful of air. "Well, we'll need a lot more chickens then." He gleams as Peter pokes at him, enjoying this peaceful moment. Moments like these are few and far between, even more so these days.

"So, it's decided," Peter starts, about to ruin the moment. "I'm going in with Shadow."

Cibor bites his lip—the smile on his face fades quick as anxiety overcomes his features. "Is that so?"

"Yes," he says matter-of-factly. "Look, I know you're upset. You've made that clear, but I also know that if we fail this mission, we'll lose more than ever. We'll lose everything we've bled for, and more importantly, we'll lose our *friend*. I am going to help her, I have to."

"I wish you wouldn't act like this." Cibor says, moving away. Peter looks hurt but he speaks anyway. "You always make me do what's right, even if it's the hardest thing imaginable."

"Well, the hardest thing and the right thing are often the same."

Cibor swallows.

"Trust me. It won't be long now until we can have all the chickens you want."

~

"I'M WORRIED ABOUT THIS, SHADOW. IT'S NOT SOME JOKE." XERO rubs his temples feverishly.

"Sure it is," she says, agitated. She'll do anything to make him upset today. Anything she can do to press his buttons, she will. Having Dax show up at her house *again* is reason enough to blow up at him.

"You need to be serious for a second. Thanthos is sniffing around for Skulls and you fraternizing with the enemy isn't going to help keep us in the dark," he snaps back. "And I need Dax protected."

She glares at him. "It's not like you weren't aware of what I was doing. Either way, what I do with Zed is none of your business."

"It is now. You didn't stop Dax before he got into the house. You weren't prepared for an attack!"

"I am always prepared."

"You were naked."

"That doesn't mean I wasn't prepared. Dax knows how to get in quietly now—I taught him that. Any guard would have caused a ruckus," she points out. She draws a circle on the floor with her boot, trying to distract herself from her anger.

"You need to stay at HQ until after the ball. Until after he's dead," he orders. He tries to make his tone seem sharp—final.

She ignores it.

"I will do as I please with who I please. I'm not your slave."

"No, but you're being naïve. You're being promiscuous! And you're putting that above what the focus *should* be."

"I could sleep with half the Skulls and none of that would be your concern, asshole."

Her words take him by surprise and he sits back in his chair, gazing at her in astonishment. He waits for her to falter, though she remains resolute for this silent stare down.

"I'm sorry," he finally says. "I just want you to be safe."

"That's no longer your worry."

Before he can retort, the door opens. Peter and Cibor walk in, clad in their black outfits and cloaks. Tonight, they'll be speaking to Noah to find out the purpose of the ball. And what to be prepared for.

"Thank the Gods." Shadow flips him off and leaves the room.

Cibor sends Xero a questioning look. Peter smirks and goes after her; he knows all about her and Zed.

IT DOESN'T TAKE LONG FOR THE TRIO TO ENTER THE INNER CITY. *T's*, the only tavern in town, isn't far away. They move in silence, watchful of the world around them. The security has been heightened yet again, with Thanthos slaughtering the innocent to find Skulls. Any suspicious activity here means the trio could be compromised.

When they reach the tavern, Shadow sneaks inside first. She spots Noah at a table in a dimly lit room. He's hiding under his usual navy cloak, his eyes fixed on the table. She slides in beside him, giving him a smile when he looks at her.

Her mouth drops.

"What the *fuck* did they do to you?"

Peter stops in his tracks when he sees Noah's face. His eye is completely gone, gouged out by the looks of it. Noah's eye is nothing but a deep wound. The rest of him is pale and bruised. Burns run down the side of his neck and cuts line his face; echoes of torture. Peter turns away, haunted by the sight.

"They know I've been feeding you information. I don't… I don't know how I even got out," he whispers. "Someone helped me. A friend. Another guard—I think."

Shadow grips his arm tightly. "You can come back with us."

"How did the Red Guard find out?" Peter whispers. "Are you being watched?"

"No. They don't know I'm here. I don't know how they found out," he answers, shivering. He looks nauseous just thinking about it. "Someone must have told them."

She squeezes his hand. "I am so terribly sorry."

"Thank you. You didn't do anything wrong, Shadow."

"*Eirho*," she whispers.

He stops, seeing Peter and Cibor tense across the table from him. This is a move they didn't expect. A long moment passes as he wraps his mind around what she said. He peers over, looking at her as if it's the first time he's ever seen her. As if he's being healed by her face. Hope floods him.

"You're alive?" His lip quivers. "Why did you hide who you were?" He hesitates. "Why are you telling me now?"

She smiles softly at him. "Because my life signifies hope... and I'm going to kill Thanthos."

Noah's throat grows dry. He lowers his head and his voice, "We killed so many people he thought were responsible for your death."

That sharp guilt stings her again. Oh, the mistakes she has made in this life. She notes a bartender passing a small envelope to a man at the bar. A bounty hunter. He could be hunting them.

"Come, it's not safe here. Let's get back to HQ."

Noah agrees, leaving the table with a large tip. It's eerie when he realizes he may never come to this place again. He may never see his old life again. If anyone understands that, it's Shadow.

When they've put enough distance between the tavern and them, Shadow removes her cloak. Noah is intoxicated by her identity. Eirho is as beautiful as the tales say. But none of them mentioned how solemn she is.

"Was it you? The ones who captured Torn and Alpha?" Noah finally says. The air is crisp in his lungs.

"Yes," Peter admits. "She revealed herself to Torn in order to save me. He was going to hang me from the end of a rope."

Cibor adjusts uncomfortably at the thought. Nothing will ever make the fear of losing Peter fade away.

"You would have done the same," she protests. "We captured Alpha outside the walls. She nearly killed me."

Noah seems surprised. "Did she know it was you?"

"That was precisely why she tried."

He clenches his teeth. "Wow, there's so much that I don't know. Are they both okay?"

"For now. Xero wants answers which means he'll have them tortured," Shadow explains, sighing. Despite what she did and what has happened, she never stopped loving the two of them. She always will love them.

"Will you let him?"

"No. I can't."

Noah sniffles, looking up at the moon that hovers in the sky.

The stars twinkle in protest of The City's lights, coming through the darkness. Exquisite, powerful, bright. A sign, he hopes, of good things to come.

"I'll set you up with one of our doctors," she says. "Then we'll find you a room and a nice hot meal. You'll be safe with us."

"Thank you. I appreciate it more than you'll ever know."

She inhaled deeply. "It's the least we can do for your sacrifice. You helped us get this far. And we will honor that by kicking Thanthos' ass."

He laughs and a sense of freedom fills him. "I hope you Skulls have steak. I'm starving."

"Hope you like porridge," Cibor teases him. He clasps him on the shoulder. "You know, you're going to look badass with an eyepatch."

Peter elbows Cibor for flirting. Noah chuckles it off, pondering how he will look.

"I'll be dashing," he insists. "Handsome, mysterious."

Shadow watches as he rants on about how irresistible he'll be to the ladies. She's grateful that Noah is okay, she only wishes she could have prevented it. That's another name to add to the list of people she has caused harm to.

Seeing Noah leads her to another question. If he's innocent, then who the hell betrayed them?

27

NOW

"Bring him in," Shadow orders, sitting on the opposite side of the table. Her personal quarters are the best place to meet, no-one would expect it. Cibor blinks at her, stunned. "Please?" she asks, thinking that's what he was waiting for.

"Uh, you really want me to bring him in here? Without guards, or locks, or...?"

"Yes."

Cibor clenches his teeth as hard as he can. Ignoring his better judgment, and the threat of the impending raids, he leaves her alone for a few minutes before returning with Jett Torn. Wearing no cuffs and a confused look on his face, he watches Shadow steadily.

"I'll be outside," Cibor announces when Shadow gives him a pointed look. He exits quickly and shuts the door.

"He thinks you're going to kill me," she tells him as she gestures to the empty chair across from her. He sits down and smiles.

"Do you think I will?"

She scoffs. "I don't care anymore."

"Ooh, that's dark Princess," he says, tauntingly. "So, why am I here? Free from my cell and my binds?"

"Don't be so theatrical. We both know if you wanted me dead, I would be."

He shrugs, not denying it. He reaches across the table for a cracker. "Can't say I love the Skulls' hospitality."

"Yeah, me neither." She leans her elbows on the table. "I need your help."

"Do you want to kill more of my men?"

"Aren't you a snarky little shit today?" She makes a face. "I want you to help me get into the Palace. I want you on my side."

Jett laughs at her—he genuinely laughs. "Really?" he muses. "You want *me* to work for the bastards who killed my men and took you away? Brainwashed you, no doubt."

"You know what he's doing is wrong."

"So are the things Marcs has done."

"He's only done what he did to protect people. To endure. We don't go out and kill aimlessly," she retorts. When she feels the anger beginning to bubble up inside, she stops and inhales until she's composed again. "Please, hear me out."

"Okay, amuse me."

She holds his stare and keeps her voice low. "I need your help."

Jett rolls his eyes, clearly annoyed. "Apparently not," he says, gesturing to Shadow.

"We both know our leaders have done questionable things, but Thanthos has been slaughtering innocent people. I know you've taken a step back from what he's done, I'm not blind. I know you know it's wrong." She watches as he ponders her words. She swears she can see him give in. *She's right,* he thinks.

"Should I be a vicious killer?"

"That's what you've pretended to be," she notes, hinting at him never taking a life despite the stories that people tell. "We need to kill Thanthos and put Alpha on the throne. Whatever happens with the Skulls will be my jurisdiction. I can handle them."

He stays quiet, contemplating the weight of her words.

"I know things can never be what they were. I've accepted that as best I can. I only want your help," she tells him quietly. "Could you at least consider it, please?"

Jett takes a drink of the ice water in front of him, watching her closely as he drinks. He keeps full eye-contact as he places the cup back down and answers, "If you plan to put Alpha on the throne, I'll help you."

Shadow nearly hugs him. She covers her face in her hands for a moment, trying to get a hold of herself. *He said yes*.

"How are you going to get Xero to agree?"

She puts her palms flat on the table. "I was having a nice moment. Why did you have to ruin it?"

He shrugs in response, crossing his arms over his broad chest. "I'm guessing you haven't thought about that, have you?"

"I'm going to take a chance on you," she says, ignoring his question. "I want you to return to the Palace with some made up story about how you were kidnapped by the Skulls and escaped. And when the day of the ball rolls around, I want your help."

"And Xero's just going to let me walk out the front door?"

"Like I said. We both know things are not what they seem." She stalls a moment, before placing an envelope in front of Jett. "Keys."

There's a knock at the door and Shadow groans angrily.

"One minute!" She places handcuffs loosely over Jett's wrists. When he seems understanding, she opens her door, appearing disinterested.

"Dax," she grunts. "What are you doing here?"

"I wanted to apologize—may I come in?" he asks hopefully, leaning on the door. "I shouldn't have followed you. I was following orders but I should have protested. I know you can handle yourself."

Shadow taps her foot. She doesn't have time for his sucking up. "I forgive you. Now, I'm busy. Could you find your way out?"

"What's going on?" Dax attempts to peek around her, only to

get shoved into the hallway. She slams the door behind her as she faces him, a predator cornering her prey.

"Mind your own business," she growls daringly. "The next time you insist on finding me, I'll insist on burying you six feet under. I'm tired of being stalked. Now, get out." Her hand instinctively finds the door while she watches Dax trudge away. She hovers her hand over the access and returns to the room.

"I don't remember this side of you."

Shadow brushes the comment off and takes a seat across from him once more. "Dax is a pain in my ass."

"Oh, I bet he is. There's something you might want to know about him. He's not what you think."

Leaning in, she says, "Let's hear it."

"WHAT ABOUT THIS, AINE?" VEX QUESTIONS AS SHE SORTS THROUGH the pile of photos and maps. She lifts up a picture of a rose carved into a rock. Studying it, she realizes that she's seen this symbol before. Maybe it has a special meaning.

"Huh," Aine squints as she studies the fine detail. "That symbol keeps popping up. I don't know how to connect it to anything though, not without sending people out to search for more. My only fear is that whatever we're looking for might already be gone."

"You're right, Alpha might have found whatever these are on her missions for Thanthos," Vex says. She keeps scanning through photos. "Who knows if there's any significance anyway."

Aine hands her another stack of papers, this time newspapers. "Look, there's been articles about the roses. From a long time ago, when King Argos ruled." Aine grabs a book that Shadow lent her. The book her mother gave her. "And this. Covered in roses. All pictures of The City."

"Interesting," Vex says as she looks through the papers.

Some articles only have pictures of the roses and a short caption. Nothing stands out as helpful in the articles, so she keeps flipping through them. There has to be something of importance here.

"Here!" Aine exclaims, handing Vex a newspaper clipping. "That rose is inside The City."

Vex looks closer, reading it. Her heart skips a beat when she sees the picture. A massive rose, spread out across a floor, leaves and vines etched into the stone and weave around each other. It takes up the entire room, its detail and beauty astounding. "It's in the Palace. The ballroom. It's under the floor. Someone carved it a long time ago and it's since been covered over with new flooring," she explains, showing off her knowledge of the Palace. "Do you think...?"

Aine nods, understanding. "He knows it's under the floor. It's like he's planning some huge grand finale."

"We have to find out what the roses mean. Otherwise we won't know what to expect going in there, head-first. It could be anything."

Shivering at the thought, Aine sketches down the rose and begins to pinpoint locations on the map that she recognizes from the photos. Many of them are outside the wall, but a few were found inside as well. It seems to be painting a strange picture for the two women.

Vex dives into books, trying to soak up all their knowledge while Aine searches. She tries to find books on The City, the government, anything she can. The Skulls' library is plentiful but seemingly not big enough. She fears she will have to look elsewhere.

"I can't help but think I've seen this rose before, as a symbol for something," Aine grumbles as she jots down some notes. "Maybe we need a fresh pair of eyes."

Vex, not hearing a word, closes one book shut and pulls another from her pile.

"I'm going to call Shadow in," Aine decides. She addresses her armband radio, calling out for Shadow who answers immediately. It will only take a few moments for her to get to Aine's research room.

The door opens and Shadow slips in, looking over both of her shoulders. Vex gives her a quizzical look but stays silent.

"Look," Aine says, organizing the pictures into rows. The rose appears in various sizes, carved into lots of different materials. "This is what we keep coming up with. No other symbols are popping up the way this one has."

Shadow skims through them quickly, turning a few of them to different angles. "I've seen this somewhere before," she tells her friends, growing more frantic. "In a couple places, actually."

"That's what we thought," Aine says. "They look familiar but they're easy to overlook. And get this, the ones in The City are bigger than the ones outside the walls."

"Seems like they're gradually getting bigger," Shadow says as she examines them. "The further inside the walls, the bigger the rose."

"Yes. We discovered something else, too," Vex says. She hands Shadow the map of The City and points to the center. "There's a rose under the ballroom floor in the Palace. It was visible years ago —rose gold and shimmering. Thanthos had it covered not long after Argos' reign ended."

"That's where I've seen it," Shadow confirms with a gasp. She grabs the map they made and studies it. "The rose under the floor is huge. It's at the dead center of all the other roses. That has to mean something. There were always whispers about underground tunnels and stuff at the Palace. Maybe this rose leads to an entryway."

Shadow grabs the book that Aine had borrowed—the one from her mother—and flips through the pages. Old pictures fill the pages. She turns to a photo of the original floor, long before Thanthos hid it, no doubt to protect a secret.

Aine processes the information and voices her thoughts, "So Thanthos sent Alpha on missions to hunt down these roses. He no doubt learned to plot them and learned there was the biggest one under his very feet. One that he covered years before."

"And that means he's found the final rose. Whatever his scheme is, he plans to complete it at the ball."

"We have less than a few weeks," Shadow says. "We have to figure out what's under there so we can be ready."

"I'll try to find it," Aine offers as she straightens her books and gets her personal handheld computer out, jotting down ideas. She begins to move about hurriedly.

Shadow stays silent as Vex sorts through the articles and puts the rest in a box for later. Only a few are left on the table.

"Okay, so we need further design layouts of the Palace," Aine says as she grabs various books. She stumbles about with her arms full.

"I can have Tools get a working blueprint. He should be able to download one into our wristbands," Vex replies. "It would be best to have it on hand. All we need is the bare minimum."

"Agreed."

Shadow takes a seat and studies the roses, looking at them every which way, touching the paper and comparing them. There has to be a way to figure out where else she's seen it. She organizes the pictures in order of where they are on the map.

Her eyes are drawn to the older photo of the rose underneath the ballroom floor. She smacks her hands down, causing Aine to jump and Vex to stare at her. *I've seen it somewhere else.*

"What's wrong?" the two say in unison.

Shadow only says, "I have to go."

But the realization makes her head throb. She has seen it before in her studies, adventures, and growing up in the Palace. It's all pointing toward one place.

The Creators' tomb.

28

NOW

"My King," Marcus nearly shouts as he pushes the throne room doors open. "My King! We have news, we need you in the courtyard! Please, it's urgent!"

Declan and Thanthos share a questionable stare, leaving their ball plans behind to follow after Marcus. It doesn't take long for them to cross the threshold of the front steps of the Palace and into the front courtyard. A few doctors and soldiers surround someone that lies on the ground.

Bloodied, beaten, and pale, Commander Jett Torn kneels on the ground, coughing and waving away any offer of help. He insists he's fine, just sore, as the doctor's pry at him and attempt to check his vitals.

"What happened to you, Commander?" Thanthos demands as he stops inches before his face. His eyes narrow darkly as he takes in the sight.

Jett glimpses up at him through a swollen eye. "The Skulls captured me for threatening to kill that Skull, Peter. They damn near killed me but I escaped," he explains. "I—can't remember much of anything though." His head drops and he holds onto his forehead.

Declan looks to Thanthos, not bothering to hide his voice. "I'm only slightly grateful he made it back alive. Perhaps we can use this to our advantage." He enjoys ignoring Jett too much.

Jett growls quietly, wishing he could tear Declan's head off. How is he not more concerned about his *wife* missing? Jett would be devastated and turn over every stone if he was Declan Snow. But he is not. He's better than that scum.

"Get him checked out. We can ask questions later," Thanthos says, ignoring his son-in-law. It's no secret that Jett is his favorite, despite how alike Declan is to him. He wants his favorite minion to be well enough to do his dirty work. "We need to make certain he isn't going to die on us."

His fellow guardsmen lift him up, taking Jett carefully to the hospital wing in the Palace—a place where he can rest and think about the consequences of his lie.

And what might happen to Eirho.

"HOW THE HELL DID TORN ESCAPE? CAN SOMEONE EXPLAIN THAT TO me?" Xero thunders in the meeting room. He grabs a file off of the table and tosses it at the wall, watching the papers flutter everywhere as it slides to the floor.

Cibor watches Shadow sit peacefully, totally composed despite Xero honing in on her every few seconds. Cibor knows what she did. But why would she help him? Cibor can only stay quiet.

"It seems as if he had help from an outsider," Tools says, going over the mountain of paperwork that piles high in front of him. Screenshots of video footage, logs of members inside the headquarters, and the empty cell number sit in front of him. "Someone from his side knew where he was. No doubt they would have let Alpha out too if she had been in a similar cell."

"Keeping them separated was a good call. To avoid this from happening," Shadow notes, studying the pictures in front of her.

Cibor watches the video footage in front of him. There's no-one visible that helps Jett. The door simply unlocks and he sprints out of the holding cell when he knows that it's safe to do so. How would the door just unlock like that?

What did you do? He watches Shadow, trying to understand. She must have given him keys and had him use them at the exact moment she scanned herself back into the headquarters; a perfect alibi. If she had simply unlocked the door, the cameras would have caught her. And if she blocked out the cameras, there would have been missing footage. She certainly knows how to get someone out without getting caught. Xero can blame her all he wants, but Cibor knows that he can't pin this on Shadow—she left no evidence behind.

"Did you let him out?" Xero demands as he slams his hands on the table in front of her. "Is this some sick game that you're playing? You couldn't protect your love, so your loyalties faltered and you let him out?"

Everyone stays silent, aside from Edet, a member who hates Shadow's guts. She watches, hoping that Shadow will be caught going against the Skulls, and maybe Shadow will be executed.

Her composed mood turns dark in mere seconds. "You better watch your tongue, Xero. I have risked my life for this mission. Why the hell would you think I'd let him out? You know he had no feelings left for me. And you know I'm too spiteful to just let someone out like that," she says in a low tone. "So, question me again."

Cibor takes a sharp breath in, watching as she challenges Xero. Her dare seems to sink in and Xero pushes himself away from the table, walking away from her.

"Alpha needs to be under constant guard. We will not lose both of our bargaining chips." He directs this at Vex, who nods compliantly. "No more mistakes. Losing Torn will be our only error."

Shadow narrows her eyes. She knows it wasn't an error. It's all part of her plan.

29

NOW

Tools and Peter watch as Shadow twirls around. One of the skilled seamstresses in the Skulls had put together a new dress for her. It's a gorgeous jade color with gold trimmings, her chest is bare as the dress hugs her curves from her breasts down. It flares out at the bottom, flowing around her legs.

"You look lovely," Tools tells her with a nervous smile. He gives a small gesture and she spins around for both of her companions to see the dress.

Peter chuckles at her spinning around like a child. "How will you wear your hair?"

She shrugs and looks into the mirror. "Braids on the left, high up top, falling down in curls on the right side. I need to be elegant and practical. My only worry is getting blood on my dress or my mask."

Peter chuckles at her. "I love it. You look incredible."

"What's the plan for the ball?" Tools asks anxiously.

She smooths the sides of the dress down as she studies herself. "Noah said that my wonderful father is having the ball in his honor. He's going all out, too. Lords and Ladies from all over, fireworks, and ice sculptures. You can imagine how it'll be. Everything in His Majesty's honor."

"As soon as he finds the magic, he will be unstoppable," Peter reminds her in a cold tone.

"And that is precisely why I am going to stop him before he can."

"I have a feeling he'll be planning a ceremony for whatever darkness he plans to summon," Shadow informs them. "Aine and Vex discovered a rose symbol that keeps popping up. I think that this magic has something to do with The Creators of our world."

Peter gasps at the idea. "So, it's an ancient kind of magic. A magic created at the beginning of time."

"Yes, I think so." Shadow nods. "From what I know of The Creators and magic, The Creators put a family on the throne who they believed would fight for what was right. That they'd be fair and just. They also gave the ruling family magic called The Heir magic. By all accounts, it should be around now, but it's been buried for years—hidden from the people of The City and the surrounding kingdoms. No-one knows what happened, but somewhere along the line, it was buried. Alpha should be the next heir —she deserves it more than Thanthos. The magic would choose her, I'm sure," Shadow steps behind a screen, beginning to slide the dress off, careful to not tear or irritate the beautiful fabric. She hangs it up carefully and slips into a robe.

"Have you had any luck talking to her?" Peter inquires. "She was quieter last time I visited Vex."

Shadow shrugs, attempting to be nonchalant. "I don't know how to get her to talk without torturing her. She has so much hatred for me. Not that I can blame her. I have failed her in many ways as a sister."

"Things happen and things change. Both of you need to let go of the past and face the present," Tools tells her, oddly sure of himself. "You have too much to focus on now."

"Tools is right," Peter says. "You need to be focusing on what happens next. The ball is a few weeks away. How will we get in?"

"*We?*" she echoes suspiciously. She does not like the sound of *we*.

"I'm going with you," Peter informs her proudly.

"Absolutely not. It's too dangerous. If anything, I can manipulate my father into thinking I was kidnapped. I can't do the same for you, not after Jett tried so hard to ruin you," she explains, frowning. "You will stay back at HQ and keep an eye on everything. Tools will hack into the security system and you can help."

"Shadow—"

"End of story. I have a solid plan. And it only involves me," she says. "You aren't going."

Peter frowns, clearly upset. "I owe you. I need to make sure you're safe."

"And you will. Through the security system."

He huffs angrily and shakes his head. There is no chance he's letting her win this argument. "Have you always been so damn stubborn?"

"You know I have." She pats his arm. "I have to see if I can coax Alpha into talking to me. I'll see you both later."

Vex reads the chart for Alpha's vitals. She's healthy and strong, the only problem is how furious she is with her sister, and the Skulls. Her blood pressure continues to rise. Vex hands Shadow the chart, showing her the numbers.

"How is she doing? Mentally?" Shadow asks, reading over everything.

"She's pissed and anxious," Vex says, sighing. "She sure has a lot of things to work through, but she'll be okay. I've been letting her walk around when she seems less likely to stab someone with a prison shank."

Shadow smiles forcibly. "Well, that's good to know."

"She's been checked for any weaponry, handmade or otherwise. You're good to go in whenever you'd like. Do you want her shackled down?"

"Nah. Maybe if we spar, she'll feel better."

Vex grunts. "She'll feel better when she kills you."

Shadow shrugs knowing it's true. "I promise I'll be okay. She can't do much to me in her current state. She's lost muscle mass just from being shackled."

Shadow hands the chart back and removes her weapons, placing them on the table outside of Alpha's cell. Best not give Alpha the chance to snatch a weapon from her.

"Good luck," Vex says as Shadow scans herself in and walks into the room.

Alpha is sitting in a chair with her back to the door. Shadow prepares for her to notice who is in the room and sprint to attack her. Death might be a sweet release from the guilt and the hurt. And it would make Alpha feel better.

"It's been a while," Alpha snarls viciously, recognizing the footsteps. "Why are you keeping me here if no-one's torturing me for information?"

"I won't let them," Shadow answers curtly. "I'm not interested in torturing my sister."

Alpha scoffs and turns around swiftly and Shadow braces herself for the battle of her lifetime.

Instead, Alpha takes her chair to the table and sits down. She gestures for Shadow to grab a chair and sit with her. Reluctant at first, Shadow relents and takes a seat across from her. She fiddles with the bottom of her tunic to keep calm. She can't ignore the suspicion that Alpha's been plotting her death. She'll know very soon whether Alpha wants her dead.

"I want to ask you some questions," Alpha states determinedly. "I want to know everything."

Shadow raises her eyebrow, nodding at the demand. "That's fair. Where do you want me to start?"

"The beginning. Why did you betray us for the Skulls?"

Leaning back in her chair, Shadow looks down at her hands. She lifts her wrist to the table and types a code into her watch. Shortly after, there's a loud, frantic banging on the door.

"I shut off their access to the room and the sound, so they can't hear us." Oh, the trust she is putting into her sister. Shadow will be dead by the time Tools fixes the system or puts the backup system into place. It's a fine line she's treading.

"Good," Alpha smirks.

"So, where to begin?" Shadow takes a deep breath. She sifts through years of obstacles, secrets, and pain. "Father wanted me to be his killing machine. He knew the fire I had inside me would be put to good use—slaughtering the innocent, of course. He tried to get me to order the execution of an innocent man, like I mentioned before. I had refused such demands before and received severe lashings for it. When I refused this time, he ordered the man to be burned to death; he was covered in gasoline." Shadow shakes her head, trying to get the image out of her head. "I will never forget the screams or the smells. I grabbed a gun from a soldier and I shot the poor man before he could suffer any longer."

Alpha waits patiently, knowing she has more to say.

"Peter had approached me with an offer of an escape. A way to get out of marrying that selfish prick, Declan, or being father's killing pawn," she continues, licking her dry lips. Her mind flickers to the fact that neither Declan or her father have been searching for Alpha or caring. They are selfish bastards but she knows that this is more about the magic than anything. "I was going to say no until that day. I couldn't allow myself to kill for him ever again."

"I'm surprised he didn't strike you," she says.

"He wanted to, but he knows my will is just as strong as his." Shadow lays her hand out. "And yours."

Alpha ignores the compliment, thinking of her next question. "Did Jett have any idea?"

"No," she replies. It is not surprising that Jett has been brought up. Sooner or later it always happens. "He thought I died in that fire. At least until Peter broke down and told him."

"How did you fake that?"

"We had a body double. I changed out of my clothes and went to my new life," she says indifferently. "Worst and best moment of my life."

Alpha shakes her head. "What did they offer you? Power? An army?"

"What? No! They offered to kill our father and protect you and Jett. I don't want power, Alpha. Our end goal is to put you on the throne," she says, offended by the idea. She isn't entirely selfish. "Xero would have given me power if I wanted it."

"How could you justify doing this? To your family?"

"How can you justify supporting a man who tortures and kills? Innocent men, and women, and *children*? How do you justify that?"

Alpha presses her lips together tightly. This hurts. It hurts so much. "Family is supposed to have each other's back. Through everything."

"If your family is a monster, why would you support them?"

"It seems to me that you're the monster."

She inhales deeply, not wanting to snap. Not wanting to say the wrong thing. Not wanting to dig her hole any deeper than it already is. "What other questions do you have?"

"Have you killed our men?"

Shadow swallows at that question. Unexpected, but not entirely surprising. "A few. Have you killed mine?"

"Yes," Alpha admits shortly. "Anything to protect my family. My people."

"I see we're on the same page."

Alpha nearly scoffs in disbelief. "I don't abandon the people I love."

Shadow clenches her hands in her lap. "Look, you have every right to hate me. I'm not saying you don't. That's never been in question."

"Good. At least you understand the severity of your actions."

"And you should understand the severity of what our father is doing." She bites back. Shadow watches as Alpha's face transforms. The hardness crumbles ever so slightly. "It's okay to disagree with him. It's okay to hate him, just like it's okay to hate me. I skipped things in your life I never thought I would miss. It killed me. I can't imagine what it was like for you to be alone for all those years."

Alpha's lip quivers, though she stays silent and watchful.

"I'm the worst sister, I know that. I was trying to do what I thought was right in order to protect you and for some stupid reason, I thought it wouldn't affect you. I was wrong. I am wrong. But I'm not wrong for wanting to make a change. Not when our father has caused so much suffering," she says, her voice trembling slightly. "The rest of it...haunts me."

"Well, I'm sorry for trying to kill you." Alpha swallows hard and looks down at her hands, fiddling with her thumbs. Something she has always done to keep herself distracted from her emotions. "But I will not apologize for being angry."

"Good, you shouldn't. I most definitely deserve it," her older sister says, feeling a sense of pride at the stubbornness of her baby sister.

Alpha snorts slightly. "So, what happens next? What happens when you face Father?"

"He's having a ball. To celebrate his accomplishments. And just so you know, he hasn't bothered to find you first," she explains. "And I'm going to sneak in with a date. When he reveals the magic he's found, I'm going to kill him."

"What will the Skulls do once he's dead?"

Shadow can't tell how her younger sister feels. Whether it's angry, or sad, relieved, or confused. Whatever is going on inside of her is a mystery.

"I told you. I want you on the throne. Then the Skulls will be disbanded. There'll be no more criminal activity when we have a fair and just leader," Shadow says. "Things will be better with you at the head of our city."

"I'm no queen. That was always a mark upon your brow. Everyone planned for you to be the leader."

"Plans change." Shadow sighs and hears more knocking on the door. "Xero promised me that you would be on the throne, The Oracles have said they'd accept it. You wouldn't be some stand-in like our father who The Oracles refuse to coronate."

"Fair enough." Alpha glimpses down. "I'm not supporting this. And I don't know if I can ever forgive you, but I'm glad you're okay."

"I'm glad you're okay, too. I love you no matter what else happens." Shadow grins. "And I'll do whatever it takes to make things right. I promise."

"Just don't hesitate when you kill him."

30

NOW

Late into the night, Shadow finds herself deep within the mountain's heart again, the forest thick and full of danger. With quick, quiet footsteps as she heads to the sorcerer's quaint home.

A little flame guides her to the house and she feels a sense of calm as she knocks on the door.

"Shadow," a voice says. He peers from inside the house, smiling when he sees her familiar face.

"Oakenstaid," she smiles. "Are you busy?"

"Never too busy for a friend," he chirps as he opens the door and guides her into the room. "Come, come. I have food ready. Get inside before the free folk kidnap you!"

Rolling her eyes at his worried ways, she walks inside and slides her cloak off. He takes it from her and hangs it up, motioning for her to take a seat. Oakenstaid has always been the best host and loves to keep her full of food and content.

"How have you been?" He grabs a mug and places it in front of her, pouring out some freshly brewed tea. "Please, drink up. It's chilly out there as winter approaches."

"As well as I can be," she responds. "There's a darkness coming. I need your help."

"Ah, of course. There's nothing better than having a friend." He sits down and gives her a knowing smile. No words passed between them and yet he knows what she's thinking. "He is close now. Close to the magic, but you already know that."

"Do you think he'll get it?" Her voice is a careful whisper.

Oakenstaid holds his hand out for Shadow to take. He admires every crease and joint before reading her palms. He studies the lines intently, analyzing the depth and length of each one. It lasts a few moments before he returns her hand.

"I would not lie to a friend. A good one at that."

Shadow feels her stomach tighten at his words. *That must mean Thanthos will win this war*. The thought makes her feel queasy and light-headed.

"It will be difficult for you. You will face enemies that you never anticipated. But if you stay true and strong, you have the chance to win." He seems oddly distracted as he gives his reading. He reaches for a vial and pours the contents onto the table. Shadow sees the bones piled on the table. Tiny ones. She isn't sure what they're from and she's not sure she wants to know. He takes a blade out and gestures for her hand again, carefully slicing her skin. The blood pools over the bones, dark and thick.

Shadow squeezes her hand until she feels the blood clot, wiping it on her dark-colored pants.

"Hmm, this is interesting. Reading you never fails to entertain," he says, attempting to lighten the mood. He senses her anxiety. Shadow shifts in her seat as the tension creeps up on her.

"I'm going to take that as a compliment," she teases.

He grins. "I am glad you came alone this time—without that strange man the size of a pecker's leg. He is someone to be watchful of but he is not the only one." His eyes darken.

"Who else is there?" Shadow asks with a hint of urgency.

Oakenstaid seems confused and shakes his head as he reads the bones in front of him. "That is something I am unable to see. Someone close to you, someone you care for," he says. "With the way your life has been lately, I cannot point out anyone specific."

"I suppose that's fair," she grumbles. "Do you see anything else? Anything of magic?"

"Ahh," he lightens up again at the word. *Magic*. "You are a believer now, I see. You must have found the items Thanthos has been searching for. You know where to find the magic."

"Yes, but I have no idea how to destroy it. And I know that you use magic."

He finds another small container and pours a syrup-like liquid all over the bones he used. It fizzles for a few moments before turning a dark purple color. Tapping his fingers, he grows deep in thought, trying to decipher the message.

"The magic must be destroyed by The Heir."

"Wait—" She slams her fist on the table, shaking Oakenstaid's things. He gives her a glare and she quickly apologizes. He always taught her magic comes with a price and she knows there is something darker to his words. "I'm sorry. You are saying that in order to end the line of the magic forever, The Heir would have to end their life?"

"The Heir must be the end of the bloodline, but yes. That appears to be what the bones are whispering," he says with a sigh, running a hand down his long, silver beard. After a moment of hesitation, Oakenstaid begins to speak rapidly, his voice high-pitched. "They say that Thanthos has persecuted and slaughtered many. The Sea people, the free folk, the sick. The magical beings hide in fear from his wicked hands. The bones scream, *no more*. We must keep The Heir out of his grasp."

"I hope that Thanthos doesn't know all this. Maybe we can hide The Heir, protect them from him."

She goes over everything in her head, trying to come up with a solution that doesn't end with someone taking their own life. That is not a sacrifice she would ask anyone to make.

Shoving the bones into a small bag, Oakenstaid places them to the side to tend to them later. He folds his hands over the table, his knuckles covered in hair and what looks like dirt. A man of age, wisdom, and nature. And a man who knows where this journey will end.

Shadow wants to ask what else he's hiding from her. She knows better than to ask though; he'd take it as a personal insult. Especially after all the trust he has put in her. It must be her worries getting the best of her.

"Thank you for doing a reading, Oakenstaid. I'm sorry to be a bother to you, I was terrified." She bows her head low—a sign of respect in the Bush.

"You have many worries, my friend. That is not your blame to take. I know you fear that you made a tragic choice, especially after seeing how others were changed by it. You need to understand that the alternative would have been far more devastating for them," he says. His voice turns into a whisper, as if he is hiding secrets from the forest itself. "You are *more* than the monsters within you, Eirho."

Her breath catches at the sound of her real name. The acid in her stomach burns and she chokes on the words rising in her throat. Of course he knows that she's been beating herself up over her mistakes. He's known her since she was small.

"You know something about my choices. What do you know?" she asks shakily.

"If you had married Declan and left for his kingdom with Jett by your side, the secret of your love with Jett would have been discovered. Declan would have made you kill Jett and your sister, Alpha. And if you didn't, he would slaughter them in front of your eyes in the most painful way he could imagine. I cannot say if he would keep you alive as his slave or if he would have been kind enough to grant you freedom from this world. Whichever option he would have chosen, you would have died miserable and they would both be gone."

His words come as a cold reality. Shadow lowers her face into her hands as she comes to terms with what that would have been like. In that life they would have still loved her, but in this life they're still alive. The choice she made had been the right one.

"I would never condone his cruelty," she says through her nausea. "He would have made me hurt so many more people, too."

"Precisely," Oakenstaid confirms with confidence. "A man who must be stopped at any cost. It's wicked souls like Declan and your father that have led magic users to hide, and the mystical creatures to migrate to other lands. I've seen this kind of darkness, and if you do not rise against it, everyone will suffer."

"I understand."

He grasps her hand and gives it a firm squeeze, his warm hands hot against her icy ones. "Good. You know what needs to be done."

"I do. But I need one last favor."

"STOP SNEAKING OUT OF THE HEADQUARTERS. STOP DISOBEYING direct orders. And stop making ignorant decisions!"

Xero is pacing up and down Shadow's room, his face as hot as the fireplace in the corner. Like the flames, Xero roars to life with every prod and poke.

"Let's stop pretending that you're in charge of me," Shadow retorts, facing him with dark eyes. The shadows that dance on her face make her more intimidating than usual. "I went to see Oakenstaid. He had a message for you," Shadow states. Xero whips round to see her smirking.

"He wanted me to tell you... the stars say fuck off."

Xero steps towards her, so close that she can feel the heat of his breath on her face. He breathes heavily—furiously. The rage inside of him knows no bounds when it comes to Shadow and her erratic behavior.

"Act up *one* more time and I will make certain that you will not attend the ball."

"I'm going either way," she challenges, eager to push him further.

Xero's nostrils flare as anger rolls off him in waves. "You can try."

Shadow glares at him. "I'm back safely. What more do you want from me?"

"Compliance!"

"It's been years and you expect to get that now? Please," she says. "I *will* be the one to kill Thanthos. Me. No-one else."

"Let's see what happens, shall we? It all depends on how you behave over the next few weeks."

Before she can make a snappy comment, he leaves the room, slamming the door behind him. She grabs a book and chucks it as hard as she can at the door, wishing she'd hit him instead.

"Damn him," she grunts.

It was her own fault really. Shadow had snuck back in unseen, much to her surprise. Everyone in the building had either been asleep, drunk, or preoccupied. Xero only discovered that she'd left when he came in to ask for a detail about the Palace; he found mud on her boots.

The war had caught fire shortly after.

She decides that it's best not to leave her room for a while, so she uses her watch to search through files. Maps of the Palace and escape plans are her two favorite things to look at. She could study them over and over. Even though she lived most of her life inside that nightmare, she wants to memorize every detail and prepare for every possibility.

As she scrolls, she stops at the roses, studying them fiercely. They have to be from The Creators. It has to hint toward something—a connection to the Heir magic, a location, maybe The Heir has a rose-shaped birthmark or tattoo? There's still so much unknown to them.

A few hours pass and staring at the watch is starting to give her a headache. She finally shuts it off and lays down on her bed, reveling in the comfort of her blankets.

This might be the only bit of peace she gets for a long while. Even if it means being stuck in her room, it's nice to have peace while she can.

~

"I TOLD YOU OVER AND OVER," JETT SAYS TO THE DOCTOR, IRRITATED by the questions and Declan Snow's satisfied smirk. "I don't know what they did to me. They could've drugged me. I don't remember much. Only that smug bastard, Marcs."

"Did you find anything that we could use against them?" Declan repeats, his tone escalates as Jett gives him the same answers. "Any location at least?"

Jett winces, feeling the pull of stitches on his abs. "I told you I didn't see anything. They attacked when I was about to kill Peter Knight. I only remember Marcs trying to question me. He was asking things about the location. Where The Heir could unlock the magic," he grumbles.

"I highly doubt you were in their captivity for weeks on end and you found out nothing." He jerks his chin forward, ordering the doctors out of the room.

When the door shuts, leaving Declan and Jett alone, Jett is the first to speak.

"Shouldn't you be more concerned about your wife? You have failed to ask if I know where she is." Jett's voice oozes resentment, years of repressed hate for the young Lord and his smug smile.

"There are more women out there, Commander Torn. I could have any that I want. Besides, Alpha is none of your concern," Declan sneers.

"It seems she's none of yours, either."

Declan leans over and grabs Jett's neck, pinning him to the bed.

"Watch yourself, *Commander*. I would hate for you to end up like Princess Eirho."

A low shot. And Declan knows it. It wasn't hard for him to see the change that happened to Jett when she died. Declan, on the other hand, wasn't fazed by his bride-to-be dying on their wedding day. He was almost grateful.

In a way, it had been bittersweet for Jett. He lost the person he loved most, but at least she wouldn't be Mrs Declan Snow.

Jett remains silent for a few moments, while Declan admires his own savagery.

"Have you ever considered," Jett muses, "that Eirho killed herself so she didn't have to marry scum like you?"

Declan's jaw drops, momentarily taken aback. He waits a second too long before biting back. "I guess you weren't important enough to get her to stick around."

For a moment, Jett considers tearing the IV out of his arm and shoving it into Declan's eye sockets. He stays silent, not caring if Declan thinks he's won or not. That smug smile flashes at him again before Declan leaves the room, slamming the door on his way out.

"LET'S GO OVER THE PLAN," TOOLS SAYS, NODDING TO AINE TO PUT the map up on their large screen. This way, the others can see it up close. When it's ready, Tools produces a small stick to use as a pointer, gliding it across the map with a serious look on his face.

Shadow and Vex share a childish giggle.

"Shadow will be going in the main entrance dressed as a fancy foreign visitor," he says pointing to the large double doors. "We'll have Skulls posted all around the perimeter to watch for trouble. I will be hacking into their security so we can keep an eye on the event inside at all times. If there are any mishaps, we'll know immediately."

Peter studies the map, using his thumb and forefinger to zoom in closer. "Has the layout of the garden changed? It seems different. Don't you think, Shadow?"

Shadow swallows hard, realizing that those bastards have turned the peaceful garden into an area for Thanthos to execute people. She can see it, written right in front of her face. *Executioner's Block.*

Her favorite part of her old home, her beautiful sanctuary, has been stained with blood and torture. Haunted by the screams of the innocent.

"Execution square," Cibor mutters darkly. "Disgusting."

"It was once the most beautiful garden in all the kingdoms," Peter adds on, disappointment filling his voice. He remembers sitting in the garden on the hardest days—the ones where he lost friends and saw the innocent being slaughtered. The garden was a comfort to him, a comfort in the midst of everything that seemed dark and empty.

He looks to see how Shadow is handling it, but she stares at the map with vacant eyes. Her face is made of stone. He knows that behind those eyes, a new fire is brewing—one that will burn the execution block to the ground.

"Yes, it seems most of the Palace has been upgraded to a slaughterhouse," Tools says with disdain. "What we really need to decide is what are the chances of Commander Torn telling Thanthos about Shadow? Is it safe to send her?"

"They wouldn't expect me to be right under their noses," Shadow says dryly. "They'll be looking for people sneaking around and planting bombs, not someone dancing in the ballroom."

Xero gives her a sideways glare. It would be so much easier to lock her in a cell until the mission is over. But he won't. He needs her too much.

"I expect you to woo them all," Peter chuckles. "And try to be subtle."

She grins and agrees to play it cool, much to Peter's satisfaction.

"If Torn had told Thanthos already, our hallways would be filled with Elite Guards," Cibor says, shrugging. "For some reason he hasn't said anything yet."

Everyone's eyes flick to a disinterested Shadow. She makes a point of ignoring any mention of Jett Torn.

"We are safe, for now," Xero grunts. "Two weeks left and we still have no idea what Thanthos is planning. Why does he want the ball to happen over the rose in the floor? We need to be prepared for every eventuality. Shadow will go in fully equipped with weapons. We have to be certain that our men and women on the ground have what they need, and those above. Our biggest concern right now is being prepared for anything."

Shadow rubs her face tiredly as the other Skulls agree mindlessly with Xero. Whilst they're all chattering about the ball, Shadow wonders how Xero will react when he realizes that she hid the truth of the rose from him. She never told him that the rose on the ballroom floor marks the entrance to the Creator's tomb.

Shadow interrupts their chatter: "Thanthos is going to unveil the source of the magic in the hope that the Heir reveals themselves. And then he's going to kill them to steal their magic. If things go according to plan, that is." Oakenstaid told her a lot more the night she spoke to him.

Vex narrows her eyes, unconvinced. "Killing them will steal their magic?"

"I don't know the ins and outs but he thinks he can take the magic by killing The Heir. I don't know who told him and who knows how true it is," Shadow says with a shrug. "But if he *is* right, someone could die."

"Has anyone taken note that there's an eclipse on the night of the ball?" Tools questions, peeking at the notes on his watch.

Shadow looks to Xero, whose face drops.

"It's an entire ceremony," he whispers, astounded. "Some mystical shit."

Shadow rests her face in her hands. "It's taken from The Creators," she growls through her fingers. The memories of being taught about The Creators flash in her mind.

"What do you mean?" Aine asks worriedly, her face growing pale.

"The eclipse represents complete darkness over the world. A symbol, kinda. The stories say that if ever a kingdom was without its rightful Heir, The Creators would wait until the night of the eclipse. Only then could they gift the True Heir with magic. Their magic represents the one light in all the darkness." Shadow leans back in her chair. "My fear is that Thanthos will attempt to get the magic and fail. He'll be humiliated in front of everyone. And that means a blood bath. And if he gets the slightest inkling of who The Heir is, he will not hesitate to kill them."

"So, either way, someone will die," Peter says shortly. He exhales at the realization. "Damn."

"Yeah." Shadow shakes her head. "And I have to protect them."

"Is that our end goal right now? Save The Heir from Thanthos' bloodlust?" Cibor asks.

Xero runs his hands through his dark hair. "If Thanthos wants The Heir, we have to keep Dax as far away from him as possible," he admits.

In an effort to hide her surprise, Shadow clenches her jaw. Keeping Dax away from Thanthos means that he needs to be protected... because Xero thinks that Dax is the true Heir. What does that mean for their plan? The uncertainty of it all makes her chest tighten.

"No. Everyone else needs to keep Dax out of there. I'm going after Thanthos." Shadow informs them. Even if Dax is The Heir, she has no faith in him. "That's the new game plan. We end this."

"We will need a way to get you out of there, quickly." Xero

looks to Tools for the answer. He nods in response, knowing he will be able to whip something up before the ball.

"Let's get this show on the road. We need to be prepared," Shadow says, rising. She looks around the room one more time before she leaves. It looks like she'll have to proceed with more caution than she had planned.

Someone else's life is in danger.

31

NOW

Quinta sits outside, her belly swollen with another life as she watches her husband and children tend to their land. She hums happily to herself, watching her family create life in the fields. Their home is a little piece of happiness in the darkness that surrounds them.

She cannot help but regret bringing another child into this world, despite how happy she is to be pregnant and how much she loves her family. The good life they had planned has already been altered, thanks to King Thanthos.

As the thought begins to weigh on her, she sees a figure approaching from a distance, clad in all-black and hidden under a thick hood. Quinta stands, grabbing the nearest gardening tool she can find. Her family senses her worry and, like a herd of meerkats, look up to see the figure nearing the house.

Together, they straighten up, ready for whatever is coming—tools in hand. Shovels and hoes are all they have to defend themselves.

"It's me," Shadow says, revealing her face from under the cloak. "It's just me."

Quinta breathes in relief, placing her tool down shakily and waddling over to give Shadow a tight hug. "Oh, my Gods! I'm so grateful you're here! And you're okay!"

Shadow laughs warmly, hugging her back. Soon she is swarmed by tiny people who wrap their arms around her legs, singing her name in excitement. They squeeze her tight and bombard her with questions, hoping she brought a sugary treat for each of them.

"I have missed you all so much," Shadow says, patting the heads of the little ones. "Where is Rye?" she asks fearfully.

"He's down by the creek getting more water," Trenton explains as he approaches, opening his arms for a big hug. "Thank you for sending medicine."

She nods. "Anything for your family."

"Come and sit, tell us about your travels," Trenton offers with a smile as he points to a makeshift picnic table. "It's been a while since you were last here."

"Yes, you promised to come more!" Oak points out, the eldest daughter always holds Shadow accountable.

Shadow grins at her and reaches into her cloak, revealing a big bag of chocolates. "My apologies, to all of you. Please accept my sincere gift," she bows with a wink.

Oak's face lights up and her eager siblings surround her as she opens up the bag. She hands a few pieces to each of them, once she gets her mother's approval, and they sit in the grass, eating their treats.

"I think you've been forgiven," Trenton laughs. "I assumed you'd be busy—what with that Commander and Princess Alpha *missing*." He knows better than to outright say things—there are ears all around them and he must keep his family safe.

"Well, one of them seems to have escaped," Shadow comments with a shrug. "I wanted to talk to you both. There are a few things you need to know."

Quinta picks up on the serious note to Shadow's words. "What is happening, Shadow?" she asks anxiously, reaching for Trenton's hand.

She reaches into her cloak again, "I need you to leave The City."

"What?" Quinta gasps, combing the open field for signs of danger.

"Why?" is Trenton's question.

Shadow hands them a bag of coins and a rolled-up piece of paper. "A map and money. I have a friend in the forest who will take you in until it's safe here. Thanthos is planning dark things and I can't let you to stay here."

"What's happening? You have to tell us what's going on," Quinta pleads. "Shadow—will you be okay?" Trenton asks.

"Oh yes, of course. I only want to make sure you're safe," she gives an assuring smile. She does everything she can to seem calm, despite feeling anything but calm. "With Thanthos' hatred corrupting The City, it's safer this way. You will be fed and taken care of. My friend has supplies and money to keep you safe and well."

"This seems strange," Trenton says with a sigh. "Tell us what's really happening. You can't keep the secrets from us forever."

He's right. She knows that, but it's easier to send them away than to tell them the truth. But they've been her loyal friends for years—more than that, they've been her family. She owes them the truth.

"Okay. Let's send the kids inside."

Quinta calls to her children, asking them to go in and wash up. They are beyond excited, taking the bag of candy with them. Washing up means no more working in the fields for the day.

When the children have gone inside, Shadow looks to her dear friends. Those who have taken her in, cared for her, believed in her.

"Here," she pushes a newspaper article to them. The color has long since faded and the edges are bent from tireless reading.

Trenton looks from her, to the paper. He sees an old headline: *Princess Eirho Killed in Church Blast.*

"What is this?" he whispers, pulling it towards himself and his wife with one finger. "Why do you have this article?"

Shadow gestures for him to continue reading. He does as she says, skimming through the words until he sees a familiar picture. It's a picture of Princess Eirho, the same one used for her memorial, six years ago.

"Did you have something to do with—" Quinta stops herself when she sees the picture. Her eyes go up to Shadow's face and she finds herself lost for words. "Oh, my heavens."

Trenton squints at the photo in disbelief. "You're *Princess Eirho*?" he whispers furtively, lowering his voice so much that Shadow has to read his lips. Trenton coughs and speaks loud enough for Shadow to hear. "You're not dead... what happened? We thought you... how?"

"It was all a ploy," she says. "A way to get me out of the Palace so I could work to fight Thanthos."

"I can't believe it's you," Quinta says, gazing between her friend and the picture. "I can't believe it."

Shadow chuckles. "It's hard to believe, I know. But it's true. I am *her*. Or whatever is left of her. I guess I've changed a lot since then."

"What made you decide to do it?" Trenton asks. It is clear by his pallor that he's still in shock. "Why not stay in the Palace?"

"Well, first of all, Lord Declan Snow is disgusting and I would rather have gnawed my own leg off like a desperate animal than be with him. And secondly, I know my father. I've witnessed first-hand the things that he'll do for power and the lengths he'll go to, to manipulate others. This just seemed like the best way to stop him."

Trenton stays silent, deep in thought. Quinta however, had a question ready: "Wouldn't it have been easier to kill him while you were in the Palace?"

"I would have had to kill him and Snow. And I wouldn't have been capable of it back then," she admits ruefully. "Since I've left, I've given my father the time to hurt so many innocent people. I will never forgive myself for the last six years. The only solace I have now is that I am ready and his death will come soon."

Quinta stares down at her hands, the thought of her friend being hurt, or worse, sticks in her head. Beside her, Trenton is still grasping the fact that Shadow isn't who she's said she is all these years. She is someone completely different.

"Why does it have to be you?" Trenton finally says. "There's loads of other Skulls. Why do you have to be the one to kill him?"

"It's what I've been training to do." She shrugs. "If anyone should right his wrongs, it's me. He has to die and it's my responsibility." Shadow pulls her hair behind her ear, thinking about the reality she will soon face. It's simple enough. All she has to do is kill her father.

Trenton grimaces at her words. "We don't want you to die at his hands."

"I won't, I promise." She assures him. "Regardless of what happens, I want you all to be safe. Please leave The City, tonight."

"It's such short notice." Quinta frowns. "Shouldn't we get everyone else, too?"

Shadow exhales heavily. "No, unfortunately we can't. It would raise suspicion. Please, just leave with your family and I will do what I can to protect your neighbors and friends," she promises. "Quinta, please? For your family and the new baby?"

Quinta wants to protest, but she knows that Shadow makes a good point. If Quinta wants to keep her family safe, she must listen. She should've known that this was coming. The herd has been unsettled lately; a sure sign that something sinister is on its way.

"We'll leave," Trenton confirms after sharing a long look with his wife. "I promise. But you need to make us a promise in return. Two, actually."

"Of course," she says, leaning forward, eager to hear what he has to say. "Anything for you, Trenton Gustus."

He gives Quinta's hand a tight squeeze. "First, you need to promise you'll come back to us."

"I will," she agrees. "I'll do what I can to make sure of it." And it's not a lie. Shadow wants to come back to this family—the people who love her as their own, without question. Gods, she hopes she comes back.

Quinta leans her head on Trenton's shoulder, taking comfort in his warmth. Shadow can tell that she's bracing herself for the next question.

Trenton adjusts himself and looks Shadow dead in the eye. A sudden gravity of washes over her as he stares at her solemnly. "If something happens to Quinta and I, we want you to be the guardian of our children."

"Really?" Shadow gasps in surprise. It's overwhelming, and so thoughtful, and kind of wonderful. Shadow grins. "I don't know if I would make the best parent but I would—"

"You would be the best parent," Trenton corrects her. "The kids love you and we love you. You would raise them to be strong, driven, and most importantly, compassionate. They would be better off if it were to happen."

"Oh, please, don't say that. You're wonderful parents! And nothing will happen to you." The thought of losing her adopted family is too much to bear. "I am going to prevent that from even being a possibility."

Trenton clasps her shoulder with his large hand. "With our children being half sea-folk, you can imagine what we face. And with Rye being so up and down with his health. The medicine has made a huge difference," he adds when he sees her about to inquire about her previous gift. "But what Rye is dealing with will catch up to him eventually. And if we're persecuted, I know that we can count on you to protect them."

Knowing the danger they face makes her skin crawl and feeds

the fire in her gut. They are not from The City, they are poor, and they're not lucky enough to fit into any social group besides the struggling farming family. All of these facts make them a target; Thanthos thinks that no-one will care what happens to them. The Sea Bloods have an accent that makes them easily spotted and unusual jade-colored eyes. Quinta tends to only speak around those she trusts, as her lingering accent is enough to put a target on her back. Everything about the way they are treated is wrong. And Shadow intends to change that.

She sits tall, trying to assume her new role as guardian for the Gustus family, their children in particular. She has to be the best she can be for them. "I'm honored you think so highly of me, but you won't have anything to worry about when Thanthos is dead. I won't let you down, I promise. The children will be taken care of."

"Thank you, Shadow, thank you," Quinta gushes, nearly in tears. "We are so grateful to have you."

"And I am grateful to have you," she replies.

Despite this, she feels a twinge of guilt stabbing at her.

She might not be here to take care of them after all.

32

NOW

"Today is the day," Peter says as he enters Shadow's room, clearly anxious about the coming events. "How are you feeling?"

She folds her hands in her lap as she stares into her mirror, peering into the old life she once had. Princess Eirho would dress up in frilly things with shiny hair and colored lips. She would dance and sing and entertain the guests until the late hours of the night. *How are your children? How is your mother? It is so wonderful to see you again*!

Shadow would never do that. She wears dark clothes and sticks to the alleys where no light hits the stone. All she knows is how to survive. Everything she does is to keep being invisible.

There are similarities though, she realizes, between her old life and her new one. Whether she's Eirho or Shadow, she possesses love, she is driven, and she is loyal to her cause. She'll do what has to be done, even if she feels guilty for it.

"I am terrified," she admits, trying to cover the full extent of her fear with a forced laugh. Peter sees right through it and wraps her in his arms. "Peter?"

"You're going to be great. You'll do what's right," he whispers. "I know you will."

She leans into his shoulder and wraps her arms around him, pulling him closer. "Stop trying to make me cry, Peter. My makeup is flawless thanks to Vex."

"Yeah, she does have an eye for that sort of thing," he admits, pulling away to admire her beauty. He smiles proudly, feeling like her older brother. "I never got to see how beautiful you were on your fake wedding day, but I hear it was a sight to be seen. Jett would always bring it up, you know."

The pain surges through her and she takes his hand, entangling her fingers within his. The thought of how Jett must have hurt...

She deserves whatever happens at this ball. She'll welcome any pain that comes with open arms.

"Jett and Alpha are better people than I am," she admits to him. "They're everything I should be striving to be."

Peter decides to distract her by remembering a much different time.

"He would get choked up," Peter reminisces, his eyes trembling as tears threaten. "He would say that he knew, in that moment, he would find a way to marry you one day. Even if you were old and weathered, he had told himself he would find a way."

She laughs warmly, feeling a sudden pang for Jett. She misses his laugh and his smile and his love. "I wonder if he still feels that way."

"I like to think he does. I think he's just working through the truth and the idea of seeing you again," Peter says. "Maybe one day you'll finally get to be Mrs. Torn."

"Ooh, what an honor," she smiles, winking at him. He helps her stand, admiring her as he holds onto her hand. "You would be the best man, Peter. Alpha would be the maid of honor. It would be a wonderful celebration."

"Xero could officiate. Oakenstaid could create some entertainment," Peter continues. "Vex would sculpt some beautiful statues in your honor, Aine would decorate *everything*, and Tools would be in charge of music."

She cannot help but laugh at the idea—the dream. What will never be. And even though she knows it will never happen—not in this lifetime, it's a nice dream to hold onto for however long she can. It is nice to pretend for a moment that there is a future to be had.

"What happens if he sees you tonight?"

She tilts her head and shrugs. "I don't know. He might decide to kill me on sight and ruin everything. Or maybe he won't."

Peter considers this. "There's a reason that he didn't tell Thanthos where our hideout was. He knows too much about us. Why hasn't he said anything?"

"Maybe he is saving it for a rainy day. Or a trap," she offers.

"I hope not. I hope that the good old Jett we loved is still in there," Peter says with a sigh. "I wouldn't be able to..."

She catches him before he spirals. "Everything is going to work out fine. I have something I need you to know, though. You and only you."

"What's that?" he asks, cautiously. "Should I be worried?"

"I have an important document, a will, stashed under my bed. If anything does go wrong, I need you to make certain that you follow my every wish. Do you understand?"

He hates the thought of anything happening to her. His first instinct is to argue back. "You're not—"

"Peter, nothing is guaranteed. You have to promise me, please?" She gives him her big, soft eyes, suckering him in once again.

"Nothing will happen," he states. "But if it does, I'll find your will and do everything it says. You have my word."

She gives him a gentle smile. "Thank you. Now, come on, I need a ride," she says, trying to sound as positive as possible.

"Okay, let's get going."

~

"Be careful, kid," Peter nudges her as he stops his car a couple of blocks away from the Palace. He is wearing a hat, glasses, and a scar to cover his features. Shadow suppresses a giggle at the sight of him.

"I will. You guys be safe too," she leans over to give him a tight hug.

Xero chimes in from her wristband. "Come on, Shadow. It's now or never. Do *not* let Jett see you."

She nods, opening the door and sliding out in her dress. She hurries to turn around the corner, sliding her cloak off and tossing it into the bushes. In her hand she holds a fancy clutch—full of blades—and waltzes right up to the front steps of the heavily guarded Palace. Her sexy dress and flirty smile gets her through in no time and she holds her head high as she enters.

Someone approaches Shadow from the side, grabbing her arm. She's too distracted to notice until she feels a warm, familiar body against her.

Xero glares at the security footage that is being live-streamed to him. He brings his face as close to the screen as he can. Shadow is being grabbed by some man. A high-ranking guard at that.

For a split second, he thinks that the man must be Zed, but then he realizes the truth. And it makes his skin crawl.

"Are you fucking kidding me? I can't believe her!" He slams his fist into the table, bruising his knuckle. Tools jumps at the noise and stares at Xero in shock. "Fuck."

Tools shakes his head at Xero and turns his attention back on the screen.

I hope you're following through, Princess Eirho.

SHADOW NEARLY JUMPS INTO ACTION, BUT WHEN SHE SEES THAT IT'S Jett, she feels a sense of calm. All she can see are his bright eyes behind his mask.

"I was about to stab you," she whispers in his ear.

She studies every inch of him. He's clad in his fanciest armor: a sleek black suit with crimson highlights. His mask is done in the same color and despite his face being covered, he is handsome. *Gods is he handsome.* Tall, broad-shouldered, and that damn charming smile.

"I know," he whispers in her ear. He waves at an admiring couple as they walk past, and says hi to a group that shake his hand.

"You seem to be the star of the show," she points out, placing her clutch under her left arm and threading her right arm through his. Shadow places her other hand on his bicep as she walks with him. When she touches his skin, she looks away, her fingertips grazing the hard muscle as he tenses up. He's a force to be reckoned with. Thank the Gods he is on her side now.

Everyone recognizes him by his fancy armor. He ignores the looks and lifts his mask up, gleaming when he looks at her. Something has changed in his features. It's like the veil has been lifted to reveal the real Jett again.

"You look handsome," she comments softly.

"And you are the most beautiful mystery in the room. Why do you think they're all looking at you?" He nods his head towards a group of Red Guards gawping at her, drinks in hand. "They're curious how I got such a gorgeous date."

She refrains from rolling her eyes at him. "Do they not see *you*?"

"Maybe they're surprised I met someone so beautiful," he says, teasing her as they walk on. It feels like the old times. He would always tease her when they were alone, locked away in her room and tangled in sheets, or sneaking through the Palace grounds, trying to lower their soft moans. What is he trying to get from this?

As they walk down the corridor, Shadow remembers, vividly, what it had been like to run down this hall as a child. To chase Alpha during tag and race her to the gardens. The marble floors, the high ceiling, the golden trim. The same artwork still decorates the corridor, paintings and sculptures that Shadow had found herself, usually in the markets or bought from those who worked in the Palace.

Being here gives her an odd feeling—all of it does. It's as if she's about to relive her old life again. Only this time, she can be public with Jett Torn. How she'd love to tell the world that she is with him and that just for tonight, they belong to each other.

"So, where's the man of the hour?" Changing the question seems like a good idea.

"He hasn't arrived yet. I would give it a while longer; he likes to make a point of keeping people waiting. A good reminder to us commoners that he's in charge," Jett explains, wryly. He tries to keep his face as playful as he can; he doesn't need guests speculating on his conversations.

"Do you know what he has planned?"

"Dancing, dinner, and then the Grand Finale," he answers. "But that's as much as I've been told. Snow has been riding my back since I came back."

"How *did* that go?" She raises her sharp eyebrow curiously.

He shrugs wordlessly and guides her into the ballroom from the large corridor, bringing back memories of when she was a princess and not a criminal.

Shadow's heart skips a beat when they see the glory of the ballroom in front of them. At least 50 tables are laid out in a horseshoe shape around the dance floor. The food smells incredible, the music is upbeat, and the guests are enjoying their time feeling fancy, powerful, and rich. A sea of dresses fills the room with masks of every shape and style. It is incredible.

There are statues of Thanthos, paintings of Thanthos, gold glasses with Thanthos' damn face on them. As wonderful as the rest of the room is, she feels sick looking at all the things he has dedicated to himself. Egotistical, selfish monster. This is the last opportunity he'll get to celebrate how great he *thinks* he is.

Jett notices her grip tighten.

"Let's get you a drink," he suggests, nodding to the table ahead. It includes a swan fountain that pours some kind of sweet drink. "What will you be having, my lady?"

"Uh, water," she says distracted as she studies the room. "How did they react, Jett? You never told me."

He orders two drinks from the bartender and looks back at her as she holds his arm tight. "Your father wasn't so worried. Snow has been following me around though, demanding I tell him every detail. I keep telling him I have no idea what really happened. That I was drugged." He smiles and thanks the bartender as he hands her the glass and takes his own. He chugs his drink quickly. "I've hardly been left alone for weeks."

"What did you do to fake your injuries?"

"I went down to a fighting pit near the Slums. There's some big guys down there who hate me," he says, shrugging. "I went a few good rounds despite having broken ribs and a bruised face."

She drinks her water and smiles around the glass. "I see you're doing better now." Shadow says, meaning more than just the fight.

"I've had time to heal," he says as he places his drink down for the bartender to take away. She places her cup down too before looking up at him. "From a lot of things."

Before he can say anything else, someone comes over to greet Jett.

Oh shit, Shadow steps behind Jett, hiding from the man in front of them as Jett reaches out his hand to shake it.

"Commander, it's good to see you're well again."

"Thank you, Private," Jett returns, giving him a strong handshake. "I see that overlooking the Slums has treated you well."

Shadow waves at a lady who looks her way, pretending to

know her. The lady looks confused at first, though she waves shortly after and continues on her way.

"Ah, you brought a date," Zed says, smiling amiably. He lifts his mask up as he drinks champagne and speaks to his Commander. He cocks his eyebrow, looking as dashing as ever. Shadow glances at him out of the corner of her eye as she tries to seem distracted by something else.

Jett nudges Shadow slightly. "Yes, I did. This is Iota, my date for this evening." Shadow looks forward, trying to hide the fact that she knows Zed. Knows, *knows*.

Oh Gods, this is awkward.

"It's a pleasure to meet you," Zed starts to say. His mouth opens when he realizes who is standing in front of him, he closes it slightly. He can tell it's her even behind the mask—he knows those eyes and the scar that runs down her neck *very* intimately. It's probably better if he doesn't send Jett into a rage.

"It's a pleasure to meet you as well, Private Zed," she says in return, trying to seem shy. She holds on tightly to Jett's arm.

Zed bows his head, eager to escape this uncomfortable situation. If Jett finds out he has been sleeping with 'Iota' he will get his ass beat in the barracks later, and no doubt he'll be damned to the Slums for eternity.

"Well, I'm off to see if there are any single ladies I can dance with," he says with a wink. He can't get away fast enough. "Enjoy your evening."

"You as well," Jett says, nodding his head.

When Zed is out of earshot, he leans over to whisper in Shadow's ear. His warm breath makes her heart race even more, she can feel it pounding in her throat. "Where do you know him from?"

She pulls away, acting confused. "What are you talking about? I just met him."

"Liar," he declares. "I didn't tell you his name. Neither did he."

"Well, fuck," she whispers back to him. "He and I drink together sometimes in the Slums."

"Also a lie. You're turning red."

She elbows him in the side and he laughs at how annoyed she's getting. He thinks it's adorable how flustered a strong woman like her can get with some childish teasing. "It's none of your business."

"Have you been sleeping with him?"

"Stop!"

He holds his hands up in surrender. "I can't say it doesn't hurt...

but you're free to do as you please," he points out. "Come, let's go find a table."

"You mean *the* table," she corrects. She's grateful for the subject change. "You have to sit next to Thanthos, don't you?"

"Yes, but he's going blind in his left eye. Keep that in mind," he says, guiding her to where they'll be sitting. "Leave your clutch under the chair. No-one will take it."

"What? But—"

"Trust me, my Princess. I didn't betray you. And I won't start now."

She gulps and places it under the chair regretfully, sliding it underneath the seat covering. When she turns to glare at Jett, she sees that he has his hand out for her, asking her to take it.

"What are you doing?" she asks, suspicious of his real motives. She slowly gives him her hand and he takes it, grinning at her.

"Well," he says, pulling her around the table and toward the dance floor. The floor is filled with twirling colors and musical laughter. "We never got to dance at your wedding like I'd hoped. You know, step in, kick the groom out. And I hate to say it, but we may never get that chance again."

He's right. She sighs as he takes her onto an open spot on the floor, his hand going to the small of her back as he holds her other hand up. Her hand slides up his chest, feeling the rock-hard familiarity under her touch. Why did she agree to this? This could definitely get in the way of her clear thinking.

"I hope that's not the case," she says, gazing up into his vividly colored eyes. She wonders how hate had even existed in such works of art. "I hope tonight goes in our favor."

"And what do you think our favor is?" He begins to move across the floor, holding her close to him. She can't tell if he's doing it to feel her body on his or to shield her from the eyes around them. Either way, it puts her at ease.

"Peter wants us to get married," she teases, watching his face lift ever so slightly in a smirk. "He is to be the best man, Alpha the maid of honor. Oh, and Xero can officiate."

Jett makes a gagging sound. "I liked it until you mentioned Marcs," he tells her. When she wrinkles her nose at him, he smiles back. "Sounds like something I once dreamed about."

She nods, agreeing. If only that were the case. The truth is, she knows that life will never let them be together. Not before, not now, not ever. She doesn't even know if she will make it through the ritual, let alone the night.

"Why the change? You wanted to string me and my supposed lover up by our toes before," she says, raising her eyebrow. "And now you want to play Prince Charming and dance with me?"

"I want to have a night where I pretend that you never left," he admits. "That everything was as good as it was back then—despite you marrying that smug bastard."

She puts her finger up to her lips. "Shh, someone will hear you."

"Does it really matter tonight?"

She gingerly draws her finger away, watching as he studies her face, seeing how it's the same and seeing how it's different. "I have a friend who uses magic to see the past, the present, the future, and what could have been," she says. "And if I had gone with Declan, you and I would have been caught. Declan and my father would have killed you and Alpha in front of me. They would have tortured you, if I didn't kill you myself."

"Another reason to hate that son of bitch," Jett grumbles darkly. "If tonight goes as planned, I hope he gets what he deserves."

"It'll go as planned, I'm going to make sure of it," she says.

"Just come out alive. We have lots to talk about."

She raises her eyebrow at him, wondering what that means. Instead of asking, she leans her head against his shoulder, letting the lull of the music and the dance guide her to a brief stretch of happiness.

33

NOW

"Please find your seats," an announcer says, booming out of the speakers.

The lords and ladies hurry to their tables whilst Jett and Shadow take their time getting to their seats; they take care to make sure no-one gets close enough to really see Shadow's face.

When they finally reach their chairs, Jett blocks her from Declan's view by sitting her on his right.

She can feel the eyes burning into her back as Jett pulls out her chair for her. It's no secret that all the women in the court want to be with Jett.

"Ah, I'm starving," Jett tells her when he sees the food being handed out.

Before Shadow can reply, the music changes. Something swift and dark reverberates around the room and the lights slowly dim. Smoke begins to creep along the floor as an ominous feeling settles.

Guards in golden armor file into the ballroom, creating an aisle from the corridor to the end table where Declan, Jett, and Shadow are sitting.

Shadow feels her mouth drying, she knows what's coming next.

The music heightens, the lights flicker in a wild pattern, and the announcer's voice thunders through the ballroom, echoing like a vicious storm.

"Please welcome our King!" A loud bellow, cheering, clapping, excitement. The room begins to sway back and forth and Jett reaches for Shadow's hand. It's the one thing that anchors her to reality as six men carry a chair into the room. Thanthos' face speaks volumes. It's clear that if his men so much as slip with him in that chair, they *will* suffer the consequences. They crouch in unison to allow their King to step off gracefully.

It's not until he steps off that Shadow finally sees him.

He looks older, that's what she notices first—especially since he wears no mask. He wants everyone else to be covered so that all eyes are on him. There's gray in his neatly trimmed beard and wrinkles that create an intricate web over his features. He is fatter than she remembers, too. And when he walks, he tends to limp on his left foot.

The villain she has wanted to kill for so long is no more than a graying man.

That's why he wants magic—to live longer.

She feels Jett yank her to her feet and they begin to clap for Thanthos along with the crowd. He ascends the stairs and makes his way to the large, golden chair in the center.

"Greetings," he says when he stops in front of the table. His voice thunders through the room, causing Shadow to shiver in fear. "Be seated," he orders. "We are here tonight to celebrate my royal accomplishments and to finally acknowledge how unstoppable our city will become."

Shadow trembles as she hears his voice—the voice of her father. She's suddenly brought back to being a young girl again, trembling before this merciless man. The man she has come here to kill. How will this end after all these years? It makes her stomach sick to think of him, of the situation she's been put in.

Her father will lose his reign by her hand, and if not, she will die trying.

And the term *will become* sticks in her head. That could only mean one thing. It confirms her biggest fear. The magic will be revealed tonight.

Under the table, Jett squeezes her hand, trying to keep her grounded as negative thoughts rush through her head.

Maybe I'm not who I thought I was. Maybe I'm weak.

Jett's grip tightens as if to tell her to pull it together. She has to focus, has to think. All those lives he destroyed, all the innocent people he brutally murdered, the terrible things he made Alpha do, the way he kept her from Jett...

She has to do this.

She squeezes Jett's calloused hand in answer: *I can do this.*

"Tonight, we shall feast and dance and laugh. Then I will unveil the big event. Enjoy yourselves," he beams. He takes his seat and the party continues, his workers are already tending to tables and handing out the first course of the meal.

A long breath leaves Shadow's mouth, one she didn't know she had been holding.

"You're okay," Jett says from next to her ear. "You can do this."

She looks at him, confused at the emotion behind his words. Everything is overwhelming her, taking over her senses. "Why do you still care?"

His brows knit together and he seems equally as perplexed. "I told you I would never stop caring about you. I wasn't lying when I said that."

"What happens if we make it through tonight?"

He places a gentle, reassuring hand on her face. "We finally get to live."

Her heart drums in her chest and she nods, placing a gentle hand over his. "I can do this," she says. "I will."

"I know you can. I believe in you." He brushes a wild hair away from her eyes and gives her a knowing smile. They will make it through this, somehow.

~

"I CAN'T BELIEVE THIS! SHE LET THAT SON OF A BITCH OUT OF OUR cells so she could play princess at a tea party!" Xero throws a radio across the room where it collides unceremoniously with a wall. Peter and Cibor share a worried glance.

"Look, we don't know that," Vex pipes up, trying to calm him down. She puts her hands up, trying to placate him. "She might have another plan, something that couldn't be shared. We don't know what happened, but I do know that if all this was some elaborate plan to betray us, she would never have hurt Torn and Alpha in the process."

Peter picks up the shattered pieces of the radio, admiring the damage Xero did with one hit. "Incredible accuracy," he murmurs. "Shadow isn't going to betray us, Xero. That's not how this is going to go down."

"And how do you know that? Did you know she let Jett free?" Xero demands, standing inches from Peter, his fists tightly clenched.

Cibor takes heed of the balled-up hands, ready to knock Xero across the room if he so much as dares to put a hand on Peter. Peter, on the other hand, doesn't seem to care.

"No, I didn't, but I know she wouldn't betray us. Shadow knows what's right and what's wrong. She won't let us down," he tells the leader. He's so confident that he smirks. "Just watch and see what happens."

"I'm going to. And if she fucks this up, you will be going down with her."

A solid threat. It's so unlike Xero that Peter actually worries.

"Let's go see how Tools is doing with the video footage download," Cibor intercepts, grabbing Peter's arm. He pulls him out of the room and into the hallway. It is not long before he stops, pushing Peter against the wall.

"Yes, my love?" Peter inquires.

Cibor narrows his eyes, seeing through his charade. "That wasn't like Xero. He never snaps like that," he keeps his voice low. "Stay away from him until this is over. I want you with Tools. I'm going to run and do my checks. I'll be back in a few."

"Fine, I hope he has snacks." He kisses Cibor's cheek and watches him walk off in a huff.

34

NOW

Declan Snow—or smug bastard as Jett calls him—sits in his chair, glancing over the lords, ladies, and Red Guards with his mouth twisted in disgust. Who knows how much time, effort, and money they spent to look nice and to come to this ball, yet he still stares at them as if they are a pile of dog feces.

He looks the same, Shadow decides as she looks at him out of the corner of her eye. He looks like the same arrogant asshole, one that Jett probably still wishes he could kill.

She thinks for a second about how he's probably treated Alpha. There is no doubt he's made her feel more alone these past few years. Shadow has to dig her nails into her leg to stop herself from assaulting him and blowing her cover.

"Did you enjoy the grouse?" Jett asks, pointing to the half-eaten food on her plate.

"I'm not hungry," she insists as she fakes a smile and surveys the room. "I don't want a full stomach for later."

He shrugs and sticks his fork into her grouse, his eyes full of hunger for the roasted meat. "Well, if you're not going to eat it."

She cannot help but laugh at him, grateful for his company. She doesn't deserve it. It was Shadow who lied to him, Shadow who deceived him. At least Peter had the courage to tell him the truth.

What was it that she had feared so much back then?

Right, she was terrified her father would slaughter Jett. And he would have, too. No doubt in her mind that Thanthos would have strung him up for even considering being with her, or helping the Skulls, if he ever found out. Jett Torn was not the man he had picked to be with his favorite daughter. His trophy.

"Is there seafood?" she asks hopefully, looking around. "I could use some crab on my plate."

"That would make your stomach hurt more," he points out, he inches closer to her. "And glaring at Declan Snow will also do that."

"Admit to me how much time you've spent in your life glaring at him," she says.

"About a third."

Shadow laughs at him, rolling her eyes. *This* feels nice. Being next to Jett, sharing food and laughter with him feels perfect. It feels right. Gods, she feels like the worst person in the world though. Sometimes she thinks it would have been better if she had died in the flames of that church. She doesn't deserve this—his kindness or his forgiveness.

"There's been a few times I considered putting poison in his shampoo," Jett admits daringly. "His damn luscious hair. He thinks it makes him invincible."

She glares at Declan, his long hair brushed neatly to his shoulders. "He probably uses the blood of virgins."

He laughs, seeing Thanthos talking to some of the higher lords in The City. One of the lords, tall with dark features is standing closest to the King; a sign of status. Jett stops chewing and drops his fork with a clunk.

"Oh no," he mouths.

Shadow follows his gaze to see the familiar face of Lord Torn, bowing for the King. That means Lady Torn is also in attendance at this soon-to-be bloodbath.

"We have to get them out of here," she says. "You have to tell them your siblings are sick or—or—"

"They wouldn't miss this ceremony. They're loyal subjects," he grumbles, swallowing on his dry throat. "I don't know how I can get them out of here. Not when it's something this important to Thanthos. They wouldn't just leave, not for a sick child."

Shadow understands what he means. Anyone who leaves, or anyone who was invited that doesn't show up, must declare their loyalty. It's either that or treason. His parents are good at playing loyalists to the crown. They've always been eager to throw money and supplies around to support their king. Anything to stay safe.

"Sickening," she mutters in disgust. "He's blackmailing everyone by threatening their lives. I can't wait to kill him."

Jett looks pale. He's worried about his family now. This could affect the plan—his emotions would get in the way and Shadow understands that, but she's not sure she can risk it.

"They will be all right; they will be your first priority when I start this. You and your parents have to get to safety before you consider coming back for me." She hopes he will listen, that for once he will let her go alone.

"No, I'm not leaving you. They're sitting by the doors so they should be able to get out first, before the stampede," he says, as if trying to calm himself down. Saying his theory out loud helps to put him at ease, as if it is a confirmation. "They will be okay."

"Yes, they will," she assures him. "Your parents will get out of here before the chaos. And if you're worried, I can order the Skulls to avoid them. That is, if Xero will talk to me now."

Jett's frowns in confusion. And then he realizes, she never told Xero about their secret plan. He is not sure what he expected, but it is a relief and makes him wonder why she didn't say anything. "You didn't tell him, did you?"

She smiles wryly at him in response. "Of course not. We had an agreement, you know. I'm not going to tell him I let you out.

Besides, if we hadn't kidnapped you, there would be more problems. Like explaining to the entire court how I'm still alive."

"It's almost time," Jett tells her. He puts his fork down, no longer feeling the hunger in his stomach. "We need to be alert."

Thanthos motions for the people in front of his table to take their seats. The cameramen settle in at his signal to display the King and the attendees on this special night. He needs this event to be televised so that the entire City—and the rest of the world—can watch as he acquires endless power.

He sits back when everything is in place, smiling proudly over the people in the audience as if they are nothing more than dirt. He takes in each one of them and sees the peasants who are here to serve him in every way he desires. Especially after tonight.

Shadow considers how lucky she is that both Thanthos and Declan are busy with others—too busy to notice that Jett has a date for the evening. She inhales and sits up straight, watching as the crowd settles in.

The rest of her life is about to begin.

~

"LORDS AND LADIES," THANTHOS BEGINS, STANDING UP AGAIN. "I AM honored to share this night with you. I have spent many years vanquishing The City of Sea People and disease, thinning it out so only the best survive. It has been an honor to serve you all as stand-in King."

The room livens up, clapping and cheering until he gestures for them to be silent.

"I have not been blessed with the magic of the ruler yet, but tonight you will see me granted the final step in becoming the full-fledged King." His voice is confident, booming through the ballroom as the guests wait quietly for his unveiling. "We will conquer the world unchallenged!"

And with that, more smoke, more lights, and louder music

sounds. Then silence. So quiet that a pin drop could be heard. Everyone waits on the edge of their seats.

The center of the ballroom—the dance floor—begins to open up as two large doors slowly shift to the side. Their cranking sounds echo in the ballroom before stopping to reveal a large piece of flooring underneath.

Shadow gasps, seeing the rose carved into the floor underneath. Its lines are deep, veining the marble floor in an elegant pattern. The roof of the ballroom begins to open slowly, the last sliver of moonlight from the eclipse glides over a few inches of the rose.

There are only a few minutes left, seconds maybe.

"The eclipse is almost here," Thanthos announces, earning a huge cheer. He walks to the center of the room, standing feet away from the rose. "It is almost time for me to unlock the most powerful magic that ever existed."

Shadow senses Jett tensing up beside her, waiting for her to act. Everything they've ever known is about to change.

Thanthos steps into the beam of moonlight, opening his arms wide and revealing his chest to the sky above. As the moon darkens, he holds his right hand out and a guard places a blade, ceremoniously, in his other hand.

The sliver of light gradually thins, until it's no thicker than a strand of hair. Thanthos has the blade pressed into the flesh of his palm, applying just enough pressure to break the skin open.

Under the table, Shadow is using a blade to cut her dress off at the knees, quietly pulling the fabric apart. Her shoes stay on—flat and perfect for this battle.

"This is the moment!" Thanthos shouts with utter excitement, nearly shaking at the thought of being blessed by The Creators. "This is it!"

Shadow slides her blades from the hidden places around her body. She readies them in her hands as she sees Thanthos slice the blade down his palm. Blood pools in his hand and he tilts his hand downwards, mesmerized as the blood falls through the air.

Shadow's mask falls to the floor.

"This is it," Peter whispers into the dark room. His eyes are focused on Thanthos, on Shadow, on Jett. Everything they've been working for... this is it.

Tools clasps Peter on the back in silence, a reminder that they're in this as a team. They started this together and they'll end it together.

Peter cocks his gun, waiting for word to storm the castle and restore peace, or attack if Thanthos' plan works.

Cibor's voice comes in over Peter's radio. "I love you. I love you so much."

"I love you too," Peter says back, trying to keep his voice from breaking. "We aren't going to lose today." He presses a button on his radio, requesting Xero's confirmation to prepare.

Xero presses his finger into the wristband when he gets the notification. A green light flashes at his touch, alerting the Skulls that it's time to strike. Peter calls the others, "Skulls—ready yourself to get the people out of there. This is it."

A drop of blood falls to the ground but Shadow is already over the table and sprinting toward him. He doesn't see her coming. In a few seconds he will have The Heir magic he so longed for and nothing will stop him.

The guards go into high alert, firing after her—but she's too fast. The sirens wail in the distance and she remembers the many sleepless nights she lived through, dealing with fear, and hatred, and war. And that's all it takes to convince her that this must end, now.

Shadow launches herself at Thanthos with blades in hand, cutting his arm and kicking him from the rose. Everyone is screaming around her, gasping in fear as they hide from the storm of bullets that rain down. Jett moves to get his family out of the ballroom, to safety. The cameras shake as they try to follow the action, many of the attendees scrambling to escape the ballroom.

Thanthos hits the ground, his eyes bloodthirsty as he glares up at his opponent, seeing her towering over him. The ricochet of bullets stops for fear of hitting him and a thick silence blankets the room.

It begins to dawn on the King that nothing is happening to him, even as his blood continues to drain onto the floor. The fear and anger begin to creep in.

Shadow studies him intently now that he's closer. Her father appears smaller, weaker, but she knows it's a façade. She knows the power that this man carries and the darkness that he brings with him. He can take on any opponent, she knows that. Men ten times his size and bigger.

His size is no indicator, his eyes tell the real truth. A darkness lingers around him and seeps out to taint the world. He will not fall easily.

He takes a few seconds to study the woman standing above him, observing her in the same way she has observed him.

Thanthos realizes exactly who his opponent is.

"*Daughter*." A bitter statement. Shadow hears the disappointment in his voice and the hunger for her head on a spike. The audience and guards gasp, yet Thanthos isn't the least bit surprised.

"You tricked me."

"I did what was necessary," she whispers into the air, moving away from him. She can feel the eyes of the cameras on her, revealing her face to everyone in The City. "I did what needed to be done."

"You're a traitor to your family," he says. "There are only a few minutes left of this eclipse. If you want to live, you better step out of my way."

She laughs grimly. "Kill me, Father."

He pushes himself up from the ground, blood smeared across the floor. Standing tall, he stares at her in complete contempt. "Gladly."

Shadow rolls out of the way, dodging an angry blow of the fist.

But she doesn't miss the bullet that hits her shoulder.

"EIRHO!" Jett screams, running up behind her, distracting her, putting himself in danger to protect her.

"No," she hisses, shoving him back as she lands a foot in Thanthos' side. "Get out of here, Jett!"

Thanthos pauses and smiles as he makes the connection between his daughter and his right-hand man. "Oh, that is so sweet, Eirho. Seducing my men to work for you. Ah, I am so proud of you."

Jett is about to protest when a fist is slammed into his face, knocking him backwards across the ballroom.

He touches his face, already feeling heat radiate from it as he raises his head. Declan Snow stands in front of him with a wicked smirk on his face. He reveals daggers in his hands as he glares in disgust at the Commander.

"Oh, I can't fucking wait for this," Jett tells him, reaching into his belt to pull out his own showcase of weapons.

"The feeling is certainly mutual, Commander."

Beside Jett, Shadow is trying to stem her blood flow as she dodges brass knuckles. He swings left, swings right. Shadow retreats backwards, over the rose to evade his blows.

She ducks underneath a hit and uppercuts him straight in the stomach. She tries to ignore the hot blood flowing down her arm as her wrist and hand become soaked—her dress turns aptly crimson as she moves to battle against her own flesh and blood.

Alongside Father and Daughter, Declan and Jett fight tirelessly. Jett serves him hit after hit giving Declan no time to recover. Declan only manages to get a couple of weak blows in and the more they fight, the closer Jett gets to ending his life.

"I've waited years for this," Declan spits the blood from his mouth. "You won't win."

"Seems like I'm doing a decent job," Jett says nonchalantly. He kicks his foot forward, winding Declan in the process. When he falls forward, Jett disarms him in two moves. "Darkness never prevails, Lord Snow."

He tosses the blades away, returning to his opponent with relish. His fists ache from the hits he's landed on Declan's body but he's not going to stop now.

"I see that working with Cibor paid off," Thanthos snarls to his daughter, blocking a hit from her good arm and kicking her backwards in return.

Shadow is propelled across the ballroom and falls over on the rose, her hands aching as they scrape the carving in the floor. A shooting pain surges through her arm and she prays the adrenaline will cover it. Of course she's gotten hurt! *That's what I get for being overconfident.* How stupid she's been to get hurt so early on in the fight. How stupid she is—

The moonlight is completely gone.

She can see Thanthos' hungry eyes through the darkness as she struggles to push herself up. The room is now clear of innocent citizens, who had evacuated when the bullets fell. The guards stand around the room, uncertain now who they should shoot. Thanthos is King, Declan is a Lord, Jett is their Commander, and now their deceased Princess has risen again.

Shadow presses her pained, bloody hand into the floor and her blood spills into the outline of the rose as she evaluates the room. Her father isn't far away. As she looks for the best spot to hit him, she notes how he avoids using certain parts of his body, especially his weaker leg. Digging her heels in, she gets ready to attack.

And then, as fast as she had been shot, the floor shifts and brilliant rays of golden light shoot up to the sky.

"YES," bellows Thanthos, spreading his arms wide once again, eager to welcome the magic into his body. "You will all perish, Eirho!"

35

NOW

"No, no, no!" Peter grabs the sides of the screen and shakes them. "No, this can't be happening! She was supposed to stop this!"

The darkness is overtaken by a bright light and Peter has to avert his eyes from the blinding brilliance of it. It's unlike anything he's ever witnessed.

Tools cries out in pain too, hiding his face from the screen as a humming noise begins.

Peter bites down on his lip, forcing himself to look back at the screen. A figure is surrounded in the light, being held up over the floor by some unseen force. It gravitates upwards and the light becomes unbearable again.

Turning away, cowering from the pain, Peter hears the noise stop. A brief, peculiar silence.

He looks back in time to see the rose turning to a million little pieces and the entire floor of the ballroom crumble into a hole below.

Everyone and everything in that ballroom falls with it.

~

THE DEBRIS SURROUNDS SHADOW AND SHE TRIES TO STAND, FEELING wobbly at first. She looks up, realizing they're nearly a hundred meters underneath the Palace. The realization makes her stumble and she coughs, hand falling against some of the fallen stones as she attempts to figure out what happened.

She peers around, her breath getting caught in her throat as she tries to push the dust and dirt away. She's standing in old ruins, ancient from the looks of it. Images forged into the walls of dragons and giant men and men with pointed ears and tiny legs. Drawings of flowers, trees, and water create a sense of harmony. And roses. Roses *everywhere*. There are even fresh roses bursting out of the walls, appearing to tear through the concrete like it is nothing more than paper. The smell of the flowers is overwhelming and intoxicating.

They cover the floors, the ceilings, and the pillars that rise above. She looks down at her blood-crusted hands and thinks back to Oakenstaid's blood rituals and wonders what happened on the ballroom floor.

"The Creators," Shadow whispers at the sight, taking everything in. "I was right! This is the tomb of The Creators. This is where it all began."

She hears a muffled cry from under the rubble and races to where Jett would've fallen. Shadow begins to lift the stones away with surprising ease, rushing to find him.

"Jett! Jett," she calls frantically. She stumbles through the stone, searching for him. "Jett!"

"Here," a voice says from a few feet away.

She climbs over the stones to find Jett pushing himself up, wiping the dust away from his eyes. He gives her a smirk. *He's okay*. She nearly falls back to the ground as relief washes over her.

"What the hell happened?" She wipes his eyes with her fingers. "Are you okay?"

"I'm fine," he dismisses. Jett studies her for a moment, checking to see what shape she's in. "Uh, Eirho?"

She takes his hand and helps him up, holding him close to her to keep him safe. "What's wrong?"

"Your wound—" His face is sick now, reaching for her with a shaky, reluctant hand. "It's... it's healed."

Shadow looks feverishly to her shoulder, stunned. Blood still smears her skin, but the wound is *gone*. "What the—" She twists her arm back and forth, confused and terrified. How?

"You conniving *bitch*!"

Pain radiates through her body as she's thrown forward into the stones. Jett catches himself before he falls, turning to peer over his shoulder to see the owner of the voice.

Of course Thanthos survived that fall. Slimy bastard.

"You took the magic from me! You stole it! I will kill you and take it right out of your veins!" He is charging at her, hands open wide. "I raised you to be loyal, not to betray me!"

Shadow grabs a stone from the rubble and throws it at him as hard as she can. The stone hits him in the shoulder with a crack that echoes. Thanthos cries out and falls to his knees, crumpling into a heap of a man.

"Stupid of me to let you live past infancy. I should have fed you to the wolves!" He snarls as he holds onto his shoulder, fumbling over the stones to reach her, persistent in his hunt. He aims a stone at her but he misses as she rolls out of the way, cutting her knees against the rocks.

Shadow gets to her feet again, rising tall above him. "I would have returned with the pack to kill you," she says, shaking her head at him. "You've taught me how to be strong, how to survive. I'm only this way because of you."

"I suppose I should be thanking myself," he scoffs, seeing her hands glow with flames that lick up her arms. He growls at the sight; this challenge is finally getting interesting. Jealousy courses through him upon seeing his hard work go to waste—his years of plotting, all the sweat and blood that he poured into it—and for what? For The Heir magic to be given to someone else. "I raised you from a shy little girl into this courageous woman. I should never have empowered you enough to challenge me."

"And now you'll face the consequences."

She crouches down in front of him, until her eyes are level with his. The fact that this mortal man has caused The City a great deal of pain, it almost makes her laugh.

"You say that, Eirho, but you're forgetting one thing. You and I too much are alike. That is why you are the only person brave enough to attempt such a mutiny." His voice is full of pride and it makes her stomach churn. He pushes himself up, slowly standing to face her. She rises with him.

"I'm nothing like you, Father," she tells him. "You're a monster, a murderer," she points out sullenly. "I'm the one person who can counter that. I'm going to save The City from your darkness."

Thanthos scoffs. "You will not save The City. You'll only make it worse. You are a monster just like me. The difference is, you are not capable of doing what needs to be done. That is why you didn't kill me sooner."

"Oh, I plan on making up for that now," she promises. She shakes his words off, noticing the sensation of heat in her hands—she looks down to see fire trailing from her palms all the way up her arms. The flames flicker beautifully in hues of purple and blue. *I am The Heir,* she thinks. *It was me all along.*

Jett lets out a gasp of surprise from behind her. His Eirho is The Heir of ancient magic. She turns to exchange a knowing look with him. When she smiles, he releases a breath. He's in awe of her.

Stay back, she mouths to him.

Thanthos uses the distraction to attack her again, hitting her in the head with a stone. She buckles, grabbing her skull as the pain throbs in time with her heartbeat. Shadow feels the warmth trickle down her neck as she attempts to stop the bleeding with a piece of her dress.

Thanthos sees his chance and crawls on top of her in an attempt to strangle her. Somehow, she musters the strength to knock him off, lying beside him for a moment before returning the favor. He moves away, ploughing a fist into her gut. She kicks at him before she rolls back, avoiding his next blow.

Before he can react, a low rumbling sound begins to fill the room, getting louder and more violent, until it turns into a deep growl. As soon as the sound changes, the entire floor of the ancient tomb starts to shake. It's like standing on a ship in a rocky ocean, swaying to and fro.

"No!" Jett shouts as he's knocked back against the walls. His heart stops when he glances down.

A deep chasm has opened up, dropping the King and the Princess further into the earth. Jett rushes toward the edge to see, but they have already vanished into darkness.

Down below, Shadow lifts herself up once more, seeing a dimly lit room encasing her. Thanthos isn't far away, somehow managing to rise to his feet again, adrenaline pumping through him. He refuses to lose.

"I hope you're enjoying this fight because it *will* be your last," he hisses to her. He moves quickly, revealing daggers in his hands. "I can't wait to leave you bleeding out on the floor." Shadow laughs.

"Oh, and Eirho, I will steal your magic."

"Please do," she challenges.

"It would be my pleasure."

~

THE SKULLS HAVE LAUNCHED THEIR ATTACK ON THE PALACE. THEY struggle to get the innocents out while killing the guards who stand in their way; the Red Guard have taken to killing anyone in their path—not just the Skulls. It's a full-on war zone. Ash coats everything as explosions shatter the air. Screams and panicked footsteps flow through the streets.

"What are you doing?" Cibor shouts, sprinting after Peter.

He has a gun in his holster and a blade in his hand as he races through the panic and devastation. People are screaming and crying right next to him, some are covered in blood or vomit. It takes everything inside of him to keep running instead of stopping to help.

"I'm getting into that Palace and I'm killing every guard that touches these people!" he yells back. "We have to get in there! Thanthos is letting his men attack civilians because of us!"

"Peter, wait," Cibor demands from behind him. He uses the hilt of his gun to knock a guard unconscious. "You don't know what dangers are waiting for you in that Palace!"

"Neither did our friends and we may have just sent them to their deaths!" Peter snaps back. He races through the gates of the Palace and up the front steps, dodging the frantic crowd in his path. "Gods be damned! Get out of the way!"

"Peter!" Cibor says, getting lost in a wave of people. "Peter, stop!"

Ignoring him, Peter feels his feet pounding against the stones toward the entrance of the Palace. He avoids guards, lowering his head to hide among the evacuees. It doesn't take him long to squeeze his way inside, hiding underneath the cover of smoke.

"Hey!"

He spins just in time to block a guard from slicing him in half with a sword. Peter spins his gun around his finger and shoots the man in the gut, leaving him on what's left of the ballroom floor to die.

"Man, that food smells incredible," he says to himself as he sprints to the edge of the pit. He leans down and peers in, trying to see where Shadow is. "Fuck. Fuck."

He sees nothing but the faint outline of bodies and a few distant figures moving about.

He sits on the edge of the pit with his legs swinging as he wonders how to do this. Peter places his gun down next to him. He'll use his blades like ice picks to descend the wreckage below, he decides. He looks down at his feet, grimacing at the drop below.

The cold barrel of the gun presses into the back of his neck and he stops, swallowing hard.

"Don't you dare move or I *will* shoot you."

Cibor comes skidding into the room, trying to locate Peter as fast as possible. It only takes him seconds to see Peter sitting with his hands up, a gun to the back of his head.

At the end of the gun is Alpha.

36

NOW

Thanthos kicks a weak pillar until it shatters into pieces but his plan to distract Shadow doesn't work. As the stones crash on top of her, the one thing that saves her is the fire that exudes from her palms. The blue flames engulf the rocks effortlessly and she keeps moving, pursuing him as he veers down a hallway.

She takes off, using the small flame in her hand to guide her through the eerie dark. How is he moving so effortlessly? It's as if he has known about this place the entire time.

Shadow descends deeper and deeper into the earth, feeling the temperature increase. She notices the heat on her skin as the flames course from her hands. A small tingling sensation emanates from her palms and travels up and down, all over her body. It's the kind of feeling she'd get from sleeping on her arms for too long. This magic is making her unstoppable. She feels like a feather as she moves now; so light that she floats above the pain.

She shrieks as a scurrying noise to her left startles her. *Get yourself together Shadow! You can't be distracted!* She hurries after her father once more. She has to catch up to him. The sound of his footsteps leads her down a winding staircase and she takes them two at a time, their feet pounding the floor in unison. After a few minutes, she realizes that something is off. All she can hear is one pair of footsteps—her own.

Shadow slows down as she reaches flat ground, hyperaware of her surroundings and her father's stillness. She swallows hard as the hair on the back of her neck stiffens and her body flushes with heat. Holding her hands out on either side of her body, she controls her breathing enough to focus her energy to her palms. She manages to light up a few feet around her with her magic.

Everything in the massive room is carved from stone, ancient like the rest of the tomb, no doubt. To her right sits a small, thin trough filled with some kind of flammable-looking liquid. She turns around—there's one on the other side as well.

"I wonder," she mouths to herself. She lays her palms in one of the troughs and the liquid catches alight instantly to create a yellow beam and spreads. Soon the entire room is lit up with light at a single touch of her hands.

As she continues her search for Thanthos, she reaches eight columns in the center of the room. They stand a few meters apart, forming an octagon. In the middle of the octagonal space is a stone table that takes the same shape of the room. The table is decorated with carvings of a rose and its vines. Whoever crafted it even etched thorns into the sides.

Shadow takes a hesitant step inward, bracing herself for an ambush as she gets closer to the table.

"Ah, my *daughter*."

There he is, standing in front of her, smiling down at her with dark intentions.

"This is where The City was created," she acknowledges as she takes another step. "This is where the first ruler was given their powers, isn't it?"

"Yes. Your mother tried to hide a map of this place from me. But I found it. Your father knew about it but he never told me."

She freezes. It takes a second to register his words. Why is he saying *your father*? *He's* her father, no-one else. He must be lying, telling her some story to distract her. But... what if he's being honest? She struggles to catch her breath as she meets his eyes.

Shadow searches his face for traces of a lie—anything that might tell her that he's joking. She scrutinizes his face and sees nothing but sincerity. He's telling the truth.

"What?" she says, her tone demanding, her head spinning. Anger overcomes her shock and she leans into the utter betrayal coursing through her. "You're not my father and you knew the whole time?!"

He snorts with amusement and walks towards her. "I had my suspicions. Your mother refused to share my bed after my brother Argos died. My own wife refused to touch me because of him. You had to be his," he says, shaking his head. "Despicable woman."

"You're lying." She's provoking him now. She needs to know more and she needs to know now—while she has the chance to ask.

He shakes his head. "Unfortunately not. Only Argos' direct bloodline could be the guardian of this city. His heir. They alone have the capability to learn The Heir magic and protect The City. Too obsessed with my wife and a bastard child, my brother never sought the magic, never cared for it, but I did."

"If you knew I wasn't your daughter, why did you treat me as such?" She feels her guard lowering as her mind reels with questions. It hurts to know that all these years she has been lied to. She is torn between feelings of betrayal and the insistent question —*why?* Now she knows how Jett and Alpha must feel.

Thanthos waves his hand around the gigantic room, gesturing at The Creators' artwork that lines the stone walls and pillars. Every inch of the room is covered with their depictions. The Creators are tall, beautiful, and powerful beyond imagination.

"I knew what you were capable of when you were born. I saw it in your eyes. I wanted to raise you to be a conqueror, a leader. I wanted you to cleanse this earth of scum," he tells her, his voice softening as he reminisces. "Strange that I loved my niece more than my own daughter."

She considers burning his face then and there for that comment against her sweet sister, Alpha. But she waits. There's more to this story.

"My brother was never concerned with magic. I had hoped I would inherit it after his death. I was his brother after all, but I couldn't find the source—and so I started my missions. It turns out that Saryss, our sister, held the magic for him. When I sent Alpha outside the walls, she found letters between Saryss and her estranged lover at that shithole the forest troll lives in." *Oakenstaid,* Shadow thinks, *of course he knew*. Shadow focuses again as she realizes Thanthos is still talking.

"Saryss locked the magic away as soon as she learned I was after it. She knew I would come for her next," he goes on. "Lucky for her, she disappeared. But it took me over two decades to discover the roses and connect them to The Creators. Roses," he trails off for a moment at the thought of the flowers. "Beautiful and pure... but their thorns can slice you."

Shadow keeps quiet, watching him as he contemplates the past and his tireless effort to possess The Heir magic. Her entire body feels alive and alert as he paces in front of her.

"When I was unable to get the magic after Argos, I knew that it was you. You were Argos' heir. For years, I convinced myself that somehow The Heir magic had been released and had passed to you. So, when you died, or so I thought, I forced The Oracles to help me find the magic again. They told me something that confirmed it all: 'realizedThe true Heir is still alive. Keep searching, King.'"

He scoffs briefly before his lip curls up in disgust. "And that's when I realized that you hadn't died in that fire. As long as you lived, I would never possess that magical gift. And so, I waited."

"If you had suspicions the first time, why didn't you kill me?"

she asks, thirsting for the answer. The fact that he tried to use her death to get magic makes her sick, yet the worst part is, she's not surprised at all.

"I knew that one day I would need a successor and I had hoped it would be you. Alpha is too weak, too dumb," he says, shaking his head. "I'm ashamed of my own seed. But you, Eirho, you were everything I dreamed of. You would have kept the powerful reign going, long after I was gone. My legacy would have been alive for years to come." He admires her now, an abrupt change from the way he had been looking at her—as if he wanted to tear her heart right out of her chest.

"Alpha would be the best leader and the greatest Queen. You underestimate her," Shadow snaps. "If anyone would create a legacy, it would be Alpha. The daughter you didn't care about when she went missing. Such a shit father." She turns to face him as he circles her like a shark, waiting for the right moment to strike.

"No. She wouldn't be able to defend The City, the kingdom. She would be a doormat to any enemy of these lands," says Thanthos with a disapproving *tsk*. "You, on the other hand, would have brought Kings to their knees. Look what you've done already."

"Why would you sell me off to Declan, then?"

Challenging him will buy her time so she can study his strengths and weaknesses and learn how to control some of the magic she has inside of her. The magic feels endless, but a wave of exhaustion threatens when she uses the fire.

He laughs, hard. "Because you would have conquered the Kingdom of Azura in due time. Declan is easily corrupted and controlled. He's a viable pawn in my court now," he explains to her. "It worked out for me."

"Things worked out for me as well. I escaped your grasp," she says. "And now I have the magic you want so badly. The magic you bled for, nearly died for. No doubt killed for."

"That is true," he admits breathlessly. "All those lives wasted for you to have what I want. Do you want to know a secret?"

She stays silent, not giving him the satisfaction of her curiosity. Waiting for him to answer, she keeps her hands behind her thighs, testing her abilities as she toys with the magic in her hands. It's not long before she conjures water and her hands grow damp.

"Your death will cause the magic to leave your body... allowing another to take it." He is sinister—watching her carefully—looking for an opening to attack her. "As I am Argos' brother, I would become the next heir."

"Imagine if you killed me and the magic went straight to Alpha," she says. "Or the magic ended with the bloodline. You'd have to wait for another eclipse like this and that doesn't happen often."

His eyes grow wide, nearly popping out of their sockets. His hands clench at the thought and his flesh turns red. Oh, he is beyond angry now. He wants to kill her more than anything. This woman he raised to be powerful and fearless is now his worst nightmare.

He throws a blade at her quickly, piercing her oblique.

Shadow thrusts her hands forward with a shout, knocking him out of the way with flames. A new blade appears in his grasp but Shadow throws it away before she is on top of him, pinning him to the stone floor, holding him in place.

"You won't do it," he snarls, trying to push her off. He kicks and rolls, earning a punch to the face. Blood fills his mouth and his teeth turn red as he spits his words out. "You are strong, but not strong enough to kill. You're the same as your weakling father, a fearful coward. Seeing such a waste of a man die by my hands was the most *satisfying* sensation I have ever felt."

Shadow instantly closes her fists, cutting off her magic supply. He looks up at her in confusion.

"I don't need magic to kill you. And I don't have to be merciless either."

He manages to roll her off just slightly, but she holds her

ground, keeping him pinned under her weight. A hit to his face nearly knocks him out cold. Shadow leaves him alone momentarily, wanting nothing more than for him to be fully awake when she takes his life.

She lands her knuckles into his stomach, causing him to cough and choke. This gives her time to pull out a gun from the holster on her hip. He tries to push her away, but she has gotten stronger. She has trained too much for this. She's ended countless lives and this one is no different.

The gun feels heavy in her hands, weighing her down. She is not one of the Gods, nor a person who wants to take a life.

And then she thinks of her wonderful parents. Her real father, Argos, was murdered by him. And so, she cocks the gun.

For The City, for the people, for Peter and Cibor, for the Gustus family. For her late father and mother and their torment faced at his hand. For Rye so he can grow big without fear, for Oak to grow into a strong warrior. For the Skulls. For Alpha to rule. For Jett... for herself.

"Alpha will be Queen," she whispers, pulling the trigger.

"ARE YOU OKAY? SHADOW, ANSWER ME," PETER ORDERS AS HE approaches her from the darkened stairs. He grabs her hands to draw her attention away from the lifeless body.

She stares down indifferently to where Thanthos lies at her feet.

He is dead.

"You know it was the right thing to do," Peter says gingerly. He cannot fight the sense of satisfaction he feels when he sees the King Thanthos dead on the stone floor. They've won. "But we need to get out of here. I have a feeling that this isn't the only struggle we're gonna face today."

She looks at Peter's face, unable to comprehend her own

actions. She actually was able to do it. She took a life again and it was her own family. Her uncle—the wicked man that raised her. Shadow's hands quiver as a shaky breath leaves her lips.

She is no better than he is. She wished for his death for so long and now her wish has been granted.

And even so, she feels an ache inside.

"Shadow! Are you listening?" Peter is in her face now, trying to reach her. She's locked away inside her own mind and Peter doesn't know how long she'll stay that way. He has to get her out of this pit while he can. "Shadow, we have to get out of here."

She finally shakes her head, rubbing her temples. "Gods," she whispers. "I'm sorry, it's just... it's always hard to take a life. And even harder to realize how badly I wanted to."

Monster, echoes in her mind, over and over.

"I know, come on. Let's start making our way back to HQ. We need to get you checked out," Peter says. He puts his hand on her back and tries to get her to turn towards the stairs. "Also, your habit of giving keys to prisoners is getting out of control, but if Alpha hadn't escaped, I would probably be dead right now. We were outnumbered by far—she may have saved me a couple of times."

That earns a tiny, proud smile. At least her sister is free. "Did you see Jett? Is he okay?" she whispers to him as they take their first few steps, comforting one another in their embrace.

Peter is about to answer, but someone cuts him off.

"Oh, he's doing fine."

Jett is tied up, thrown on the ground. His face is colored with rage and bloody cuts line his brow. Luckily, there are no severe injuries. Shadow is relieved until she sees the gun pointed at her face.

37

BEFORE IT ALL

Xero Marcs balances a blade in between his fingers, tossing it high in the air before catching it again. He waits patiently for his apprentice Peter to arrive, the newest addition to the Skulls. Peter is a young buck, no doubt, fresh into the Red Guard and as wide-eyed as they come.

And the perfect person for Xero to train.

A knock sounds at his door and he opens it, seeing Peter waiting patiently for him.

"Oh, hello, sir," Peter says, bowing his head. He's rarely been this close to Xero, but now that he is, he can't help but notice that Xero isn't much older than he is. Actually, they're probably around the same age. He feels weird after calling Xero 'sir'.

"Peter, come in," Xero says. He closes the door as Peter hurries inside. The leader gestures for him to take a seat. "Thank you for coming on such short notice. I can't imagine how hard it is to get out of the Palace without being followed."

"They know I like to go out for drinks," Peter says with a shrug.

Xero seems entertained by this idea and hands a flask to Peter. "Might as well play the part when you get back," he insists.

Peter is grateful as he swigs the whiskey, feeling the fire seep into his core. "Damn, this is the good stuff."

"Only the best from the outside," Xero says with a wink. He sits down next to Peter and studies him for a long moment. "Peter, I've heard you're a very talented young man. Cibor told me all about you."

"Oh, thank you," Peter says as he struggles to ignore the heat on his cheeks. He takes another sip, grimacing at the burning in his throat.

"And you're close with Princess Eirho?" Xero adds.

Peter nods. "Yeah, my best friend is sweet on her, but we're all really close. Like family," he says without a second thought.

"Best friend? That's Lieutenant Colonel Torn, right?"

"Yeah. Best friends since we were knee high," he explains. "You won't say anything though, right? Princess Eirho is engaged to that conceited bastard Declan Snow and Jett's scared of her getting in trouble because of him."

"Oh, no. I wouldn't say anything. I mean, who would I tell? It's not like Thanthos is my number one contact," Xero chuckles. "I just know that Princess Eirho is going through a hard time. And Declan Snow is a piece of work if I've ever seen one."

Peter frowns. "Yeah, he's a piece of shit, if we're being honest. All that man cares about is himself. He doesn't care about her. That's what kills Jett the most."

Xero nods in understanding. "Peter, what if we offer Princess Eirho a way out? A way out of a loveless marriage and a way for her to escape her Father?"

Hesitating, Peter places the flask down and screws the lid back on. He looks back up at Xero. "What exactly are you proposing?"

"I think she should join the movement. Princess Eirho would be a powerful piece in the fight against Thanthos. Not only that, we could save her."

He has to think about it. What would happen if she joined the

Skulls? What would Jett say? And not only that, what if Peter asks her and she tells Jett or worse—Thanthos? It's definitely a risk.

He thinks about Declan Snow and the life that she'll be forced to live with him. And he thinks about Jett and all he can offer her. It's not fair to send her to some hell when she has someone who would give her the heavens.

"I think she should join too," he concludes. "We should try to convince her, at least."

Xero smiles. His plan is going to work. "Yes, we can save her."

"What do I need to do?" Peter asks apprehensively.

"I need you to try to talk to her about it. Thanthos—or even Snow—might do something that will set her off. She knows right from wrong; she knows what Thanthos does isn't okay," Xero tells him. "You just have to wait until the moment is right."

"How will I know?"

"Oh, trust me, you'll know. She'll be upset, hurt. Your job is to take that opportunity to offer her a solution—an escape from the darkness. It's a win-win. We can help her and she can help us. Together we can create a better world," Xero says. "Can you do it, Peter?"

Peter swallows hard and nods. "Yes, I think I can. I'll talk to her."

38

NOW

"*What* are you doing here?"

Xero keeps one gun pointed at Jett as the other is trained on Shadow, a smirk growing across his face as he takes her in. She is covered in blood—hers and the blood of Thanthos. Her dress is torn to shreds, hanging down in tattered strips. Her legs are marked with dirt-filled cuts and littered with bruises, much like her face.

"I'm getting what I've wanted from the beginning," he responds, kicking Jett in the back as hard as he can. Jett moans in pain through the gag in his mouth, trying to stay upright. "Crawl, *Commander*."

Peter stares at him, taking his bait. "And what's that?"

Xero groans in exasperation as Jett struggles to crawl across the sharp stones on his hands and knees. After a few painful seconds, he kicks him back to the ground, tired of waiting. "I got Thanthos to lead me right to the magic."

"You're not The Heir," Shadow states calmly.

She can't believe that Xero was using them to get the magic for himself! Using her as a pawn this entire time. No wonder he would never let her go in and kill Thanthos—he had been using her to gain the magic he wanted. He has lied to the Skulls about his true intentions since the beginning. Maybe it is possible to hate someone more than Thanthos.

"She's right," says Peter, "you won't be able to hold the magic. You're not in the same bloodline."

Xero shrugs as if their words mean nothing. He digs his gun into Jett's head, just for his own amusement. "No, but he is."

Xero gestures over his shoulder to Dax as he steps out of the shadows. He has a smirk plastered on his face as he approaches. He's completely unscathed, giving him a huge advantage if it comes to a fight.

"I fucking knew it!" Shadow exclaims proudly. Jett and Peter give her peculiar looks as she changes her expression to one of frustration.

"You better hope he can hold your magic. Otherwise Jett is going to be eating a bullet in a few minutes." Xero sneers, making her skin crawl.

The reality sinks in as Shadow analyzes the tomb around her. Xero is a liar and a traitor. He might decide after this that Jett needs to be killed. Or perhaps he's already decided to kill him. His hatred for Jett Torn is one of the few things that has always been real and that makes her worried.

"Let him go and I'll let you have whatever you want." Shadow stands resolutely, holding her hands above her head. "Peter and Jett leave. And you and I can talk about the magic." *That I know nothing about because I inherited it about half an hour ago.*

Dax's betrayal is no surprise to her and she's not worried about him in the slightest—mainly because she anticipated it. She knows how he fights and how incompetent he is. Dax's deception could never hurt as much as what Xero did. She knew he had ulterior motives but she never thought it would be this.

Xero looks to Peter and throws something metal to Dax. "Handcuff Peter and sit him next to Jett. Now."

Peter hesitates for a long moment, knowing ultimately he is keeping his friends alive for a while longer by complying. With a sigh, he steps forward to let Dax cuff him. Dax sits him next to Jett as the metal closes around his wrists with a loud click. He nudges Jett into a sitting position and lets him lean on his shoulder.

"Now, you get to come with me," Xero says with a confident smile. "The fun part is... I have some very loyal comrades up above and if I don't return, they'll unleash hell upon this underground tomb."

He grabs the front of Shadow's dress and pushes her towards the octagon. Spitting on Thanthos' limp body as he walks by, he pats her on the back as if to congratulate her for a job well done. It nearly makes her sick. She allowed him to manipulate her further than she ever thought. She wasn't just his pawn in the Skulls, he used her for his own selfish gain.

The regrets she carries and tries to make right because of Thanthos are nothing compared to what Xero has manipulated her into doing. And she had let it happen all these years. What is wrong with her?

"Are you going to tell me why you did this? Why you lied?" Shadow questions as Xero's gun digs into her skin.

"I might," he says. "Or I might just do what needs to be done." He pushes her toward the stone table in the center. She notes the words etched into the side—an ancient language that she cannot speak. He makes her lie back onto the stone as he produces straps to tie her down to the table with.

"Who else was involved?" she asks as he tightens the strap around her leg.

"Dax, but you knew that already. You suspected it the entire time and I made you think you were paranoid," he tells her with a proud laugh. He makes the straps around her hands extra tight to restrict her magic and movement. Shadow winces as they dig into her skin. "His little magic powers made me believe he was The Heir for a long time. When I manipulated Peter into bringing you to me, I only thought of you as a powerful pawn in my plan to kill Thanthos and take the magic. And then, years later when I brought Dax in and he couldn't harness enough magic to kill a dog—" He looks over his shoulder and addresses Dax, "No offense."

Dax doesn't respond as Xero turns his attention back to Shadow. "I had a feeling it was you. *Princess Eirho,* you were more important than I thought."

Nausea runs through her stomach and her head pounds. She knew that he had other plans for Thanthos, but she never imagined they would involve using her to this degree. For years she confided in him, killed for him, nearly died for him and it was all a façade. He had become the father figure she never had. If her hands were free right now, they'd be wrapped around his neck.

When all she does is give him a cold, hard look, he continues his rant, picking up a shiny pebble. He is distracted for a moment by the strength of this tiny stone, rolling it between his fingers. He drops it when he hears Peter struggle against his bonds. Jett is equally distraught, but he tries to calm Peter down with a soft elbow, reminding him that he's there too. Xero smirks.

"I saw how you began to challenge me so I drew you back in with your precious Commander. You've always had a weak spot for him as he has had for you. Even Dax started to have a soft spot for you, despite you being such a bitch to him. He started to see through the lies I told about you." His lip curls up. Dax having sympathy for her must have been such an inconvenience. "I had to remind him of the reason he joined me—to get magic at any cost, which meant killing you. And to top it off, fighting with you about the ball only made you want to come more, you're such a rebel." Xero chuckles. "Thanthos did some horrible things but I'll let you in on a little secret… sometimes I did things to innocent people just to encourage you. I worked hard to discredit you with the others for the past few months and distract you with Dax, so you wouldn't see what I really was planning. You almost killed me though that night at the Gustus'. I had to keep you on edge. Dax worked hard to do the same, all these years we searched for what our fathers wanted—the bloodline magic. And the key was you."

She balls her dusty hands into fists now, wishing she could launch them into his smug face. Traitorous, monstrous bastard needs to feel the pain she feels. He manipulated everyone to get what he wanted, no matter who got hurt or worse. Anything to get what he wants, even at the cost of life.

"Of course, he's part of this all along. That fucking bastard." Shadow spits, glaring in Dax's direction with bloodlust in her eyes.

"Yeah, he is. It was his idea to trick you into joining us so we could have insight into what Thanthos was searching for after Thanthos removed him from his Guard," he informs her. He's proud of his dark plan that he built up. "And getting you to kill him and lead us to this magic! Ha! I was worried you'd be trouble for a while and I'd have to kill you, but you proved to be useful."

Dax must have been trying to get Princess Eirho and when she died he tried to get into the Red Guard to stay close to Thanthos and the magic. This has been the place all along.

Placing a hand on the side of her face, he strokes it gently, admiring her in such a vulnerable position.

"Hmm... maybe I should have some fun with you first," he coos suggestively, sliding his fingers down her neck, her chest, and over her stomach. He lets his fingers linger for a moment before he takes them away.

Shadow's face grows hot from a mix of murderous rage and embarrassment from being in such a compromising position. In front of the two people she is closest to, too. He would love to make Jett watch too. Sick bastard.

"What are you going to do with the magic?" Changing the subject might distract him from touching her. He's making her stomach grow sick.

"I'm going to have revenge for Thanthos skinning my family alive. I'll kill you—his most precious family member—and take the magic in the process. Dax will be given the magic and we will conquer The City and every kingdom we can touch." He strokes her golden hair again. This time, he keeps his touch deliberately soft to make her skin crawl in disgust. "There's been talk that this couldn't be done. But I know it can."

"What do you mean *'give it to Dax?'* Why not take it for yourself?" She struggles against her bonds, ignoring the looks from the others. It's just her and Xero now. She has to focus if she wants to survive this.

"The magic can only be given to a member of the royal bloodline. Dax just so happens to be a part of it. He discovered a picture of the ballroom in your house. I knew when I saw it that the rumors were true and that this would be the final battle and I knew if I protested, you couldn't stand staying away. He also discovered a picture of Argos in that little box of yours. They're almost twins, *Princess*. Seeing the likeness proved that Argos is his real father, just as I thought—which makes Dax your brother. The Oracles told me that if I tear your heart out while it's still beating, and let Dax eat it, he will be granted the magic from your very flesh. He already has magic, so taking yours will only make his magic stronger and give him what you owe him."

She laughs at him mockingly, waiting for him to hit her, but he remains calm. She laughs at the irony of everything and then the shock settles in. Dax is her *brother*. Of course he is. At this point every person she knows is somehow tightly connected to her.

That night in the cell, Jett had told Shadow about Dax's adopted father. Watten Ryer had been seeking The Heir his whole life. He was on Thanthos' hit list so Jett knew all about him and his history. Jett told Shadow that Dax and Watten had been trying to find and kill her for years because of the rumors about young Princess Eirho stealing magic for herself.

Dax had slipped into the Red Guard to work for Thanthos and his connections had no doubt fed him information about Peter at the town square, which led Shadow to reveal her true self to Jett. Xero and Dax planned that as they had planned many things, including taking the magic. The fire in Dax grew when he learned who he truly was; he was meant to be The Heir. That night, Jett had told her everything she needed to hear.

And so, she went to the ball with Jett on her side. Xero and his little spy could no longer be in her inner circle.

The least of her worries is Dax. Dax can hardly move a feather with his magic. Some power that guy has.

"That's the most ridiculous thing I've ever heard of," she says, "and I've heard my fair share. The magic isn't stored in my heart. You are wasting your time."

He snorts at the assumption, patting her head again. "Oh, dear one, if you really think I care, you're wrong. I get to see you suffer and that's enough for me, whether eating your heart works or not, I will find a way. The Oracles told me what I needed to know and this is a sacrifice worthy of Dax taking the magic. Then we'll have all the power in the world." He looks over at Jett and Peter, shaking his head at the Commander. "I knew you would be trouble after you let *him* out. I wasn't planning on killing you in such a painful way, but you ruined that."

"So, we trusted you and this is what we get?" Maybe this is what she deserves for all the pain she caused. She had hoped that Xero would never cause her pain though. Thinking of Xero causing her pain, it flashes in her mind that Xero had attacked her that night at the Gustus'. He wanted to kill her then but she saved herself.

"Yes," he says. He reaches into his bag and yanks out a dagger, swinging it back and forth. He tests the weight in his hand, teasing her with it. Shadow exhales sharply as she sees the blade, recognizing the movement in Xero's hand. It is the same tool that was used to cut her that night, the dagger with gems. Xero framed Dax to keep her suspicious and focused on him. All the while, Xero tried to tear her down. He wanted to get the magic the night he attacked her but she beat him. After that, he learned that he needed her alive longer. What a bastard.

Studying his sister with a long, hard stare, Dax thinks of all the things that Watten planted into him. He said Eirho was a conniving, greedy, spiteful Princess who was ungrateful and 'deserved what was coming to her.' When he found out that she was alive, Dax felt bittersweet. It is a shame that this power-hungry woman didn't die in that fire, but at least he can do Watten proud by taking her life with his bare hands. Then he'll finally have the power to take control of the kingdom.

Dax had been told every day of his life that his duty was to kill The Heir and take the magic for him and Watten. He never knew the truth until Xero recruited him and he stumbled upon it in Shadow's closet. For many years, Dax thought that the man who raised him was his real father, until Watten passed and the family told him that everything he knew was a lie.

There had to be some truth to his childhood. The truth that he wants to believe is that Watten thought he had a shot at being King. This is his chance to make that a reality.

"Anyway, let's not waste any more time. We have a princess to torture." Xero winks at her sardonically.

Jett starts to yell into his gag, Peter screaming from beside him. They are begging, bargaining, pleading, cursing him. They shout whatever they can think of at him. They'll do anything that they can to beg for her freedom.

But Xero Marcs no longer cares as he hands the weapon to Dax. The dagger with jade gems glows slightly in Dax's hand. His magic works, no matter how weak it may be.

Dax leans over and says, "Hey big sis," as he plunges the blade downward to her heart.

SHADOW IS OFF THE TABLE IN A SPLIT SECOND, THE STRAPS BURNT with the magic she conjured. Dax's blade is stuck deep in the stone and he tries frantically to yank it out.

"Fuck," he shouts, hoping to pull it free. It's exactly where her heart had been. If she was a second later, it would have it pierced into her chest.

Xero steps to his rescue but is met with the full wrath of Shadow, who sets her entire arm on fire. She throws her body into him, burning the side of his face. He screams in pain and falls over, allowing her time to kick him in the back. He curls in on himself and cries out.

"I'm about to do something really stupid!" she yells as she races to Jett and Peter, grabbing Peter's hands first as he's only cuffed. She grabs the handcuffs and holds onto the middle chains as her hands grow hot. "Stupid, stupid. This is stupid."

"Shadow watch—"

A painful kick throws her to the side and as she swiftly jumps up, she sees Xero clutching his face as he holds a blade at Jett's throat. Her heart thumps with apprehension as she realizes what he's about to do.

"Oh, you think you're so fucking sneaky!" Xero pulls hard against Jett's head. Jett winces in pain, his body is already damaged from the fall and from Xero's earlier attack.

Jett darts his eyes to Shadow quickly telling her to not risk it—to let Xero do what he pleases and not let him get to her. They risked too much to allow this bastard to win. Dax has finally freed the blade and is sauntering toward her, ready to try again.

"I'm going to kill Jett. And then Peter, then I'm going to slice your beating heart out of your chest while you're still breathing," Xero growls darkly. He's practically foaming at the mouth, ready to hunt her to her death.

Shadow pushes Peter away from her and bends down. "Wait!" she orders, confusing Xero. "You need my heart pumping for this to work, right?"

Xero narrows his gaze, tightening his grip on Jett. Xero growls at him to stop moving. "Yes. He needs to absorb its power while it's beating."

His eyes flicker to Dax's momentarily, both curious why she would ask.

"Perfect."

In one quick motion, she uses her foot to flip a gun up from the ground into the air, catching it in her hand. She aims it at her chest —right in front of her heart. She cocks the gun and watches Xero's face drop.

"Let them go or I will pull the trigger."

"Eirho, no!" Jett shouts out hoarsely. "Don't you fucking dare!"

Peter tries to move towards her, but she looks at him, daring him to take another step. She will shoot herself if she has to. Dax backs away slowly, looking to Xero for guidance.

"Release him," Shadow says in a firm voice. "*Now.* Or my heart will no longer be beating and the line of magic will end here. In this room."

Xero pulls harder on Jett's hair. "You wouldn't dare. That will not destroy the magic! The magic will go to another. What if it's Alpha? How selfish can you be?" He tries to move his hair from his eyes, jealousy and hatred contorting his features. He wants the magic and he'll do anything to take it. "You know Alpha will die if you dare try it. I'll just kill her instead. I'll kill everyone who gets it until Dax has it. Do you want her to suffer the same fate?"

"I would never condemn her to that. But there's something you need to know about The Heir magic," she says, a sly smile forming on her face.

He hesitates in his response, unsure what to do. It seems to him like she's setting a trap for him. Damn her for being smart.

"If the bearer sacrifices themselves to end the magic line, it will be gone forever."

Xero nearly drops the blade from Jett's throat. "*What?*"

"I learned that from a good friend. Oakenstaid knew what you were up to, you son of a bitch. He didn't warn me directly, but I pieced it together," she says, feeling successful. She presses the gun further into her chest. "So, let him go or else the magic will end here forever."

He stays still for a long moment, ignoring the words and muffled grunts from Peter and Jett.

Jett is fighting back tears that come to his eyes—he is about to lose her again. She doesn't have to end her life this way. Not here, not ever. Not for this sickening men who deserve death.

"I will kill him either way," Xero finally says. "Do you want him to die?" He points his blade at her. "Yes or no?"

She hesitates and drops the gun by her knees. She hears Peter and Jett sigh in unison, their relief flooding the room. Once the gun is on the ground, she puts her hands up and walks towards him as Dax moves to grab the gun.

"Fine, let him go," she bargains. "Me for Jett. No more tricks."

Xero seems as if he is about to cooperate with her for a mere second, then he flashes a deadly smirk and raises the blade up to attack.

Shadow tackles him.

The blade falls.

~

ALL SHE SEES IS BLACK. THE DARKNESS OF HER EYES, THE ROOM? Blood? Is blood covering her?

Her body trembles and she hears a loud shot ring through the room. She falls onto something hard. The ground, maybe. Her knees and hand get cut when they touch it; her ears pulsing from the noise.

Arms are around her. None of them feel like Jett's.

Where is Jett? What happened? She remembers tackling Xero, knocking him away from Jett after he dared to slice the blade. She had been too busy attacking him to look back and see what had been happening with Jett and Peter.

She can feel her eyes grow wet.

She feels someone lifting her up high, holding her close. Their heart is beating like a drum. It soothes her slightly despite the immense pain that radiates throughout her entire body. What happened?

There are voices now. Lots of voices. Hurried ones, crying ones. Ones full of confusion and anger. Shadow tries to open her eyes and fails.

Everything is a chaotic blur.

And then, nothing.

39

NOW

The sun comes through the curtains and Shadow tries to open her eyes. It stings as if she's never seen light before but she manages to open them despite the pain.

She's in a white room; the curtains, the walls, even the sheets that cover her are pure white. All she can see from where she lies, is the corner of the window and the pillow edge. It's fluffier than she's used to, but it feels amazing against her skin. Her head feels like it weighs a ton. It pulses slightly, making her want to sit up—maybe that'll stop the thumping.

Pushing herself up, she realizes her left leg is numb. It must be asleep from lying here for so long. It takes a few minutes, but she sits upright against the headboard, looking around the room. It's a hospital room, no doubt in the Palace if she's remembering correctly. How'd she end up in this place?

The pain seems to subside slightly as she sits upright. Her neck is stiff and she brings her chin to her chest to stretch it. That felt good. She rolls her shoulders, feeling them click as someone appears outside the door. They knock very softly, so much so that she barely hears it.

"Ah, you're awake!"

"Peter!" She tries to sit even more upright and he places his arms around her neck in a light hug. He lingers for a couple minutes before pulling back.

He tilts his head, admiring her. "You don't look too shabby," he says with a grin. "How are you feeling?"

"Like I died," she admits. Hearing her own voice scares her a bit, the hoarseness taking her by surprise. It's almost as if she's forgotten how to speak. "And came back."

He chuckles lightly and beams at her. "I'm just... I'm so glad you're okay."

"Yeah, I'm fine, my leg is just falling asleep a lot. My left one," she makes a face as she wiggles her legs around. "I can't feel anything."

Peter's face drops. "About that. I have some things to tell you," his voice gets lower, graver. "About what happened with Xero and Dax."

She stays quiet, but nods for him to continue.

"Well, it all happened so fast. You saw that he was going to stab Jett with that blade," he begins, "so you jumped on top of him and Dax shot you in the leg. You ended up losing your leg. They couldn't save it."

Shadow laughs brightly at him. "What? No. No I didn't," she insists, shrugging him off.

"I'm not kidding," he says. He gestures to the sheets covering her. Their eyes lock. He would never joke about something this serious.

Her smile fades away as she slowly plucks the blankets off one-by-one until she gets to the sheets. The lower part of her leg is flat. It takes a whole lot of courage for her to lift the blanket.

"Oh no," she whispers. Her knee is bandaged and the rest of her leg is gone. "Oh no, no. No!"

"You defeated Xero with a bullet in your leg. Xero was furious. You burned that fucker's face completely off while getting shot and

Alpha finished him off with an arrow," Peter tells her. "Dax escaped, but as far as we know he's long gone."

She shakes as she looks down to where her leg once was. She looks at her hands to, wondering if she can remember what it felt like to burn human flesh to the bone. She doesn't remember, thankfully.

The room begins to sway and her stomach churns as her thoughts wander.

"Tools is working on a fully functional robotic leg for you," he adds. "It honestly looks really badass."

"Uh, uh—you said Alpha," she says from behind her hands, trying to forget her leg and the sickness in her gut. "Let's go back to that."

Peter covers her legs—or what is left of them—up again. He needs her to focus. The world has changed since she's been knocked out with sleeping pills and pain medications. She's already been through so much, Peter hopes to keep the stress at a minimum.

"Alpha got out somehow. She escaped and was angry as hell," he starts. "She was going to kill me until I told her why the ballroom looked the way it did. I told her I thought Xero was going to come after you. He'd been acting suspicious all week and as soon as he told us to strike, he made a beeline straight for the Palace. He didn't stop to help anyone. Even shoved a few out of his way. It took some convincing, but she agreed to help. She ordered the guards to stand down from hurting the citizens and get them to safety. Then she came back for us and shot Xero with an arrow. Bullseye. Right in his tiny brain."

"Wow, that's something," she comments. "I lost a leg, our leader was killed, and Alpha saved us. How long was I out?"

"A few days," he says. "I think your magic would have healed you, except for how deep the wound was."

She nods and exhales with dismay. "I lost my damn leg." Reality sinks in and the sickness is wearing off, she is more aware now. "So, where's Jett? Is he okay?"

Peter hesitates. She pushes his shoulder.

"Peter, *please*. What happened?"

"He has some bumps," he tells her, avoiding her eyes. "But he's fine."

She smacks his shoulder as hard as she can manage. "You sick jerk!" she exclaims lightheartedly. "How dare you?"

"I wanted to liven up the mood!" Chuckling, he leans over and kisses her forehead. "He wouldn't sleep while he was in here so I gave him a sedative and Cibor helped me take him to a room a few doors down. He wouldn't leave you alone."

"That sounds like him. So... what happens now?"

"Well, Dax is missing in action," he grumbles. "But our other enemies are dead. You're fit for the throne now, as our leader. The true Queen."

"No. Alpha will sit on the throne." She throws the blankets off. "Get me some crutches. I want to see Jett."

"Eirho, come on. You have the magic, you would be strong and just!" He tries to convince her while stumbling around looking for crutches. If he isn't quick enough, she might hop there instead.

"Where is my sister?" she asks when he hands her the crutches. "I want to see her after I see Jett." She shoves them under her armpits and begins to hobble out of the room.

"Jett's asleep. You'll have an easier time talking to Alpha. She was in the garden last time I checked—and shouldn't you put clothes on?" He rushes after her, stunned by how quickly she can move on crutches. "You only have a shirt and those can barely be classified as shorts!"

She ignores him and makes her way to what's left of the garden. Peter races back to her room to find a robe to bring her, but she's hobbling in the garden long before he returns.

She struggles to stay upright on the rocks, managing to make her way through the flowers and the trees that remain. She keeps the execution area to her back; she doesn't want to see that right now.

When she spots Alpha, she picks up speed. Alpha sits on the bench, watching the fish beg her for food.

"What are you doing? You're nearly naked!" Alpha says, standing up. Somewhere in the distance Peter is trying to catch up with a robe.

"I'm not, I'm not," Shadow insists. She hops to the bench and sits down, glancing over the missing part of her leg, nausea passing through her briefly. This will take some getting used to. "I wanted to see you."

Alpha sits beside her. It looks as if she is opening her mouth to say something, but she is quick to engulf her sister in her arms.

"I am so sorry," she whispers into her hair. She tightens her embrace. "I should have understood—he was making a terrible choice, Rho."

That name, *Rho,* sends chills down her spine. The nickname is haunting coming from her sister. It reminds her of a past she secretly wishes she could forget, and that includes the pain she caused Alpha. But it also reminds her of the times she spent chasing her little sister through corridors and tickling her when she got caught. It reminds her of challenging Cibor and sneaking out with Jett. There are many great memories to outweigh the dark ones.

"I know, it's okay," she soothes, stroking her younger sister's hair. "It's okay, Alpha." Alpha's body begins to shake, trembling with tears that threaten to spill. "Hey, it's okay. You and I are together now. Forever, I promise."

Alpha enjoys a few minutes of soaking up her sister's attention and care before she pulls away, wiping her eyes. The tears dry quickly as she watches the fish dance around the pond. For years she sat here—alone—and now she finally has her sister again.

"I'm sorry," she repeats. "I'm glad you're okay."

"I heard you saved me. Thank you," Shadow says earnestly. "I am beyond lucky to have you as my sister."

Alpha catches her gaze and nods with a smile. "Yeah. Yes," she says. "I did. I didn't want to lose you. Again."

Shadow nods in understanding, knowing it's her turn to apologize. "I am sorry about what I did. I had good intentions. I only wish they hadn't hurt you. I promise that was never my goal."

"Well, we have the future to make up for everything."

"Yes, with you as the queen," Shadow says.

Alpha freezes. *Queen*? Is that what she's going to be? "No, you have the magic. You should be Queen."

"Not in my plans," Shadow insists. "You will make the best queen and I'll be your Hand. My magic will still serve the crown and the head wearing the crown will be yours. You were made for this, you know? You're compassionate, strong, thoughtful, just. You'll make a great queen."

"You really think so?"

"I know so. And I'll never leave your side again," she says. "I promise you, Alpha. Never again."

Alpha grins. "You know, Declan made it out of that pit. My men caught him trying to flee The City when he realized you had the upper hand. He's trapped in a cell right now. I hear Jett wants to see him again."

"Did he beat Jett?"

"Oh, heavens no!" Alpha retorts. "Jett is the best fighter in the Elite Guard. He let Declan escape when he noticed you went after Father."

Father, Shadow muses. Alpha needs to know the truth. "There's another thing. My father, it turns out, was Argos."

"Wait. So, we're cousins *and* sisters?" Alpha gasps wildly, confused. "Gods."

"Yup. I was confused and concerned. It seems there's so much that we don't know yet. Dax is also Argos' son. I could never read him, much like I struggle to read you. My siblings are bred with a thick shield to protect themselves. I should've known." Shadow looks down, seeing Cerberus still swimming in the pond. He appears as white and fat as ever. "You've been feeding him."

"Too much it seems," Alpha laughs. "What the hell kind of lies were we living?"

"Take this!" Peter grumbles as he reaches the sisters. "Good grief. Jett will kill me if I don't take care of you," He's out of breath as he hands Shadow the robe. She begrudgingly slides into it and smiles. "You're right. It's better if you're not Queen."

Both sisters laugh playfully at his words, Shadow nudges him after sliding into the robe. Peter rolls his eyes in return. This is nice.

"I'm having a crew clean out the ballroom now," Alpha says. "They're also knocking down that forsaken executioner block in the gardens. We'll turn that into a memorial."

Shadow seems pleased with that idea. She leans onto Alpha's shoulder, Peter taking a seat on the opposite side of her. This is strange, something old and new pushed together. But it is nice and peaceful. She hopes things will be this way for a long time.

"OF COURSE YOU'RE IN THE LIBRARY."

Shadow glimpses up from the book her mother had given her to see Jett leaning against the doorway, smiling at her with relief on his face. She closes her book and puts it on the table, wanting to rise to welcome him. Wobbling a bit, she manages to find her balance on her right foot.

"You're finally awake," he says gratefully, striding towards her. He's excited to get to see her again, especially now that there's peace.

"I could say the same to you," she teases back. He engulfs her in his arms, cautious of her wounds. Her head falls onto his chest and she breathes in his scent. He smells the same as she remembers. "I'm grateful you made it out. Is your family okay?"

"Yes, everyone's safe now," he tells her. "I am glad that *you're* okay."

She chuckles and pulls back. "I would love to say I made it out in one piece but..." she trails off as she wiggles her left thigh around. He grins at her joke and shakes his head. "Tools is making me a new leg."

"You look beautiful, you know that right? Even if you're down a leg," he promises. He steps back and studies her, taking in every detail. She's as attractive as ever.

"Thank you," she says. "Thank you for having my back. Even though I hurt you by lying and leaving. If I could change it, I would. I let Xero manipulate me into doing the worst things."

Jett exhales, wearily, scratching the visible scruff that forms on his chin. "Hurt aside, I'm happy you're alive. And I know you're with Zed, so I'll keep my distance."

She chuckles at him. "I don't know what Zed and I are, to be honest. When I figure it out, you'll be one of the first to know," she offers. "Hopefully you won't be taken by the time I talk to him. Those ladies at the ball loved you."

"I mean, who wouldn't?" He jokes.

She can't help but smile at him. Through everything they've faced—both together and apart—they've come back to each other with a sense of support. They have each other's backs through everything now, and that has to be the most important thing of all.

"Alpha has agreed to become Queen," she says, looking down and smiling as she caresses across a book cover. "She's going to turn everything around."

"Alpha will make a great Queen. But, where does that put you?" he asks worriedly. Shadow has the magic gifts, not Alpha.

"I will serve the Queen as her Hand and greatest protector," she says in a grand voice. "I'll keep this city safe with my iron fist. And iron leg."

He places his thumb and forefinger on his chin as if he has to think about it. "Are you sure you can scare off the big, bad guys?" he asks jokingly.

"Oh, hush up."

She laughs at his smile. Despite facing her greatest threats, she has so much to figure out about how the world works now. So many people to talk to and straighten things out with. And Jett needs his space—until he can figure things out.

"I should get back to reading the history of the Creator's tomb. I'll talk to you soon," she says, giving him a one-armed hug and a wink. "And don't worry, things are going to be okay."

"Oh, I know," he taunts before he walks out, leaving Shadow behind with her thoughts.

I really need to talk to Zed. Her eyes follow after him and she smiles.

~

"Are you certain I should do this?" Alpha asks fearfully, frowning into the mirror. "I mean—what if it's a bad choice? What if I shouldn't become Queen? I've done some fucked up things for our father. Er—my father."

Shadow pats her head gently and smiles. "You should be Queen," she says. A brush in hand, she finishes off her sister's hair and lays it down neatly. "Ah, gorgeous."

Last minute doubts are plaguing her, despite Alpha being confident beforehand. Cold feet, maybe. Shadow knows that her sister is going to change the lives of so many. Whether or not she realizes it, is another story.

"Thank you," Alpha says with a grin. "I'm nervous."

"Alpha, you've led armies, you've won battles, you've ventured into the wilderness," she says. "This is just another challenge for you. And another one that you'll overcome."

Alpha stands up to grab her coronation gown. "How's that new leg treating you?" she asks.

Shadow shakes it around a bit, moving her limb around. "I'm lucky to have Tools, that's for sure. Those crutches were *killing* my armpits."

Alpha chuckles as she slides into the gown—a beautiful gold color with long sleeves and a modest cut. "I'm glad, too. I'll need you healed and ready to go."

"I'm much better now that you'll be our leader."

Alpha grins wider this time. "We are going to change this city."

"Alpha, we are going to change *the world*."

The strawberry haired sister nods and straightens up. "What do you plan to do about Dax? And... what will you do now that you have magic?"

She has put plenty of thought into Dax and the future, but Shadow feels queasy at the thought. How can she know what's ahead when she barely knows what's inside of her now? There's also the question of her real lineage—the one where her father is Argos, not Thanthos.

"I have to hunt him down and I have to find someone who can help me learn about myself." She stares down at her hands, thinking about the unknown. "And I want to know about my father."

A strange look crosses Alpha's face—she still hasn't grasped that her sister has a different father. Shadow wants to comfort her through all the truths they've uncovered.

"We have to get you on the throne and get The City running smoothly again. Then I'll start the hunt."

Alpha beams at the idea and gasps as if she's remembered something. Careful not to ruin her dress, she hurries to her closet and pulls out something flat and rectangular. It is covered carefully with a cloth and she places it on her table.

"I started this when you gave me new brushes. Before you left," she says. Alpha lifts the cloth from the painting, earning Shadow's full attention. "I added to it as the years went on and I finished it while you were in the hospital wing. I made it for you."

The painting is a glory in itself—with a combination of elegant hues and precise lines. But the use of paint isn't what intrigues her, it is the picture. Alpha, Shadow, and their mother stand dressed in the most glorious gowns of purple and blue and green, with gold and silver trimmings. They stand in the garden, surrounded by roses, embracing one another.

Shadow falls to her knees to come face-to-face with the painting. "This is the most beautiful painting I have ever seen," she whispers. Tears cloud her eyes and she tries to push them away, unsuccessfully.

This is what she fought for and will always fight for. Family. Her sister. The life she could have had if Thanthos hadn't been such a wicked bastard.

"Thank you, Alpha. I love it. Thank you so much."

She stands up and hugs her sister tight. "I am so sorry."

"Just promise you'll never leave me like that again. I might actually kill you next time," Alpha says solemnly. When Shadow pulls back, she laughs.

"Alpha, I promise."

The Queen smiles with satisfaction. "Good. Let's go change the world."

After the coronation, Alpha spends her time with her new council, getting to know them and encouraging them to think about a progressive new world. It's clear that she is busy, excited about what she will accomplish and the darkness she will defeat.

Shadow watches her as she snacks on finger food—still not full from the main course she ate earlier. Delicious platters of meat and cheese are her favorite. She seems to have forgotten how good the Palace chefs are compared to the cooking at the Skulls HQ.

This is delicious.

"You're looking spiffy." Cibor stands next to her and swipes up a piece of cheese before Shadow can shove it in her face. "Are you starved?"

She tries not to laugh with food in her mouth. Shaking her head is the only response she can offer. She pokes him playfully and swallows her snacks.

"This is what we worked for," he says, beaming. "All we sacrificed for. Evil has been defeated."

"For now," she reminds him. "Who knows where Dax is. I should've carved that little shit when I could."

"Oh, how princess-like," says another smooth voice from behind them.

Ah, Jett. Always coming into the conversation at the best of times. She snatches up another cheese and pepperoni stick and pops it into her mouth before Cibor can stop her. It will give her time to gather her thoughts.

"How you doing, Commander?" Cibor offers his hand, Jett ignores it to give him a tight hug and clasp him on the back. Cibor is taken by surprise.

"I'm doing well. Back to my normal self, mostly," he replies, taking a cheese stick. Much to Shadow's dismay; that means less cheese for her. "Alpha wants me to be head of the entire military—not just the guard. General Torn."

"No way," Shadow gasps. This is the first time she's heard of it. "Jett that's fantastic, congratulations! You'll make a great military leader."

He's grateful for her kind words. "I hope so. The last one was an ass." He chuckles to himself and wolfs down another stick.

"I'm going to go find Peter," Cibor says happily, patting the Princess and Commander on the back. His smiles is suggestive when he glances between them. "I'll see you two later."

Shadow waves after him as he vanishes into the crowd, excited to have the cheese mostly to herself. That is, until the guests start to notice what's on offer.

"Are you ready for your new position as Hand of the Queen?" Jett asks, studying her face.

He wants to read her, fully—no lies or shenanigans this time. He wants to know how she truly feels now that there's peace and prosperity. Once he knows that, he can determine how he feels. But for now, he wants to know first.

Shadow takes a deep breath. "I'm ready. I'll serve her and protect her in this life and the next. We have lots of work to do, but I'm not worried anymore. Everything has somehow fallen into place."

Jett mouth barely lifts into a smile and his eyes drop to the ground. "Yeah, so it seems. Once everything has settled, we will need to work together to get Dax tracked down."

"And skinned alive," she adds.

"I'll let you do the honors."

She chuckles, feeling her stomach ready to burst. Maybe she should stop eating soon. It's just so delicious! Placing her hand on her bloated stomach, she lets out a long breath.

"DOE!" a squeal comes out of nowhere as an army of little arms wrap around her tightly. "You're okay!"

Shadow wants to cry. *The Gustus family*, she swells with joy. Kneeling, she hugs the kids, one-by-one and then in a group. They're crawling all over her until Quinta pulls them away and scolds them:

"Be careful! She's been through a lot," Quinta tells them. "Rye, calm down! They had a lovely time in the forest, Shadow. They love their 'little tree friend'."

Shadow laughs at their nickname for Oakenstaid and lifts her dress up slightly, revealing her leg to show the kids. "I'm okay now," she winks. "I'm part robot."

"Woah!" Oak says, bending down to check out the new leg. "That looks so awesome!"

"Cool!" Rye coos, admiring it beside his sister. His eyes are wide as he examines the colors and designs. "You're like a superhero!"

Shadow laughs, grateful for them. She's struggled with the idea that her leg will never be the same, but hearing how cool the Gustus kids think it is makes her feel better. Even with her flaws, they think she's strong and capable. That's much more credit than she's been giving herself.

"Thank you," she whispers. A hand pats her shoulder, seemingly understanding her thoughts. "Oh," she says, spinning around. "Trenton and Quinta, this is Commander Jett Torn."

While Quinta looks cautious, Oak walks up to him and stares him dead in the eye. There's no fear in that little girl's heart. For a while she studies him, her parents anxious about what she might say.

"You're handsome," she tells him bluntly.

Shadow laughs, seeing Jett's face turn a hue of red. It's a new look upon the Commander's normally solemn face. He has been warming up to his old self since the battle.

"Thank you," he says with a chuckle. "You're quite pretty yourself and a fearless little lady by the looks of it."

Shadow swears Oak nearly faints.

"It's a pleasure to meet all of you," Jett says. "I'm going to go see how Alpha is doing."

Quinta slowly edges toward Shadow while the kids eye up the food that still lines the tables. Leaning over, Quinta whispers, "Mr. Tall and Handsome seems quite smitten with you."

Shadow raises her eyebrow but stays quiet, watching as Quinta pokes her teasingly. She chuckles and gives her a hug, just wanting time to relax and regroup. Her eyes scan the area around them, seeing a happy and healthy Theta befriending Oak and Rye. The other kids laugh and dance around, the guests are gleeful. Things are easing up on The City.

"I'm glad you made it out okay."

40

NOW

The balcony is peaceful. The stars hang across the sky as a visible reminder that there's no such thing as being alone as she stares at the bench her mother carved all those years ago. Loneliness fades away whenever she sees the bench.

Shadow wiggles her new leg about, trying to get used to the new sensations she feels. Many things have changed since she left the Palace—her leg, surprisingly, being the smallest.

It's strange without Thanthos, eerie even. It feels like he haunts the hallways every day, searching for his vengeance. What a funny thing it was, to be loved by such a terrible human. To have been raised under the eye of a tyrant who would kill children. Even his own.

She exhales and lowers her head.

He isn't the only ghost, though. Sometimes she senses her father—her *real* father—watching her. Or watching out for her.

She whispers to him that she wishes he could be here and that she could know him. He's dust now, though. She looks at her slender hands, wondering what he had been like. Sure, there are stories about him. He had been tall and golden-haired with a beard. He was a strong man, like an ox. They say he was driven, passionate, and determined.

Most importantly, they say he was kind.

Shadow knows she needs to be like him—to show compassion above anything else. There's been a time or two when she's faltered, but now, she has a new drive. If one good thing comes from this war, it will be a gentler soul.

Her hands grow warm as the magic courses through them. This is a gift that she was chosen for. Only those with the most love in their hearts can possess such a gift.

What high standards she has to live up to. She doesn't quite know how she'll manage but she is willing to rise up to the challenge.

"So, are you a princess again?"

She looks at Jett and grins. "I suppose so," she says. She turns to her side, leaning over the rail.

"Should I refer to you as your royal highness?" A joke, naturally but he says it to earn a grin.

"Yes. I will accept nothing less."

He leans on the rail beside her, handing her a glass of champagne. Jett has one of his own, swirling it around softly. Smirking as he gazes up at the stars, he says: "You would spend so much time out here when we were kids. It was never hard to find you. It was a fifty percent chance between the garden or here. Still so predictable."

"Yes. I'm a creature of habit," she chuckles. "Things seem strange now. I don't know what to do with this magic. I need something—someone to help me. How do I control this? How do we go back to pretending things are what they were?" Her eyes fall on her hands, recognizing the immense power inside of her that she can't control. She must learn.

"We don't," he tells her. "We take what we have learned and we get better. We do better than the ones before us. Better than we used to do."

She swallows. "I need to find someone to teach me," she sighs. "I may have to step away from my duties until I can learn how to not be a danger to Alpha and everyone else. Where will I find someone? Magic has been hidden for ages! no-one practices anymore without the fear of being caught."

"There are other kingdoms. I'll help you if you need me to. With whatever you need, I promise," he says. "We will find someone to help you learn and we will keep Alpha safe. Just take a while to enjoy the peace."

He's right, she tells herself. She needs a break after everything she's been through. She fiddles with her hands, studying her fingers and her palms. Little flames grow from her hand and she lets it rise and fall. In her other hand, an icicle forms into a tiny blade.

"I'm still trying with this one," she admits as he watches her magic thrive. Finally, she smothers them, drying her hand off. It's been a challenge to have water completely vanish when she stops her flow of magic, but she is getting better every time.

"It's incredible," he comments.

"Yeah, it truly is." She pauses and studies his handsome face in the moonlight. Every memory with him comes to life when she gazes into those ocean eyes. "I spoke with Zed."

He cocks his eyebrow sharply, trying to hide the flutter in his chest. "Oh, yeah?"

"Yeah. He was really interested, you know. We have been seeing each other for a long time and it seems like we made the right choice."

He adjusts uncomfortably, trying to keep positive despite what he thinks is coming. To his best efforts, he keeps his face mostly indifferent. But Shadow catches the tiny squint in his eye as the hurt courses through him.

"I ended things."

His head snaps to the side and he pushes himself away from the rail. "Really?"

She lets out a peal of laughter at his reaction. "I have too many other things to focus on now. Magic, Alpha, finding Dax. I have to make this new life work. I wanted to destroy the magic for good, but here we are."

He leans over the railing and grins, a sigh of relief leaving him. "It's fate. You will find a way, you always do."

A few minutes pass and the sun begins to clear the horizon of stars. The blanket of darkness over The City retreats for the sunrise. Shadow hopes that this feeling of peace lasts. Hopefully for a long time. The people deserve it. Shadow and Jett deserve it.

"Thank you, Jett."

"For what?" he says, confused.

"Everything. You helped me when I least deserved it," she points out. A smile crosses her lips. "I can never repay you for that."

Jett shakes his head. "No," he protests. "You don't owe me anything. I told you I would always care for you and that's all I have ever done."

Yeah, he did. Despite the pain and chaos she caused, despite the monsters within her, he has stayed true to his word. The Oracles predicted the events happening and their dark magic had been right. Maybe Marcs' dark magic about the heart is true too. Jett must keep her safe, it is his duty.

Shadow is grateful for him, grateful to be standing next to him after all these years. Luck is on her side for once.

"We should toast," Jett says, straightening up and holding his champagne glass out. He stands confident as he waits for her to join, his shoulders back and head held high.

Shadow mimics him and asks, "What are we toasting to?"

"Well," he begins. "To The City and the people. To no longer being sworn enemies." He looks over the edge of the balcony. "To our new Queen. To those who have lost their lives and sacrificed everything for the peace we experience now."

Chills run down her spine as she taps his glass, but he moves away. She frowns until she realizes that he's not finished.

"And to us. To whatever the future holds, Princess. I hope we get to experience it together." Jett Torn smiles.

Shadow taps her glass with his, making a light ringing sound.

She'll drink to that.

~

As Shadow sips her drink, her eyes fall to where the execution stand once haunted the gardens. Flowers have begun to climb the walls—roses are bursting their way through the cracks as they take over the blood-stained planks. Shadow shivers as goose bumps creep up her skin. She has a horrible feeling that The Creators are trying to tell her something…

Her war has yet to be won.

ACKNOWLEDGMENTS

I want to thank Josh, Jenna, Alicia, Soph, and El for their support, love, and encouragement. My editor, illustrator, and cover artist deserve a huge thank you for helping my story come to life. I also want to thank my cousin, David, for expanding my library and helping to drive my dreams regardless of the obstacles.

For the little ones Malachi, Monet, and Kailani: I hope you love stories full of heroes, magic, and wonder even when you're my age. For Jasper: you are stronger and smarter than you believe—never forget that.

And to all my loved ones who wanted to read my story or sent encouragement, I thank you for being there for me and want you to know how moved I am by your support.

In memory of the light who brightened the darkness out of every corner of the world and believed in everything I did: my auntie Darlene. I hope I can make you proud. This book, and this series, is for you.

CPSIA information can be obtained
at www.ICGtesting.com
Printed in the USA
LVHW092149301120
673086LV00023B/203/J